ANNIE'S SONG

Annie couldn't imagine why Alex was so upset. He looked ominously angry; initially she'd believed he was furious with her.

But no . . . Gazing up at him, she saw dark shadows of regret in his eyes, and she couldn't believe that emotion like that could be feigned. The grip of his hand on her chin was incredibly gentle, the caress of his thumb over her mouth so light it made her skin tingle.

Past experience warned Annie to be wary. But another part of her wanted desperately to believe in this man. Maybe it was the gentleness with which he touched her or the remorse she read in his eyes, or perhaps she was just tired of feeling afraid.

She only knew that the warmth of his strong fingers on her skin made her feel safe. Wonderfully safe.

CATHERINE ANDERSON

"Catherine Anderson has established herself as a Western romance writer of unusual power, emotional depth and exceptional storytelling."

Romantic Times

Catherine Anderson

Annie's Song

AVON BOOKS ◆ NEW YORK

ANNIE'S SONG is an original publication of Avon Books. This work has never before appeared in book form. This work is a novel. Any similarity to actual persons or events is purely coincidental.

AVON BOOKS
A division of
The Hearst Corporation
1350 Avenue of the Americas
New York, New York 10019

First Avon Books Printing: January 1996

AVON TRADEMARK REG. U.S. PAT. OFF. AND IN OTHER COUNTRIES, MARCA REGISTRADA, HECHO EN U.S.A.

Printed in the U.S.A.

RA   10 9 8 7 6 5 4 3 2 1

To our wonderful son John and his lovely new wife, Deanna. May God, in His goodness, bless you with a future filled with joy, laughter, and wishes that come true.

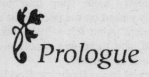

Prologue

HOOPERVILLE, OREGON
SUNDAY, APRIL 6, 1890

When he was sober, Douglas Montgomery was bearable to be around, but when he drank, Alan Dristol was afraid of him. Why, Alan wasn't certain. As far as he knew, Douglas had never done anything truly vicious to anyone. But even so, Alan couldn't shake the feeling that he might.

It was an unsettling thought because it forced Alan to examine his own character. If he didn't like Douglas, why did he associate with him, let alone drink with him? It was a question Alan had asked himself a dozen times, and the answer, though unpleasant to admit, was that he was afraid to tell Douglas no. *No*—such a simple word. But saying it to someone like Douglas wasn't simple.

Slowing his horse's pace, Alan squinted against the bright morning sunlight to study the backs of his four companions as they rode along in front of him. Douglas Montgomery, a head taller and broader across the shoul-

ders than the others, led the group. As though to emphasize his authority, he frequently sank spur into his
gelding's flanks and continually jerked on the poor beast's
reins. Observing the mistreatment, Alan felt a little sick.
The gelding was well-behaved, and there was absolutely
no need for Douglas to handle it so harshly.

Shifting his gaze, Alan observed James Radwick, Roddy
Simms, and Sam Peck, the other three young men who preceded him. They had been his best friends since way back
when he still wore knickers, and he felt he knew them
nearly as well as he knew himself. He suspected each of
them feared Douglas as much as he did. What a pitiful lot
they were, forsaking everything they'd ever been taught,
following along behind Douglas last night like ducklings in
a queue, visiting the brothels with him, then drowning their
guilt in drink, only to pay the price this morning with fierce
headaches. Christ. It was Sunday. Their families would be
at church right now, wondering where they were. Did none
of them have a will of his own?

Wheeling his mount sideways in the road to block their
way, Douglas swept off his gray felt derby and wiped the
perspiration from his forehead with his sleeve. It was an
uncommonly dry April; there had been little rain the last
two weeks, and the road was dusty. He grimaced at the
dirt that came away on his white cuff. "I say we sober
up with a swim," he said with a challenging air. "Last
one in is a mama's boy."

Misty Falls and their favorite swimming hole were
nearby. Scarcely able to believe he had heard correctly,
Alan glanced in that direction. Douglas loved to do wild,
crazy things, the more daring, the better. But coming on
the heels of last night, this was too much. "A swim? Have
you lost your mind? We'll freeze our asses off."

"Jesus, Alan, you're such a little mollycoddle. It's hot-
ter than blazes out here. I'm sweating and so are you."

"Fully clothed and dry, yes, I am sweating," Alan conceded. "But I won't be if I get in that swimming hole."

"The water in that pool is melt off from the snow in the mountains," Roddy pointed out. "It'll be uncomfortably cold, Douglas, without a doubt."

"Uncomfortably cold? Are you a man, Roddy? Or a mewling girl dressed up like one?"

Roddy's face flushed with humiliation, but he said nothing in defense of his manhood. None of them ever stood up to Douglas.

With a snort of disgust, Douglas spurred his gelding off the road and into the drainage ditch that ran alongside. Waving his derby, he let out a caterwaul as his horse sprang up the bank. Alan looked dubiously at his three friends, knowing without asking that none of them wanted to go swimming. Sadly enough, he also knew they'd kowtow to Douglas's whim because no one had the guts to buck him.

"Well?" Roddy said.

Sam sighed. "Sometimes I wish it was just us again, that we'd never gotten involved with him."

"I'll second that," James put in.

Alan shared the sentiment, but it seemed a moot point. The fact was, Douglas had not only joined their group but had taken over. The four of them turned their horses and headed reluctantly toward the falls. As if in forewarning, the wind suddenly picked up, brisk and refreshingly cool on Alan's face. Against wet skin, he knew it would feel icy.

Instead of taking the trodden path, Douglas cut through the woods to reach the swimming hole, and it was rough terrain. Madrone, laurel, stunted oak, and twisted fir tangled together like an old woman's arthritic fingers to block the way, their stout, gnarled trunks shooting up from thick clumps of undergrowth. It was impossible to see the ground. Afraid his horse might stumble into a chuckhole and break a foreleg, Alan slowed his pace to a cautious walk. His friends, fearful of getting on Douglas's bad side if they dallied, made no such concession. The cost of a ruined horse aside, Alan felt they showed no humane regard for their mounts by pushing them across such uneven ground. But he was only a follower, not the leader. Whatever Douglas insisted upon, the others did, no questions asked, their horses and everything else be damned.

Arriving last, Alan heard the voices of his four companions drifting back to him through the pine and fir trees. Whoops and hollers. Despite his resentment of Douglas, he smiled, imagining Sam, Roddy, and James leaping naked into the freezing water. Crazy fools. They'd get pneumonia for this day's work, and all only to humor Montgomery. Blast the Montgomerys. Blast their fancy house up on the hill. Blast their money. Sometimes Alan wondered if their self-appointed leader didn't come up with these outlandish suggestions just to see how far he could push them.

Breaking through the trees at last, Alan was surprised to note that no one had entered the water yet. He cupped a hand over his eyes to see what all the commotion was about and determined that there were five figures near the swimming hole, his four companions and a slightly built girl. Douglas had taken possession of the girl's shawl and was holding it beyond her reach. Typical. Any time Douglas got a chance to bully someone, he took it. Though it disturbed Alan, he supposed the teasing was harmless enough.

Then he recognized the girl. Annie Trimble, the town moron. Though nearly twenty and well past girlhood, she cut a childish and pathetic figure in her shapeless blue frock, black stockings, and high-button shoes smudged with dirt. Because his mother was a frequent visitor to the

Trimble home, Alan knew that Edie Trimble tried to keep her daughter tidy, but Annie ran wild in the woods so much it was an impossible task.

His heart caught at the panicked expression on her small face as she grabbed wildly to reclaim possession of her shawl. Because Annie frequently forgot articles of clothing in the woods, her folks were strict with her about bringing her things home. Alan knew she'd get a scolding, or worse, if she went back to the house without her wrap. Her father, the judge, didn't believe in sparing the rod, and, given Annie's affliction, he used a firmer hand with her than he ever had with his three older daughters.

Alan didn't fault the judge for that or think him cruel. A girl of Annie's limited intelligence was difficult to control, and her parents were to be commended for keeping her at home. Most people would have committed a child like Annie to an asylum. If not for the fact that the Trimbles managed to keep the girl pretty much out of sight when they had callers, they might have been ostracized by polite society. A good many individuals found someone like Annie off-putting. Despite that, Annie's parents had not institutionalized her, choosing instead to keep her existence obscure.

Why the Trimbles bothered, Alan couldn't say. Money was certainly no object; they could easily afford to foster the girl out, and given the judge's political aspirations, it was a wonder they hadn't done just that. Though it was a well-known fact that Annie had been of normal intelligence until a childhood fever affected her mind, there were still those individuals in town who whispered behind the Trimbles' backs, claiming one of Edie Trimble's uncles was mad and that mental imbalance ran in their family. Talk like that could destroy a politician's credibility.

Damn it. Douglas had to know Annie didn't understand he was only playing with her. That was evident in her frantic attempts to reclaim possession of the shawl. The poor creature was several bricks shy of a full load, and anyone could see it. The bewildered expression in her large blue eyes was a dead giveaway, not to mention the odd way she tipped her head whenever Douglas spoke to her. She clearly didn't grasp anything he said.

"Haven't we outgrown this sort of behavior?" Alan called out. "Come on, Douglas. Leave the poor girl alone."

"Saint Alan speaks," Douglas retorted. "As if you've never made sport of her?"

He had Alan there. "We've all been guilty of tormenting Annie a time or two, but that was when we were kids. Grown men don't do such things."

"Yeah. Come on, Douglas," Roddy cajoled. "Leave her be."

Douglas didn't appear to be listening. Leaning forward, he grinned broadly at Annie and dangled her shawl just beyond her grasp. "You want it, sweet thing? Come and get it, then."

As he lured her ever closer, Douglas swept his gaze over Annie's frock, which was damp, probably from the waterfall farther upstream. Everyone who lived in and around Hooperville knew that Annie had a penchant for lounging about on the rocks surrounding the falls. Why, God only knew. The continual mist that rose off the cascading water was icy cold, but it didn't seem to discourage her, no matter the weather.

The wet cloth of Annie's dress, soft from many washings, clung to her body, revealing far more than it concealed. The feminine curves beneath were delightfully ample and unfettered. Smelling trouble, Alan swung down from his horse. Surely Douglas couldn't be thinking what Alan feared he might be. To even entertain the notion was unconscionable. But, then, who had ever claimed Douglas had a conscience?

To look at Douglas, one would think him to be a nice young man with his neatly trimmed, tawny hair and laughing brown eyes. He had everything going for him, money, privilege, and an impressive education from an exclusive eastern college. But all of that wasn't enough, not for him, and it probably never would be. There seemed to be a need within him for power, a need to control others. That need had long since manifested itself with Alan and his friends and was now being unleased on Annie.

Only Annie wasn't capable of fighting back.

Alan took one look into her bewildered blue eyes and turned on Douglas. "Damn you! She isn't right in her mind, Douglas, and you know it. Pick on somebody who can give back as good as she gets."

"Her mind may be tetched, but the rest of her is in fine form," Douglas countered. "Holy revelations, I can see her titties plain as day." Giving a low whistle that boded ill for Annie, he added, "Makes my mouth water just looking at 'em."

Alan turned to his friends for help. Hands buried in his pockets, Sam bent his head and shuffled the toe of one boot in the reddish dirt, as if he thought ignoring the situation would make it disappear. Roddy snickered, and James's ruddy face had turned scarlet. Despite their embarrassment, neither seemed able to drag his gaze from Annie's bodice. Reluctantly, Alan took a quick look himself. It was true that her nipples stood out in sharp relief. To make matters worse, her skirt clung to her thighs. Disgusted with himself for even noticing, Alan tore his gaze from the forbidden. Like a cold fist, fear for Annie clenched his guts.

"Your mama's crazy, girl, for letting you traipse all

over the countryside half-dressed,'' Douglas said softly, still dangling the shawl as bait.

''Mentally she's still a child, and not a very bright one at that,'' Alan reminded him in a voice gone high-pitched with anxiety. ''I'm sure her mother dresses her that way because she runs about in the woods so much. She trusts in the common decency of anyone who may encounter her, and rightly so. She isn't fair game, Douglas, and you know it. Give the girl her shawl and let her go home.''

''I'll give it to her,'' Douglas assured him. ''All she has to do is come and get it. Come on, love. Come and see Douglas.''

Clearly oblivious of the carnal bent of her tormentor's thoughts, Annie lunged for the garment. The instant she came within his reach, Douglas caught her around the waist. She didn't scream, but the terrified little panting sounds she made seemed even worse. Alan's stomach lurched. He didn't like this. He didn't like it at all. The expression on Douglas's face was evil. Evil and cruel. His whiskey-colored eyes gleamed with unholy excitement.

Alan stepped forward. ''Let the girl go, Douglas. I mean it.''

''Girl?'' His prey ensnared, Douglas discarded the shawl to press his hand over Annie's well-rounded posterior. Judging by the way his fingers sank in, the bite of his grip was deliberately cruel. ''You're blind, my friend. No girl this, but a woman fully grown.''

With a low laugh, he tried to steal a kiss. Shoving ineffectually at his shoulders, Annie, her sable hair hanging in silken tangles down her slender back, her eyes clouded with confusion, managed to arch her back and avoid his mouth. Douglas settled for nibbling along the column of her throat.

''Damn, she's sweet,'' he murmured as he claimed a

handful of breast with the same biting grip he had used on her backside.

Rage surged through Alan. He'd be damned if he'd stand aside and watch the girl be hurt. This had gone far enough. He curled a hand over Douglas's well-muscled arm. "I said let her—"

Whatever else Alan meant to say was cut short by the flash of a knife. He stared in mute astonishment as Douglas released Annie to assume a fighting stance and threaten him with the weapon, which seemed to have come out of nowhere.

"Don't you *ever* interfere with me," Douglas warned with deceptive softness.

Alan's knees nearly buckled at the thought of that blade ripping open his middle. His only consolation was that in his anger, Douglas seemed to have forgotten Annie. Alan wanted to yell at her to run but knew that if he did, Douglas would remember what he had been about and grab her. He could only hope Annie had enough sense to flee of her own accord.

"Come on, Douglas. You're drunk," Alan observed shakily.

Run, Annie. Get the hell out of here! Alan felt sweat trickling down his spine. From the corner of his eye, he saw Annie casting about frantically for her wrap. Her breath came in shallow little pants, the sounds like those of a mewling kitten. She was obviously afraid and wanted to get away. But she wasn't about to leave without her shawl. With a sinking sensation, Alan realized that, to her, the wrap was of utmost importance. If she returned home without it, her father would punish her. The poor thing didn't comprehend the extent of the danger she was in. No surprise, that. He doubted any other man had ever even looked at her lustfully, let alone laid hands on her. She couldn't anticipate something beyond her experience.

In that moment, Alan's definition of the word *innocence* took on new meaning, Annie its epitome.

Fixing his attention on Douglas, Alan decided to try to reason with him. If nothing else, he might at least gain some time for Annie. "Just calm down, Douglas. You don't want to run afoul of the law, do you? Mess with an idiot girl, and you sure as hell will. She's old Judge Trimble's daughter, for Christ's sake. Retired or no, he'll see you hang by your balls from the flagpole on Main if you touch her."

"How will he know? She can't tell, remember?"

Because it was inarguably true, the observation made Alan's blood run cold. Annie couldn't talk. Even if she recognized them, she probably didn't know their names and couldn't repeat them if she did. He dared a quick glance in her direction and saw her tugging to free her shawl from an exposed tree root. *Jesus.* Her parents had trained her well. So well that she was prepared to risk her hide rather than leave that worthless length of wool behind. Alan knew Annie had borne the brunt of cruel teasing for most of her life. She had no way of knowing this time was different, that Douglas had more on his mind than simply tormenting her. Far more.

James, who'd lowered himself onto a fallen log, rose to a half crouch, his gray eyes filled with incredulity, whether at the knife or at Douglas's lurid suggestion, Alan wasn't certain. "Surely you aren't serious, Douglas," James cried. "Whether she can tell or not, there's the moral aspect to consider."

"What moral aspect?" Douglas laughed. "You four are such namby-pambies. I don't know why I waste my time with any of you. She's probably hungry for it. Hell, she's eighteen or nineteen if she's a day. Most girls her age are already married and have a child or two. This may be her one big chance to have some fun."

Fun. The word hung in the air, ugly and discordant. Alan prayed he could hold Douglas's attention, if only for a moment. Behind him, Annie had finally tugged her shawl free. As if he had eyes in the back of his head, Douglas reached back and caught her wrist as she turned to flee. She staggered under the force of his grip. When she saw the knife he wielded, her face drained of color. Alan guessed it had finally sunk into her dim little mind that Douglas might be truly dangerous.

Punctuating his warning to Alan with the sharp tip of his knife, Douglas asked, "Any of you want to take me on? If so, make like a frog, and hop on it."

None of them was that foolish. Douglas was capable of killing. The glint in his eyes testified to that. He continued to wave the knife, his cold smile promising reprisal should any of them challenge him. When he was satisfied no one had the courage to do so, he returned the blade to its sheath on his belt and fixed his attention on Annie. She twisted helplessly, prying at his fingers to loosen his grip.

"You can't do this," Alan cried.

"Who's going to stop me?"

Not Annie, certainly. She was a slightly built girl, Douglas a strapping six feet plus. With an agile twist of his body, he threw her to the ground, pushed up her skirts, and raped her as effortlessly as he might have a child.

One

Holding a lantern high to light his way, Alex Montgomery strode briskly along the alley that led through the stable. The pungent odor of fresh manure blended with the dusty smell of alfalfa hay to lay heavily on the crisp night air. Nickers of welcome drifted to him from the shadowy stalls. Under other circumstances, Alex might have stopped, but he didn't have the time or inclination to hand out sugar lumps to the horses tonight.

Jerky splashes of golden light from the lantern and the quick motions of his shadow playing across the plank walls indicated the depth of his anger. Grinding his back teeth to keep from roaring, he reached the end of the corridor and kicked open the planked door to the tack room. As he hoped, his brother Douglas lay sprawled on a pile of scattered straw along one wall, one of his favorite places to sleep off a drinking binge.

Swallowing before he spoke to control the anger in his voice, Alex said, "Wake up, little brother. We need to talk."

A whiskey jug in one hand, the other shading his eyes, the boy groaned and rolled over, presenting Alex with his back. "Go 'way. It's the middle of the night."

Seven in the evening could scarcely be termed the middle of the night, and observing Douglas with the whiskey jug reminded Alex that it was high time he stopped thinking of his twenty-year-old brother as a boy.

"Wake up, I said." Alex moved farther into the room and hung the lantern from a rafter hook. "There has been a very serious accusation lodged against you, young man, and I want to get to the bottom of it."

Douglas groaned again. "Can't we discuss it later?"

Planting his hands on his hips, Alex spread his jean-clad legs and jutted his chin. "Old Judge Trimble just paid me a visit. His daughter Annie has been raped, and Alan Dristol claims it was you who did it."

That seemed to get Douglas's attention, and he flopped onto his back to peer out from under his cupped fingers. Hope filled Alex. Lies, it was all lies. A horrible misunderstanding that could be cleared up with a few words from his brother. No Montgomery man would ever stoop so low as to force his attentions on a female, let alone one as helpless as Annie Trimble. Besides, why would Douglas bother? He was a handsome young man from an affluent family. Nearly every girl in town vied for his favor.

Douglas blinked as though trying to assimilate what had been said. "Alan claims what?" After a moment, he drew back his lips in a sneer. "That traitorous little bastard. Just wait till I get my hands on him."

Like wet, icy fingers, the words snuffed out Alex's last spark of hope. For a moment, he simply stood there, mired in disbelief. There wasn't a trace of pity for Annie Trimble in Douglas's voice, nor had he denied the accusation.

Dust from the straw floated up to sting Alex's nostrils. A searing sensation washed over his eyes. "Tell me you didn't do it, for God's sake," he demanded hoarsely.

Even as he spoke, he heard the ring of desperation in his
tone.

"I didn't do it. Now, then, can the rest of this discussion wait until morning?"

"No, it damned well can't." Alex stepped closer, his
body taut, his temples suddenly throbbing. "A girl has
been raped. How can that possibly be left until morning?
Old Judge Trimble is beside himself, and who can blame
him? I want the truth, Douglas, and I want it now. What
in heaven's name happened? Why would Alan say such
a thing?"

"Because he's a chicken-livered little turncoat, that's
why. I had too much to drink and things got out of hand.
That's all."

"That's all?" It seemed to Alex that the lantern light
pulsated, glowing brightly one second, dimming slightly
the next. "Dear God, Douglas, the girl has been violated."

"It's not like I did her any permanent harm."

Permanent harm? "We're discussing a *rape*, for
Christ's sake."

"Rape." Douglas huffed under his breath as though the
charge was preposterous. "By definition, rape occurs
when a man forces his unwanted attentions on a female.
Annie Trimble got exactly what she's been angling for."

"What?"

"Only look at how she dresses and comports herself!
Wearing naught but a thin camisole and bloomers under
her dress, no corset or petticoats to conceal her shape.
Flitting about like a wood nymph, unchaperoned! She's
been issuing an invitation to every man in Hooper County
since she first developed bubbies. What's a fellow to do,
pretend he's stone-blind? I was drunk, I tell you. A man
can only withstand so much temptation. Her mother

should know better than to let her run around dressed like that with no one to attend her.''

''My God,'' Alex whispered. ''You did it, didn't you? You raped that poor girl.''

His jaw muscle ticking, Douglas angled his forearm over his golden-brown eyes. ''You're such a bleeding heart, Alex. Annie Trimble's brains may be baked, but she's right as rain from the neck down. She wanted it as much as I did. And even if she didn't, what does it matter? She can't remember her own name, let alone what happened to her five minutes ago. The way you're acting, you'd think I diddled Amy Widlow, the preacher's daughter.''

''Amy Widlow, Annie Trimble, wherein lies the difference? Rape is rape.''

Once again, Douglas gave a derisive snort. An unholy urge came over Alex to jerk him up from his bed of straw and shake him sober. Instead he simply stared, praying this was a bad dream. Douglas had always been a hellion, but for all his unruliness, he had never done anyone serious harm. Because he hadn't, Alex had fooled himself into believing he never would. *He'll grow out of it*, Alex had assured himself time and again. *He's just high-spirited.* Now Alex knew better. No matter what his age, a man either had the ability to feel compassion or didn't. It wasn't something that could be taught. What burdened Alex the most was that he might have saved Annie Trimble this heartbreak if only he had opened his eyes sooner; if he hadn't refused to accept the glaring truth, that Douglas was no damned good and never would be.

Folks in Hooperville claimed Alex and his brother were almost exact lookalikes. It was a resemblance Alex had always taken pride in. Now all he wanted to do was note the differences between them and shout to the world that they were only half brothers, sired by Bartholomew Montgomery but born of different mothers. Alex's own mother, Sarah, had died of food poisoning shortly after Alex's third birthday. As a renowned breeder of thoroughbred horses, Alex had always placed a lot of stock in bloodlines and grasped at that now as an excuse, assuring himself that Douglas must have inherited a bad strain from Alicia, Alex's stepmother.

The bitter taste of shame rose up his throat. *Rape.* It was an ugly word, and one that he had never dreamed might be connected to him. His own brother? He couldn't credit it, yet there Douglas lay, his every action testimony to his guilt.

"How could you?" Alex drove shaking fingers into his hair, started to pace, and then swung back around to stare. "What kind of monster are you? To harm a helpless little girl like Annie Trimble?"

"She isn't a little girl." Gingerly touching a scratch along his neck, which Alex had failed to notice until now, Douglas added, "And not helpless, either."

Alex dropped his arms to his sides and knotted his hands into throbbing fists. "Yet you claim you didn't force her? From the looks of that scratch, I'd say she fought you with all her might."

Giving his head a shake as if to clear it, Douglas pushed to a sitting position, yawned lazily, and draped his arms over his bent knees. His white dress shirt was smeared with reddish dirt. Like most of the earth in the foothills around Hooperville, the earth near Misty Falls was a rust-red clay. Alex felt sick. And defeated. Since the accidental deaths of his father and stepmother fourteen years ago, for which he had always blamed himself, he had done everything he knew to atone for the loss and give his little brother a decent upbringing, to instill in him the values and morals that their sire would have taught him had he lived. His efforts had gone for naught. Under that handsome exterior, Douglas was as rotten as a week-old string of fish, and nothing Alex ever did was going to change him.

"What a miserable excuse for a man you've turned out to be," Alex whispered. "Thank God our father isn't alive to see it."

Narrowing his eyes against the light, Douglas met Alex's accusing gaze. "Would you listen to yourself? Annie Trimble is a moron, for Christ's sake. So I had a little fun. You can bet she doesn't even remember it now. I don't see what the big fuss is about."

Alex didn't feel himself move. The next thing he knew, he had his brother by the throat and pinned against the wall. Though tall and well-developed, Douglas had never turned his hand to an honest day's work. His frantic efforts to dislodge Alex's grip were in vain. His face went from breathless red to purple before Alex realized what he was doing and relaxed his stranglehold.

"God help me, I could throttle you. My own flesh and blood, and I could kill you without a second's hesitation."

Douglas squirmed between Alex's work-hardened body and the rough planks of the wall, his thighs hugging Alex's knee where it was lodged threateningly against his groin.

"You're crazy!" Douglas croaked.

Wanting to do far worse but holding himself in check, Alex settled for giving his brother a hard shove. Douglas's shoulders hit the wood with a jarring impact. Whiskey breath gone sour from sleep blasted Alex in the face and drove home the point that this young man, whom he'd loved so dearly and singularly, had become a rowdy, conscienceless drunk. "Not crazy, Douglas. The way I see it, I've just regained my sanity. I've made excuses for you and bailed you out of trouble all your life. But not this time. If they hang you for this, I'll be in the crowd to watch the trap fall.''

"I just had a little fun, I tell you."

"At poor Annie's expense."

Alex released his brother as though the touch of him was contaminating. Never had he come so close to killing a man. Though he had glimpsed Annie Trimble only a few times and always from a distance, he kept picturing her, small and fragilely built, a fey, harmless creature who frequented the surrounding forests, more shadow than substance, always skittering into the trees to hide when she encountered strangers. How must her parents be feeling tonight, knowing that she had been so cruelly attacked? And not by just anyone, but by Douglas Montgomery, whose brother's wealth had always made him invulnerable to the law.

Oh, yes. Alex had become adept at doling out bribes. Over the years, he had learned that nearly anyone could be bought if the offer was substantial enough, and he had gotten Douglas's ass out of a sling more than once by crossing palms with money. But not this time. This time Douglas had gone beyond the boundaries of decency. His offense was one that not even Alex could excuse, the brutal rape of a girl who couldn't even comprehend the meaning of the word.

The rage within Alex was frightening in its intensity, and he knew beyond a shadow of a doubt that if Douglas didn't get the hell away from him, his life would be forfeit.

"Get out," he said softly. "Go to the house, get some money from the safe and what clothing you want. Then get out. If I ever lay eyes on you again, I won't be responsible for my actions."

"Out?" Douglas echoed. "You're kicking me out of the house? Don't be absurd, Alex. I'm your brother."

His brother. Alex gazed at Douglas's sharply chiseled features, so very like his own, at his tawny hair and burnished skin, at the broad set of his shoulders. How could two people be so much alike on the outside and so wholly different within?

"I don't have a brother," Alex said succinctly. "As of now, my brother is dead to me. Get out of my sight before I make that sentiment a reality."

For the first time in Alex's memory, Douglas's cocky attitude deserted him. His face twisted with an emotion that could only be panic. "You don't mean it." He pushed from the wall and shrugged to straighten his shirt. "Where will I go? What will I do?"

"I don't care."

"But I—" Douglas broke off and gave a shaky laugh. "Come on, Alex. Give me a chance to make things right. Everybody gets a second chance."

"You're out of chances."

Slack-jawed, Douglas just stood there gaping. "For Christ's sake. Take away my allowance for a month! Confine me to the house! Do anything you want, but don't kick me out."

"Those are punishments for children, Douglas," Alex said tiredly. "You didn't take a club to some farmer's pumpkin patch this time or set fire to an outbuilding." In a twinkling, Alex recalled the many pranks his brother had perpetrated over the years, most of them harmless but always with an underlying viciousness he had refused to recognize. Kerosene-soaked sacks of shit placed on people's front porches and set aflame so the unsuspecting inhabitants would run outside to stomp out the fire. Outhouses moved after dark to sit directly behind their sewage pits so visitors would step off into the putrid sludge. Harmless pranks, Alex had always told himself, but in truth, he had known differently. "The damage you wrought today can't be recompensed with money, Douglas. Can't you comprehend that?''

The muscles around his brother's mouth began to twitch. "But it *can* be fixed." He lifted his hands in supplication. Yesterday, Alex might have pitied him, but now he felt nothing. Absolutely nothing. "To make things right, I'll even marry the little idiot, Alex. Just say the word."

"Marry her? I wouldn't wish that fate on a dog, let alone a retarded girl."

With that, Alex spun and left the tack room. As he gained the alley, he paused only long enough to say, "If you're not out of here before I return from the Trimbles' house, I'll hand you over to the law myself."

"The Trimbles' house? Why in hell are you going there?"

Why, indeed. "To try and make amends," Alex said softly, "though God only knows how. Being a Montgomery doesn't give you license to destroy other people's lives, Douglas. You're finished in these parts. Clear out before they set the hounds on you."

The lee of the high porch steps protecting her from the chilly night breeze, Annie huddled behind the holly bush, her back pressed firmly against the brick foundation of the house. *Safe here.* No one could sneak up on her from behind. Hands couldn't grab her unexpectedly. The only way anyone could approach her was from the front.

She tried to see through scalding tears as she scrubbed compulsively at her legs with the hem of her white nightgown. *Dirty, sticky, ugly.* She couldn't bear to have anyone look at her, not her mother with that aching sadness in her eyes, or her father with that burning anger. She had done nothing wrong, nothing. Yet the way they stared at her made her feel as though she had. Here, in the darkness, she didn't have to endure the accusing expressions on their faces. She took a shuddering breath and held it trapped at the base of her throat to prevent herself from sobbing.

The branches of the holly bush swayed in the breeze. The muscles in Annie's arms and back twitched and knotted with relentless tension. Moonlight frosted the front yard with silver, lending the shadows eerie outlines and making the harmless seem threatening. When the airless pounding inside her head finally forced her to breathe, she did so with a frantic gulp to swallow back any sound she might accidentally make. Someone might hear, and then Papa would come with the strap to make her be quiet. Her whole body already ached. She didn't think she could bear to get a licking, not tonight.

Even the air around Annie seemed filled with menace. Though she knew it was silly, she kept looking up, half afraid the bad man who had hurt her might swoop down from out of nowhere. That was how it had seemed to happen this morning. She had stopped to gaze at her reflection in the water, and suddenly his face had appeared beside hers.

She should have left her shawl and run. She realized that now. *Stupid, stupid Annie.* Perhaps that was why her parents looked at her the way they did. They were angry because she had lingered there to fetch her wrap. At the time, that had seemed the thing to do. Alan had been there, after all. Because his mama visited hers all the time, she had felt safe. There had been no reason not to. People tormented her a lot, but no one had ever really hurt her.

Not until this morning.

Sinking her teeth into her bottom lip, Annie trembled at the remembered pain. That man. She had seen him before. He lived in a house even bigger than hers, the one on the hill with all the horses in its fields. From a distance, she had seen him out riding. He didn't look mean. She'd had no reason to think he might hurt her.

He could be out there in the darkness somewhere. Annie yearned to close her eyes against the memories that swamped her, but she didn't dare. Her eyes were her only defense.

Why had he hurt her like that? The question had bedeviled her all day and evening, and there was no answer for it. She had done nothing wrong, nothing to make him mad at her. She remembered the glitter in his eyes. Pretty eyes, the color of Mama's Christmas toffee. He had laughed as he hurt her. Annie didn't think she'd ever be able to get the pictures out of her mind.

She locked her arms around her bent knees. Her stomach ached, and she felt raw and torn inside. Though Mama had helped her bathe away the stickiness, she still felt so dirty, as if his touch had left a stain that could never be washed away. When she thought of the things he'd done to her, she wanted to vomit.

A movement in the darkness caught Annie's attention. She leaned forward to peer through the prickly leaves. The shadowy figure of a man on horseback was coming up the driveway. As he drew nearer, a litany resounded inside her head. *Don't let it be him. Please, God. Please, please, please.* She tried frantically to recall the words to the prayers her mother had taught her when she was little, but they all jumbled in her mind. As if prayers would help. They hadn't this morning.

The man drew his horse to a stop near the hitching rail and swung from the saddle, the toe of one suede boot gaining purchase on the ground as he caught his balance and drew his left foot from the stirrup. Dressed in tan corduroy knee breeches and a gray serge suit coat, his face concealed by the brim of a matching felt fedora, he wasn't immediately identifiable. Tall and heavily muscled across the shoulders, he had a similar build to that of the man who had hurt her but was outfitted much more casually. The cuffs of his knee breeches were red-plaid flannel, the black stockings that skimmed his muscular calves were common ribbed cotton.

He looped his horse's reins over the rail and swatted away the horsehair that clung to his pant legs as he strode toward the porch. At the bottom step, he paused. Annie saw his chest expand as he drew a deep breath and straightened his shoulders, a gesture that hinted at nervousness. Then he swept off his hat.

The tawny glint of his hair in the moonlight was unmistakable. Panic chased all rational thought from her mind. One look at that face, which would haunt her nightmares for years to come, and Annie forgot all her well-conceived plans to remain hidden with her back protected on all sides. It was he! She had to get away. But if she moved, she was afraid he might see her.

As though he sensed her eyes on him, he squinted against the light that spilled out the windows and across the porch. His toffee-colored gaze routed through the darkness that shrouded her, and he leaned forward slightly to peer through the holly leaves. His face was partially in shadow, and when he spoke, Annie had difficulty making out the words. As if he realized she didn't understand, he inched closer and repeated himself. With his movement, light from the house played across his face so she could see his lips.

"Hello, there."

Hello, there? After what he had done to her, Annie could scarcely believe he was greeting her as if nothing had happened. Remembering how quickly he could move and the punishing grip of his hands, she was terrified that he might grab her again. She made fists in the dirt and dug in with her heels to crab-walk sideways. The silence that pressed against her ears became a soundless drumbeat as he reached to part the branches that formed a bower around her.

No, no, no. Annie could almost feel his weight crushing the breath from her. The bruises he'd left on her body throbbed as her pulse picked up and sent a rush of blood to the surface of her skin. She shook her head in denial as the claw of his huge hand reached toward her.

Scrambling madly along the brick foundation of the house, she ignored the tearing of her flesh where the holly pierced her nightgown. Twisting onto her hands and knees, she butted her way through a section of rose bushes, not caring that the thorns grabbed her by the hair. She had to get away before he caught her and hurt her again.

Two

Searching the shrubbery for another glimpse of the girl, Alex remained frozen, one foot resting on the bottom step of the Trimbles' porch. The thickness of the greenery foiled him. A soft panting sound drifted to him, and the bushes swayed. Leaning his weight backward, he saw a flash of white. The next second, she burst from the foliage, her slender shape seemingly afloat on a cloud of zephyr.

"I won't hurt you, Annie! Don't be afraid." Before his words could die away, she had disappeared into a thick stand of trees that bordered the yard. "Damn."

Convinced that it wasn't safe for her to be alone out in the woods at night, Alex nearly went after her. Then he thought better of it. She clearly believed him to be Douglas, and her terror of him would lend her speed. Even if he could catch her, he doubted he could make her understand that he meant her no harm. Poor little thing. Her lot in life had been cross enough to bear without Douglas adding to her woes. Alex didn't want to compound her troubles by scaring her half to death. She probably couldn't comprehend what had happened to her today or understand that it was unlikely to occur again.

He shook his head and continued up the steps. Dear God. Just the thought that the poor little creature believed he was her rapist made Alex want to rush back home and give Douglas the beating of his young life. The unleashed anger made him rap his fist against the Trimbles' door with more force than he might have otherwise. Blood was thicker than water, and for that reason Alex didn't want to see his brother dancing at the end of a rope. But, on the other hand, if Douglas was caught, he had whatever he got coming to him, in spades.

Edie Trimble, the judge's wife, answered Alex's knock. He was mildly surprised not to be let in by a servant, but then he realized tonight was extraordinary for this family, a time for discretion and hushed whispers. Having a mentally retarded child was undoubtedly difficult enough. If word got out that the girl had been raped, the gossips would never let the Trimbles hear the end of it. The staff had undoubtedly been given the evening off to make sure that didn't occur.

Alex thought it was a pity that the Trimbles had to be concerned with such matters at a time like this. But he couldn't really blame them, either. As accepting as the majority of people were of handicaps, there were always those few narrow-minded individuals. Even though Annie was never taken to town and her parents reputedly kept her out of sight when they had callers, Alex had heard that Edie had still been snubbed more than once by other ladies of her station because of her daughter. Rumor also had it that the Trimbles' other three daughters visited home infrequently, not because of the distance, as the Trimbles maintained, but because their husbands felt uncomfortable being around Annie.

Though impeccably turned out in a green alpaca shirt-waist, her graying sable hair swept up and twisted into a tidy knot atop her head, Edie looked exhausted. Her blue eyes were puffy from weeping, and her delicately sculpted face was pale, the skin drawn tautly across her high cheekbones, her finely drawn mouth pursed and bracketed by deep crevices. She was startled to see him but managed to hide it fairly well, the only telltale sign a nervous plucking of her fingers at her skirt.

"Mr. Montgomery." She inclined her head as she addressed him, her manner stiff and formal. "To what do we owe this . . . honor?"

That last word sounded as though it nearly gagged her to utter it. Not that he blamed her. The Montgomerys couldn't be at the top of her list right now. He imagined it was her fondest wish to claw his eyes out. If Annie were his daughter, that was how he'd feel. Enraged. Violent. Wanting his pound of flesh.

"I came to speak with your husband," Alex managed. "I trust he's at home?"

She nodded and opened the door more widely, beckoning him into the foyer, albeit with obvious reluctance. Feeling like a weevil in the flour sack, Alex turned his hat in his hands, wishing to God he were anywhere but there. What did one say to the parents of a girl his brother had violated? *I've come to make amends*? As if he could. An apology wouldn't begin to undo the damage that had been wrought. He'd felt ashamed a few times in his life, but this took the prize.

Usually self-assured and oblivious to what others might think of him, Alex regarded the fine cut of Edie Trimble's gown and found himself wishing he had taken the time to dress a bit more formally. Bad enough to be the brother of a rapist without appearing tasteless, to boot.

Ah, well. It was too late now. Though blessed with substantial amounts of money and a home that could encompass this one on its first floor, Alex spent most of his time with the hired hands, working his horses or the fields.

When he socialized, which was rarely, he preferred the company of common people who eked their livings from the soil. Unless he planned a trip to town, he usually dressed in blue denims and a sensible shirt, collar open, sleeves rolled back to the elbows. Before coming here, he had washed up, shaved, thrown on knee breeches, and a suit jacket, and called himself presentable. With all else that had been on his mind, he'd forgotten that Trimble was a man who placed a lot of importance on appearances. After having been a judge for over thirty years, he didn't even keep livestock on his place, let alone stoop to getting his hands dirty.

"The judge is in his study," Mrs. Trimble informed him, her manner faultlessly gracious but frosty.

Acutely aware that she hadn't offered to take his hat, Alex followed her from the foyer into a long, door-lined hallway. Halfway down the corridor, she paused and tapped lightly on gleaming oak. "Judge? You have a caller."

An indiscernible grumble came from within. Mrs. Trimble opened the door and moved back to let Alex enter. As he stepped into the room, some of his tension eased. It was a study very like his own, with large, comfortably stuffed chairs positioned strategically around colorful tapestry rugs. A room where a man could relax and feel at home. Leather-bound books lined gleaming oak shelves along three walls, the fourth boasting a river-rock fireplace. Firelight flickered cheerily in the grate, the only other illumination that of two gas jets above the mantel.

The judge sat behind his desk, his white court shirt rumpled, the collar open, his crimson tie loosened. A tendril of smoke drifted up from an ashtray near his elbow, the smell of it sharp. Alex settled his gaze on the cigar. Even after fourteen years, just the sight of one made him think of his father and filled him with sadness.

"Alex," Trimble said wearily. "I take it you've spoken with your brother?"

It didn't take clairvoyance to realize the judge expected him to launch into a tirade, denying Douglas's involvement in the attack on his daughter. Alex only wished that were the case. "Yes." Gazing at the books along one wall, he tried to make out the titles. The gold lettering blurred and danced in his vision, as jumbled as his thoughts. He didn't know where to start, or what to say. "I, um . . ." He swallowed and scrubbed his mouth with the back of his hand. Then he slapped his pant leg with his hat. "Douglas did it," he finally blurted. "I've come to offer my abject apologies for the injury he has done your daughter and make amends in any way I possibly can."

In response to that, the judge said nothing.

Alex rushed on. "If you intend to prosecute, I won't stand in your way. But you'd better be quick about notifying the sheriff. I've kicked my brother out of the house, and he's probably hightailing it for parts unknown about now."

Resting both elbows on his desk blotter, the judge rubbed at his temples. "Prosecute?" He gave a bitter laugh. "Ah, yes, one would think so. It seems the natural thing to do, doesn't it? But in situations like this, matters of right and wrong become blurred." At that admission, he laughed again, but there was no humor in the sound. "A judge for over half my life, and for the first time in my memory, there seems to be a very wide area of gray between the black and white."

The pain in the judge's voice made Alex fix his gaze on the floor. Safe territory, that. No accusing eyes stared back at him. He could think of nothing he might say, so he took refuge in silence.

Finally, the judge resumed speaking. "I appreciate your

offer not to interfere. He is your brother, after all. But I'm not sure restraint on your part will prove necessary.''

Forcing himself to look up, Alex said, ''I'm afraid I don't follow you.''

Trimble lowered his hands and met Alex's gaze. ''I know it may sound heartless, but there is far more to be considered here than the injury done to Annie.'' The judge shoved back his chair and came to his feet. For a man of small stature, he had a large presence, his eyes a piercing sapphire-blue, his features a striking blend of character and strength. Alex had always admired him and applauded the fairness of his decisions on the bench. He was a hard man, but just, a person people instinctively trusted.

''Scandal, Alex, a politician's nightmare,'' he said softly. ''If what happened today gets out, the backlash could be extreme.'' Looking a little shamefaced, he shoved his hands deep into his trouser pockets and studied the toes of his highly polished black shoes. ''Not just to Annie, but to me and the rest of my family.''

Alex was still confused but refrained from saying so.

With a sigh, the older man took a turn before the crackling fire, his gaze fixed on the stone hearth, his manner dejected. ''Douglas should be hanged for what he did to my little girl today. There's no question in my mind about that. But to what gain? Annie has been violated, and I can't undo that. For that reason, I'm inclined to do nothing. As I'm sure you know, I've retired from the bench to try my luck at local politics and possibly go on from there to serve in some capacity at a state level. A scandal of any sort could ruin me.''

It seemed to Alex that the scandal would besmirch the Montgomery name, not Trimble's. ''Your daughter has been raped. You can't be blamed for that or in any way held accountable. If anything, public sympathy will be aroused.''

''Ordinarily, yes. But our Annie isn't normal. She's tetched, no question about it, an affliction brought on by a high fever in early childhood. Unfortunately, people being given to gossip as they are, there have been those who have speculated about her idiocy, hinting that it could be inherited.'' He pinned Alex with a direct, intense gaze. ''How many mad politicians have you voted for recently?''

There was nothing Alex could say to that. No one could question the judge's sanity, but if gossips painted him as having madness in his family, the voters' faith in him might be shaken. All it would take to ruin his chances at the polls was a seed of doubt.

''We've kept Annie out of sight as much as possible so folks won't talk. If Douglas's attack on her is made public, all our efforts to keep her out of the limelight will have gone for naught.''

Alex nodded. ''So you intend to keep this hushed up, then?''

''I do.''

Even though it was his brother's salvation, Alex felt it was a misguided decision, and he was disappointed in the judge for having made it. If Douglas would attack one girl, there was nothing to say he might not victimize another. The only way to ensure he didn't was to prosecute him to the full extent of the law.

When Alex pointed that out, the judge replied, ''Douglas Montgomery's threat to society isn't my problem or my responsibility. I have to think of my family and myself, of our future. Going into politics has been my life-long dream, and I've worked toward that end my entire career. Why should I let your brother's actions snuff that out? I can't afford the scandal, I tell you, and at best, there would be a nasty one. Even if Annie were normal, which she isn't, the gossip would spread like wildfire. In her case, the talk could be even more vicious. I can't take that risk. I won't. Out of sight, out of mind. That has been my motto in raising Annie, and it will continue to be.

"In addition to the damage to my reputation, I also have to think of the consequences for her. Until now, she's been left alone by the young men in this area. But once word of this gets out, who's to say? Soiled goods, and all of that."

Alex found that line of reasoning appalling, and his feelings must have shown, for the judge's gaze turned fiery.

"Damn it, just you think about it, Montgomery. My daughter is a moron. All her life, she's been a target for torment. Why do you think she skulks away to hide in the woods whenever she spies people? Children throw stones at her. At every opportunity, they play cruel tricks on her. Today your brother simply carried the abuse a step further. If it becomes public knowledge, another young man may figure it can't hurt to do the same. To protect her, we'd have to keep her locked up, and if it comes to that, we may as well institutionalize her. My wife would be heartbroken if that happened."

Alex could think of nothing to say. Absolutely nothing except, "I'm sorry, Judge. I'm so very sorry."

The older man sighed again, the sound incredibly weary. "Yes, I know you are. But sorry doesn't undo what happened today." As if he suddenly realized how harsh that sounded, he added, "Don't take it so personally, Alex. It's a sad fact, but true. A man can choose his friends, but not his relatives."

"No." Alex looked helplessly around the room, searching his mind for something, anything he might do to set things right. There was nothing. He had said what he had come to say. "If there is anything I can do, anything at all . . ."

The judge shook his head. "I wish to God there were, son. As it is, we can only pray her dimwittedness gives her quick release from the memories."

Recalling the way Annie had clawed her way through the bushes to escape him a few minutes ago, Alex had reason to wonder if terror wasn't more reflexive than anything else, an instinctive emotion inherent in morons and geniuses alike. He wished she might forget quickly, but somehow he doubted she would.

His throat felt parchment-dry. The faint scent of wood smoke coming from the hearth blended with the acrid smell of the cigar. "If there should be complications, please feel free—"

"God forbid!"

Alex didn't blame the man for rejecting all thought of a pregnancy, but that being a natural consequence of what Douglas had done, it was a possibility neither of them could completely eliminate. "All the same, please contact me if problems of that nature should arise. I'll happily lend assistance in any way I can."

The judge gave a disheartened nod. Coming abreast of Alex, he reached up to pat his shoulder, his expression reflecting his utter dejection. "I appreciate your coming over. It took guts."

More than he could know. Alex felt heat crawl up his neck. It wasn't in him to hang his head, but he wanted to. "You know how to reach me."

"Rest assured I'll be in touch if it should prove necessary."

There seemed nothing more to say. Alex exited the house, his mind swimming. Incredible though it seemed, Douglas had once again gotten off scot-free. Alex knew he should feel relieved. But he didn't. It wasn't fair that Annie should be the only one to pay for the wrongs that had been committed this day.

Not fair at all.

Three

FOUR MONTHS LATER
AUGUST 16, 1890

S aturday. Pressing her forehead against her knees so
her mother could scrub her back, Annie mouthed the word
exactly as she had seen her mother say it and tried to think
how it might sound. Some words were easy because she
could remember hearing and saying them when she was
a small girl. But *Saturday* was more difficult. In her recollection, she'd never heard the word spoken. Not that it
mattered if she imagined the sounds wrong. Her mama
slapped her mouth whenever she tried to talk. Annie
wasn't sure why and had long since ceased to wonder.
The rules were different for her than for other people, and
she had come to accept there were lots of things she
wasn't allowed to do.

She didn't really care. Not anymore. When she went
up to her secret place in the attic to play, she could do
anything she wanted. Except for her pet mice, no one was
up there to see and tattle on her. In the attic, she could

35

dress up like a lady in old clothes from the trunks. She could have tea parties just like her mama did and pretend she could talk. Sometimes she even danced. And when she grew bored with doing all of that, she could sketch with the pads and pencils she'd sneaked from Papa's study. The attic was a lot of fun, and being able to do forbidden things there made up for not being able to do them the rest of the time.

Saturday. Annie mouthed the word against her knee again and promised herself that the very next time she went to the attic, she'd practice saying it in front of her mirror. In her younger years, before she had completely mastered lipreading, she had believed the word *Saturday* meant ''bath'' because her mother always said it with great emphasis as she shoved her into the tub. Now Annie realized Saturday was the day preceding church day, and in preparation, everybody in the family had to bathe.

Since Annie hadn't been allowed to attend church in a very long while, she didn't think it was fair that she had to take a bath right along with everyone else. In the morning, she wouldn't be allowed to put on a pretty dress like her mama and three sisters always did, and when it came time for everyone to leave for services, she would be left behind with the servants. Who was going to notice if her ears were clean, let alone care? Certainly not her.

As if guessing her thoughts, her mama grabbed her earlobe and gave it a hard pull. Like a turtle, Annie drew her head down close to her shoulders and squeezed her eyes closed. She hated this part. Hated it, hated it. To scrub her ears, her mother always wrapped a cloth around her fingertip then shoved the lot into her ear hole. Even when the ministrations didn't hurt, which was rarely, they were highly irritating. Annie wished she were allowed to scrub her ears by herself, but for some reason, her mother didn't believe her capable of doing a thorough job. Annie had learned long ago not to resist. It only earned her a cuffing, and in the end, her mother shoved the washcloth in her ear, regardless.

Thump, thump. The sharp rap of her mother's knuckles on the top of her head brought Annie's eyes open. Knowing what was expected of her, she raised her face and suffered through the suffocating experience of having it washed. Then, obeying the motion of her mother's hand, she rose, streaming water, so her torso and legs could be scrubbed. Annie knew the ritual by heart and turned this way and that.

Suddenly her mama stopped scrubbing. Annie peered through the wet strands of her dark hair, wondering what was the matter. Her mother's blue eyes were bugging, and her mouth hung open as if someone had knocked the breath out of her. Annie looked down at herself, half expecting to see something horrible. But as far as she could tell, there was nothing wrong. She turned her gaze back on her mother, silently questioning.

As if in answer, her mother's lips formed the words, "Oh, dear God, you're increasing."

Increasing? It was a word Annie was unfamiliar with. As she struggled to sound it out inside her head and determine its possible meaning, she saw that her mama was staring at her stomach. Embarrassed, Annie tried to suck in the slight bulge. She had noticed the thickening of her waist a lot lately and had determined only that afternoon that she should cut back on her eating. Spending so much time wandering in the woods, she had oft observed the wild animals as they prepared for their winter sleep and had figured out by herself that too much food made creatures fat. Annie could only suppose that she'd been snitching too many cookies and sweetbreads from the kitchen.

Her bulging stomach seemed a small problem to Annie, one that she could easily cure. But her mother seemed to think the problem was much more serious. After staring at her for a moment, she dropped the wet washcloth to the floor and covered her face with her hands. By the jerk of her shoulders, Annie knew she was sobbing. She didn't know what to do, and before she could think of anything, her papa stormed into her room, the tails of his nightshirt flapping around his bare, hairy ankles.

Annie crossed her hands over the juncture of her thighs and sank back into the water. Her papa never entered her bedchamber while she was bathing.

"What the blazes is the matter?" he asked.

Annie fixed her gaze on her mother, hoping to watch her reply so she could learn the answer to that question herself. But her mother's hands still covered her face. Whatever she said to Papa made him grow pale. He turned aching blue eyes on Annie.

"Dear God, no."

He moved slowly toward the tub. Grasping Annie's arm, he drew her to her feet. Annie couldn't recall the last time her father had seen her without clothes, and an awful hot feeling washed over her. She bent forward at the waist and splayed her hands over her private place again. In response, Papa gave her a hard shake. She glanced up just in time to see him say, "Stop that! Stand up, girl, so I can look at you."

Annie didn't want him to look, but look he did. She was thankful that the humiliation lasted only for a moment. Then he released her arm and, cupping a hand over his eyes, wheeled away. Growing alarmed at their behavior, Annie clamped both palms over her stomach. She'd seldom seen her parents so upset. Surely she wasn't as fat as all that.

Saying something over his shoulder that Annie couldn't catch, her father left the room. Her mother wiped at her cheeks with shaky hands, then lifted the towel, beckoning

Annie from the tub. Shivering, she stepped into the warm folds of flannel and drew the cloth around her body. Her mother gestured at the fresh nightgown she had laid out for her on the bed. Then, clearly expecting Annie to dry off and dress by herself, she scurried from the bedroom.

After tugging on her gown, Annie crept to the door and cracked it open. She felt the vibration of her father's footsteps in the floor before she saw him coming down the hall. To her surprise, he had thrown his clothes back on and was hastily buttoning his shirt. His shoelaces flopped as he walked, but he didn't seem aware that he had forgotten to tie them. She watched as he descended the stairs. A moment later, she felt the walls tremble as he slammed the front door on the way out.

Annie couldn't imagine where he might be going. On Saturday evenings, he always retired early and read in bed until he fell asleep. In her memory, he had never gone out after retiring unless something bad had happened.

Afraid her mother might catch her spying, she eased the door closed. Pressing her back against the wood, she hugged her waist and went back over all that had happened. Her parents couldn't be this upset because her waist was thickening.

Unable to make sense of things, she turned down the lamps then hurried into bed by the dying glow of the wicks. Even though the summer night was warm, the sheets were cool, and she shivered, snuggling deeply under the quilt. As darkness settled, she closed her eyes, determined to go to sleep. Whatever her father was so upset about, it didn't concern her. Surely not. Lots of people were far fatter than she, and no one got into such a dither about it.

Alex took a slow sip of brandy, savoring its taste as it flowed over his tongue. This was his favorite time of evening, his workday finished, supper over, the quiet hours before bedtime stretching before him. The fire popped cheerily, its amber flames and most of the heat rushing upward to the open chimney vent. Winter or summer, Alex always liked to build a fire at night, for warmth during the cold months, for mood when the temperatures grew sultry. Very little heat radiated from the flames, but the friendly glow flickered into the farthest corners of his study.

After doing a little paperwork, he hoped to catch up on his reading. A week's worth of newspapers from Portland were stacked beside his chair, none of them so much as unfolded. At both the horse farm and the rock quarry, spring and summer were his busiest times of year, beginning with the foaling season and not ending until harvest time in September. In between stretched week after week of backbreaking toil, filling orders for crushed rock, attending mares in labor, caring for foals, tilling the fields, then planting and irrigating. The chores seemed endless, the leisure hours few. On those rare occasions when he found spare time, he usually spent it at the rock quarry conferring with his foreman.

Stretching out his long legs, Alex crossed his ankles. Basking in the glow of the fire, he felt as lazy as a cat. Drowsiness slipped over him like a downy comforter, and he allowed his eyes to close, his snifter cupped loosely in one hand and perched on his chest.

"Sir?"

At the sound of his butler's voice, Alex jerked erect. Brandy sloshed over the front of his shirt, and he swore under his breath.

"I am sorry to disturb you, Master Alex, but James Trimble is in the foyer, and he insists he must see you about a matter of great urgency."

Alex set the snifter on the marble table beside his chair and rubbed his hand over his face. Trimble? He glanced at the mantel clock and saw that it was only ten after seven. Giving himself a shake to wake up, he pushed to his feet and began tucking in his shirt. "Show him in, Frederick."

Black coattails floating behind him, the butler pivoted and exited the study. A moment later, the gleaming mahogany door swung back open and Trimble stepped inside. With one glance, Alex knew something was wrong. The judge's left shoelace was untied, and his right stocking lay in folds around his ankle, his pant leg riding above it. His shirt was buttoned straight, but only one tail had found its way into his trousers.

"Dear God, Judge, what's happened?"

The older man made a beeline for the sideboard, never breaking stride until his hand curled around the brandy decanter. Without so much as a by-your-leave, he sloshed a generous measure of liquor into a glass and downed it in one gulp. Given the fact that the judge had called at his home only one other time, that being the evening of his daughter's rape, Alex found his behavior rather odd, to say the least. He watched with a raised eyebrow as the man poured himself more brandy.

After taking another belt, he finally turned toward Alex. "She's pregnant."

The words took Alex completely off-guard. Four months had passed with nary a word from the Trimbles, and he'd thought the possibility of a pregnancy long past. His knees buckled, and he barely guided himself into his chair. Eyes burning, his throat frozen with shock, he could only stare at the older man. After several endlessly long seconds, he finally said, "You're just now discovering it?"

The judge waved his hand, accidentally sloshing liquor over the edge of his glass. He didn't seem to notice the spill on the Persian carpet. "Her mother never told me."

He broke off and closed his eyes for a moment. "She hoped the cessation of her flux didn't mean anything." He raised his lashes to fix Alex with an anguished gaze. "She was wrong. Annie's breeding, no doubt about it."

Alex sank back in his chair. "Damn."

"The question now is what do we do? I believe she's too far along to terminate the pregnancy without endangering her life."

Alex knew there were disreputable physicians who, for a price, would perform such procedures, but the thought sickened him. His brother's child? His own niece or nephew? Even if a termination were possible at this late date, he wouldn't allow it. To him, children were an unattainable dream and precious beyond measure.

As if reading his thoughts, the judge downed the remainder of his brandy and said in a shaky voice, "My Annie isn't capable of raising a child, Montgomery, and my wife and I are too old to take on such a responsibility. We'll be doddering old fools before it ever reaches its majority." He shook his head. "If she weren't so far into the pregnancy, I'd have it terminated without batting an eye. Probably that's why Edie wouldn't admit the possibility to me."

"You're forgetting my responsibility in this. Has the thought occurred to you that I might be willing to raise the child?"

"That isn't an alternative."

"Why the hell not? Because of your political career?" Alex snorted. "There are ways to get around a scandal, Trimble." Though the admission came with difficulty, Alex knew this was no time to mince words. "I'm sure you've heard the rumors that I'm sterile. They're true. Mumps in my early twenties." Feigning a casualness he was far from feeling, Alex shrugged. "Because I'm unable to father children, I have no intention of taking a wife. If nothing else, I'd be willing to marry Annie and claim this child as my own.''

The judge shook his head vehemently.

Alex rushed on to argue his point. "Aside from the young men who witnessed the rape, and I doubt they'll talk, no one will know the babe isn't mine. Given Annie's affliction, there might be some speculation about why I'd marry her, but that would reflect badly on me, not you. After an acceptable period of time, I could claim irreconcilable differences and seek a separation. Annie could return home to be with her mother. It'd be the perfect solution for all involved. This is my brother's child we're discussing, after all. I've a responsibility for its welfare as well as for Annie's.''

"No.''

With that pronouncement, the judge slapped his glass back down on the sideboard. Like a blind man, he made his way across the room toward the fire, hands groping for support on the chair backs he passed. When he reached the hearth, he grasped the mantel and pressed his forehead against the rock. Alex was shocked when he heard the man sob.

"If you ever breathe a word of this,'' Trimble whispered raggedly, "I'm ruined. Swear nothing I say will go beyond this room.''

Alex shot a glance at the door to be certain it was securely closed. "Of course you have my word.''

"I know you think I'm a hardhearted bastard for wishing we could do away with the babe, but you aren't aware of all the facts. Our Annie, she—'' He broke off and heaved a jerky breath. "Well, you've heard the story. About the childhood fever that affected her mind?''

"Yes.''

The judge brushed his cheek against the shoulder of his jacket. "She *was* stricken with a fever. That isn't a lie.

When she was five or six, somewhere around then, and her strangeness began after that, coming on slowly, growing progressively worse as time wore on until she became what she is now.''

Alex didn't know what to say or if the judge even expected a reply.

"The thing is," he went on, "I'm not absolutely *sure* her affliction was caused by the fever. Edie insists it was. And because spreading that story has made it possible for us to keep the girl at home without it reflecting too badly on our family, I've pretended to believe it. But the truth is, one of Edie's uncles went mad. Stark raving mad. The mental imbalance began in childhood, just as Annie's did, and he grew progressively worse until he had to be physically restrained and institutionalized.''

Alex clenched his teeth, not wanting to hear this.

The judge slowly straightened and turned to face him, his blue eyes sparkling with tears, his face pasty white. "Until now, the truth was never that important. I just bided my time and prayed Annie would never get so bad I'd be forced to send her away. It'd kill her mother to put the girl into an asylum. Even the best of them are horrible places.''

Alex had heard the stories.

The judge lifted his hands. "But now—well, I can't continue to bury my head in the sand, not with a child on the way. Annie's affliction could be hereditary. Knowing that, I can't allow you or anyone else to adopt her child. A few years hence, it might go mad.''

Alex dropped his gaze, shamed to his core that he voiced no objection. Madness. Dear God. Not even he would want to take the risk of being saddled with a child like that.

"Now you see the problem.''

Alex pushed up from his chair and started to pace. He

wished to hell Douglas were here right now to witness the pain and heartache he had inflicted, not just on Annie, but on everyone around her.

The judge pinched the bridge of his nose. "The way I see it, I've only one option, and that is to send Annie away until the child has been born and can be put in an orphanage. I'll see to it that those in charge understand that it should never be adopted out."

Alex nodded. It seemed to be the only alternative to him as well. "Where will you send Annie? Have you relatives who might take her in?"

The judge shook his head. "A couple of elderly aunts who are too feeble to be of help. My brothers died of influenza back in the seventies, and Edie was an only child, conceived during her mother's change of life when she thought she had become infertile. Because of the uncle, her parents thought it best never to have other children for fear the madness might be hereditary."

In light of that, Alex was dying to know why the judge and Mrs. Trimble had had four daughters, but he bit back the question. It was none of his business, after all. "Then you'll have to foster Annie out to a home of some sort?"

"Yes, and that's where you come in. I'll need a bit of help financially. Care for her will be expensive, especially for that long a period of time."

"Name the amount. I told you in the beginning that I'd help in any way possible, and I meant it. As it happens, money is something I have plenty of, and I'll happily pay all the expenses."

The judge rubbed a hand over his face. "I'm comfortably set, but, contrary to what folks believe, my financial resources aren't inexhaustible."

His heart going out to the other man, Alex clasped his shoulder. "You know, James, not that I doubt your judgment, but wouldn't it be wise to have Annie's condition confirmed by Dr. Muir before we go off half-cocked?''

"She's pregnant, no doubt about it. Her waistline is already beginning to thicken.''

Alex recalled the many times he'd thought a mare to be with foal only to discover later that it wasn't. "Sometimes looks can be deceiving. Trust me on that. We may be panicking over nothing. The girl could be putting on a bit of weight, nothing more.''

"If only that were so. Dear God, if only it were.''

Alex shared that sentiment. It would be better for all concerned if Annie wasn't carrying Douglas's child, especially for the babe's sake. An orphanage. The thought of his own flesh and blood being stuck in an institution and labeled unadoptable made him heartsick.

The judge drew himself up and took a bracing breath. "Well, I guess I'll go get Dr. Muir.''

"Tonight?'' Alex couldn't conceal his surprise. It seemed to him that calling in the doctor could wait until morning, for Annie's sake, if nothing else.

"Edie is so upset, I want this settled as quickly as possible,'' the older man explained.

"I see.''

"While we're on the subject of Edie . . .'' The judge ran a finger under his collar, clearly uncomfortable with what he meant to say. "I'd appreciate it if you wouldn't mention anything we've discussed tonight in front of her. About her uncle, I mean. I, um . . . well, the madness in her family, it isn't something we talk about.''

It wasn't something they talked about? Considering the fact that their daughter might be mad, Alex found that bit of information peculiar in the extreme.

Four

Doing his best to conceal his anger, Daniel Muir eased himself down onto the edge of Annie Trimble's bed and took her hand. The wariness in her wide blue eyes caught at his heart, and for at least the dozenth time since Alex Montgomery had fetched him from town, he had to swallow his ire at her parents. How two people as good and charitable as James and Edie could be so callous in their dealings with their youngest daughter was beyond him. If the girl was indeed pregnant, she'd be no less so in the morning. But they had insisted her condition be confirmed tonight.

Daniel didn't believe in frightening his patients, and there was no mistaking the fact that Annie was afraid of him. Small wonder. He'd attended the girl no more than half a dozen times in her entire life, only once since the fever that had rendered her mentally impaired, and was a virtual stranger to her. Now here he was, waking her from a sound sleep to examine her. Behind him, Edie stood guard, wringing her hands, wailing, and weeping. That alone was bound to terrify the girl. To make matters worse, James was across the room, wearing a path in the gleaming hardwood floor. For two highly intelligent peo-

47

ple, they were sorely lacking in horse sense.

"Well?" James said impatiently. "Is she, or isn't she?"

Enough was enough. Daniel rose from the bed and drew himself to his full height, which was diminutive, at best. Leveling a glare at the distraught couple, he barked, "Out! I haven't examined her yet and don't plan to with all of this going on."

Edie jumped. James spun to a stop and fixed him with a startled gaze.

"You're upsetting the girl," Daniel said more gently. "Please, step out into the hall. When I've come to a determination, I'll call you back in."

"Well," Edie said with an indignant sputter. "I never!"

At the moment, Daniel didn't particularly care if he had offended Edie Trimble. His patience with the woman was in short supply, and it was all he could do not to lace her up one side and down the other. Moron or no, Annie still had feelings, and her mother, of all people, should appreciate that. Raped, no less, and Daniel hadn't been summoned to examine her? Edie had to have known the girl might have had internal bleeding or, barring that, could have contracted an infection. Yet he hadn't been brought to the house. It was almost as if Edie were afraid to let him examine Annie for fear of what he might conclude. Why, that was the question, and it was one for which Daniel had no answer.

After showing the Trimbles to the door, Daniel sighed and turned back to regard Annie. She watched him nervously, her eyes the size of dinner plates. Trying his best to look harmless, he walked slowly back to the bed. Resuming his seat on the edge of the mattress, he took her hand again and gave it a kindly pat.

"Do you remember me, Annie?" he asked softly.

Keeping her gaze fixed on his mouth, she tucked in her chin and rubbed her cheek against the shoulder of her nightgown. Daniel took stock of her finely sculpted features, thinking what a shame it was that a fever had incapacitated her. Though the older Trimble girls were all married and, because of the distances they had to travel, visited home infrequently, Daniel recollected each of their countenances quite clearly. Of the four sisters, Annie was without question the loveliest. A person had to look closely to see that, of course. She had an uncommonly thick mane of sable hair that clouded in silky, unruly waves about her face, nearly obscuring what was an almost cameo-perfect visage. Her mother wasted little coin to clothe her, probably because the girl ruined her garments running in the hills. The result was that Annie went about in shapeless, unflattering frocks made of low-quality fabric. To make matters worse, no one had bothered to teach the child any social graces. To be fair to the Trimbles, maybe she was incapable of learning, but Daniel still thought it a shame they hadn't at least made an effort to give the girl some polish. As it was, her manners and behavior were those of a six-year-old.

"When you were a very small girl, I used to hide candy in my pockets when I came to see you, but I don't suppose you can remember that."

Her gaze flicked to the breast pocket of his jacket. Grasping the lapel, Daniel turned the inner compartment out, glad that he always carried treats to win over his younger patients. Leaning forward slightly, he released his hold on her small hand and said, "Go ahead. Help yourself."

Her finely arched brows drew together in a frown. Instead of reaching for the candy, she placed a palm over her abdomen and shook her head slightly.

"Not in the mood for a sweet, hmm?" Taking care not

to make any sudden moves, Daniel drew back the quilt and placed a hand beside hers on her stomach. "Tummy ache?" He kneaded gently with expert fingers. As her parents had forewarned, her abdomen was slightly distended. He took gentle measure of the swelling, then pulled the quilt back up to her waist and smiled at her. "Everything seems to be in fine order to me."

The distrust in her eyes told Daniel that unless he used restraints, an internal examination would be nigh unto impossible. Undaunted, he bent to open his black bag and withdrew his stethoscope. He hadn't been working in this profession for over forty years without learning his way around shy patients. After cupping the stethoscope's receiver between his hands to warm it, he placed it just beneath her collarbone and made a great show of listening to her heart, gently flattening his palms against her chest as he did so. When she didn't protest, he moved the instrument lower, then lower still until he had it positioned over her small breast. While pretending to listen, he quickly palpated the area, his heart sinking when she winced and he felt how swollen she was.

Without doing a thorough exam, he couldn't be absolutely positive she was pregnant, but the distension of her abdomen and the tenderness in her breasts were two undeniable counts against her. He sighed as he returned the stethoscope to his bag. Given the cessation of her menses, he felt ninety-nine percent sure her parents were correct in their diagnosis. He didn't relish the thought of relaying the news to them. Edie would no doubt shriek and carry on, which would only alarm the girl all the more.

Straightening, he regarded Annie with saddened eyes. What was to become of her? he wondered. A home for unwed mothers, at best. Possibly a nightmarish stint in an asylum. The thought nearly broke his heart. She was a wild little creature, accustomed to running free in the woods. Being locked up anywhere would be hard on her, especially when she couldn't be made to understand it was only for a few months.

Acting on impulse, Daniel smoothed her dark hair back from her face. The loveliness of her delicate features made his breath catch. He drew a piece of hard candy from his breast pocket and enfolded her hand around it. "Maybe you'll feel like a sweet in the morning, hmm?"

Long after the doctor doused the lamp and left her room, Annie lay still, staring at the shadows on the ceiling. The candy in her hand was beginning to melt, and it felt sticky against her palm. Dimly she could remember the doctor coming to see her when she was small. His hair had been black then, not gray, and his face hadn't been so lined. But try as she might, she couldn't recollect his bringing her sweets. That he had done so tonight was a puzzle. She hadn't missed the concern in his expression when he felt her stomach. If her growing fat had everyone so worried, why would he bring her a treat that would only make her grow fatter?

There was a strange feeling in the air tonight, like right before a lightning storm. Occasionally she felt vibrations emanating from the floor and walls and wondered what made them. Doors opening and closing? Footsteps? She wanted to sneak from her room and peer over the banister to see what was happening downstairs, but she was afraid her mother might catch her. Sometimes Annie could watch the goings-on without getting into trouble, but she sensed that tonight wasn't one of those times.

Rolling onto her side, she placed the piece of candy on her bedside table. Then she licked the stickiness from her palm, savoring the sweetness and hoping such a small amount of sugar wouldn't make her any fatter. She'd never seen her parents so upset, not even the time she'd run up to the front of the church to touch the organ.

Drowsy, Annie drew the quilt up to her chin and closed her eyes. Tomorrow, she vowed, she wouldn't eat anything but a small breakfast and dinner. In no time at all, she'd be thin again, and her parents would stop looking at her so sadly.

Alex had a pounding headache, and Edie Trimble's shrill voice made the pain explode behind his eyes. He sat before the hearth in the judge's study and wished himself far away from here. A woman's tears always made him feel a little panicky, probably because he hadn't been around many females. Maddy, his housekeeper, a stalwart old gal of fifty-three, wasn't given to tearful displays, and he could scarcely remember much about his stepmother, Alicia.

"Please, James," Edie pleaded. "Let me take care of her here. She won't understand if we send her off to a strange place to stay with people she doesn't know."

The judge raked a hand through his thinning hair and cast a flustered glance at Dr. Muir. "Daniel, say something."

The physician shrugged. "What can I say? Edie is absolutely correct. The girl won't understand, and she's bound to be upset if you farm her out to strangers."

His temper fraying, the judge threw up his hands. "What else can I do?"

Daniel rubbed his chin. "Keeping her at home isn't possible?"

"What of the scandal?" the judge cried.

"Ah, yes, the scandal."

By the physician's tone, it was abundantly clear he was unsympathetic to James Trimble's concerns about his political career. Personally, Alex was of the same bent. If Annie were his daughter, he liked to think her welfare would be his first priority, his professional endeavors second.

"Perhaps I can do some checking around and find a suitable home in which to place Annie," Alex offered.

Edie turned tear-swollen eyes on him. Alex pushed up from his chair and braced an arm on the mantel. "The ideal thing would be to find a grandmotherly sort to care for her, someone who'd be willing to take Annie in for the duration of her pregnancy. I'm sure that we can find such a woman if we look hard enough." To emphasize his point, Alex held up his hands. "The girl is only four months along. We have some time to play with." Looking to Edie, he said, "As for her being confused and upset by a change of residence, there's nothing to say you can't go with her and stay until she's settled in."

Edie touched a hand to her throat. She looked to the judge for confirmation. "Could I do that, dear?"

Trimble nodded. "I don't see why not. The trouble will be finding such a woman." Flashing Alex a hopeful look, he added, "If we could, it'd be ideal, the answer to everything."

Feeling guilty beyond measure because his brother had caused all of this upheaval, Alex was quick to say, "Leave it to me. Dealing in horseflesh as I do, I've made acquaintances in other towns. I'll begin writing inquiries in the morning and will post them Monday. It may take a bit of time, but we'll find someone who'll take Annie in."

Edie stepped into her husband's arms and dissolved into another bout of tears. Though he sympathized with her, Alex was eager to get out of there. Once again assuring the Trimbles that he would begin making inquiries come morning, he escaped into the hall and made a beeline for the foyer. He was outside on the porch before he realized the good doctor was right behind him.

"A bad bit of business, this," Daniel Muir observed.

To Alex, that seemed an understatement. He couldn't forget, not for an instant, that Douglas was responsible. "Yes, it is that. God knows, I wish I could undo it, but I can't."

As they descended the front steps, the doctor took off his jacket, hooked it by the collar with his thumb, and slung it over his shoulder. "It's fair to middling warm tonight, isn't it? I was about to suffocate in there."

Accustomed to working out of doors during the heat of the day, Alex hadn't noticed the stuffiness. He looked up at the starlit sky. "We could do with some rain."

"Isn't that just the way of it? We complain of the wetness all winter, then come mid-August, we pray for a downpour."

Drawing up beside his horse at the hitching post, Alex observed, "Human nature is contrary."

Muir glanced toward the house. "You aren't telling me anything I don't already know. Those folks are certainly a puzzle, and that's a fact."

Believing he referred to the judge's concern about his political career, Alex said, "It's not always possible to understand another man's priorities."

"True." Squinting to study Alex through the moonlit gloom, Muir said, "Take you, for instance. I took you for a smart man, always on the lookout for an opportunity. Now, an opportunity's knocking, and you're passing it up."

"Pardon?"

"Little Annie. Her breeding, and all," the doctor clarified. "There you stand, creeping up on thirty, not yet married and convinced you can't have children. Seems to me you'd jump at the chance to marry that girl and claim Douglas's child as your own. You can't get much closer to having your own child than your own brother's."

Knowing how it must appear to the doctor, Alex looked away, unable to explain because he'd given his word not to repeat what Trimble had divulged to him. "Yeah, well, as much as I'd dearly love to have a child, Doc, I have my reasons for hesitating."

Muir sighed. "Edie's mad uncle, you mean?" The physician stepped around the hitching rail to his horse. After tightening the belly strap, he looked at Alex over the saddle. "Oh, yes, I've heard the stories. And I'm telling you, Alex, that girl isn't mad. I was with Edie when Annie was born, and I was the attending physician all during her early years. She was right as can be until that fever struck. There's not a thing wrong with that girl that she'll pass on to her children. I guarantee you that."

Alex curled a hand over the rail and gripped with such force his knuckles ached. "You could be wrong."

Daniel chuckled. "Water may start running uphill, too. I don't say it lightly, Alex. I realize the consequences if I'm wrong. But I assure you, I'm not. That girl was as bright as a new penny before that illness struck."

"You're certain it's not hereditary?"

"Dead certain."

Alex swallowed and glanced toward the house, his mind racing with possibilities. "I don't know. If I married her, it'd cause a heap of talk, her not being right and all. People would think me lecherous, and who could blame them?"

"That's probably true. If you're sensitive to gossip, I guess you'd best stay clear of the situation."

Alex drew a deep breath. "And that's not to mention the responsibility I'd be taking on. A girl like Annie. Well, she's bound to be a handful."

The doctor smiled. "She's a docile little thing, happy as a clam with her simple pleasures. With your money, you could hire a live-in nurse to look after her and scarcely realize she was in the house. There's Annie's welfare to consider as well. Moving to your place might unsettle her for a bit, but it'd be a sight less upsetting than if she's sent away to God knows where. Living with you, at least she could wander in the woods she's so familiar with, and when she took a fancy, she could mosey home to see her mama. Not that you're responsible for the misfortune that's about to befall the poor little thing, but if you were to marry her, you could make things a hell of a lot easier on her.''

Alex fixed his gaze on the dark woods that bordered the Trimbles' yard. ''I don't know, Doc.'' He took a deep, bracing breath. ''If you're wrong about the girl—'' He broke off and shrugged. ''A child with mental problems? I didn't do such a great job of raising Douglas, you know. Look how he turned out. To consider bringing up a child with an affliction—well, just the thought makes me run scared.''

The doctor conceded the point by inclining his head. Then he delivered the killing blow. ''And if I'm not wrong and the child is normal? It'll spend its entire life in an orphanage, with no hope of being adopted.'' The doctor mounted his horse, laying his coat over the saddle horn. ''Just you think about that, young man. If you can turn your back, more power to you. I hope you'll be able to sleep nights.''

With that, the good physician spurred his horse and rode down the drive toward the road.

Feeling as though someone had kicked his feet out from under him, Alex stepped to the porch and sat down. Crickets sang in the darkness. The moon hung like a gigantic silver dollar over the mountains, its glow frosting the distant treetops. From inside the house came the muted sound of Edie Trimble's weeping.

Closing his eyes, Alex tried to sort his thoughts, but

the doctor's last words hung foremost in his mind. How could he turn his back on his brother's child and sleep nights? He had the financial resources to hire a live-in nurse to care for Annie, and the doctor was probably correct that in his monstrosity of a house, he probably wouldn't even realize the girl was residing there. The child could be born in wedlock. It would have the Montgomery name, as was its birthright, and all the advantages that came with it. Though it might take Annie a few days to adjust to living in a different home, she'd eventually settle in, and it would be much easier on her, not being entirely separated from her family and all that was familiar to her.

After circling the problem for several minutes, Alex pushed to his feet and climbed back up the steps. Not bothering to knock at the front door, he let himself inside and traversed the dimly lit corridor to the judge's study. The Trimbles looked up in surprise when he reentered the room, Edie with bleary, swollen eyes, her husband with bewilderment.

"I thought you'd gone," the judge said.

Feeling unaccountably nervous, Alex raked a hand through his hair. "Yes, well, I had a long talk with Dr. Muir, and I've been thinking that there's another solution to this problem." Alex met the judge's gaze. "Despite what you mentioned earlier, sir, I've decided the best thing for everyone concerned is for me to marry your daughter."

Before either of the Trimbles could protest, Alex rushed on.

"I'll hire a competent live-in nurse to care for her. On occasion, she'll be able to come here for visits, and both of you would be welcome at my place any time. The child will have my name." Alex waved a hand. "It's the perfect situation, if you think about it."

All the color had drained from Edie's face, and she pushed unsteadily to her feet. Alex expected her to agree with him wholeheartedly. Instead, she cried, "No!"

It was the last thing he expected her to say. "Why, for God's sake?"

"Because," she cried, turning to the judge. "I won't have it, James. After the baby is born, I want Annie to come back home where she belongs. I don't want strangers caring for her the rest of her life. She's *my* child and *my* responsibility."

Alex was too exhausted to argue. "Shortly after the child is born, Annie and I could separate. We could put it out and about that there were difficulties within the marriage that couldn't be resolved. She could return home. I'd raise the child."

Edie pressed the back of her wrist to her forehead and started to pace, her agitation apparent in every rigid line of her body. The judge watched her for several seconds. Then he looked at Alex, his gaze filled with questions. Well aware of what he must be thinking, Alex softly said, "I'm aware of the risks, Judge. I'm willing to take my chances. If it should happen that there's something wrong with the child, I'll see that it's kept quiet and have it institutionalized, just as you originally planned. No gossip, no scandal. We'll say the child died or that I sent it away to relatives."

The older man shot him a warning glare, then glanced at his pacing wife, clearly afraid she might have overheard. He relaxed slightly when she continued circling the study, apparently oblivious of the exchange.

"I don't know," he said under his breath. "If word got out, it could ruin me. I really think it's best if we simply—"

"I'm not giving you a choice," Alex inserted.

The judge's pupils dilated, turning his irises nearly black. "Is that a threat?"

"A promise," Alex corrected. "Fight me on this, and you can kiss your chances for public office goodbye."

The man's neck turned dull red. After staring at Alex for a long moment, he returned his gaze to his wife. "Edie, it's the best solution we've come up with yet. Annie wouldn't be with Alex forever, only for a few months."

Mrs. Trimble shook her head vehemently. "No. I'd rather do as we planned earlier and find someone out of town to care for her until she has the child."

That made absolutely no sense. His patience fraying, Alex settled onto a chair and fixed the judge with a relentless gaze. "There's more to consider here than just Mrs. Trimble's wishes," he said carefully. "My plan would be better for Annie, certainly. And the child won't be put into an orphanage."

Edie whirled on Alex, her eyes sparking with anger. "The child is not your concern, Mr. Montgomery! None of this is."

It was all Alex could do to keep his temper. "I disagree. The child is very much my concern, and if there's a way to avoid its being raised in an institution, that's what we have to do."

"Edie," the judge said softly, "why don't you go to the kitchen and prepare some tea?"

She made fists in her skirt. "Tea? You're deciding my daughter's future, and you expect me to brew tea?"

"Yes." Though softly spoken, the judge's reply was an unmistakable order. "I'm still the man of this house. Ultimately, I must make the decision, and you must abide by it."

Turning a murderous glare on Alex, Mrs. Trimble

swept from the room, her cheeks spotted with crimson, her mouth drawn into a tight line.

Immediately after her departure, some of the tension in the study dissipated. Alex took advantage of the momentary privacy to relate to the judge what Dr. Muir had said, namely his assurances that Annie's affliction had been caused by a high fever.

"And if he's wrong?" the judge asked.

"What if he isn't?" Alex countered. "A perfectly normal child stuck in an orphanage and tagged as unadoptable? The way I see it, I have to take the chance. And, like it or not, you're going to take it with me. This is your grandchild and my niece or nephew we're talking about. We owe it at least this much."

Trimble considered that for a moment, then he finally nodded. "Just so long as you're going into it with your eyes open. Muir means well, and I'm sure he believes what he's saying, but that doesn't mean he couldn't be wrong."

"Let's pray he isn't."

That settled, the two men discussed the particulars, and within five minutes, both had agreed that a marriage between Alex and Annie should take place as quickly as possible. When Edie returned to the room, the judge gently informed her of their decision about the marriage, which both men hoped would take place within the week, the only prerequisite being that Alex find a competent live-in nurse.

When his wife began to protest, the judge cut her short with, "That will be enough, Edie. This is best. Trust me on that."

Defeated, Mrs. Trimble sank onto the settee beside her husband and folded her hands tightly on her lap. "But, James, he knows nothing of how to handle her."

"Neither would a nurse in another town," Alex pointed out.

"At least then I might have exercised some control in matters," she shot back. "Putting our daughter into inexperienced hands could undo all the years of training I've worked so hard to instill in her."

Alex rubbed his temple, silently cursing the headache that throbbed behind his eyes. Though he couldn't understand the woman, her concerns still had to be addressed. "Mrs. Trimble, I'll happily allow you to confer with the nurse I hire, if that's your worry. You can instruct her in Annie's care, just as you would have a nurse elsewhere."

Some of the rigidity eased from her slender body. "You truly wouldn't mind?"

Alex dredged up a smile, albeit a weak one. "Of course not. It isn't as if this will be a marriage in fact. It's a convenient arrangement, nothing more. If anything, I'll be grateful for your input and experience in dealing with Annie."

For a long moment, she searched Alex's gaze. Then she finally returned his smile. "Perhaps this will be a workable situation, after all," she conceded.

"I certainly hope so. Otherwise, I wouldn't offer," Alex assured her.

"Annie is a difficult girl," she hurried to add. "She must be made to follow strict rules, you understand, or she becomes intractable. You may pooh-pooh my worries, but the fact is, if Annie becomes uncontrollable, it will necessitate her being committed to a sanitarium, and as her mother, I want to avoid that at all costs."

Finally, Alex began to understand what drove the woman. As upset as she had been about Annie's being sent away, at least then she would have had some control over her care. Her objections to Alex marrying Annie stemmed from fear, nothing more. "I give you my word that I'll adopt all your rules for Annie and strictly enforce them,'' Alex promised her. ''And you can spend as much time as necessary instructing the nurse I hire so she will carry on with Annie exactly as you would if you were there to supervise.''

Edie heaved a relieved sigh. ''Thank you, Mr. Montgomery. That makes me feel much more at ease with this situation.''

Hoping that was the end of it, Alex rose from his chair, only to sit back down again when Edie Trimble launched into a long list of instructions regarding her daughter's care. Annie was never to be taken to town; crowds of people unsettled her. Pencils or pens were taboo; the girl might injure herself with them. Never, not under any circumstances, was Annie to be allowed to make sound; once she got started, it was impossible to silence her, and the din she could raise was earsplitting.

By the time the woman wound down, Alex's head was swimming and he seriously doubted he would be able to remember anything she had told him. Even so, he promised to observe each and every rule to the letter. Anything to get out of there.

Before taking his leave, Alex shook hands with the judge on their agreement and promised to begin his search for a live-in nurse immediately. As he left the house, he paused in the foyer to gaze at the second-story landing, wondering which door along the upper hallway led to Annie's room. As ashamed as it made him feel to admit it, until that moment, Alex hadn't given much thought to Annie's reaction to all of this. Recalling her terror of him four months ago, he could only pray she had forgotten all about Douglas and what he had done to her. If not—well, it didn't bear thinking about.

Five

The wedding date was set for one week later, and Alex arrived on the Trimbles' doorstep at precisely ten o'clock on the appointed morning to make Annie his lawfully wedded wife. The plan sounded simple enough: a quick marriage, a few months of looking after Annie, and then he would send the girl back to her parents. What could possibly go wrong? It seemed to Alex the answer to that question was everything. The instant he stepped into the house, he began to have doubts, a whole host of them.

Like a curious child who'd been sent upstairs while guests were present, Annie sat on the landing that overlooked the foyer, her small face bracketed by mahogany balusters, her eyes wide with bewilderment as she watched all the goings-on below. Reverend Widlow, the minister who was to officiate at the ceremony, had arrived just seconds before Alex and was being shown into the parlor by a servant. Two hired men were carrying one of Annie's trunks downstairs. Maids were scurrying to and fro. Anyone could see that something out of the ordinary was about to occur.

As Alex stepped into the foyer, Annie went absolutely

still, and every drop of blood seemed to drain from her face. It didn't take a genius to figure out that she believed him to be Douglas. Given her intellectual disabilities, he could think of no way to disabuse her of the notion. As people were so fond of reminding him, he was the "spittin' image" of his brother. To Alex, the resemblance didn't seem quite that pronounced, but to Annie, who undoubtedly recalled everything about Douglas in a nightmarish blur, the differences between them might not seem so apparent.

Afraid of making her panic, Alex came to a dead stop. Even at a distance of twenty feet, he could feel her fear. Electrical, it hung in the air between them, raising goose flesh along his spine.

Six-two in his stocking feet, he stood a head taller than most men. For a score of different reasons, there had been a number of times when he wished he were smaller, but never quite so much as in that moment. Before entering the house, he'd removed his hat, so he couldn't jerk it off now to make himself look shorter. Judging by the stark terror in Annie's eyes, slumping his shoulders wasn't helping much, either. He was a big man. There was little he could do to disguise that fact. With a girl like Annie, who had every reason to be frightened, that was a definite strike against him.

If she'd been able to communicate, he might have been able to reassure her. As it was, all he could do was stand there and try to convey with his gaze what he couldn't express with words, namely that he was not cut from the same cloth as his brother. He would never dream of harming her, or allow anyone else to, for that matter.

"Hello, Annie," he said softly.

As he spoke, her attention shifted to his mouth, and an expression of total bewilderment crossed her face. Alex's heart sank, for he had hoped she might understand a few words, at least. Seeing that she didn't, he shoved his hands into his trouser pockets and made tight fists.

The way she stared at him made him feel like a monster. A very large monster. He flashed what he prayed was a harmless-looking smile, but his face felt so stiff he feared it was more a grimace. Deciding she might realize he wasn't Douglas if she got a better look at him, he moved a bit closer.

For some reason, he hadn't imagined her as being so small. Narrow shoulders, tiny feet, fragile limbs. He doubted she'd tip the scales at a hundred pounds fully clothed.

Over the years, he had met a number of women he might have described as delicate, but even that seemed too sturdy an adjective for Annie. She put him in mind of handblown crystal. Her face was heart-shaped, her features finely sculpted and as close to perfect as any he'd ever seen. Her short, straight little nose slanted from between dark, elegantly arched brows.

As he drew closer, she shifted her position slightly. By her tenseness, he guessed she meant to bolt if he made any sudden moves. A smothered smile spread warmth through his chest when he saw she had lifted one knee slightly. From her vantage point, she was decently covered. But looking at her from the ground up, such was not the case. Like most bloomers, hers had an opening at the crotch, and she wore no petticoats to obstruct his view.

He jerked his attention back to her face. Scalding heat inched up his neck. Looking into her eyes, he tried to ascertain if she'd noticed where his gaze had wandered. *Those eyes.* Startlingly large and the color of a cloudless sky on a hot summer day, they were completely guileless.

A practical man to the marrow of his bones, Alex had never believed in all the nonsense men spouted during courtships. While looking into a woman's eyes, the closest he'd ever come to drowning was when he broke out in a sweat, and that from lust. But Annie's eyes were different. He didn't feel as though he were drowning, exactly. But close. Mighty damned close. Sort of like a fish gaffed through both gills, her big blue eyes the line that was hauling him in.

She was such a helpless little thing. And so horribly vulnerable. Marrying her was the lesser of two evils, no question about that. But even so, he hated to be instrumental in bringing her more pain. It was like having a wobbly fawn in his rifle sights and pulling the trigger.

As he studied her, Alex noticed a bit of blue on a baluster to her right. To his surprise, he saw that she'd wrapped her hair ribbon around the post in a perfect spiral, similar to that on a barber pole or a peppermint stick. He wondered if she liked candy canes and made a mental note to buy her several the next time he went to town.

Sweets for the sweet . . .

"Alex, my good man."

The unexpected greeting made Alex jerk. He turned to see James Trimble emerging from the parlor. Given the reason for this gathering, he couldn't fathom why the man was grinning so broadly. As far as Alex could see, this was no occasion to celebrate.

"James," he said evenly.

By way of polite greeting, Alex knew he should probably say something more, but for the life of him, he couldn't dredge up a pleasantry. What could he say? That he was glad to see him? Frankly, he wasn't. Over the last week, he had come to like Annie's father less with each successive encounter. For years, he had admired the man. Now, after getting better acquainted with him, he knew him for the self-centered, insensitive bastard he really was. And those were his fine points.

Drawing up beside Alex, Trimble hooked his thumbs

under his jacket lapels, rocked back on his heels, and said, "It's a fine morning for a wedding, wouldn't you say? Yes, indeed, absolutely perfect." When Alex didn't concur, his smile faltered, and with a true politician's knack for equivocation, he amended, "A trifle warm, perhaps. But at least we can count on it not to rain. Not that we couldn't use a good downpour."

The way Alex saw it, it was not, by any stretch of the imagination, a fine morning. As far as that went, it had been a rotten week as well. He was about to marry a girl without her consent. Whether Annie understood that or not, he did. Night after night, he'd lain awake to stare at his ceiling, telling himself that the end would justify the means, that he was doing the right thing. But was he? It was a question Alex couldn't answer with any certainty, not without a crystal ball and a seer to foretell the future. Not that he believed in such bullshit.

He gave his future father-in-law's attire a scathing glance. With a total lack of regard for the significance of the occasion, Trimble wore a loosely cut tan sack suit over a lightly starched white shirt and a V-necked, rose-colored cotton sweater. His matching tie was an even deeper shade of pink. It was a decidedly casual outfit, more appropriate for entertaining guests out on the lawn than for a wedding, even one as informal as this.

Conversely, Alex had been uncharacteristically particular about what he wore this morning. He'd ended up choosing a dark gray tailored suit and a heavily starched white shirt, the front of which was so stiffly polished it threatened to crack when he moved. Since he detested the smell of shirt enamel, a blend of wax and spermaceti that filmed his nostrils and clung bitterly to the back of his tongue, he couldn't help but resent the other man's informality.

With another broad grin, James slapped Alex's arm.

"Got the bridegroom jitters, do you? Step into the parlor. I've got just the cure." With a conspiratorial wink, he leaned closer. "My special stuff. Peach brandy, the likes of which you've never tasted."

As he was drawn toward the parlor, Alex looked back over his shoulder at Annie. Her big blue eyes were still riveted to him. He flashed her another smile, hoping to reassure her. Before he could read her reaction, James led him through the archway into the other room.

Brandy and pompous asses. Over the next few minutes, Alex decided it was a particularly nauseating mixture. Neither Trimble nor the minister seemed to realize the magnitude of what they were about to do. Alex could think of nothing else. True, his intentions were good, but that would not lessen the impact all this would have on Annie. Shortly after this mockery of a wedding took place, she would be carted away from the only home she'd ever known by a man who terrified her. The more Alex thought about that, the more inclined he was to agree with his housekeeper, Maddy, that this entire arrangement was a sin against God and all that was holy.

Finishing his brandy, the minister drew his watch from his pocket. A tall, portly man with thinning black hair the exact same shade as his suit, he made Alex think of funerals. He realized why when he noticed the man was wearing a black collar instead of the customary white. "Well, James?" he said. "Let's get on with it, shall we? As I mentioned when we talked earlier in the week, I've a busy schedule. I managed to fit this in, but only just barely. I've two christenings and another wedding to do this afternoon, plus a funeral yet this morning that I didn't plan on." He gave a raucous laugh. "That's the trouble with dying parishioners. They never choose a convenient time."

A muscle began to twitch under Alex's eye, a purely nervous reaction to anger, one of the few outward signs he hadn't learned to control over the years. This wedding, he realized, was nothing more than a bothersome chore for both these men, an irritating necessity to be gotten out of the way with as little fuss as possible.

"When it comes to busy schedules, no one understands better than I." James set his half-empty snifter on the mantel. "Well, Alex? Has that brandy given you enough false courage to say the two most dreaded words in the English language?" He guffawed and winked at the reverend. "I've never known a bachelor yet who could say 'I do' without getting a case of cold feet, myself included."

Alex tightened his grip on the glass and set his back teeth to prevent himself from saying something he might regret. While James stepped to the archway to hail his wife, Alex gazed into the fireplace.

Had the good reverend been informed of the reasons for this sudden marriage? Given James's confident manner, Alex had a nasty suspicion that his future father-in-law had ensured the minister's cooperation by making a substantial donation to his church. Stained-glass windows and fancy steeple bells didn't come cheap. The thought sickened him. Money spoke with eloquence; no one knew that better than he. But men of the cloth were supposed to be above taking bribes.

Kitchen smells drifted into the parlor from somewhere at the back of the house—cinnamon, vanilla, and yeast dough—to mix nauseatingly with the sticky sweetness of his brandy. For a dizzying instant, he could have sworn the roses on the wool rug were moving. He blinked, craving the bracing effects the liquor might provide, but half afraid his stomach might rebel if he drank the rest of it.

Annie . . . She was definitely not a cherished daughter.

A well-kept secret, more like, one that was about to be
spirited by sleight of hand from one household to another.
*And in a few months, after her child is born, she'll be
spirited back home*, he reminded himself.

That thought, along with the remainder of the brandy,
bolstered his flagging determination. A week ago, he had
made a decision for the good of Annie and her child. All
his reasons for reaching that decision still stood. He could
not allow his niece or nephew to be branded as unadoptable and raised in an orphanage. He absolutely could not.

When Edie Trimble entered the parlor, dragging her
daughter behind her, Alex clenched his hand around his
empty glass with such force that the crystal nearly shattered. Her eyes gigantic in her pale face, Annie glanced
first at him, then at the minister, and lastly at her father.
She was clearly not accustomed to being in the presence
of guests, least of all a man who so greatly resembled her
rapist. Plucking frantically at her mother's fingers to
loosen her grip on her wrist, the girl dug in with her heels
and put all her weight, slight though it was, into balking.

Edie rewarded Annie's efforts by digging her fingers
into her forearm and giving her a hard shake. "Stop
that!" she fairly shrieked.

Annie flinched and threw up her other arm to shield
her face. It was patently obvious to Alex that Edie might
have slapped her had there been no one else in the room.
His gaze shifted to the red fingerprints the woman had left
on the girl's arm. With precise movements, he placed his
snifter on the mantel and turned toward the minister.

"Let's get this business over with," Alex said with ill-
concealed distaste.

Edie, perfectly turned out in a pink shirtwaist and a
rose-colored skirt that coordinated nicely with her husband's outfit, cast him a startled glance. Alex met her

gaze. He didn't give a rap if she guessed what he was thinking. Just because he had never struck a woman and had no intention of starting with her, that didn't mean he was above entertaining the notion.

As he strode toward the minister, he gave Annie's shabby blue frock a long look. A man of Trimble's means could certainly afford to dress his daughter in something better, especially on her wedding day. Farce or no, this was still a wedding. The toes of the girl's black shoes were worn down to rough leather. Her white ribbed stockings, revealed from the shin down by the schoolgirl length of her frock, were grass-stained. He'd seen orphans turned out more nicely.

At his approach, Annie began to struggle against her mother's hold again. He drew up several feet shy of where he had originally planned to stand. With her hair in a wild tangle of dark curls around her face and dressed as she was, she looked more like a child than a woman. A terrified child.

Not wishing to frighten her by staring, Alex tore his gaze away and focused his attention on the minister, who had opened his prayer book and was leafing quickly through the pages to find his place. His black suit had seen better days, he noticed, and standing so close to the man, he detected the acrid smell of stale sweat emanating from his whipcord jacket. Given the warm morning, the rank odor was almost overwhelming. It was enough to turn Alex's stomach, and he wasn't pregnant. He shot a concerned glance at Annie.

Evidently unnerved by his scrutiny, she bent her head, concealing her face behind the thick curtains of her dark hair. Alex wondered what she was thinking, if she had any inkling at all of what was about to happen. When her mother released her wrist, she glanced longingly over her shoulder at the door. Then, obviously afraid to test Edie's temper by running, she began to fidget, scuffing the toes of her high-top shoes against the nap of the rose-patterned rug and tugging nervously on the buttons of her bodice. He had to smile when she suddenly intertwined her fingers, turned her hands palm out, and extended her arms to pop her knuckles. A knuckle-popper himself, he understood how soothing the popping sensation could be when a person was nervous.

"Annie, stop that!" Edie scolded.

"Leave her be," Alex inserted in a low voice.

Edie's eyebrows, so very like her daughter's, shot nearly to her hairline. "I beg your pardon?"

"She's not hurting anything." Glancing toward the minister, he said, "Widlow, given the circumstances, let's skip the unnecessary parts and get down to business."

More than happy to oblige, the reverend found his place and marked the spot with a tattered red ribbon. Smiling vacuously at no one in particular, he coughed to clear his throat and, in a singsong voice, began the nuptials.

When the moment finally came for Annie to say "I do," Edie Trimble caught the girl's face between her hands and none too gently prompted her to nod her head. The minister never gave so much as a pause and rushed to finish the short ceremony.

Forgoing the privilege of kissing his bride, Alex gave her a wide berth and followed his parents-in-law and the minister to a small parlor desk, where the marriage documents awaited their attention. After scrawling his name on the appropriate line, Alex stepped back so Annie might approach without feeling threatened. Duly witnessed by those present, her mark, which her father helped her to make, sufficed where her signature was required.

Just that simply, they were married. Alex could scarcely believe it. Ignoring the beaming faces of the minister and

Annie's parents, he fixed his gaze on his bride. Still hovering near her mother, she stood with her head hanging again, a dejected posture that was beginning to wear on his nerves even as it caught at his heart. It occurred to him that she might be growing weary, and given her condition, that couldn't be good for her.

He met Edie Trimble's gaze. "So all would be ready after the ceremony, I instructed my driver to park my carriage out front and see to the loading of the trunks. If we head directly for Montgomery Hall, Annie will still have most of the day to settle in before you have to leave her there alone tonight."

Edie caught her lower lip in her teeth and glanced uneasily at her husband. Standing slightly behind Alex, James Trimble coughed nervously. "Dear God, did I forget to mention that we've had a change of plans?"

Alex shot the man a look. "A change in what plans?"

"Well, you see, Alex, I forgot to check my calendar when we arranged for the wedding to take place this morning." He glanced at the minister. "As I'm sure you gathered from our earlier conversation, Reverend Widlow was booked solid every other day this week, so we couldn't reschedule for another time."

"What exactly are you saying, Trimble?"

"I'm hosting a garden luncheon this afternoon. Edie is going to have her hands full, I'm afraid. You'll have to manage without her until tomorrow."

"Manage without her?" Alex knew his voice was rising, but he couldn't seem to help himself. "My managing without her isn't the problem, James, and you damned well know it. If Edie will be busy today, I'll leave Annie here until tomorrow. When she makes the move to Montgomery Hall, she should have her mother with her. We all agreed on that."

James tugged on his ear, then glanced at the floor, the

wall, everywhere but at Alex. "Well, you see, it's a little more complicated than that. Some of my guests are from out of town, and I've invited them to sleep over. Annie's room will be occupied." He lifted his hands in a gesture of helplessness. "I thought she'd be staying at your place."

Silence settled over the room, an awful, tense silence broken only by the monotonous ticking of a pendulum clock standing against one wall. When he had first seen James this morning, Alex had thought his attire too casual. Not so. The man was dressed perfectly for the garden party he planned to host.

A garden party that obviously took precedence over his daughter. It seemed that just about everything took precedence over Annie, Alex thought scathingly. Funerals. Garden parties. Overnight guests. *Damn him.* It wasn't that Alex had expected a fancy wedding with all the trimmings. The very idea was ludicrous. But it seemed to him there was a principle involved here, one that James Trimble had overlooked. *Respect.* When it came to his daughter, that seemed a commodity he had in pitifully short supply.

"Let me clarify what you're saying," Alex said softly. "Edie can't accompany Annie to help her get settled in at Montgomery Hall, and it's impossible for me to leave her here?"

James nodded, looking aggrieved. "It's not as if I deliberately arranged things this way, Montgomery. It's just one of those"—he coughed again—"unavoidable wrinkles."

An unavoidable wrinkle. Alex had long since pegged James Trimble as being self-centered and insensitive, but this exceeded even his expectations. He had an unholy urge to grab the pompous little bastard by his lapels and shake him until his eyes bugged. If it hadn't been for the fact that such behavior on his part would frighten Annie, he might have done just that.

Turning his gaze to Edie, Alex managed to say in a relatively calm voice, "You promised me that you would accompany Annie to Montgomery Hall to help me get her settled in, Mrs. Trimble. Surely you can come, if only for a couple of hours."

Edie glanced guiltily at Annie, then at her husband, and began wringing her hands. "I know I promised, Mr. Montgomery, but that was before I learned of the garden party. James needs me here to be his hostess. This luncheon is so *very* important. To his political career, you understand. I simply—" She broke off and swallowed. "Well, with an entire houseful of company coming, I can't possibly be gone for two hours."

"What do you expect me to do, madam? Grab your daughter by the hair and *drag* her out of here?"

James settled a thoughtful gaze on Annie's bent head. "I have it. Edie, run along upstairs and fetch the laudanum."

"*Laudanum*?" Alex bit down hard on his back teeth. After a stinging silence, he finally said, "I won't have the girl drugged. She's pregnant, for Christ's sake. It might be harmful to the infant."

"Nonsense! Make her groggy, nothing more."

Evidently uncomfortable with the building tension, the minister chose that moment to thrust out a hand to James. "I do have to be going, Trimble. The funeral, you know." Turning toward Alex, he added, "It's been my pleasure, Mr. Montgomery. I wish you and your bride every happiness."

Alex was too outraged to reply. Ever conscious of appearances, James hastily excused himself to see the minister out to the foyer. As the two men departed, Alex waited for Edie Trimble to answer his question. "Well?"

he finally prodded. "Is that your plan, Mrs. Trimble? That we dope the girl with laudanum? Or that I simply drag her out?"

"It won't be necessary for you to *drag* her anywhere. Nor must we resort to laudanum. I will see her comfortably settled inside the carriage myself. After that, it's only a short drive to your place. When you arrive, you can turn her over to the nurse's care. I'll be there tomorrow afternoon, just as we originally planned. You're behaving as though this is a great inconvenience to you."

Alex could see that trying to reason with these people was useless. "Tussling with a hysterical girl won't prove to be any great inconvenience for me. I'm more than capable of handling her. My only concern is how she may feel about it."

She dug her teeth into her lower lip, looking miserable. "James is very . . . exacting," she said in a whisper, clearly afraid her husband might overhear. "He insists I be here for this gathering, and I can't go against his wishes. If I did—well, he'd be *dread*fully angry!"

And that would be catastrophic? It would have done Alex's heart good to see Trimble get so mad he ruptured a vessel. His patience gone, he gestured toward the doorway. "My driver is waiting. If you can help me get your daughter into my carriage, I'd greatly appreciate your doing so. She looks tired, and I'd like to get her home so she can rest."

"Certainly."

With that, Edie curled an arm around Annie's shoulders and guided her from the room. Alex followed, wondering with every step how the woman planned to get the girl into his vehicle without a tussle.

James, who had just bidden the minister goodbye, was still in the foyer when they emerged from the parlor. Muttering under his breath, he dashed into his study to get something before joining Alex and the women on the porch. "I do hope you understand about the sleeping arrangements for tonight," he said to Alex. "It wasn't intentional, I assure you. When I scheduled the wedding for this morning, I totally forgot the luncheon."

Alex might have believed the judge had made an honest mistake if it hadn't been for the fact that he'd promised Annie's room to one of his guests. If not for the wedding, his daughter would have been occupying the bedchamber. Alex understood, all right. Perhaps a little too well. And since it made him so blisteringly angry, he preferred not to discuss it with the bastard.

Descending the steps, he opened the carriage door and then stood aside. To his surprise, Mrs. Trimble led Annie down the steps and to the vehicle without incident. Glancing at the girl, who was eyeing the strange carriage with wide-eyed curiosity, Alex decided she was probably too dimwitted to comprehend what was about to happen.

Gathering up her skirt, Edie Trimble made as if to enter the carriage. Caught off-guard, Alex hurried forward to lend her assistance. At his sudden movement, Annie lurched backward and nearly tripped on the step behind her. Only his quick reflexes saved her from a nasty tumble. Grabbing her arm, he steadied her until she caught her balance. The instant she had done so, she shrank away from him. Mindful of her fear and the reasons for it, Alex released her.

Turning back to assist Mrs. Trimble, he said, "You've decided to come, after all?"

"Good heavens, no." Edie sank onto the front carriage seat, then leaned forward to see around Alex's shoulder. Patting the spot beside her, she said, "Come along, Annie. We're going for a little jaunt. Won't that be fun?"

A tight sensation closed around Alex's throat. Edie Trimble couldn't possibly be planning to trick the girl. To do such a thing would be indescribably cruel. Yet, as Alex stood there and watched, that was exactly what Edie did. Pretending she meant to accompany them on a ride, she lured Annie into the vehicle, waited for Alex to enter and take his seat, and then exited the carriage by the opposite door.

For all her dimwittedness, Annie seemed to realize her predicament quickly enough. She took one look at Alex and then tried to bolt after her mother. Left with no alternative, at least none that came immediately to mind, Alex forestalled her by blocking her way with his arm and jerking the door closed. As he hastily fastened the latch, James Trimble closed and locked the other door behind them. Like a lamb herded into a chute, Annie had been trapped, neatly and with a minimum of fuss, just as her mother promised.

Trimble rested a folded arm on the edge of the open carriage window, his face creased in a smile. "You see, Alex? Nothing to it."

Glancing at Annie, who was frantically rattling the door handle, Alex was sorely tempted to plant a fist in her father's mouth. He might have done just that if he hadn't heard the door latch click. Reaching past Annie, he relocked the mechanism to keep her from making good an escape.

As Alex sat back in his seat, James added, "And if all else fails, there's always this." He thrust a thrice-folded length of leather through the window and into Alex's hand. "Just the sight of it is usually enough to keep her in line. On the rare occasion that she gets stubborn, don't hesitate to use it."

Dumbfounded, Alex had already closed his hand around the leather before he realized what it was. *A razor strop.* Annie recognized what he held at almost the same moment he did. She ceased her attempts to unlock the door and shrank back against the seat. The look on her face was one that he doubted he would ever forget. Not just fear. As unpleasant as that was, he expected it. No, what broke his heart was the shattered trust he saw reflected in her eyes. Like any child, she'd believed in her parents, and they'd both just betrayed her.

Suddenly the carriage lurched. The motion was all it took to send Annie into a full-blown panic. She dived for the door again, her slender fingers clawing frantically at the lock. Before she could get a good grasp on the latch, Alex was upon her.

As he closed his arms around her body, it struck Alex just how slightly built she actually was. In the everyday course of his work, he frequently grappled with stubborn horses six times his weight, and it took all his strength to control them. With this girl, he had to make a conscious effort to hold back. Afraid of hurting her, he didn't want to exert undue pressure with his grip or embrace her too forcefully.

Annie had no such compunction. With the flexibility of a contortionist, she somehow managed to slip from his hold, not once but repeatedly, twisting and bending her body in places that Alex had heretofore believed to be humanly impossible. As a boy, he'd once tried to catch a greased pig at the county fair. Trying to hold on to this girl was every bit as frustrating. Not to mention humiliating. She was half his size, for Christ's sake.

In the end, Alex realized he had no choice but to play catch-as-catch-can, taking advantage of any opportunity that presented itself. The carriage was moving at too fast a clip to take any chances. If she managed to get a door open and tried to jump, she could do herself a serious injury.

Barely saving his face from being lacerated by her fingernails, Alex caught both her wrists in the grip of one hand, wrapped an arm around her midriff, and, with no slight difficulty, turned her so that she sat between his spread thighs with her back pressed to his chest. By angling one leg across both of hers, he brought a quick halt to her digging the heels of her shoes into his shins. Not in time to entirely save his shinbones, but at this point, he was thankful for small blessings. The girl had at least twelve elbows, he felt sure, and half again as many knees.

During the struggle, the only sound Annie had made was a shallow panting. Alex scarcely noticed her silence until after he had subdued her, and even then he didn't ponder on it overmuch. He was too busy slumping in the seat and striving to catch his breath.

Kerwhack! The sound splintered inside his brain. Pain, its center point the cleft of his chin, radiated along his jaws and exploded in his temples. Spots danced before his eyes. Momentarily stunned by the blow, he blinked, trying desperately to clear his vision.

''What the—''

In a blur, he saw Annie tuck in her chin and hunch her shoulders. In barely the nick of time, he shifted sideways so that when she reared back again, her head connected harmlessly with his shoulder.

The little minx! He'd taken blows from the fists of stout men and felt less dazed. Hovering somewhere between outrage and amazement, Alex gaped at her, not quite able to credit her daring. Poleaxed! And by a slip of a girl. Jesus. He could easily break her neck with one well-placed blow. Didn't she comprehend that?

Evidently not. Realizing her target had moved, she flung her head sideways, nailing him on the ear.

''Ouch! You little—''

Whoever said the earlobe had no feeling?

''Annie, don't—''

Kerwhack! Agony lanced along his cheek. He hooked his chin over her shoulder to minimize her swing. Her temple promptly connected with the side of his skull, causing her more discomfort than it did him, he felt sure.

"Annie . . . Whoa, there, love. I'm not going to hurt you. Stop it, now."

Kerthunk—kerthunk—kerwhack! Alex clenched his teeth, beginning to feel as if his brains were marbles in a bag and someone was giving them a shake. He bit down hard to stifle a curse. Whether she understood him or not, it went against his grain to use bad language in front of a female.

As if she realized the futility of trying to bludgeon him with her head, she tensed her body in one last, valiant effort to break free of his hold. Then she shuddered, the force of it vibrating through him and conveying her terror more eloquently than words.

Alex closed his eyes, swamped with equal measures of guilt and regret. After what Douglas had done to her, it was criminal for her to be put through this. Her parents should be shot, and he along with them.

"I won't hurt you, sweet. Just calm down."

She shuddered again. Then she went limp. He wished he knew of some way to ease her fears. But there was nothing he could think of to say or do. Nothing.

After a few minutes, the rhythmic sway of the carriage seemed to lull her. Judging it to be safe, Alex dared to straighten. He half expected her to lambaste him with her head again, but nothing happened. Eyeing the dejected slump of her thin shoulders, he decided that sheer exhaustion had claimed its victory.

Studying the back of her bent head, he couldn't fail to notice the sweet curve of her neck where her sable hair had parted. The skin there looked as soft as silk. Remembering her sitting on the landing earlier, he smiled slightly.

Despite the vague, confused expression in her large blue eyes, she had a lovely little face.

A beautiful shell, that was Annie. There was no way he could accurately determine what degree of intelligence she might possess, but he guessed she had the mind of about a six-year-old, and not a very smart six-year-old, at that. It seemed such a waste. Such a terrible waste.

Lulled by her stillness and preoccupied with his thoughts, he relaxed his hold on her slightly. Sensing a chance for escape, she gave a sudden jerk and twisted violently in his arms. He grappled to reestablish dominance. In doing so, he shifted his grip on her ribs and encountered a breast. Long after he moved his hand, the fleeting impression of feminine softness seared his palm.

Right as rain from the neck down, Douglas had once said of her, and now that he'd had his hands all over her, Alex was in complete, though reluctant, agreement. Annie Trimble might be sorely lacking between the ears, but nature had generously compensated for the deficiency. Hidden under the shapeless frocks she wore, the tempting curves of her body weren't apparent to the eye. They were, however, *very* apparent to the touch.

In proportion to her size, her breasts weren't as small as he had originally thought, and despite her pregnancy, she still had a slender waist, accentuated by gently rounded hips. Judging by what he'd seen in the foyer, a chemise and bloomers were the only underthings she wore. Except, of course, for stockings. During their tussle, he'd felt a garter encircling one of her thighs. A very soft, warm thigh.

His throat tightened, and a sheen of perspiration broke out on his brow. *Jesus Christ*. Only a lowdown blackguard would get notions about a girl like Annie. Thoroughly disgusted with himself, Alex tried to recall the last time he had spent an evening in town with a sporting woman. From spring until fall, he didn't have much time for that sort of thing. Usually, he didn't notice the lack. Not so with this girl stuck to him like a label to a bottle.

Evidently still hoping she might escape, Annie squirmed again. Alex nearly groaned. There wasn't enough room between them for a flea to wiggle.

The thing to do, he told himself, was look out the window, enjoy the passing scenery, and concentrate on something else. Trees. Mountains. Anything. It was a simple case of mind over body. The instant he got the girl to Montgomery Hall, he would turn her over to Mistress Perkins, the nurse he had hired. And from that moment on, he would endeavor to see as little as possible of her.

Out of sight, out of mind, as the old saying went.

Six

Annie had seen the slate-roofed, stone house from a distance, but, intimidated by its size, she had never ventured too close. Outlined against a backdrop of forest green, it stood four stories high, including its attic floor, atop a grassy knoll crisscrossed with white fences. Its exterior was saved from severity by generous touches of white trim: a columned porch with an overhanging balcony, shutters at all the windows, and curlicue woodwork, the likes of which Annie had never seen, along the eaves.

Stone walls with white coping bordered the front lawn, the driveway entrance marked by white-topped gate pillars that had lanterns sticking up out of them. Lanterns, of all things. To Annie, that seemed completely crazy. Lights outside? When her papa had to go outdoors after dark, he just carried a lamp.

As the carriage shook and jiggled its way along the drive, she gazed at the house through a blur of tears, her panic mounting. Her mama and papa had given her away . . . As relentlessly as a knife, the thought kept slicing through her brain. They must not love her anymore. Because she was growing fat, she guessed. So they had given her away. And to this man, of all people.

Oh, God . . . Annie gulped and held her breath, terrified she might accidentally make a noise. The stranger had Papa's strop. It was lying there, within easy reach, on the seat beside him. One wrong move, and she would get it for sure.

She knew this wasn't the same man who had hurt her up at the falls. When he stood below her in the foyer, she'd gotten a good look at his face. Tiny lines fanned out from the corners of his thickly lashed, toffee-colored eyes, an indication he was older than the other fellow by several years. And she thought his sun-burnished features were a little sharper as well. But, otherwise, the differences were so slight they were scarcely noticeable. The same whiskey-colored hair, shot through with streaks of gold. The same straight nose, jutting from between tawny brows, a perfect offset for his high cheekbones and squared jaw.

The resemblance was too marked to be a coincidence, that was for sure. Except for the difference in ages, he looked enough like the other man to be his twin. That had to mean the two were close relatives, maybe even brothers. Just the thought made her stomach turn.

Brothers . . . Annie figured that brothers were probably a lot like sisters, living in the same house and bearing a lot of similarities to one another, not just in looks, but in other ways. If one brother was nice, the other probably was. If one brother was mean, the other might be as well.

Annie knew for a fact that this man had a close relative, possibly a brother, who was *very, very* mean. That scared the stuffing out of her. To make herself feel better, she kept reminding herself that he could have hurt her already if he wanted. And so far, he hadn't. But that didn't mean he wouldn't if the mood struck.

The carriage rocked to a stop. Filled with dread, she stared at the house, stricken by yet another thought. The other man, the one from up at the falls, might be in there. Waiting for her, maybe.

Her heart gave a sickening lurch, and she glanced around, searching for any way she might escape. No matter what, she couldn't go inside that house.

As if he sensed what she was thinking, the stranger tightened his arm around her. It was all Annie could do not to scream, and she began to tremble so that her teeth started to clack. She couldn't hear the sound. But she guessed that he probably did. If so, he would know how afraid of him she was. Bullies were always meaner when they thought she was afraid.

Keeping a firm grip on her wrists, the man released her with his other arm to grab the razor strop and open the carriage door. Before Annie guessed what he meant to do, he stuffed the strop in his pocket, caught her to his chest, and exited the conveyance. Clasped in his embrace as she was, her feet dangled uselessly several inches above the ground.

She thought about giving him another sharp kick on the shins or smacking him in the mouth again with her head, but she quickly discarded the idea. Now that he had her here, there was no telling what he might do to her if she made him mad.

As if she weighed no more than a rag doll stuffed with goose down, he carried her up the flight of steps to the house. Then, never turning loose of her, he somehow managed to open the door and fling it wide. After taking three long strides into the entrance hall, he drew to a stop and lowered her feet to the floor. Because he continued to hold her with one arm clamped around her ribs, Annie didn't think about trying to run. Even if she managed to get away, where might she go? He would find her if she went home.

His house was bigger than it looked from outside. Lots

bigger. Oak wainscoting adorned the lower walls of the entry hall, above which rose a landscape mural done in the colors of early autumn. Midway to the opposite end of the hall, a gleaming oak staircase swept up from the rust-red tile floor to a second- and third-floor landing.

Awestruck, Annie stared up at the mural. The leaves falling from the trees looked absolutely real, as did the small stream that wove lazily through a stand of cottonwood. The focal point was a rearing black horse, similar to those she'd seen outside in the pastures, forelegs striking the air, luxurious mane lifted by the wind, tail streaming.

Never had she seen anything so beautiful. Living in this house, one would never grow weary of the winter rain, for a feeling of sunshine had been brought indoors. Looking at the painting, she could almost feel a warm breeze touching her cheeks.

With a start, she realized the warmth she felt was the stranger's breath. He had leaned around to watch her expression, the pride in his own unmistakable.

"Well, do you like it?"

For a long moment, Annie stared up at his dark face, acutely aware of his height and the breadth of his shoulders. Then, with a shiver, she jerked her gaze from his, fighting down another surge of panic.

A tremor in his chest told her he was speaking again, and by the force of the vibration, she guessed that he was calling to someone. Like chipmunks from their holes, a butler and several uniformed household staff emerged from doorways along the hall. When they spotted Annie, they politely inclined their heads and withdrew again.

A moment later, a stoutly built woman in a black dress appeared on the second-floor landing. Annie had never seen anyone quite like her. Like a huge black crow, she swooped down the curving staircase. As she gained the first floor and walked toward them, she spread her hands in a gesture of welcome.

Annie gaped at her. The only cheerful thing about the woman was the end of her hooked nose, which was apple-red. She wore her steel-gray hair skinned back so tightly into a chignon at the nape of her thick neck that she looked squint-eyed.

"So this is our little Annie," she said with a broad smile that showed decayed front teeth. Flicking a glance at the man, she added, "My, my. That hair of hers is certainly in a tangle, Mr. Montgomery. Doesn't her mother ever tend it?"

Annie couldn't see the man's face to tell what he said in reply, but she felt the vibration of his voice thrumming through her shoulder blades. Mr. Montgomery, the woman called him. She filed the name away in her memory.

The woman smiled at whatever it was he said to her. "Ah, well, no matter. I'll have her set to rights in no time." Turning her attention back to Annie and stretching out a plump hand, she said, "I am Mistress Perkins, your nurse. We're going to get along wonderfully, you and I. Oh, yes."

Annie was almost grateful for the solid length of the man's body behind her as she shrank from the nurse's touch. The woman's smile was friendly enough, and she seemed nice. But there was something about her that made Annie nervous. Her eyes, she decided. With no trace of warmth, they gleamed like polished chips of black rock.

The man grasped Annie firmly by her shoulders. She felt his chest give another rumble. Then he handed her over to Mistress Perkins. Initially, Annie was relieved to escape his clutches. But not for long. The nurse's grip on her arm was biting as she pulled her up the stairs and along a corridor. At any second, Annie expected one of the closed doors to fly open and the man who had attacked her to leap out. Not being able to hear, she had only her eyes to forewarn her. At every shadow, she jumped, which made Mistress Perkins grip her arm all the harder.

The woman led her into a bedchamber that looked as if it had once served as a nursery. In one corner stood a wooden rocking horse, its paint faded and completely worn away in spots. Postioned along two of the interior walls were a battered but serviceable armoire, a matching chest of drawers, and a rice-carved four-poster bed. The third wall was taken up by a massive rock fireplace. Only one window let in sunlight. Before it sat a scarred pedestal table where she presumed the young occupants of the nursery had once taken their lessons.

Shortly after she and Mistress Perkins entered the room, a wiry man in work clothes arrived bearing one of Annie's trunks. A few minutes later, he reappeared, huffing and puffing from the climb, carrying another trunk balanced on his shoulder. Immediately after he left, Mistress Perkins locked the oak door, dropped the key into her skirt pocket, and began rifling through Annie's things. Once she located a brush and hair ribbon, she motioned for Annie to sit on one of two straight-backed chairs at the table.

Accustomed to doing as she was bidden, Annie sat down to have her hair brushed. After the woman dispensed with all the tangles, she set herself to the task of plaiting Annie's long tresses, pulling and twisting at the strands until Annie felt as if the hair at her temples was about to part company with her scalp.

At her beseeching look, Mistress Perkins flashed a cold smile. "We'll get along fine, missy. Just fine." Then she wagged a finger. "Just don't try me. I have no patience with nonsense."

Annie curled shaking hands over the edges of her chair.

''You sit tight. When I've finished with the unpacking, I'll ring for our lunch.''

Annie didn't want any lunch. Or any dinner, either. Her only thought was to get out of this place, and to do that, she had to get skinny so her mama and papa would want her back.

She hugged her waist and watched as the older woman took all her things from the trunks and put them away in the bureau and armoire. Watching her work drove home to Annie that Mr. Montgomery had plans to keep her here for a long, long time. *Why* was the question. The possible answers made her stomach feel sick.

Her fear rekindled by the thoughts plaguing her, she glanced at the locked door and then at the window. Her heart sank when she saw there were iron bars on the opposite side of the glass. Nursery windows on upper floors were often barred to prevent little ones from accidentally falling. But she wasn't little. If Mr. Montgomery had no intention of doing anything horrid to her, why would he lock her up?

As promised, Mistress Perkins rang for lunch as soon as she finished unpacking Annie's things. Shortly after a maid delivered the food, the stout nurse took her place at the table and became so intent on her meal of sliced roast beef, vegetables, and freshly baked bread that it took several minutes before she noticed Annie wasn't eating. When she finally did, she wiped the corners of her mouth, placed her crumpled linen napkin beside her plate, and pushed up from her chair.

''What a bother. I wasn't told you couldn't feed yourself. Trust me to land a job where I must play nursemaid to an idiot.''

The woman speared a piece of meat and pushed it at Annie's mouth.

''You have to eat, missy. If you don't, you'll take sick,

and that'll look bad for me. Understand? I can't be losing this position.''

Normally, Annie would have felt sympathy for the lady. The servants at her parents' house needed their jobs as well, and she knew by things they said that employment was hard to find. But in this instance, she couldn't afford to be charitable. No matter what, she had to get skinny. And she had to do it fast.

When, after a nudge with the fork, Annie refused to open her mouth, Mistress Perkins got an unholy gleam in her eye and jabbed. Annie blinked, at first with pain, then with disbelief. One of the tines had punctured her lip. She could feel blood trickling down her chin.

''The nice thing about idiots, missy, is that they can't carry tales. If Alex Montgomery notices ought amiss, I'll tell him you did the injury to yourself.'' Arching a black eyebrow, she added, ''You'll not be difficult. Not with me. Do you understand?''

Annie understood, all right. This woman was as vicious as she was ugly.

Rebellion was usually completely foreign to her nature, but this had been no ordinary morning. In the space of two hours, she'd been tricked by her mama, betrayed by her papa, and roughly handled by a man who frightened her half to death. And now she was being jabbed with a fork? An awful, hot feeling washed over her. Short of grabbing the other fork and jabbing the woman back, there was little she could do but take the abuse.

And take it, she would. Nothing this woman or Alex Montgomery did was going to make her eat. Nothing.

When another jab with the fork tines didn't encourage Annie to open her mouth, Mistress Perkins chose other forms of persuasion that wouldn't be quite so evident to her employer. She pulled Annie's hair, slapped her sharply on the back, and then resorted to pinching her in places where the resultant bruises would be hidden by her clothing.

Through it all, Annie sat there glaring up at the nurse with her teeth tightly clenched.

Just before dawn the next morning, Annie slipped from her bed and crept across the room on her tiptoes, wincing every time she felt a floorboard give beneath her weight. One of the disadvantages of being deaf, of which there were many, was that it could be very difficult to sneak about. She couldn't tell, with any accuracy, whether she was making noise. It was ever so bothersome, especially when she wanted very much to do something and was afraid she'd be punished if she were caught.

Like right now . . .

Reaching the window, Annie carefully inched the table to one side. When there was adequate room before the double-hung panes, she unfastened the lock and braced the heels of her hands against the lower sash bars. *Quietly, Annie, quietly.* Momentarily forgetting her run-in with the fork yesterday, she caught her lower lip in her teeth. At the ensuing pain, she opted to bite the inside of her cheek instead. She wasn't sure why, but in her experience, to do something exactly right, she had to hold her mouth just so, and biting the inside of her cheek seemed to work best.

Slowly, she pushed the window open, almost afraid to breathe. She could only hope that Alex Montgomery was one of those fussy sorts who kept the window jambs in his house well-oiled. If not, she was probably making enough noise to wake the dead.

Not that the dead were her concern. It was Mistress Perkins she didn't want to wake up. Last night before retiring, the crazy woman had tied her to the bed, of all things, with strips of linen. From things the nurse had said, Annie knew she believed her to be hopelessly stupid. And maybe she was. But even a dummy was smart enough to untie knots.

Fresh air wafted through the iron bars, molding Annie's zephyr nightgown to her body. Before she allowed herself to relax, she ''listened'' for any movement coming from the room adjoining hers. *Nothing*. No footsteps vibrating through the floor. No tingles at the nape of her neck. Nothing. She allowed herself a satisfied smile. The fat old thing was still asleep.

Grasping the bars and letting her hands slide down their length, Annie knelt on the wooden floor. Ignoring the grit that pricked one bare knee, she fastened her gaze on the heavens. *Dawn*. To her, it was the most beautiful part of the day, and unless she was sick, which was hardly ever, she never missed watching it. Right now the sky looked blue-black, just as it did in the dead of night, but she knew by the lackluster glimmer of the stars that day was about to break.

It never ceased to amaze her when it happened. Catching her breath, she watched as a rose-pink crack zigzagged across the horizon. A few minutes later, glorious shafts of light spilled forth from it, lending everything they touched a magical luminance. When the mountains became visible, their peaks were wreathed by a low-hanging mist the color of pale pink rose petals. Then, like a smile that slowly gained radiance, the light beams streaking the sky began to turn a brilliant gold.

Awestruck, Annie tightened her hands on the iron bars, thinking that, in place of music, God had given her the sunrises. Even without her ears, she heard the song in her heart, but it was no less moving for all that. Beautiful music made of light.

Closing her eyes, Annie remembered all the sounds that usually came with first light, the crow of a rooster, the strident outbursts from little birds, the distant barking of a dog, the whisper of the morning breeze as it picked up. Those sounds were forever lost to her, and yet she had filed them away in her memory, hers to recall and enjoy whenever it pleased her.

As she opened her eyes, a movement in the yard below caught her attention. She focused on a flash of gold that rivaled that of the sunbeams: Alex Montgomery's hair. She knew with absolute certainty that it was he by the way he walked, his strides long and sure, the muscles in his thighs bunching and stretching the cloth of his biscuit-colored riding breeches.

Moving alongside the house as he was, he presented her with a frontal view. He wore a white cotton shirt, the sleeves rolled back over his thickly roped forearms, the front hanging open, the tails loose around his narrow hips. Annie had never seen a man's bare chest, and she stared with curious fascination. Instead of pale bubbies with pink tips like hers, he had sun-burnished ones that not only looked hard but rippled peculiarly when he moved. In the center of each was a brown splotch about the size of a copper penny. Upon closer inspection, she saw that he also had golden hair on his chest, short, furry-looking stuff that she felt sure had to itch. It ran clear to his bellybutton, then narrowed into a line that dived under his belt.

As he passed beneath her window, which gave her a rear view of him, he began shrugging out of his shirt. Craning her neck, she stared in startled amazement as he wadded the white cotton in one fist. Across his back, under bronze skin that gleamed as if it had been rubbed with oil, muscle worked, bunching in one place, flattening out in others.

Leaving the yard, he went to a small outbuilding near the stables. Beside it stood a rusty old pump, the spout of which was positioned over a weathered washstand. After tossing his shirt over a nearby fence, he worked the pump handle until water spewed forth, then thrust his head and shoulders under the flow. Annie shuddered, imagining how cold it must feel. When he straightened, he shook himself like a doused raccoon and rubbed the water from his eyes.

His hair stood out from his head as if someone had stirred it with a whisk. She couldn't help but smile at how silly he looked. He quickly remedied the situation by raking his fingers through the darkened strands. His upper torso still sparkling with droplets of water, he grabbed his shirt and put it back on, evidently not caring that the cotton absorbed the wetness and clung to him like a second skin.

Mesmerized, Annie watched him brace a hand on the top fence rail and vault over it without any apparent effort. There was a brown horse in the enclosure. When the beast saw him, it flung its head and repeatedly struck the earth with a front hoof. Alex approached the animal slowly. When he came within about ten feet of it, the horse pivoted on its hind legs and galloped away. Making no sudden moves, Alex followed. As before, just when he had almost closed the distance between himself and the animal, it bolted.

Again and again, Alex made his approach. Annie's sympathies were all with the horse. While Alex wasted no energy, the animal kept breaking into a gallop, and in its panic was making unnecessary circles inside the fence. Soon its coat glistened with sweat, and its sides heaved with exhaustion.

Annie realized that Alex intended to keep approaching the animal until it no longer had the strength to run from him. The poor horse seemed to realize it as well and watched him warily, its body aquiver with overexertion.

To Annie, it seemed a cruel game, and seeing him put the animal through such an ordeal cemented in her mind that he wasn't a very nice man.

At the thought, Annie's throat tightened. She pushed to her feet with a suddenness that made her head swim. Turning her back on the window, she hugged her waist and swung her gaze to the locked door. At her back, sunlight spilled through the window, throwing the striped pattern of the iron bars across the floor. *Trapped.* That was how she felt.

Perhaps it was simply memories of that day at the falls getting the best of her, but she could almost see Alex Montgomery entering this room and stalking her, just as he did the horse, with that same relentless determination, until she was too spent to run anymore.

Unable to stop herself, she glanced back at the window. Through the bars, she saw that the inevitable had finally happened. The horse stood with its rump pressed into a V of the fence line, trembling but no longer able to resist the touch of its master's hands upon its body.

Seven

For the remainder of that day and the two following, Alex studiously avoided the upstairs nursery but met daily with Mistress Perkins to be updated on Annie's progress. Edie Trimble visited, and after a lengthy stay, she seemed satisfied with the nurse's credentials and performance.

Mistress Perkins, a kindly, middle-aged woman, had come to Montgomery Hall with glowing letters of recommendation and appeared to be the epitome of efficiency. She informed Alex that Annie was settling into her new routine quite nicely, and that he shouldn't have a moment's worry about her welfare. From now on, she said, that was her concern.

Alex was more than willing to leave the woman to it. He couldn't forget his physical reaction to Annie in the carriage, nor could he forgive himself for it. The farther he stayed away from the girl, the better.

Fortunately his was a large, rambling old house, and as Dr. Muir had predicted, Annie's presence there could be virtually ignored. Alex went on with his usual routine, working days in the stables and fields or at the rock quarry, spending the evenings doing accounts or taking his leisure in the study.

On the third evening, he had just settled into his favorite chair with a snifter of brandy and a recent issue of the Portland *Morning Oregonian* when a piercing screech reverberated through the room. He shot straight up in his seat, the hair at the nape of his neck standing on end. The screech was soon followed by screams.

With a curse, Alex rushed from his study into the hall where he collided with his housekeeper Maddy, who had also been alarmed by the noise. After a bit of scrambling to regain their balance, the two of them made for the stairs, Alex gaining a considerable lead in the ascent; Maddy, plump and short of leg, huffing for breath behind him. When Alex reached the nursery door, he found it locked from the inside.

Rapping sharply on the thick panel of oak, he yelled, "Mistress Perkins! What the blazes is—"

"Help me!" the woman shrieked. "Oh, God, have mercy! Help me, please!"

"Jesus, Mary, and Joseph," Maddy cried, and quickly crossed herself.

Alex shouldered her plump form aside. Rearing back, he gave the door a sharp kick. The thick slab of oak stood fast. Prodded by the screams coming from the room beyond, he withdrew several steps and put all his weight into butting the door with his shoulder. Upon impact, he reeled backward with such force he nearly had to peel himself off the adjacent wall.

"Son of a bitch!"

Maddy pressed her hands to her temples. "Dear God, what's happenin' in there?"

From the sound of things, all hell had broken loose. Alex eyed the door, grimly determined. All his life, he'd heard stories of men kicking their way into locked rooms, and he was a larger man than most. There had to be a trick to it. Focusing on the doorknob, he backed up as far as the opposite wall would allow, took two steps to get momentum, and planted his foot directly beneath the brass backplate. The wooden frame splintered, the door gave way, and Alex entered the nursery in a staggering rush. He swayed to a stop only a few feet shy of Mistress Perkins and Annie, who seemed to be locked in mortal combat.

Such was the confusion of writhing bodies that it took Alex a moment to figure out what was going on. When he finally did, his eyes widened in amazement. Annie, the docile little creature whom Dr. Muir had assured him would never cause any trouble, had her teeth sunk into Mistress Perkins's finger, her intent apparently to relieve the woman of the appendage. The nurse, dancing about in agony, was slapping her charge about the head and shoulders in an attempt to get free. Before Alex could step in, the woman evidently decided mere slaps weren't going to work and resorted to using her fists.

"Say now!" Alex shouted.

He leaped into the fray, not at all certain whom he meant to save—Annie, who was being bludgeoned, or Mistress Perkins, who was in danger of being dismembered. Dimly he realized that Maddy skirted the battle, grabbing clothes here, arms and hair there, her shrill Irish brogue adding to the din. There ensued a four-person bout, Annie and Mistress Perkins in an inseparable tangle, Alex and Maddy trying, without much success, to separate them. Just as Alex was finally managing to pry Annie's clenched jaws apart, the frantic nurse missed her mark and dealt him a blinding blow to the nose.

Freed at last and holding her injured finger, she staggered backward, her black eyes blazing. "You little she-bitch!"

"Now, just one minute!" Alex cut in. "I'll have no talk like that." He swiped at the blood pooling on his upper lip. "What in blazes prompted the girl to bite you?" Turning, he saw that Annie had fled to a far corner of the room, where she huddled on the floor with her back pressed to the wall. He shifted his gaze back to the nurse. "Well?"

"Nothing prompted her! With no provocation, she attacked me."

Wiping at his nose again, Alex studied the hefty woman, his instincts telling him that there was more to this than she was revealing. "How, exactly, did your finger come to be in Annie's mouth?"

"She bit it."

Recalling his own experience with Annie, Alex had no difficulty believing she might bite, but he found it rather peculiar that she'd latched onto a finger instead of a more accessible body part. "What did you do? Stick your finger out to accommodate her? I'm sorry, Mistress Perkins, but something about this strikes me as odd."

"I was *feeding* her! That's all. Correct me if I'm wrong, but I believe that's my job. And while I was about it, the little bitch bit me!"

Alex didn't lose his temper often, but then he very seldom got his nose bloodied. "You'll watch your language, madam, or be dispatched without references for your trouble."

"Dispatched? Without references? I have several letters of reference, sir, as you well know, and if those won't suffice, I can write others. There are always fools like you who don't bother to check them out."

Stunned, Alex stared at her. Then he winced, for he had indeed been a fool. Due to lack of time, he hadn't verified this woman's credentials.

She gave a shrill laugh. "As if I'd stay on in this position! The girl's mad! You'll never find someone to take care of her. Mark my words on that, sir. I was trying to make her eat, nothing more. She's been refusing to take her meals. What was I to do, let her starve?''

"If you were having a problem with Annie, you should have come to me. As it is, you've let the situation get out of hand, and I'm left with no choice but to let you go. I can't allow someone in my employ to strike my wife, no matter what the provocation.''

"Your wife? Ha! As for this position, I'll gladly quit and walk every step of the way back to town rather than spend another night in this house!''

"That won't be necessary. I'll arrange for your transportation.'' Drawing his handkerchief from his pocket, Alex clamped it over his bleeding nose and glanced at Maddy. "Can you see to the girl while I take care of matters downstairs?''

Her grizzled red hair gleaming in the lamplight, her face pale by contrast, Maddy threw an uncertain look at Annie. Then she straightened her round shoulders and nodded. "Go ahead, Master Alex. We'll manage, I'm sure.''

Alex wished he felt as certain. He hated to leave Maddy to cope alone, but he saw no other alternative. Motioning for Mistress Perkins to precede him, he exited the room.

Alex had just seen Mistress Perkins off in the carriage and was heading back up the front steps to the house when Maddy appeared in the open doorway, her ample frame outlined against the backdrop of light that spilled from the entrance hall. Planting her hands on her hips, she gazed after the departing conveyance.

"It's a good thing she's gone, and that's a fact! I'd have taken her apart with me bare hands, let there be no question about it!''

Since the death of his mother when he was three, Alex had regarded Maddy, with her kindly green eyes, as more of a parent than a housekeeper. In his recollection, he'd never seen her in such a temper. Heavy-breasted and wearing a dark blue dress with a white bib apron, she put him in mind of a small schooner with a high wind billowing her topsails.

Gaining the porch, he gazed down at her face, trying in vain to read her shadowed expression. When her Irish was up, Maddy could be a corker, no doubt about it. Alex could only be grateful that Mistress Perkins had made good her getaway.

"I'm not exactly pleased with how the woman handled the situation myself," he admitted. "Striking Annie with her fists was uncalled for. But I suppose, in her frenzy, that she might not have realized what she was doing."

Maddy crossed her plump arms. "That beastly woman has been downright cruel to that poor girl, no frenzy about it."

Maddy had an excitable streak and quite often overreacted. Alex couldn't help thinking she must be doing so now. "Mistress Perkins was out of line, Maddy, but I think the word *cruel* is a little too harsh. Annie was about to relieve her of her finger."

"She was cruel!" Maddy insisted. "I am appalled that such goings-on have been allowed to occur in this house. Absolutely appalled."

"I admit it was a nasty scene, but let's not make it into something worse than it actually was."

"Worse than it actually was? The woman is a *fiend*. How could ye neglect to check her references? I can't believe ye'd be so careless."

Caught off-guard by the attack, Alex couldn't immediately think of a response. When he finally spoke, his tone was defensive. "I needed a nurse, if you'll recall. There wasn't time to correspond with her former employers. She seemed respectable enough and kindly."

"Kindly? I wouldn't entrust a mongrel dog into that witch's care. A nurse, ye say? What ye really wanted was a keeper, and anyone would do, just as long as the lass was kept quiet and out of yer way till her babe was born."

"Maddy, you know that isn't—"

"Ye give yer mares better care. There isn't a lowly stableboy in yer employ whose references ye haven't checked. God forbid that an injury should befall one of yer blasted horses."

"I believed the woman was competent, Maddy."

"But ye didn't make certain. Therein lies the shame of it." She wagged a rigid finger under his nose. "I told ye from the start that no good would come of this. Feeble-minded or no, the girl's not a piece of breedin' flesh to be passed back and forth between ye and her parents as the mood strikes. It's a sin against God and all that's holy."

He thrust a hand through his hair. "Let's calm down a bit, hmm?"

"What ye're really sayin' is that *I* should calm down. Well, calm isn't how I'm feelin'. If ye were still a lad in knickers, I'd wear out yer hinder with a hickory switch for this piece of work."

In Alex's opinion, dancing to the tune of a hickory switch might have been less lacerating than hearing Maddy's words. "I made a mistake, Maddy. I don't deny that. But you know it wasn't intentional."

"The road to hell is paved with good intentions."

"Yes, well . . . I promise you it won't happen again. I'll make sure the next nurse is of sterling character."

"The next nurse? Why not just put the lass in a horse stall?" At Alex's stunned expression, she went on, "Well? She'd not be a bother to ye that way. When her labor comes on, ye can have Deiter deliver the babe like he does all the foals. Ye'll get yer heir. Annie can be packed off home. Everyone but the lass will be happy. Isn't that essentially what ye've got in mind, anyhow? Why fancy it up by hirin' a nurse?''

Alex's temper snapped. "That will be quite enough. This is an ugly predicament, true, and I wish it had never happened. But it did, the girl is pregnant, and I've tried to remedy the problem as best I can. What more can you ask of me?''

"That ye be a husband to the lass?'' she suggested with scathing sarcasm.

"Besides that."

"Well, barrin' that, yer payin' the wee thing a bit more attention wouldn't hurt. That *nurse* ye hired has been tryin' to shove food down the girl's throat! That's how her finger came to be in Annie's mouth. The woman deserved to get it bit clean off, if ye ask me."

"Shove food down her throat?" Alex repeated in amazement.

"And that isn't the half of it. Pinchin' the poor wee thing all over her person. Every time I think of it—" She hauled in a shaky breath. "Well, words can't describe me anger. The lass has so many bruises, she looks like a bolt of polka dot. All under her frock, of course, where they can't be seen. Ye should look at her back where that horrible woman has been slapping her."

"Bruises?" Alex's heart caught. "Jesus. How badly is she hurt?"

He started to step past Maddy, but she caught his arm. "Don't race up there like chaff in a high wind. Ye'll frighten the lass."

Knowing she was right, Alex withdrew from her grasp but made no further attempt to enter the house. A long silence fell between them, during which time Maddy made a visible effort to calm down. When Alex felt she had regained at least a margin of her composure, he said, "Should I have Henry fetch Dr. Muir?"

"I don't think she'll be needin' a doctor, no. I can tend her. But there is another small wrinkle ye need to iron out."

"What's that?"

"The reason she's been refusin' to eat is because she thinks she's gettin' fat. Somehow ye've got to make her understand it's a baby thickenin' her waist, not too much food."

Alex studied his housekeeper's round features. "How can you possibly know what Annie thinks?"

"Well, I got it from Annie, of course."

"The girl can't talk."

Maddy raised her chin. "Not like we do, that's a fact. But she can get her point across if pressed."

"How?"

"Come upstairs and see for yerself." With that, she spun and headed for the stairs, muttering angrily under her breath every step of the way.

Not wishing to startle Annie, Alex entered her bed-chamber after Maddy. Still hiding in the shadowy corner, the girl sat with her arms hugging her bent legs, her blue frock tucked modestly around her ankles. Apparently exhausted, she rested her head on her knees. So he might see better, Alex stepped over to light the bedside lamp before crossing the room to her. At his approach, she straightened and fixed him with a wide, wary gaze. In the depths of her blue eyes, he read several emotions: fear, no small amount of distrust, and a dreary hopelessness.

Christ. He had brought her into his home to give her his protection. A fine job he'd done of it. She'd been pinched, pummeled, and God only knew what else. Little wonder she looked at him the way she did.

Hunkering down in front of her, he took a moment to study her, searching carefully for signs of abuse. As far as he could tell, there were none. Aside from the fact that she had dropped a bit of weight that she could ill afford to lose, she looked well-scrubbed and healthy, her dark hair confined in tidy plaits that fell to her waist.

"Maddy tells me that Mistress Perkins has been treating you badly, Annie," he began. "Would you care to tell me about it?"

In response, she gave him the usual uncomprehending look, her gaze fixed intently on his mouth. Alex got the feeling he might as well be speaking Greek. The girl obviously didn't understand the simplest sentences. That she had somehow managed to communicate with Maddy stretched credibility to the utmost. Yet Alex had never known his housekeeper to lie.

Intent on seeing the girl's bruises, he reached to draw the neckline of her frock slightly aside. At his movement, she shrank against the wall, her eyes going dark with fear. His hand hovering in midair, Alex made a fist in frustration. As limited as her mental capacities seemed to be, she clearly had no difficulty remembering what Douglas had done to her and believed he might do the same.

Glancing up at Maddy, who stood off to one side, he shook his head. "It's no use. If she's hurt, I'll have to take your word for it. Are you certain I shouldn't send for Dr. Muir?"

"As I said, I can tend her bruises," Maddy said with a sniff. "What blisters me, Master Alex, is that I don't think ye believe what I said. She showed me how the woman shoved the food down her throat, I'm telling ye. And conveyed to me that she thinks she's getting fat."

Alex pushed to his feet and stepped away from Annie to lean a shoulder against the wall. "I'll believe it when I see it."

Maddy shot him a frosty glare and marched over to the small table to snatch up Annie's supper plate. Forking up a lump of cold potatoes, she retraced her steps, smiling broadly at the girl. "Come now, Annie love, be a good girl and eat some of yer supper fer Maddy."

Annie shook her head, which in itself amazed Alex. She actually seemed to understand what Maddy had said to her.

"But ye have to eat, love. Ye'll take sick if ye don't," Maddy cajoled. "One bite, for me?"

Once again shaking her head, Annie shifted a wary glance toward Alex, then puffed out her cheeks and tried, without much success, to double her chin. Though she was far too thin to make herself look fat, no matter what faces she pulled, the message was clear. Alex gaped at her in absolute astonishment.

"My God," he whispered.

Keeping her gaze fixed on Annie, Maddy continued to approach her, fork extended. "There's a good girl. Eat yer supper for Maddy."

Growing increasingly agitated, Annie straightened her legs and curled her hands over her waist to pat her stomach. Then, as though she held an invisible eating utensil, she pretended to stuff food into her mouth and chew. Afterward, she puffed air into her cheeks again and gave her head another shake.

With a victorious flourish of the fork, which nearly sent the potatoes flying, Maddy turned to Alex and said, "There, ye see?"

Alex pushed away from the wall. Goose bumps rose on his skin as he regarded the girl before him. For several long seconds, he couldn't gather his wits enough to speak. When he finally did, all he managed was another, "My God."

"What did I tell ye?" Maddy said smugly. "If that

isn't gettin' her point across, I'll put in with ye.''

"Maddy . . ." Alex's voice was hushed. "Do you have any inkling what this means? For her to draw a correlation between weight gain and eating—well, it's downright incredible. She must have conceptual reasoning capabilities."

"Not as stupid as ye thought, hmm, Master Alex? Why, when a body starts to think about it, it fair addles the mind." She presented Annie with her back to return the plate to the table. "If she can understand somethin' like that, one has to wonder what else she might be able to understand. Or feel. When ye snatch her babe from her arms, I wonder if she'll pine for it?"

A horrible, weak sensation attacked Alex's legs. Still reeling with amazement, all he could do was stare at his charge. No, not his charge, his wife. His pregnant wife, whom his brother had raped and he had married. So he could take her child.

A piece of breeding flesh, Maddy had called her. A mindless object to be passed back and forth between him and her parents. The thought made him feel so sick he squeezed his eyes closed.

"Dear God, Maddy, what have I done?"

A weighted silence settled over the room. Finally Maddy said, "Ye can't undo what ye've done, Master Alex. What matters now is what ye do from here on out."

Eight

Deeply troubled by the discovery about Annie, Alex paid a visit to her parents the following morning. After being shown into the parlor, he took a seat in a wing chair near the hearth so he might face Edie and James, who sat together on the horsehair sofa. Not exactly sure how or even where to begin, Alex pressed his fingertips together and studied the rose-patterned carpet to collect his thoughts, which at the moment seemed as difficult to gather as dust kittens in a high wind.

In the end, he decided that coming right out with it was his best course of action, and he recounted the events of the night before. He finished by saying, "After seeing Annie interact with my housekeeper, I am convinced she may be more intelligent than any of us thought."

At Alex's words, Edie went deathly pale. After a moment of silence that seemed to crash against his eardrums, she said, "Stuff and nonsense. Our daughter was beset by a high fever that rendered her mentally disabled, Mr. Montgomery. We've explained that to you at length!"

"And you may be absolutely right. The question is, how severe is the mental disability? Have you ever tried to find out? The girl is capable of conceptual reasoning,

Mrs. Trimble. A true imbecile is not." Moving forward to the edge of the chair, he gestured vaguely. "James, you're an educated man. Surely you understand what I'm saying. Your daughter can note a relationship between two seemingly unrelated events. If she were as feeble-minded as you both believe, how would she be able to do that?"

Her spine snapping taut, Edie stood. "We *both* understand what you're saying. We simply do not agree."

"I'm not placing blame here," Alex assured them in a more soothing tone. "Please don't misunderstand me. I'm simply saying that Annie's affliction may not be as severe as you think. I'd like to take her to Portland. Have a few tests done. There are some excellent physicians up there who might—"

"No!" Edie cried shrilly. She glanced resentfully at her husband. "I feared this would happen! I begged you to arrange for her to be sent away until the baby was born. Now look! He wants *tests*!"

She said the word *tests* as though it were a vulgarity. Alex sighed. "Just a routine examination, Mrs. Trimble. Nothing extensive. What harm can come from that?"

"What harm?" she asked thinly. "It's just the beginning. The next thing we know, you'll be wanting to keep Annie at Montgomery Hall and never let her come home."

James reached up to clasp his wife's hand. "Now, Edie. Alex hasn't said that. You're jumping to conclusions. Isn't she, Alex?"

A suffocating sensation filled Alex's chest. "Well, actually, James, I would like to talk to you about—"

"I *knew* it!" Edie tore her hand from James's grasp. Glaring at Alex, she cried, "You gave your word, sir! A temporary arrangement, you said. In name only. You promised!"

Alex rubbed a hand over his face. "That was before I realized—"

"Before you realized what?" she demanded. "How dare you? You have the girl for three short days, and suddenly you think you know more about her than her own mother? You're thinking about making the marriage permanent? How dare you!"

"I only want what's best for Annie," Alex said softly. "If she isn't as retarded as you believe, Edie, imagine the heartache she'll suffer if I separate her from her baby."

"What's best for Annie?" She gave a bitter laugh. "Shall I predict the future if you act on this madness, Mr. Montgomery? After it's too late, you'll discover I am correct, that our daughter is indeed an imbecile. And in the end, you'll do the easy thing and have her stuck away in one of those terrible sanitariums. She'll be locked in a room and tended as though she's an animal. I've spent fourteen years doing everything I can to *prevent* that."

"I would never put Annie in an institution."

"Wouldn't you? You're a young, attractive man. One day you'll meet a normal young woman you'd like to marry. What will become of Annie then?"

"I have never broken my word in my life," Alex retorted. "I certainly won't begin with my marriage vows. Annie will always have a home at Montgomery Hall."

"You're breaking your word right now," she shot back. "You promised to return my daughter to me, and now you're shilly-shallying."

"James," Alex said wearily, "talk some sense to her. Please? If there's a chance, no matter how minute, that Annie may be trainable, how can we ignore it? What harm can a few tests do?"

The judge avoided looking directly into Alex's eyes. "Do you really believe that we would neglect to have our daughter tested if we believed, even for a moment, that there was hope? The only person I'll try to talk some sense into is you, Alex. Edie is Annie's mother. She has cared for the girl since she was a newborn babe. Who knows better than she how severe Annie's disabilities are?''

Under ordinary circumstances, Alex couldn't have argued with that. But because of the judge's previous candidness, he knew there was a whole lot more involved here than met the eye. *Hereditary madness.* They were ugly words and constituted the Trimbles' greatest fear. A fear so overwhelming that neither of them could acknowledge it, both for different reasons, James because of his career, Edie out of guilt.

If Annie were tested . . . if it were discovered that her mental disorder was due to hereditary madness and not from the effects of a high fever, then both of them were afraid they would pay a price, Edie in her marriage for deceptions she'd perpetrated thirty years before, the judge by losing his political credibility. Rather than take that risk, they kept Annie, their guilty secret, hidden from the world.

''We could keep the trip to Portland confidential,'' Alex tried. ''No one need ever know a physician examined her.''

''I will not give my approval for any tests,'' James said firmly.

Alex didn't need the man's approval, and the Trimbles both knew it. He didn't feel it was circumspect to say as much, however. ''I see.''

''Please trust that we love our daughter,'' James added.

Drawing his lips into a grim line, Alex regarded this man, whom he'd once admired so greatly. If he thought he loved his daughter, then he had an entirely different definition of the word than Alex did. It wasn't just his reluctance to have the girl tested, but everything else that had gone before—the drab wedding ceremony, the garden party taking precedence over Annie's needs, and a dozen other things Alex couldn't immediately call to mind. Love? That Trimble even used the word was a travesty.

"If we thought tests would bring anything new to light, anything at all," James continued, "we'd have taken Annie to Portland ourselves years ago."

Silence. A throbbing, accusing silence. In that moment, Alex knew that the Trimbles would fight him to their dying breath to keep Annie from being seen by any doctors. If he bucked them, things were going to get ugly. Very ugly.

He needed to think things through carefully before he reached any decisions, not because he particularly cared about safeguarding his relationship with his in-laws, but because Annie's happiness might rest in the balance. If, as Maddy suspected, the girl was capable of feeling affection, then she undoubtedly loved her parents, whether they deserved it or not. For her sake, Alex didn't want to cause a rift, not without good reason.

Evidently mistaking his silence for a change of heart, Edie had regained some of her composure. In a quieter, more reasonable voice, she said, "I know how deceiving Annie's behavior can be, Mr. Montgomery. On occasion she can display a measure of what may seem to be normal intelligence, but then she immediately regresses. Trust me on that. Though I detest the word, my little girl is an imbecile. All the wishing in the world can't alter that."

Exhausted beyond words, Alex sighed and ran a hand over his face again. He'd scarcely slept a wink last night. Annie . . . with her sweet face and bewildered blue eyes. He couldn't get her off his mind. Maybe he and Maddy were grasping at straws. But, damn it, he had to be sure.

"I'm sorry," he hedged. "I guess I shouldn't have come. I've upset you both, and if you're right, I've done so for absolutely no good reason. It's just that I—'' He shrugged. ''Last night—watching her—I was so sure there might be some hope.''

Looking into Edie's eyes, Alex could see her pain and knew she believed with all her heart that her daughter had inherited a strain of madness from her side of the family. Could it be she believed in it so strongly, and was so consumed with fear that her husband would divorce her over it, that she was blind to any other possibility?

''There is no hope,'' she said shakily. ''God knows I wish there were. For Annie's sake, you've got to put all these doubts out of your mind.''

For Annie's sake. Alex ground his teeth to keep from saying anything he might regret.

''In the space of three days, her condition has already begun to deteriorate,'' Edie pointed out. ''And to such a degree that she physically attacked her nurse. Allowed to continue, that sort of behavior will land her in an institution, Mr. Montgomery. I know you came here this morning with all the best of intentions and that your heart is in the right place. But you must trust me absolutely in this. I didn't dream up a bunch of rules for Annie to follow because it pleased me. I did it to safeguard her future. To do likewise, you must enforce them, just as you promised me you would. Otherwise she will become uncontrollable and all my years of work will go for naught. I don't want my little girl in a madhouse.''

''That's the last thing I want as well. Please believe that.''

''Of course we do,'' James inserted.

Alex pushed to his feet. ''I'm sorry that I've intruded on your morning.''

''Nonsense,'' Edie scolded. ''Annie is our daughter, and we love her.''

There was that word again. *Love.* Alex longed to ask

these people if they even understood what it meant.

James rose and slipped an arm around his wife. "Exactly so. I'm glad you came directly to us with your concerns. Neither of us would want it any other way."

As Alex made his farewells to the Trimbles and left their home, his head was swimming with questions, none of which seemed to have easy answers. Were Annie's parents so wrapped up in their own concerns that they had become blind to Annie's? Or was it he and Maddy who were tilting at windmills?

"Mr. Montgomery! Mr. Montgomery! Wait, please!"

Alex heard the voice just as he gained the road at the end of the Trimbles' driveway. Reining his black to a stop, he turned slightly in the saddle to see Edie dashing from the shade of a sprawling oak to cross the lawn, her ankle-length, flared skirt whipping like a blue flag behind her. From a distance, with her sable hair and slight build, he could almost believe she was Annie. At the thought, his throat went dry. If Edie was correct, Annie would never speak, much less call out to anyone.

At the drainage ditch alongside the road, she drew up, one hand pressed to her midriff as she struggled to regain her breath. Alex waited patiently for her to speak. Even after running such a distance, she was still pale, he noticed. Her eyes pleaded with his as she sought his gaze.

"I couldn't let you leave without speaking with you about a matter of great concern to me," she finally managed.

"I see. And what is that?"

The muscles in her throat grew distended as she swallowed and hauled in another ragged breath. "I must ask a great favor of you, Mr. Montgomery. In future, please don't ask questions about Annie's condition in front of the judge. If you have concerns, you must consult with me privately.''

''Why must I keep my concerns from the judge?'' he asked, trying without success to read her expression.

''My husband is not well. He mustn't be bothered with such trifles.''

Trifles? It was all Alex could do not to turn the air blue. Annie's future was a trifle? To protect her position as the estimable judge's wife, just how far would this woman go? Alex had a feeling he didn't care to know. Not when Annie was the lamb she sacrificed. ''I'm sorry,'' he said stonily. ''I didn't realize the judge was in poor health.''

''Yes, well, it isn't something he wants talked about. He has his career to consider, after all.''

Oh, yes, the judge's damnable career. How could he have forgotten?

''I'm hopeful that James will grow better with proper treatment and rest,'' she went on. ''For the time being, however, it would be best if he doesn't become overset. I'm fearful that turmoil of any sort, especially regarding Annie, may cause him to have a relapse.''

Looking into the woman's eyes, Alex saw fear, all right, but he suspected it was for herself, not her husband. She had her secret to protect, after all. The irony of it was that her husband already knew that madness might run in her family and, for reasons beyond Alex, had neglected to inform her of it. Alex supposed that Trimble must be a believer in the old adage that to acknowledge something was to lend it strength.

How could two people live in the same house, make love, create children, and yet have so little honesty between them?

All Alex wanted was to get away from both of them. Away so he might think. He had some decisions to make.

Damned important decisions. For Annie's sake, he had to be sure he made the right ones. "I'll bear the judge's poor health in mind before approaching either of you with my concerns again. As I said, I had no idea he was ill."

Edie closed her eyes briefly. When she lifted her lashes, tears spilled onto her pale cheeks. "I know you think badly of me, Mr. Montgomery. You think I'm a poor excuse for a mother, don't you?"

That didn't say it by half, but Alex could see no point in wounding her. She was already so pathetic he could scarcely bear to look at her. "I am not a man to make snap judgments about anyone."

"No matter how it may appear, I've done what I thought best for my daughter," she said shakily. "Always. It hasn't been easy. The rest of my family demands my time as well. But I've kept her at home, never once begrudging her the hardships she has caused me. I believe many mothers would have taken the easy way out."

Alex didn't doubt that. He supposed that Edie in her own pitiful way had made her share of maternal sacrifices. She blinked and brushed at her cheeks. Something in her expression—Alex wasn't certain what—almost made him feel sorry for her.

"I'll bring my concerns to you from now on," he promised her. With that, he tipped his hat and started to nudge his horse into a walk. "Good day, Mrs. Trimble."

She threw up a hand. "Wait! Please. A moment more of your time, and then I'll let you be on your way."

"Yes?"

She caught her lower lip between her teeth. After a moment, she ceased worrying it to say, "I know you've given your word that Annie will be returned to us after the birth of the baby. But meanwhile there are some things about her you should know, things that I didn't mention the other night in front of the judge. Because of his poor health, you understand.''

"And what might those things be?''

Wringing her hands, she blurted, "Whatever you do, don't ever allow Annie to be around a cat without supervision. And should you have guests in your home who have young children, you should never leave her alone with one of their infants. Not under any circumstances.''

"Would you care to explain why?''

"Isn't it obvious? She wouldn't do it on purpose, you understand, but I can't help but be afraid she might do a small child or animal unintenional harm.'' Fresh tears sprang to her eyes, and the corners of her mouth started to quiver. "Just heed what I say. Please!''

With that, she whirled away and retraced her path across the yard. For a long while, Alex stared after her.

After returning to Montgomery Hall, Alex retired to his study where he hoped to find some solitude. Maddy had different ideas. Before he could get comfortably settled in his chair, she tapped at the door and then entered without permission. One look at her told Alex that she would settle for nothing less than a complete recounting of his conversation with the Trimbles.

"Well?'' she said.

Alex rose and stepped to the sideboard where he poured them each a measure of brandy. Because he seldom imbibed so early in the day, the housekeeper's eyebrows lifted when he handed her a snifter. "That bad?''

Taking a turn before the multipaned windows that looked out onto the west gardens, Alex replied, "Let's just say that after speaking with Annie's parents again, I'm more confused than ever.'' He stopped for a moment, running a critical gaze over the sculptured shrubs that bordered the rose beds. "Damn it, Maddy. I was so hopeful last night. I lay awake until daylight, a hundred possibilities racing through my head—that she's not as retarded as her parents think, that maybe the fever affected her in some other way we haven't even considered. Her ability to speak, perhaps? Or her hearing.''

Looking as frustrated as Alex felt, Maddy said, ''Well, it isn't her hearing, rest assured of that. Most of the time when I call her name, she turns at the sound.'' With a thoughtful frown drawing her brows together, she rubbed her glass between her palms. ''I thought that was the whole reason fer wanting to have her tested, Master Alex, to find out exactly what's the matter.''

Alex laughed bitterly. ''If I decide to have her tested or even so much as *suggest* that I'd like to keep her in residence here after the baby's born, I'll have a battle on my hands.''

''The Trimbles have no legal rights, not anymore. Ye can do what ye like.''

''True, but they are Annie's parents. If you're correct, and she's capable of developing emotional attachments, then an estrangement . . .'' Alex let his voice trail away. After a moment, he said, ''I don't want her heart broken for no good reason.''

''No, we don't want that. I've a feelin' that the poor wee thing has suffered heartache enough in her short life.''

As briefly as possible, Alex related everything else that had been said during his conversation with the Trimbles, including Edie's peculiar warnings, that Annie should never be left alone with a cat or anyone's infant.

''That's preposterous,'' Maddy said with a huff. ''The lass is harmless.''

''She wasn't harmless last night when she attacked Mistress Perkins,'' Alex reminded her. ''She wasn't exactly anybody's angel when I brought her here in the carriage, either.''

''But she was provoked!''

Alex couldn't deny that. He gazed into the amber depths of his brandy. When he glanced back up, he had made the decision to tell Maddy everything, even about Edie's uncle and the Trimbles' fear that their daughter might be mad. He didn't let himself think about breaking James Trimble's confidence. What he said in this room would never go past Maddy, and Annie's future was at stake.

As he spoke, Maddy turned frighteningly pale. ''Dear Lord in heaven,'' she whispered when he had finished. ''The lass isn't mad, Master Alex. I'd stake me life on it.''

That was Alex's feeling as well. ''Nevertheless, I think that both the Trimbles are afraid she may be, which explains their reluctance to have her examined.''

Maddy shook her head sadly. ''Because a doctor might discover she's not simply tetched, but crazy?''

''That could destroy James Trimble's political career, and if it did, I think his wife believes he would divorce her over it.''

''In other words, they can't see the forest for the trees.''

Alex sighed. ''I don't know. Maybe it's you and I who aren't looking at things clearly. Only time will tell, I guess.'' He met Maddy's gaze with a slight smile touching his lips. ''Luckily, we have that time. It's not as if we'll be fiddling while Rome is burning. She's only four months along. That gives us five more months to watch her and make a decision. If, after a few weeks, we both feel sure that she might be helped, I'll take her to Portland, the devil take her parents.''

Maddy raised her snifter. ''I'll drink to that.''

Alex couldn't help but grin. ''It won't be pleasant. If I

decide to go against their wishes, they're going to fight me with everything they've got.''

"They'll find their match in the pair of us." The housekeeper's eyes teared slightly as she swallowed the rest of her brandy. Waving a hand before her face, she blinked and sucked air through her teeth. "Lands, but that stuff burns a path clear to me toes!"

Alex chuckled. "Well, have we reached a decision then?"

"More a decision in lieu of a decision, but, yes, we've reached one. We'll be takin' the lass to Portland for tests."

"*If* we see signs that she may be trainable," Alex amended.

"We'll see signs."

"Don't get your hopes up, Maddy," he cautioned her gently. "I don't want to see them dashed."

"They won't be," she assured him with a challenging glint in her eyes. "The lass may never do arithmetic and the like, but she's trainable. I'll bet me garters on it."

"I hope you're right." Feeling more relaxed than he had in hours, he rested a shoulder against the wall. "There's another problem we haven't addressed, that of a nurse. I know you're busy, and I can't expect you to assume the added responsibility of caring for Annie as well. We're going to have to hire someone. Which reminds me. Where is she right now?"

"In her room. I asked one of the maids to sit with her while I came down to talk to ye. The door is repaired, by the way. Henry got the facing and lock replaced. Good as new."

"He got to it quickly."

"Yes, well, I did a bit of naggin'. Ye know Henry. If it can be put off until tomorrow . . .'' Her voice trailed away.

"I'm sorry about the extra work, Maddy."

She waved his apology away. "I don't mind lookin' after the girl. As far as I can see, there's no reason she can't tag along behind me while I attend me duties. She wasn't kept locked in her room at home, was she?"

"No."

"Well, then? If she gets away from me and runs off, it isn't as if ye won't know where to find her."

With a nod, Alex conceded the point. His main concern was that, given to wandering in the woods as she was, Annie might venture away from the house and sustain an injury. Until her pregnancy was over, special measures had to be taken to safeguard her well-being. "If you're sure you don't mind looking after her. For obvious reasons, I don't want her going outdoors without supervision."

"I don't mind." Maddy studied him for a moment. "As fer not letting her go outdoors alone, mayhap ye could make time to accompany her?"

"Me?" The suggestion caught Alex by surprise. After his physical reaction to Annie the other morning in the carriage, he didn't relish the thought of being alone with her. "It might be better if I assigned one of the household staff to escort her."

Maddy pursed her lips. "Master Alex, after what happened with Mistress Perkins, how can ye even think of it? Annie should be treated as a member of yer family. She isn't a pet or some such that ye can have walked by whoever's handy."

Knowing the housekeeper was right, Alex sighed. "I'll look at my schedule and see if I can't get away to spend some time with the two of you each afternoon." He prayed she didn't ask why he required her presence. Pulling his watch from his pocket, he checked the time. This afternoon, he had appointments with two men who were interested in purchasing one of his mares. "Well, now that we have that settled, I guess I should—"

"There is one other small matter," Maddy interrupted.

Alex lifted an inquiring eyebrow.

"As I mentioned last night, somehow ye have to make Annie understand that her increasin' proportions are from carryin' an infant. She's still off her food."

Alex groaned. "Maddy, I don't think she understands a word I say to her."

"Then draw her a picture."

"A picture? I can't draw. Besides, given her nervousness around me, wouldn't it be better if a woman explained it to her?"

A twinkle came into Maddy's eyes. "Don't be lookin' at me. I can't draw either. As fer me bein' the one to explain it to her, that's nonsense. Ye're the lass's husband."

"I am her husband only by the loosest definition of the word."

She raised her empty glass to him. "Which is a state of affairs ye should rectify. I've said so from the beginnin'."

"The girl is—"

"Lovely."

"No man with a shred of decency—"

"And she's sweet as well."

"Maddy, for God's sake, be reasonable."

"It seems perfectly reasonable to me," she informed him cheerfully. "By law, she's already yer wife. She's carryin' a child who'll bear yer name. Ye've said yerself a dozen times that ye've no intention of marryin' anyone else. Why not make this a marriage in fact?"

Leaving that question to hang in the air behind her, Maddy set her snifter on the sideboard and exited the room. After her departure, Alex gazed blankly at the floor. A marriage in fact . . . He closed his eyes on the thought, but shutting out the world around him did little to alleviate the ache of loneliness deep inside him.

Nine

That evening after Annie's supper, most of which she had once again refused to eat, Alex, with sketchpad and pencil in hand, went up to the nursery. Not wishing to frighten Annie any more than was necessary, he had arranged for Maddy to remain in attendance during their exchange. Happy to oblige, the housekeeper was already seated on the edge of the bed when he arrived.

Annie sat at the small table near the window, her hands clasped on her lap, her feet crossed at the ankle and hooked over a chair rung. When she caught sight of Alex opening the door, the little remaining color in her cheeks drained away. Despite her obvious fear of him, she made no attempt, as she had the previous night, to vacate the chair and seek obscurity in a dark corner. Since he doubted she had suddenly developed a courageous streak, he could only assume her daring stemmed from the fact that Maddy sat nearby. She obviously felt safe as long as the older woman was there to protect her.

Annie's erect posture afforded Alex a better look at her than he'd gotten last night, and he was dismayed by what he saw. In the last four days, she had dropped an alarming amount of weight. According to Maddy, she had eaten almost nothing since Mistress Perkins's dismissal, a few bites at each meal and nothing more. Judging by her thinness, he guessed she had eaten as lightly the first three days of her stay, which explained, but did not excuse, the nurse's bungled attempts to make her eat.

After this meeting, Alex hoped Annie would be a little more cooperative and stop starving herself. Otherwise, he'd have no choice but to improve upon Mistress Perkins's methods. Though he didn't doubt his ability to overpower the girl and force her to eat, he hated for it to come to that. She had already suffered enough in this house without that being added to the list.

Lamplight shimmered in the unruly sable curls that framed her small face, accentuating the color of her eyes, which, at the moment, reminded him of blue pools of crystal-clear water. Her frock, a faded pink garment better suited to a child, hung on her even more loosely than before, the well-worn cloth clinging softly to the subtle curves of her body. Perfection in miniature, that was Annie, lovely in a way that somehow outshone the more voluptuous beauties he'd been attracted to in the past.

Maddy's suggestion that he should make this a bona fide marriage chose that moment to reenter his mind. As much as he hated to admit it, even to himself, it was tempting to do just that. Incredibly tempting. The physical aspects of marriage to such a beautiful girl would be no great hardship for him, or for any other man, as far as that went. But more than that, making this a marriage in fact would be far less complicated than his original plan. Unfortunately, the guilt he felt for even thinking along those lines constituted a barrier he couldn't seem to work his way past. There were codes of decency to be observed if a man wanted to respect himself, and a girl with Annie's disabilities was not fair game.

After turning up the lamps, Alex joined her at the table,

positioning his chair across from hers in the hope that she might feel more at ease if he kept his distance. Since it was his plan to communicate with her by drawing pictures, he took it as a good sign that she seemed fascinated by the sketchpad and pencil.

"Hello, Annie," he said softly.

Pulling her gaze from the drawing pad, she stared fixedly at his mouth. Her expression said more clearly than words that she hadn't grasped what he said. It was *not* an encouraging start. Somehow he had to make her understand that her intake of food had nothing to do with her increasing waistline.

Neatly covered by a towel, Annie's supper plate sat at his elbow, the nearly untouched helpings of food forming telltale mounds beneath the linen. Shoving aside the pad and pencil, he grabbed the plate, uncovered the food, and forked up some green beans. Her expressive eyes reflecting a willfulness that surprised Alex nearly as much as it amused him, Annie immediately clamped her mouth closed. She obviously had no intention of surrendering without a fight.

Feeling far more nervous than the situation warranted, he flashed her what he hoped was a confident smile and touched her lower lip with the tapered end of a bean. At the contact, she jerked back, almost reflexively, and looked down her nose at the fork tines. With her movement, the light from a wall lamp fell directly across her face.

For an endlessly long moment, Alex stared at her mouth, then slowly lowered his hand. Forgetting all his good intentions to watch his language in the girl's presence, his voice raspy with rage, he said, "That heartless bitch!"

Startled by his tone and the sheer volume of his voice, Maddy shot to her feet. "Holy mother, what is it?"

Alex pushed up from his chair and circled the table. At his sudden advance, Annie scrabbled to get away. Before she could make any headway, he caught her by the shoulder. Though her terrified expression caught at his heart, he anchored her where she sat and cupped her small chin in one hand. Eyes wide, her face as pale as milk, she went instantly still, as if she were afraid to so much as breathe.

Naturally she was afraid, he thought with scathing self-derision. What reason had she not to be? Douglas had committed the most heinous of crimes against her, and now she was being held prisoner by a man she must surely believe was a monster.

Trembling with emotions difficult to identify, let alone control, Alex rubbed his thumb lightly across her lower lip. *Puncture marks!* Impotent anger roiled within him. "Oh, honey, I am so sorry."

Maddy hovered at his elbow. "Master Alex?"

Managing to keep his voice carefully even, Alex said, "The nurse jabbed her with a fork." *My fault*, a little voice whispered inside his head. *All my fault*. Never again, no matter what the time constraints, would he fail to verify an employee's references. He might not have felt so bad if he'd had to pay the price for his own neglect, but instead a helpless girl had suffered the consequences. For that, he would never forgive himself.

Her green eyes aching with sympathy, Maddy leaned forward to see the marks on Annie's lip for herself. "Oh, ye poor wee lass. Was there nothing she did not think to do to ye?"

"Apparently not," Alex ground out.

"And us going about our business downstairs, never guessing." Maddy touched a hand lightly to Annie's hair. "I swear to ye, lass, if I'd known, I'd have snatched the old witch bald."

Annie couldn't imagine why they were both so upset

over a couple of tiny sores that were nearly healed. Maddy had tears in her eyes, and Alex looked ominously angry. Initially she'd believed he was furious with her.

But no . . . Gazing up at him, she saw dark shadows of regret in his eyes, and she couldn't believe, even for a minute, that emotion like that could be feigned. To add to that impression, the grip of his hand on her chin was incredibly gentle, the caress of his thumb across her mouth so light it made her skin tingle. He clearly felt bad about the way the nurse had treated her.

His reaction was the exact opposite of anything Annie might have expected from him. Relentless, that was how she had imagined him, the kind of man who took what he wanted, the devil take anyone who got in his way. Yet there he stood, the features of his face taut, his large body shaking with rage that was directed not at her, but at the woman who had hurt her.

For days, she had lived in constant fear of him. In the dead of night, when she knew the household was asleep, she'd lain awake until exhaustion claimed her, staring at the door, terrified that he might come, convinced that it was only a matter of time until he would. Now that impression of him was being shattered, not measure by measure so she might slowly grow accustomed to the change, but with one fell blow.

Like a band of rubber that had been stretched taut and then released, Annie went limp with an overwhelming sense of relief. Past experience warned her to be wary. A part of her couldn't so easily forget all the times she'd been tricked into trusting people, only to discover too late that they meant to harm her. But another part of her wanted desperately to believe in this man.

It was undoubtedly the height of foolishness, but mistake or no, she couldn't resist doing just that. Maybe it was the gentleness with which he touched her or the remorse she read in his eyes, or perhaps she was just tired of feeling afraid. At this point, she was too weak from hunger and too heartsore from being abandoned by her parents to analyze her reasons. She only knew that the warmth of his strong fingers on her skin made her feel safe. Wonderfully safe.

Crazy, so crazy . . . But it was how she felt.

When he finally released her to resume his seat, Annie was so preoccupied with studying him that she scarcely heeded Maddy, who ambled back to the bed. Tonight he wore a white shirt with a turned-down collar and wide cuffs, similar to the ones her father favored. But there all similarity ended. His sleeves were folded back over his muscular forearms, and instead of a tie, he wore his collar open, the front plackets hanging loose to reveal an expanse of well-padded chest. In the lamplight, his burnished skin gleamed, its darkness striking a startling contrast to his amber eyes and perfectly straight, white teeth.

Unlike her papa and all of his haughty acquaintances, Alex Montgomery dressed more for comfort than fashion, she decided, his manner one of careless disregard. Yet, despite that, he managed to project a commanding presence.

The flickering light from the wall lamps played over him, molten in the tousled waves of his sun-streaked hair. With his head slightly bent, his carved features were limned with amber, the planes of his face in shadow, which defined the sharp blade of his nose, the square angle of his jaw, and the deep slashes that bracketed his mouth. Mesmerized, she gazed at his lips, the upper sharply etched, the lower full and moist.

"Shall we try again?" he asked.

Though she knew it had to be her imagination, Annie thought she actually heard his voice, its timber low and deep. It was something that happened to her a lot, imagining she heard things she knew she couldn't. Pretend sounds, she called them, but for all of that, they seemed absolutely real. Always before, it had happened with ordinary, familiar things—her mother's voice, the barking of a dog, the slamming of a door. The only explanation Annie could think of was that she saw the sound being made, knew it from memory, and, because her brain expected her to hear it, she thought she actually did.

Only she'd never heard Alex Montgomery's voice. Her father's was thinner and less husky, so Annie knew she wasn't recalling that and making a substitution. No. As unexplainable as it seemed, she'd imagined hearing *this* man's voice. This man's, and no other.

A prickly feeling crawled up her spine.

After what had happened to her up at the falls, she couldn't dredge up much enthusiasm for being friends with any man. Despite her yearning to trust Alex, he looked alarmingly wide across the shoulders to her in that moment, a huge wall of muscle that stood between her and everything she held dear—her childhood home, her parents, the forests she loved.

He reclaimed the fork, speared more beans, and pressed them upon her. Annie glanced uneasily at Maddy, hoping she might intervene.

By lightly nudging her mouth, Alex reclaimed her attention, his eyes glinting with determination. "You're dealing with *me* now, Annie, and I say you have to eat your supper."

Annie preferred to deal with Maddy, thank you very much. She wished she could tell him that, among other things. Did he think she wanted to remain here, locked up in this cheerless room, day after endless day? She wanted to go home. To accomplish that goal, she had to be thin the next time her mother came to see her.

Recalling the strength in his fingers, she gulped in nervous dismay. If he decided to force her . . . An awful, achy sensation centered in her chest, reminding her of the time she'd accidentally swallowed an unchewed mouthful of apple. Tears stung her eyes, and she blinked furiously to chase them away.

His face went hard, a muscle along his jaw bunching and then relaxing as he ground his teeth. Studiously avoiding her eyes, he said, "No foolishness, young lady. I am not a man easily affected by tears. You're going to eat. We can do it the easy way or the hard way. That's entirely up to you."

In the vain hope that she might sway him as she had Maddy, Annie started to puff air into her cheeks. The instant she did, he gave his head a shake and tossed the fork back onto her plate. At his sudden movement, she jumped with a start and ducked, just in case he had a mind to box her ears as her mother so often did. Freezing with his hand suspended in midair, he stared at her for a long moment. Then, barely moving his lips in a way that suggested he might be whispering, he bit out a word she'd never seen or heard anyone say before. She frowned in puzzlement.

At her look of bewilderment, he groaned visibly. Then he ran a hand over his face and blinked to bring her back into focus. Annie had the unpleasant feeling he regarded her as an extremely vexatious problem and was wishing with all his heart that she would miraculously disappear. She wished she could oblige him. Blink, gone. No more Annie.

After hauling in a deep breath, he said, very slowly and succinctly, "Annie, love, you are not fat."

If not fat, then what did he call it? Her stomach wasn't extraordinarily large yet, but at the rate it was growing, it soon would be. At the beginning of butterfly season, she had been able to look down between her bubbies and see her toes. Now all she saw was her belly. And what was worse, her frocks always seemed to get dirty there. Little wonder her parents didn't want her anymore.

"Honey, you have to eat," he said, his expression going from stern to cajoling. "Won't you do that for me? I don't want to have to force you, and I'm sure you don't want me to."

He leaned even closer, and to her surprise, he curled his hand over her cheek. His palm was so large and wonderfully warm that she was sorely tempted to bury her face there so he wouldn't see her cry. He was going to think she was nothing but a big old blubber baby, at this rate, and for reasons that totally escaped her for the moment, she didn't want him to think that.

"Listen to me, hmm? You are *not* fat." Smiling slightly, he repeated the last two words. "*Not fat!*" With that, he shoved her plate out of his way and reached for the sketchpad. "I had hoped to avoid this, but it looks as if there's no help for it. Pay close attention, all right? This will only take a few minutes."

As he began to draw, an intent frown creased his forehead. Curious in spite of herself, Annie swiped at her wet cheeks and sat a little straighter so she might see. Though she had always done so secretly, she loved to sketch. Alex seemed to be fashioning a full-length figure of a woman standing in profile.

As she watched him draw, Annie detected a movement of his lips from the corner of her eye. She glanced up in time to see him finish with" . . . not very good at this, I'm afraid."

She had to agree; he had very little, if any, artistic talent. The woman he was trying to draw had a head that more resembled a misshapen ball, and her hair looked like a crop of wiggly worms. From there, she went from bad to worse, with a nose more like a bird's beak and arms that resembled thick lengths of rope with frayed ends for fingers. As drawings went, it wasn't just poor, it was *awful*.

Because her mother had allowed her to utter no sound for so many years, Annie very seldom got an urge to laugh. But this was one of those rare moments. Alex looked so serious about the drawing, his lower lip caught in his teeth, his thick brows pulled together in concentration. He was clearly giving this his very best effort. But even when he tried to make the sketch look better, it remained one of the poorest attempts she'd ever seen.

To stifle the horrified giggle that was trying to come up her throat, she had to hold her breath. He glanced up just then, and for a moment, he seemed to forget all about the sketch. Filled with questions, his eyes searched hers. She had a feeling he sensed she was about to laugh. He didn't seem disgruntled about it, only confused. And troubled.

In that moment, Annie had the strangest feeling. It was as if he looked into her instead of at her, that he saw things in her eyes that others never had and probably never would. The breathless sensation in her chest intensified. She couldn't drag her gaze from his, couldn't move to break the tension.

Whatever was bothering him, he finally seemed to shake it off and began drawing again, this time to give the woman a huge stomach. Under the table, Annie touched a hand to her waist. His sketch was of her? As if he sensed her reaction, he looked up again, his mouth quirking slightly at the corners.

"Not very flattering, I know. But bear with me."

Flattering? It was a word she didn't know. Bewildered, she glanced back at the sketch.

Alex added some finishing touches to his drawing.

Then he sat back to examine the work. Apparently satisfied, he turned the pad so she might view it. To her complete surprise, she saw that within the woman's protruding abdomen he'd drawn an infant, recognizable as such only by its ruffled bonnet, gown and booties. For several endless seconds, she stared at it.

"Baby," he said with exaggerated slowness, tapping the drawing as he spoke. Gesturing at her supper plate, then pointing to the infant's slit of a mouth, he added, "You have to eat. To feed the baby. Do you understand, Annie? You're not getting fat. There's a baby growing inside you."

Staring at him in stunned amazement, Annie hugged her waist. Her incredulity must have shown in her eyes. As though frustrated beyond endurance, he tossed down the pencil. "Maddy, you come try. She doesn't understand."

Maddy rose from the bed and approached the table. Pretending to hold an infant, she began to rock to and fro, smiling broadly. Then she pointed at Annie's middle. "A wee one, lass. Isn't it a wonder? Ye're own wee babe. But ye must eat so it'll grow hale and hardy."

Annie understood all of that. The problem was, she couldn't credit it. A baby? They were saying she had a baby inside her? She looked down at her stomach.

As Annie regarded her waistline, Alex took advantage of the moment to study her. At one point while he'd been drawing, he could have sworn she'd been about to laugh, and every once in a while, her expression had implied a certain cognizance.

Not that her mental abilities or lack of them were the issue right now. What mattered was that she finally understood what was making her waistline increase. He could tell she'd gotten the message by the startled look in her blue eyes and the way she was leaning back in her chair to rest her hands over her stomach.

She was obviously wondering how a child had managed to take up residence inside of her. How could he possibly explain that to her? Through the thin layers of her clothing, she plunged a fingertip into her navel and wiggled it around.

Alex shot a glance at Maddy. With an expectant lift of her grizzled red eyebrows, the housekeeper met his gaze.

"Don't even think it," he said.

"But she thinks—"

"I don't care if she thinks she swallowed a seed and it sprouted, I am *not*, I repeat *not*, drawing her a picture."

"The poor wee lass!"

With that assessment, Alex was in complete agreement. Annie was, without a doubt, a poor wee lass, and it was nothing short of criminal that she'd been thrust into this predicament.

Looking at her now, he could almost see her holding a child in her arms, its downy head nestled against her breast. Even if she was daft, that didn't mean she was incapable of feeling love. Who was he to say what she thought or felt about anything? Or in what measure?

As those questions filled Alex's mind, a dozen others rose to bedevil him, none of which he could answer. He only knew, with sudden and almost blinding clarity, that Maddy was absolutely right; no one had the right to snatch a babe from its mother's arms. No one. He must have been mad to even consider it.

Before marrying Annie, he had convinced himself it was the only decent thing to do. He had seen it as his duty, not just to Annie, but to his brother's child. Right now none of those reasons held water.

A searing sensation washed over Alex's eyes as he watched Annie continue to poke curiously at her bellybutton. With a loud scrape of his chair, he pushed to his feet. No matter what he had promised her parents, how would he find it in his heart to separate her from the infant after its birth?

The answer to that was simple: he couldn't.

A little over an hour later, Annie was finally alone. Measured in broad stripes by the barred window, moonlight spilled into her bedchamber. Limned with silver, the utilitarian furnishings and long forgotten children's toys in the room took on a lifelike quality. Starkly defined by shadow, the carvings in the armoire door looked like a person's face. The rocking horse in one corner actually seemed to move slightly, its mane and tail rippling as though touched by a light breeze. Annie imagined she could even hear the sound of children's voices and laughter, ever so faint, ever so distant, from a time long past.

A sense of wonder filled her. If Alex Montgomery and Maddy weren't lying, she would soon have a child of her own. Her very own little baby. The thought made her throat tighten with gladness. Sometimes it was lonely, living in silence. The only pets she'd been allowed to have were wild creatures she had tamed—the animals in the woods and some mice in her parents' attic. She had no human friends and little hope of acquiring any.

A baby . . . Annie hugged her waist, so happy that it was difficult to contain herself. Someone of her very own to love. It was the nicest thing that had ever happened to her, barring none. So nice that she was almost afraid to believe it might be true.

After positioning herself cross-legged in the center of the bed, she held her hands reverently over her waist. Alex had seemed convinced a baby was in there. Try as she might, Annie couldn't imagine how it had gotten inside her. More importantly, how would it ever get out?

Jerking up her nightgown so she might better explore, she dived her fingertip into her navel again, wondering if the hole could possibly go clear through to her stomach. It didn't seem to. Frowning, she pushed as hard as she could, not easing up until it began to hurt. No, a baby had definitely not sneaked in that way, and it wasn't likely to get out that way, either.

When Annie had been a small child, her mother told her that babies were brought by fairies and left on people's doorsteps during the night. It had always seemed a perfectly logical explanation to Annie, for if not from fairies, where else could babies come from? Even the newborn creatures in the forest seemed to appear at their mother's sides as if by magic. Except for birds, of course. Annie knew they came from eggs. Mother birds, like domestic hens, laid the eggs and then sat on them until their chicks hatched.

Could it be that human babies came from eggs as well? Maybe her mother had lied to her, and babies weren't brought by fairies, after all. The thought made her heartbeat quicken. Spreading her hands over her waist again, she palpitated the slight roundness. If there was an egg in there, it was already bigger than most. Surely it was due to come out soon.

And then what? She weighed far too much to sit on an egg without cracking it. So what was she supposed to do with it? If allowed to get cold, the chicks inside eggs never hatched. Annie suspected that they died.

Despite the warmth of the summer night, she felt chilled at the thought of her baby dying inside its egg for lack of warmth. Lying down, she drew the down comforter to her chin. She couldn't let her baby die. She just couldn't. She had to think of a way to keep it warm. But how?

As the warmth of the comforter began to envelop her,

Annie found an answer to that question. When her egg came out, she could lie with it under the quilt. The heat from her body would keep her baby nice and toasty until it hatched.

Alex poured himself another glass of whiskey, tried to recall how many he'd already had, and then said to hell with counting. He didn't want to think. He didn't want to feel. To get staggering drunk, that was his aim.

To Annie, he thought, upending the glass. With two gulps, the whiskey was en route to his stomach, burning a path every inch of the way. He clenched his teeth and wiped his mouth with the back of his hand.

"Master Alex!"

Maddy's scandalized whisper pierced the silence. Alex sat forward in his chair, turned, and with painstaking care, finally managed to focus on her. "Hello, Maddy. Care to join me?"

Planting her hands on her ample hips, she marched across the Persian rug. Casting a fiery glance at his whiskey jug, she tutted in disgust. "What are ye about with all of this imbibing here of late? Just this mornin', ye were tippin' the bottle, and now here ye are at it again. It isn't like ye at all, if ye don't mind me sayin' so. And whiskey? I thought brandy was yer drink."

"Every now and again, Maddy, a man needs something with a little more bite than brandy."

"As if that'll solve yer troubles?"

She had Alex there. "It isn't my hope to solve my problems," he admitted. "Only to forget them." He tipped the glass to her. "All the best to you."

"Hmm. And what problems are ye tryin' to forget?"

Alex considered that question at length. "Be damned if I can recall."

"Lord help us." She perched on the arm of the chair

catty-corner to his. After studying him for several moments, during which time Alex refilled and once again emptied his glass, she finally said, "It's the wee lass, isn't it? That's what's troublin' ye. Ye feel bound by yer oath to return her to her mama, but yer heart's tellin' ye that would be wrong, terrible wrong."

Leave it to Maddy to hit the nail on the head. Alex poured himself another drink and sat forward again to brace his elbows on his knees. Finding his knees proved to be a slight problem. When he managed, he discovered that they wobbled worse than a three-legged chair. "What the hell am I going to do, Maddy?" he finally asked.

"What ye always do," she said gently.

"And what's that?" he snapped, irritated by what he interpreted as evasiveness.

"The right thing."

He groaned. "And just what *is* the right thing? I gave her parents my word, damn it. I've never gone back on my word in my life."

A long silence fell over them. At last, Maddy said, "Ye also gave God yer word, did ye not? It seems to me that if it comes to a choice between honorin' yer promise to God or to man, ye've got to choose God every time."

Alex gave a bitter laugh. "Put like that, it sounds so simple, but it isn't. You're probably going to go hunting for the shotgun if I tell you this, but I'm going to anyway. Since bringing Annie here, I'm discovering that my sterling character is a little tarnished around the edges. I'm half afraid to be alone with her."

"Why ever not?"

Alex glanced up, feeling suddenly sober. "Good God, Maddy. Do I have to draw you pictures as well? The girl's mind may be impaired, but otherwise, she's lovely." At his housekeeper's blank expression, he swore under his breath. "To put it in terms you will understand, I'm a lecherous bastard. Is that clear enough for you?''

Maddy's green eyes began to twinkle. ''Ah,'' she said.

''Ah? Is that all you can say? Jesus, Maddy. I'm not joking about this. The morning I brought her home, I—'' He broke off, swirled the liquor in his glass until it sloshed over the edge, and then heaved an exhausted sigh. ''If I keep her here, she'll be constantly at hand. Over a period of time, I'm worried that the few scruples I have left may get swept under the dust ruffle.''

''Ye'd never lay a hand on the lass unless she was willin', and well ye know it. Why, I'd venture to say ye'd kill any man who tried. I'm amazed ye let Douglas walk away from here in one piece.''

''He very nearly didn't,'' Alex admitted. ''There was a moment when I came just that close to strangling him. Now I'm beginning to wonder if I'm not more like him than I thought.''

''Don't be absurd. Ye're nothin' alike. Never have been, not even as young lads. He shot wee birds from the trees. Ye set their wings and nursed 'em back to health. He kicked the dog. Ye begged a treat from the kitchen to make it feel better. Over the years, he just got meaner, and ye went around behind him, tryin' to set his wrongs aright.'' She leaned forward to settle a kindly hand on his shoulder. ''Alex, me boy, ye are no more like Douglas than day is like night.''

He squeezed his eyes closed. ''What he did to Annie can't be fixed, Maddy. And I'm terrified that by keeping her here, I'll only wound her more.''

''Love has no sharp edges,'' she reminded him. ''And lots of love is what ye'll be givin' Annie if ye keep her here. Mayhap not the kind of love a man usually has fer his wife, but love nonetheless, and that will be more than she will ever have otherwise. As fer yer fears? The way I see it, ye've already plucked the goose by marryin' the lass. Now all ye can do is wait to see how the feathers settle.''

With those words of wisdom, Maddy left the study. For a long while after the door closed, Alex sat and stared at the intricate pattern in the carpet. When he told the Trimbles of his decision concerning Annie, feathers were going to fly, all right. A veritable blizzard of them.

Ten

A lex awoke shortly after dawn the next morning to a nasty headache and a ruckus loud enough to wake the dead. Shrill voices. The disturbance reminded him of the other night when Annie had sunk her teeth into Mistress Perkins's finger. Not something he could comfortably ignore, hangover or no. Wondering what sort of trouble his wife might be perpetrating this time, he groaned and swung out of bed.

After throwing on his clothes, Alex rushed from the master suite into the second-floor corridor and tracked the sound of raised voices directly to the nursery. Still barefoot, his shirt only partially buttoned, he stepped into the room, half expecting to see combatants writhing on the floor. Instead he found Maddy, three of the maids, Frederick the butler, and Henry the handyman, all gathered around Annie's bed. One of the maids held a stack of neatly folded sheets in her arms.

"What in blazes is going on in here?" Alex barked.

Apparently at a loss, Maddy turned to face him with her hands uplifted in a gesture of helpless quandary. "Yvonne just came in to do the cleanin' and change the sheets, as she always does each mornin'."

"So?"

Stuffing his shirttails into his trousers, Alex crossed the room. With a sweeping glance, he took stock of the situation. Annie, *en déshabillé* in a long-sleeved, nearly transparent white nightgown, seemed to be the center of attention. She sat cross-legged in the center of her rumpled bed, both shapely legs bare to the knee, arms extended as if to ward off encroachers. Looking down at her, Alex was put in mind of a skater who had just taken a spill on thin ice and was terrified that the people gathered around her might come charging to her rescue, go crashing through, and take her down with them.

He rubbed a hand over his face and blinked, partly to clear the sleep from his eyes, but mostly because it was a nervous habit. Maddy said it made him look idiotic. But, oh, well.

When his vision cleared, Annie was still sitting there, her posture conveying more clearly than words that she wanted them to stay back. Regarding her, Alex couldn't rid himself of the feeling that she was trying to protect something. The question was, what? A bunch of rumpled bedding?

"I don't understand it," Maddy mused aloud. "Yesterday mornin' she got up without a fuss." She looked to Alex. "What should I do?"

Alex had several ideas, the first of which was to dispense with Frederick and Henry. He couldn't believe Maddy had allowed two men in here while his wife was so immodestly clothed. Through the bodice of her gown, her nipples shone like rosy little beacons. If he had noticed, he knew damned well Frederick and Henry had as well.

Hooking a thumb over his shoulder, he barked, "Out!"

Everyone but Annie jumped. Frederick went slightly wall-eyed, and a bright red flush crept up his neck. Henry, the less intelligent of the two, scratched above one ear and fastened a questioning blue gaze on his employer. "We just come to help, Mr. Montgomery."

"Out!" Alex repeated through clenched teeth. His head was beginning to feel like a melon that had been dropped on cement. "*Now*! This is my wife's bedchamber, for Christ's sake!"

The maids, all three as nervous as titmice, hurried to leave with the men. Alex caught Yvonne, the sheet bearer, by her elbow. "Not *you*!"

With a frightened squeak, the maid froze, looking up at Alex as though he had sprouted horns. Since he'd never so much as raised his voice to the woman, he could only wonder why she seemed afraid of him.

Releasing Yvonne's arm, he waited until both men and the other two maids had departed. Only then did he turn back to regard Annie. At the apex of her slender thighs, a shadowy triangle of darkness was clearly outlined under her gown. Cross-legged. She had actually been sitting *cross*-legged in front of two men.

Shooting a glare at Maddy, he said, "Would you care to explain yourself, madam?"

"Just like I was sayin', Master Alex. For reasons beyond me, she refuses to get out of bed this mornin'."

"Not *that*! I meant—" Alex broke off. After looking into his housekeeper's guileless green eyes for a second, he groaned and rubbed a hand over his face again, striving to regain control of his temper. "In future, Maddy, I would appreciate it if no other men were allowed in my wife's bedchamber until she is properly *dressed*!"

Light dawned in Maddy's expression. "Oh." She glanced sideways at Annie. "Oh, of course. It was just—well, we had a bit of a situation in here, Master Alex. An emergency, if you will. And I—"

"A *fire* is an emergency. A tree falling on the house,

that is an emergency. *This*''—he gestured with his hand—''is not! I do not appreciate your allowing her to be ogled. She may be daft, but you're certainly not.''

''Yes.'' Two bright spots of pink flagged her plump cheeks. ''Now that ye mention it, I can see yer concern. Indeed I can. I apologize. I just didn't think, ye see. Her bein' so childlike and all, it just didn't occur to me that—'' She broke off and blushed to the roots of her hair. ''Well, Frederick and Henry, they're like part of the family.''

Alex's gaze cut to the front of Annie's nightgown. In his estimation, *childlike* did not describe his wife's anatomy. Grasping for a calmness that continued to elude him, Alex drew in a deep breath and slowly exhaled. He was behaving like a possessive husband, and overreacting, at that.

Turning the full blast of his glare on Yvonne, he asked, ''Is there a particular *hurry* to change my wife's sheets?''

''N-no, sir. It's just that since she came, I've made it my habit to do her room first. Before bringing up breakfast and dusting and the like.''

With exaggerated patience, Alex said, ''Well, this morning, since my wife seems disinclined to begin her day, change your routine, Yvonne, and do her room *last*. Perhaps by the time you return, she will feel more enthusiastic about leaving her bed.'' He started to check his watch, then realized he hadn't gotten it off his dressing table. ''It's rather early, isn't it? I'd be none too pleased if you rousted me out at this hour to change my sheets.''

The blond-haired Yvonne nodded and bobbed a little curtsy. ''Y-yes, sir.''

Alex glanced at Maddy. ''If Annie wishes to stay abed on a Sunday morning, I can only applaud her good sense. Let her sleep, for God's sake.''

With that, he returned to the master suite, his intention

to follow Annie's good example and be a layabout for the rest of the morning. It was the Sabbath, after all. Once in a blue moon, a man had a do-nothing day coming to him.

He had just unbuttoned his shirt when another loud knock came at the door. The sharp retort sent a pain lancing through his temples that made him wince. Striding across the room, he jerked the door open. "What now?"

Maddy stood in the hall. "I think ye'd better come. Annie's behavin' beyond peculiar, and I just can't figure what to make of it."

Before Alex could respond, his housekeeper, clearly beside herself, executed an abrupt about-face. Left with little alternative, he followed her back to the nursery. As he stepped into the room, he saw that Annie had finally chosen to vacate her bed and seemed to be searching through the layers of bedding for something.

"It looks to me as if she's lost something," he observed in a mild voice that belied his irritation. "What's peculiar about that?"

"What's peculiar about it? What could she have lost?"

"God knows." His headache growing worse by the second, Alex nearly groaned at the sound of his own voice. He'd think twice before upending a whiskey jug again. "What difference does it make what she's looking for?"

Closing the distance with three long strides, Alex gained the bed. Annie, apparently unaware until that moment that he'd entered the room, gave a violent start when he came to stand beside her. Then, bending forward at the waist, she spread her arms protectively over her bedding. To indicate he had no intention of touching anything, Alex folded his arms and watched as she lifted the top sheet and peeked beneath it. Curious, he leaned sideways and craned his neck to see as well. *Nothing.* The girl was obviously daft. Since that wasn't exactly news to anyone, least of all to Maddy, Alex couldn't fathom why she'd summoned him. A peculiar girl behaving in a peculiar manner was not, in his books, peculiar.

"Maybe there are bedbugs," he said, knowing even before he made such a suggestion that Maddy would burst her seams at the mere thought. "In *this* house? Bite yer tongue!"

Perversely satisfied to have pricked her ire, he returned his attention to Annie to find that she had gone from peering under her bedding to searching under her pillow. Finding nothing there, she began to pat her comforter, carefully palpitating the folds as though feeling for lumps. "She's definitely searching for something," Alex said. "And hasn't found it." He lifted an eyebrow at Maddy. "A hair ribbon, perhaps?"

"She wasn't wearin' one when she went to bed."

Alex glanced at the girl's hands. No ring. It occurred to him he needed to rectify that. A simple gold band. He should purchase one straight away, he supposed. But, then again, maybe it would be better to wait and speak with her mother first. For all he knew, there could be a reason Annie had no rings or necklaces. She might swallow them or some god-awful thing. "A piece of jewelry?" he asked, knowing even as he did what Maddy's reply would be.

"She has none."

He heaved an exasperated sigh. "Well, she's convinced she's lost *something*, Maddy. Maybe an *imaginary* something. Why can't you just humor her?"

"But don't ye find her behavior strange?"

Alex shot the woman an amazed look. "What do you expect? Normal?" Nearly blind with the pain pounding behind his eyes, he headed for the door. "Humor her, I said. Help her search. Have yourself a cup of coffee while she searches. I don't really care, Maddy. Just leave me to my rest.''

Maddy bristled at his tone and called after him, ''I think ye be needin' some hair off the dog what bit ye. That's what I'm thinkin'.''

Just the thought made his stomach roll.

Shortly after noon, Alex awoke to another knock at his chamber door. He couldn't quite believe that on the one occasion he chose to sleep late, he could get so little peace.

''I'm coming!'' he called. ''Quit that blasted pounding! I'm not deaf.''

After dragging on his pants, he reached for his shirt and began putting it on as he crossed the room. He had one arm down a sleeve when Maddy cried, ''Do hurry, Master Alex. I've lost her!''

''You've *what*!'' Picking up his pace, Alex lunged for the door, his shirt bunched around one elbow. Throwing the portal wide, he fastened an incredulous gaze on his housekeeper. ''*Where* have you lost her, for God's sake?''

''Well, if I knew that, she wouldn't be lost, now would she?''

Ignoring the sarcasm, he stepped past her into the hall. ''Has she left the house?''

Maddy trotted alongside him as he moved toward the nursery. ''When I brought her downstairs, I locked all the doors. If she got out, she had to go through a window.'' She made a squeaky sound of distress and pressed her knuckles against her mouth. In a muffled voice, she cried, ''I'll never fergive meself if somethin' has happened to her. There one minute and gone the next, she was. Just that fast. I really was watchin' her, Master Alex. I swear it as I breathe.''

Drawing to a stop on the landing, Alex grasped the

balustrade and leaned over to cast a glance about the hall. Forgetting his headache, he bellowed, "Annie!"

"It won't do any good, I tell ye. I've looked high and low. As much as I hate to say it, I don't believe she's in the house."

His pulse beginning to pound like a sledge in his temples, Alex headed for the stairs. Annie, pregnant and on the loose, unsupervised. He imagined her shinnying up a tree and falling. Or tripping over a tree root. A dozen different accidents could befall her. Descending the steps three at a time, he called back over his shoulder, "Just calm down, Maddy. If she's outdoors, it isn't a major catastrophe. She knows her way about. I'm sure she probably went home."

Taking jarring little steps, the plump housekeeper raced to keep apace with him. When he gained the first floor and began trying the front doors, she planted her fists on her hips and said, "I told ye I locked 'em all. Do ye doubt me word?"

"Of course not. I'm just checking to be sure." Alex moved swiftly through the house to try all the other exits. All the doors were locked, just as Maddy claimed. "I don't suppose you latched all the windows?"

Maddy pursed her mouth. "No, I didn't think to do that. I'm sorry, Master Alex. I never dreamed she'd go out a window."

Because he knew Maddy was usually pretty careful about relatching the windows after she'd had them open, Alex said, "It can't hurt to check all the latches. If we find one unfastened, it'll be a good indication she's slipped outside."

Yelling for the staff, Maddy organized an efficient team to assist them in making their rounds. Within minutes, Alex met her back in the hall. "The parlor window was unfastened. She might have gone out that way." At the housekeeper's stricken expression, he softened his tone and clasped her shoulder. "Maddy, would you stop? She'll be fine. I'll dress and ride over to the Trimbles'. I'm sure I'll find her there."

She nodded and sniffed. "I just pray nothin' has happened to her. Such a sweet little thing, she is. I'll never fergive meself."

"I'm sure nothing has happened. As much as I hate to admit it, now that Douglas is gone, I doubt there's a man in the area rotten enough to bother her, and aside from what Douglas did to her, she's been wandering in the woods for years without getting hurt. The only reason I don't allow it now is because of her pregnancy. Stop fretting. I'll have her home in two shakes of a lamb's tail. Mark my words."

Annie was not at the Trimble place. Even more surprising to Alex was that neither of her parents seemed to be alarmed when he appeared on their doorstep, looking for his wife. Edie suggested that Alex might find her in the woods. Not that it was necessary for him to go out searching. It was Annie's habit to roam, she reminded him, and had been for years. Along toward dark, she would come home, either to Alex's place or to the Trimbles'. If she chose the latter, her parents assured Alex they would send him a message so he could come collect her.

Still uneasy despite the Trimbles' reassurances, Alex searched the woods before heading home. It was like looking for the proverbial needle in a haystack. Open country stretched in all directions, and he knew Annie could be almost anywhere. In the end, he had no choice but to return to Montgomery Hall and wait. If she hadn't shown up by dusk, he would organize a search party.

As far as he was concerned, evening couldn't come quickly enough. Until Annie was home again, he wouldn't draw an easy breath. True, she'd been roaming the hills for most of her life. But that had been before her condition had become so delicate. He couldn't quite credit her mother's indifference. All manner of accidents could befall a pregnant woman, especially someone like Annie who didn't comprehend the dangers. Just the thought of her getting hurt made him feel panicky. Annie, with her tangled dark hair and big blue eyes. In an amazingly short time, she had wormed her way into his heart and become more important to him than he cared to admit.

Expecting Maddy to still be in a stew, Alex didn't tarry when he reached the stables. Quickly dismounting, he turned his horse over to a stableboy and went directly to the house. As he entered the hall, Maddy leaned over the upstairs balustrade and called down to him.

"She's back. Safe and sound."

Relief made Alex's legs feel weak. Needing a moment to regain his composure, he leaned against the carved entrance doors, his gaze uplifted to Maddy's beaming face. "Where was she?"

The housekeeper lifted her hands in a bewildered shrug. "I've no idea. We were searching the house, and suddenly, there she was. If I didn't know better, I'd think she oozed out from under a mopboard."

Alex frowned. Recalling the unlatched parlor window, he said, "More likely, she came back in the way she went out."

Annie suddenly appeared on the landing. Giving her a once-over, Alex was quick to note the telltale dirt smudges on her pale blue frock and white stockings. Her dark hair in its usual tangle of curls, she gazed down at him with those gigantic blue eyes, her expression unaccountably solemn. Alex guessed that she realized, however vaguely, that she'd done something wrong and might be in trouble. So she would know he wasn't angry, he made it a point to smile and wink at her. As nasty a scare as she'd given all of them, she couldn't really be blamed; holding her accountable was out of the question.

The way to handle this, he assured himself, was to take extra precautions so it wouldn't happen again. He looked at Maddy. "Have you a minute or two you might spare? I think we need to set down some new rules around here, not just for the household staff, but also for ourselves. We can't have her slipping outdoors again. Until the baby's born, it isn't safe. If she got injured while away from the house, she could very well bleed to death before anyone found her."

At the suggestion, Maddy went as pale as whitewashed pickets. "I'll be right down."

Minutes later, Alex and his housekeeper met in his study. Between the two of them, they outlined some safeguards they could enforce that would discourage, if not prevent, Annie from sneaking outside again, the most important being that, henceforth, all the exterior doors would be kept locked from the inside, day and night, and only Alex or Maddy would have the keys. The first floor windows, equipped with interior latches instead of locks, presented a bit more of a problem. It was decided, however, that if they were all kept closed and latched, Annie's use of one of them as an escape route would be easy to detect. Once outside, the girl would be unable to relatch the window she'd used, and they would know for certain she had left the house. In that event, Alex could initiate an immediate search of the surrounding woods for her.

Comfortable with the preventive measures they were taking, Alex drifted off to sleep that night, confident that Annie was safe. Beginning tomorrow, he promised himself, he would set aside an hour or two every afternoon so he could spend some time with her. Doing what, he wasn't certain. How did one entertain a feebleminded girl?

Ah well . . . Maddy seemed to think it was important that he and Annie become better acquainted, and to that end, Alex would happily sacrifice a bit of his time. Not that it would be easy. He usually spent his mornings doing paperwork in his study, and during the afternoons, he saw to the care of his thoroughbreds and the farm, or went to the rock quarry. As it was, he sometimes felt he was burning his candle at both ends, especially during the summer.

Nonetheless, the last thing he wanted was for Annie to feel frightened in her new home. If he could assuage her fears by spending an hour or so with her each day, it would be well worth the effort.

Alex's plan proved to be a little more difficult to execute than he hoped. He juggled his schedule to make time for her the next day, but when he arrived at the house, Annie was nowhere to be found.

"What do you mean, she's disappeared?" he demanded of Maddy.

"Well . . ." The housekeeper's green eyes sparkled with unshed tears. "It's just like yesterday, Master Alex. One minute she was there, and the next she wasn't. Frederick was just leaving to go tell you."

Spinning on his heel, Alex asked, "Have you checked the windows?"

"Yes. We checked 'em all. Nary a one is unfastened."

The housekeeper's response brought Alex to a quick halt. He turned to regard her. "None of them? Are you absolutely sure?"

"Nary a one."

"Then she has to be in the house somewhere."

"So one would think. Only she isn't. We've looked everywhere, Master Alex. It's like as if—" She broke off and hugged her waist. "It's like as if she disappeared into thin air."

Alex had seen that expression on his housekeeper's face before and knew it boded ill. "Now, Maddy. Don't let your Irish imagination get the best of you. The girl is flesh and blood. She can't disappear into thin air any more than you or I."

"Are ye sure?" she whispered. "There's no denyin' she's a bit fey. Like that business of her searchin' her beddin'. Did it again this mornin', she did. Beyond peculiar, if ye ask me, a body searchin' fer somethin' she hasn't lost." She shivered slightly. "I know fer a fact that fey folks aren't like the rest of us. Sometimes they see things we can't, and they got talents that border on magic. Ye've heard the stories about how she tames the wild animals in the woods. That isn't normal, and ye can't argue it is."

"I'm not saying she's normal. I'm just saying that, for all her differences, she's still very much human, Maddy, and thereby limited in what she can do. Disappearing into thin air? That's silly. She's either found herself a hidey-hole somewhere in the house, or she's exiting by an upstairs window."

"An upstairs window?" Maddy gasped and crossed herself. "Dear Lord, if she fell, she'd break her fool little neck!"

"Exactly." Alex headed for the stairs. "From now on, all the windows on the second and third floors must be kept fastened, too. We'll attend to that right now. Then I'll gather up some men to help me comb the woods. She's probably wandering around out there, happy as a clam and completely oblivious to the panic she's causing us."

*　　*　　*

Ten minutes later, Alex was checking window latches in the ballroom, situated on the third floor, when he sensed a presence behind him. Skin prickling, he looked over his shoulder to see Annie standing in the open doorway. As had been the case yesterday, her shapeless frock was smeared with dirt, and there were smudges of dust on her cheeks. Since Alex knew she couldn't possibly have gotten so dirty inside the house, he could only surmise she'd done as he suspected and climbed out a second- or third-floor window.

Just the thought made his pulse skitter. While doing roof repairs in the recent past, he had learned the hard way how treacherous some sections of that slate could be. One false step was all it might take. In most places, there was nothing to break a person's fall. He had a good mind to drive nails through all the bottom window rails.

"Annie," he said weakly. "Honey, where have you been?"

At the question, she retreated a step.

"Don't be afraid. I'm not angry with you. Just concerned. I know you've been outside somewhere, and if you went out through one of these windows, you might have fallen."

She backed up another step.

Moving slowly, Alex tried to close the distance between them. He had covered only a few feet when she bolted. "Annie! Come back here. I won't hurt you."

His words fell on empty air. Alex heaved a disheartened sigh and pinched the bridge of his nose. So he was supposed to spend time with her, was he? And how, exactly, was he going to accomplish that? By tying her to a chair, perhaps?

He followed the third-floor corridor to the landing. Grasping a newel post, he swung his weight onto the stairs and took the descent three steps at a time. Once on the second level, he headed directly for the nursery. Maddy, who was busy scolding Annie and checking her for injuries, didn't notice when he entered the room.

"Oh, lass, ye can't be takin' off like this!" the housekeeper cried. "Me old heart won't take it, ye understand? What did ye do? Go out an upstairs window? Lord help us! Ye could've broke yer silly neck. Don't ye realize that?"

Alex made his way to the table where Annie was sitting. Hunkering in front of her chair, he gazed solemnly into her eyes. The emotions he read there baffled him. She was afraid of being punished, that much was clear. But she also looked confused and a little self-righteous, as if she were being unjustly accused.

Alex gave her a thorough inspection, starting with her hair, which had bits of what appeared to be cobwebs clinging to the tendrils, and ending with her white stockings, which were smudged with dirt. Grayish colored dirt. Not red. Most of the soil thereabouts was a rust-red clay.

"Maddy, is there anyplace inside the house—say a closet or a storage room?—that might be filled with cobwebs and dust?"

Maddy sputtered at the suggestion. "Only the attic, and ye know very well it's always kept locked. I have the only key, and I haven't let it out to anyone since ye bought the new safe after Douglas left."

Alex frowned. "You're sure it's locked?"

"Positive. With all those spiders and mice thereabouts?" She shuddered. "It's always kept locked."

"Someplace else then?" Alex pointed out the smudges on Annie's clothing. "If she'd been outside, the dirt on her frock would be reddish." He touched a smudge on her knee. "This looks more like dust to me."

"Dust?" The housekeeper glared at him. "I'll have ye know that every crack and cranny of this house gets a thorough and regular cleanin', no exceptions. I'd never allow any room, closet or otherwise, to get so filthy.''

Alex knew that to be so. But he still couldn't put his suspicions to rest. Had Annie found a hidey-hole somewhere that Maddy had overlooked? "Tomorrow, I want you to keep a closer eye on her," he instructed the housekeeper. "If you have to, enlist the help of a maid or two. When she slips away again, I want to know which direction she takes.''

Maddy's Irish brogue became more pronounced with her building indignation. "She went out! Just look at her, all covered with dirt. She couldna get so soiled inside me house!''

Alex pushed to his feet and patted the older woman's shoulder. "I'm sure she couldn't, Maddy. But all the same, do as I ask, hmm? I'd really appreciate it. And meanwhile, when I'm up at the stables working, I'll keep an eye on the exterior of the house to see if I can spot her sneaking out a window.''

Returning his gaze to his wife, Alex considered the situation and possible solutions. Because the girl had been allowed to wander at will when she lived at home, she probably found her existence at Montgomery Hall pretty confining in comparison, and he couldn't really fault her for that. Arrangements needed to be made so she might have daily outings. Maddy didn't really have time to accompany her. For that matter, neither did Alex.

He sighed with resignation. Annie was ultimately his responsibility and no one else's. If she needed to be taken for daily walks, which she obviously did, then he was the likely candidate. Now that he'd decided to make her a permanent resident at Montgomery Hall, he couldn't avoid being thrust into situations where he would be alone with her. Not indefinitely. To even try would be ludicrous. A marriage in name only or not, they were still married, and though his role as such would be limited, he *was* her husband.

A little self-control was in order, he thought determinedly. If he didn't have a good measure of that at his disposal already, then he'd damned well better acquire some.

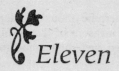

Eleven

When *Alex* suddenly grasped Annie's hand and drew her up from the chair, she couldn't have been more surprised. On the heels of her surprise came dread. He meant to take her somewhere? It didn't require a great deal of thought to guess his intentions. Both he and Maddy mistakenly believed she had sneaked outdoors and were upset with her. To ensure she wouldn't break the rules again, Alex obviously meant to punish her.

In the past, Annie had endured her share of lickings, most of them meted out by her father in his study, all with his razor strop. From experience, she knew that the sting only lasted for a short while and that the bruises would go away within a few days. But that had been when her papa punished her. Alex Montgomery was twice his size and far stronger.

For the space of a heartbeat, she seriously considered running from him. But before she could act on the urge, she remembered the baby she was supposedly carrying. If, as she suspected, it was enclosed in a fragile egg, she couldn't take any chances. Trying to run from Alex Montgomery would definitely pose a risk. His legs were long and powerfully muscled. In a footrace against him, she wouldn't have a prayer. And when he caught her? That didn't bear thinking about. Eggs, Annie knew, broke very easily. She doubted hers could withstand the crushing force of his arms around her waist.

As he led her out into the hall, she frantically searched her mind for some way she might tell him she hadn't sneaked outside. All she'd done was go to the secret place for a little while. Where was the harm in that? At home, she'd done it all the time. Nearly every day during the rainy season. Her mama had never cared, let alone been angry.

Pulling her along behind him, Alex walked with a loose-hipped, powerful stride that made her blood run cold. Watching the sway of his shoulders, she recalled the morning she'd seen him without a shirt. All that strength, and now he was about to unleash it on her.

Annie expected him to take her to his study as her papa had usually done. Instead, when they got downstairs, he headed straight for the entry doors. Keeping a firm hold on her wrist, he used his other hand to fish in his trouser pocket. Within seconds, he had drawn out a key, unlocked the doors, and pulled her onto the porch.

Guessing his intent, Annie's heart began to kick violently against her ribs, and she glanced wildly around. Where did he plan to take her? In her estimation, there could only be one reason why he was taking her outside; he didn't want anyone in his household to see how severely he punished her.

Oh, God . . . Annie was so frightened she could scarcely think. She threw him a pleading glance, but he was too preoccupied with looking around to notice. Suddenly he smiled, his expression decisive, and led her down the front steps, angling right when they struck the drive. As they went around the corner of the house, they entered a beautiful garden, artfully crisscrossed with white stone paths. Roses bloomed in profusion, the varying shades of pink and red making brilliant splashes against the deep green backdrop of sculptured shrubs and grass.

Drawing her abreast of him, he slowed his pace, for all the world as though he wanted her to enjoy the stroll. All Annie could think about was the beating that was in store for her. Sneaking glances at his dark face, she saw the breeze catch his molten hair, whipping it into lazy waves across his high forehead. As though he sensed her regard, he turned and caught her studying him. She quickly looked away, then jumped with a start when he brushed gently at her cheek to push a tendril of hair from her eyes.

Their gazes locked. Annie's feet suddenly felt numb. If she didn't watch where she was going, she knew she might stumble. But for the life of her, she couldn't look away from his gleaming amber eyes.

"Do you like roses, Annie?"

Roses? He was taking her someplace to beat her, and he expected her to admire his roses? Her attention became fixed on his smile—a lazy, slightly crooked grin that flashed his white teeth and deepened the creases at the corners of his mouth. He didn't look angry, not in the least, and that frightened her more than anything else. A man had to be utterly coldhearted to inflict pain on someone when he wasn't even mad at her.

Averting her face, Annie saw the stables up ahead of them, and her footsteps faltered. Once, a long time ago, her papa had taken her to the woodshed to punish her. In her recollection, that trip to the woodshed had preceded the worst licking of her life. A watery sensation attacked her legs. Between that and the numb feeling in her feet, it was difficult for her to remain standing, let alone walk.

As she expected, Alex headed directly for the outbuildings. When they reached a long, narrow structure with an open-ended alley running lengthwise through its center, he turned to her and said, "I understand you like animals."

Only if they had four legs, she thought acidly, and caught the inside of her cheek between her teeth, hoping the pain might distract her from worrying about what he might do to her. The entrance of the building yawned before her like a gigantic mouth. A little hysterically, she remembered the story her mother used to read to her years ago about Jonah being swallowed by a whale.

Left with little choice because his grip on her hand was relentless, she followed him into the alleyway. As the shadows fell over them, Annie's nostrils were assaulted by a strong but not entirely unpleasant blend of scents, that of animals and hay, grain and leather, all adrift on a current of fresh air. As her eyes grew accustomed to the dimness, she glanced nervously around. Hanging from large nails along the wall to her left were all manner of riding accessories and grooming tools—gig saddles, brushes, mane combs, blanket pins, muzzles, harnesses and lunging lines. Taking a fast inventory, she spotted several leather straps. A bead of sweat broke loose near the nape of her neck and trickled icily down her spine.

Her worst fear was realized when Alex released her hand and stepped over to the wall to take something from a nail. As he turned back toward her, Annie glimpsed a loop of leather dangling from his fist. When she jerked her gaze back to his face, she saw that he was smiling still, his expression oddly tender. That look chased away the last shreds of her courage. If he meant to punish her, which he surely did, how could he stand there and smile at her that way?

Running was out of the question now. Her feet felt as if they had put down taproots. She settled frightened eyes on his shoulders—broad muscular shoulders that blocked out the wall behind him. The loose fit of his white shirt did little to conceal the defined contours of muscle across his chest and along his arms. She didn't want to think about how it would feel when he struck her, but unfortunately, her traitorous mind could focus on little else.

With no warning, he swung up the hand that held the leather. Annie glimpsed the strap coming toward her face and reacted instinctively, bending forward and hugging her waist to protect her baby.

Alex was so startled when Annie jackknifed forward that for a moment all he could do was stand there and stare at her with his mouth hanging open. He'd been about to take her to the opposite end of the stable. Rosy, one of his mares, had recently dropped a foal. Though the horse was an incurable biter, her colt was a cute little bugger, all legs and ears, with a penchant for suckling on whatever caught his eye, buttons, fingers, elbows, or anything else that looked as if it might yield milk. Alex had thought Annie might enjoy seeing him.

"Annie?" he finally managed to say.

She didn't look up when he called her name. Judging by the way she was hugging her waist, it struck him that she might be in pain. His first concern was for the baby, and a dozen possibilities chased through his mind. Had she hurt herself while wandering in the woods? Horrible visions of her miscarrying right there in the stable swamped him. Dropping the muzzle he'd just taken from a nail, he grasped her slender shoulders and tried, with little success, to make her stand straight.

She was trembling. Trembling horribly. Alex threw a helpless look toward the house, wishing Maddy were with them. When it came to female complaints, especially those involving pregnancy, he was at a complete loss. Should he carry her to the house? Make her lie down?

"Christ!"

Leaning sideways, he pushed ineffectually at her hair, trying to part the wildly curly tresses so he might see her face. He finally resorted to going down on one knee and craning his neck so he could look up into her eyes.

"Annie love? Do you hurt someplace?"

By her pallor, Alex knew she was frightened half to death. Every awful story he'd ever heard about pregnant women miscarrying and bleeding to death came back to haunt him. The thought of Annie dying—God, she was so sweet, so impossibly and wonderfully sweet.

Half expecting to see blood soaking through the pink cloth, he glanced in anxious torment at the knee-length hem of her frock. *Nothing*. That was a good sign, wasn't it? No hemorrhaging. Then again, maybe she just wasn't bleeding that heavily yet.

"Honey, where does it hurt? Can you show me?"

Blue eyes that rivaled the size of saucers stared out at him from her small, pinched face. Smoothing her hair back, he cupped her cheeks between his hands.

"Annie, did you hurt yourself? Show me, honey. Here?" He dropped one hand to touch her waist. "How bad does it hurt?"

She jerked violently away and executed an awkward sidestep. Then she froze, staring at something on the ground. He followed her gaze to the discarded muzzle, his brain not making a connection until she jerked her eyes back to his hand.

His empty hand.

It hit Alex then. For an awful moment, his stomach knotted so violently he thought he might vomit. Reenacted in slow motion, he saw himself drawing her up from her chair immediately after Maddy had scolded her. Taking her downstairs. Outside. Through the garden. Into the stables. When he had swung the muzzle toward her, he had only been pointing the way to Rosy's stall, but Annie had thought he meant to strike her.

Rage . . . It exploded inside Alex's head in blinding shades of red. If James Trimble had been within his reach at that moment, he would have killed him. He balled his hands into throbbing fists.

Annie was all that mattered, not her bastard of a father. Calm, he had to stay calm. To that end, he forced his lungs to expand, drawing in a shuddering breath. As he exhaled, her face broke through the haze of his anger. He'd never seen anyone look quite so terrified. Wanting desperately to wipe that look off her face, he searched his mind for some way—any way at all—that he might re-assure her. The poor little thing didn't understand anything he said to her. The one and only time he had been successful at communicating with her, he'd had to draw her a picture.

A picture . . . Actions spoke louder than words. All he had to do was think of some way to look harmless. No easy task when the girl he wanted to convince was half his size and badly frightened.

Only vaguely aware of his movements or the decision that prompted them, Alex folded a leg under himself and sat unceremoniously on the dirt. It was the best idea he could think of, his hope being that she would feel less threatened if he placed himself at a physical disadvantage. Not that it gave her much of an edge. After working with horses for the majority of his life, he'd learned to move more quickly than most people, an ability that had saved his hide more than once. If she decided to run, he could be on his feet before she could execute a full about-face.

Something cold and wettish was seeping through one leg of his trousers. Not caring to think about what manner of muck he might have encountered, he kept his attention focused on Annie. Bless her heart, she didn't look capable of running. Her legs were shaking so badly, he was surprised her knees weren't knocking.

Unable to think of anything else he might do to assuage her fears, Alex made a valiant attempt to smile. A horrible, artificial, crack-your-face smile, but it was the best he could muster. Through the tangled curtains of her dark hair, she gaped at him as if he'd gone mad. And perhaps he had. A grown man, lolling around in horse shit and grinning as though he *liked* it? If that didn't qualify him for the madhouse, nothing much would.

On legs that still didn't look capable of holding her up, she manage to retreat a step. Then she spun and ran from the stable. Alex followed her with his gaze, relieved beyond words when he saw that she was heading for the house. The thought of having to pursue her through the woods right now didn't hold a great deal of appeal. Neither did the thought of catching her. The little minx didn't fight fair.

As was his habit when nothing in his life seemed to be going right, Alex started to rub a hand over his face. At the last second, he caught himself short. Something brown was smeared across his palm. He took a cautious sniff. Then, in spite of himself, he snorted with laughter.

"Master Alex?"

The amazed male voice came from behind Alex. He shot a look over his shoulder to see Deiter, his head groom, standing in the tack room doorway. Wiry and gray-haired, the man had a face that resembled a strip of beef jerky. "Yes, Deiter?"

"Are you all right?"

The question made Alex start to laugh again, harder this time. When his mirth had finally subsided, Deiter asked, "What are you doin' down there, anyhow?"

"I'm really not sure. It seemed like a good idea at the time."

"Need any help?"

Alex sighed. "As a matter of fact, I believe I'm going to need all the help I can get."

Despite all of Alex and Maddy's efforts to prevent it, Annie disappeared nearly every afternoon of the next week, her destination unknown to anyone but her. Maddy tried to keep an eagle eye on her, but somehow Annie managed to sneak away. After each of her vanishing acts, Alex was summoned to the house, the staff was divided up into teams, and the windows on all three floors were checked.

None of them were ever found to be unlatched.

So . . . if not outdoors, where was Annie going? The question bedeviled everyone at Montgomery Hall, from Alex and Maddy on down to the youngest stableboy. By the end of the week, Alex was so baffled, he was about ready to put in with Maddy and start believing that Annie had a magical ability to disappear into thin air.

Except for one small thing. How did she get so dirty?

One afternoon, a week to the day after Annie's first disappearance, Alex was summoned to the house and informed by Maddy that their mystery had finally been solved.

"I outsmarted her," she told Alex proudly. "Pretended I was preoccupied with somethin' else, I did. Waited fer the lass to slip away, and then I followed her. Ye'll never guess where it is she's gettin' off to, Master Alex. Ye'll never guess in a million years."

Alex gazed at his housekeeper expectantly. When he realized she intended to say nothing more, he ground his teeth. "Maddy, tell me, for God's sake. Where does she go?"

"The attic!" she informed him, beaming with satisfaction. "Up to the bleedin' attic."

"How? You assured me—absolutely no question, re-member—that you kept it locked. Didn't you check it?"

"I have the key," she reminded him. "I didn't see a need to check, knowin' as I did that it couldn't be un-locked."

"But it obviously was!"

"Henry again," she said by way of explanation.

"Henry?"

"When ye replaced the safe in yer study, I had him take the old one up to the attic. He must've forgot to lock the door. When I asked, he assured me he did, and I saw no call to question his word."

Alex sighed. "Trust Henry to think he locked it when he didn't. I should've checked it myself." Glancing up at the second floor landing, he frowned. "The attic? Of all the dirty, nasty places—" He shook his head. "Why in God's name would she go up there?"

"Ye got me. That's why I sent fer ye, to go fetch her down. I'd go, but ye know how I hate mice. Frederick offered to go up, but Annie doesn't see much of him, and I didn't want her to get frightened. Our luck, she'd try to run and step in one of those rat traps."

The unsprung traps in the attic weren't Alex's only con-cern, even though, as he recalled, the uppermost floor was littered with them. What worried him more was that the attic was probably stifling at this time of year, not to men-tion dark, dusty, and infested with spiders. Black widows being indigenous to the area, that was not a comforting thought.

Alex pushed past Maddy and made for the stairs.

"Do ye want me to send Frederick up to help ye search?" she called.

He never broke stride. "I think I can find her. Go on about your work, Maddy. I'll bring her back down."

The stairway that led to the attic was located on the

third floor in the west wing. Envisioning Annie with a fatal spider bite, Alex took the treacherously steep and narrow steps at a breakneck speed. The door, rusty from disuse, squeaked eerily as he pushed it open. Wishing he'd thought to bring a lantern, he stepped into the semi-darkness. The only source of light came from strategically placed dormer and gable windows, their efficiency undermined by grime. The smell of dust and mildew burned his nostrils.

While he paused to get his bearings and allow his eyes to adjust, he heard faint scurrying noises that made his blood run cold. *Rodents.* Though he would never admit it to anyone, he harbored an irrational fear of the nasty little creatures. He wasn't sure why. He could handle snakes. Spiders scarcely gave him pause. He wasn't even particularly wary of large carnivores. But mice? On the rare occasion when one was spotted downstairs, he wanted to follow Maddy's example and stand on a chair until Frederick came to dispense with it.

Sweat beaded on his forehead. From his right came a scratching noise, then a gnawing sound. The skin along his back and arms shriveled. *Jesus.* Over the years, he'd conquered his fear enough to face the occasional mouse. For the sake of his pride, he'd had no choice. But a legion of them? He felt like Goliath must have while facing David. Only, in this confrontation, David had multiplied.

As his eyes grew accustomed to the dimness, Alex could make out the shapes around him. The replaced safe. Old pieces of furniture. A mirror that had once graced the parlor and was now so grimy it no longer reflected any light. Propped between two stacks of boxes, he saw several oil paintings covered with sheets and bound with twine. In a clutter at their base was an assortment of what appeared to be cooking pots. Over everything lay a thick coat of dust, and stretching from object to object were filigreed webs, their intricately woven fibers adorned with dead moths and other hapless insects. The place wasn't fit for man or beast. Yet Annie was up here somewhere.

Stepping forward, he barked his shin on an old trunk. *Son of a bitch.* "Annie!" he called gruffly. Venturing a few more steps, he stumbled into a huge iron caldron that had once been used for boiling laundry. "*Damn it!*" he said under his breath. Then, more loudly, "Annie, where are you?"

As he wove his way through the haphazard assortment of castoff items that had collected there over the years, Alex reminded himself that his wife wasn't able to answer him. Fool that he was, he was yelling as though he expected a reply. On the other hand, the attic was nearly as large as the three floors below, and he didn't relish the thought of searching every square inch. Not when lack of light rendered him half blind and mice scurried in the shadows.

"Annie? Come on out, honey. Maddy has tea and cakes waiting for you." It wasn't exactly a lie. When he got the girl downstairs, he'd see to it she was given a treat of some sort. Anything to cajole her out of hiding. "Did you hear me? Cakes. *God damn it!*" Alex bent to rub his knee, which had connected painfully with the sharp corner of the antiquated safe. "Honey? I know you're up here somewhere. Won't you come out? Please? It's not safe up here."

As he straightened, Alex heard a sound that he thought came from the east wing. Not a scurrying noise, but more of a thump. Definitely too loud for a mouse or—God forbid—a rat. Relieved to have at least pinpointed Annie's general location, he turned and headed in that direction. To his immense relief, he found that the way had been cleared a few feet beyond the door, almost as if she had set things aside so they wouldn't obstruct her path. He cringed at the thought of her moving heavy furniture. If worry was fatal, the girl was going to drive him to an early grave.

As he drew near the east section of the attic, the light seemed to grow stronger. Pondering its source, he remembered there was a flank of dormer windows in this wing. Drawn to the illumination, he made steady progress, calling out loudly every few seconds. Even if Annie didn't understand him, at least she wouldn't be startled when he found her.

Stepping around a partition wall, Alex finally spotted his quarry. He stopped, not quite able to believe his eyes. Annie . . . only not the Annie he knew. Dressed in a pink morning dress and black kid pumps that she must have ferreted from his dead stepmother's trunks, she was a veritable fashion plate, albeit an outdated one. With her dark hair drawn into a tousled and slightly off-center topknot of curls, which she'd secured with a bit of lace, she presented a perfect cameo in profile, the loveliest woman he had ever seen, barring none.

"Annie, what in the world?"

No response. Not even a twitch to indicate she'd heard him.

So stunned he couldn't move, Alex simply stood there and gaped. Annie went on about her business, and busy business it was. With odds and ends of furniture, she had created a parlor of sorts, which he noticed was free of cobwebs and dust. On a three-legged table propped up with crates at one corner, she'd laid out chipped china and was pretending to serve tea.

Her imaginary guests, male and female dummies she'd fashioned by stuffing old clothes, occupied two of the three mismatched chairs she had appropriated from somewhere in the attic. The gentleman was a dapper fellow in a moth-eaten gray suit, the lady proportionately elegant in a faded blue gown trimmed with yellowed lace. Their heads, made from stuffed white stockings, were adorned with hats, the man's a felt derby, the woman's a wilted arrangement of silk flowers with a veil that swept over the upper portion of her face.

Alex couldn't help but smile. It was a wonder that Maddy hadn't been complaining about Annie's dwindling supply of stockings. From the looks of things, the girl had sneaked berries from the breakfast table as well. Her stuffed guests had painted faces done in a suspicious shade of raspberry-red.

"Annie, this is incredible!" Alex exclaimed, and sincerely meant it. "Ingenious! Is there anything you haven't—"

He broke off to watch as she poured imaginary tea. With a gracious smile at her guests, she began moving her lips. Though she uttered no sound, she looked for all the world as if she were speaking. Her every movement was precise yet fluid, exactly as a lady's should be.

"*Sugar?*" she asked the gentleman as she proffered the sugar bowl. Then, glancing toward the sunlight spilling through the windows, she said, "*My, isn't it a lovely day?*" At least, that was what he thought she said. Inexpert at lipreading, he couldn't be positive. After that, she continued to speak, but he had difficulty following the words.

Words . . . Dear God. Soundlessly or no, she was *talking*. Actually talking. It was like watching a child play make-believe. Only she wasn't a child. And this wasn't just make-believe to her, but reality. Her only reality.

Annie hadn't been disappearing into thin air, as Maddy half believed. She'd been slipping from one world into another.

Once, years ago, Alex had been kicked in the gut by a full-grown stallion. The blow had staggered him. For several endless seconds, he hadn't been able to breathe. His vision had blurred. For a crazy instant, he'd even felt as though his heart had stopped beating. That was how he felt now. As if, for a suspended moment, everything inside him lurched to a stop.

As feeling slowly began to return to his body, pain accompanied it—a relentless, mind-numbing pain centered in his chest. He'd heard people say their hearts were broken. A few times in his life, he had even used the expression himself. But until now, the saying hadn't really had meaning. The human heart didn't actually break, after all. It didn't come apart, piece by piece, and drop, along with a man's stomach, to the region of his boots.

Like hell, it didn't.

Annie Trimble, the town moron. Only she wasn't a moron at all. She was deaf. Stone-deaf. And, God forgive him, he had been stone-blind.

Twelve

Stunned, Alex watched Annie touch a hand to her throat and coyly bat her lashes at the stuffed gentleman. Then, to his amazement, she stepped around the makeshift table, took the dummy's arm to embrace him, and fell into a perfectly executed waltz step, her skirt swirling as she swept around the room.

A beautiful young woman, dancing to music no one else could hear, in the arms of a man she'd created with talented hands and a vivid imagination. With the dummy, she could be someone, a privilege that the rest of the world, including Alex, had denied her.

Without intending to, Alex shifted his weight, and a floorboard gave slightly beneath his foot. With the sharpened senses of a deaf person, Annie felt the wood give and immediately froze, her eyes huge and wary as she searched him out in the gloom.

Alex could see that she was frightened. After what had happened between them in the stable, knowing as he did that she expected him to beat her if she sneaked off, he was surprised she'd even found the courage to come here again. Not that he blamed her for taking the risk. In this make-believe parlor, she could be whoever she wished, do whatever she wished. In comparison, the world that awaited her downstairs probably seemed like a prison. Stupid Annie, locked inside the house for her own protection. Stupid Annie, expected to eat what was set before her, to bathe when told, to dress like a ragamuffin child. She was a lump of flesh they tended, kept in a room with a barred window half the time, watched over as though she were a toddler the rest of the time. In her shoes, he would have risked a beating to come up here, too.

A beating . . . From her stricken expression, Alex guessed that physical punishment was not the only thing she feared. In coming here, he had discovered her secret. This world she had created was sacrosanct, and she undoubtedly saw him as an intruder who might destroy it. With the simple turn of a key, he could lock her out of the attic, prevent her from ever returning. Worse yet, and again with only the turn of a key, he could lock her in a room with a barred window and never let her out. Power. Ultimate authority. If he chose, he could make her life more of a hell than it already was.

Only he wouldn't. Not for anything.

Seeing her like this, Alex was awestruck. And helplessly fascinated. All he wanted was to pass from his reality, which suddenly had very little to recommend it, into hers. Not to destroy, but to seek some small margin of common ground with her, if only for a few brief seconds.

Moving cautiously, ever so cautiously, he closed the distance between them. It was a gamble. He knew that. This was her world—a secret world—and he hadn't been issued an invitation. But it was the only way he could think of that he might reach her.

When he came within arm's length, he tapped her lifeless dance partner on the shoulder. Executing a polite bow, he said, ''May I have the honor of this dance?''

A study in motion, Annie still stood frozen with one

foot extended to take a step, her slender body slightly off balance, the dummy clutched to her breast. Limned by silvery light from the windows behind her, she might have been an ice carving, too fragile and delicate to withstand the touch of a man's hands. In the hollow of her throat, he could see a pulsebeat, and by its frantic rhythm, he took measure of her fear. He knew she might try to flee. He couldn't blame her for that. After Douglas's treatment of her, he hadn't come into her life with much to recommend him, and in the time since, he'd done little to rectify the lack.

"Please, Annie? Just one dance," he said huskily. "Surely your card isn't full."

There it was again—that confused, uncomprehending expression in her eyes. He'd seen it dozens of times before and mistakenly believed it to be a reflection of her stupidity. Wrong. If anyone was an idiot, he was. While executing the bow, he had bent his head as he was speaking. The reason she looked bewildered was because she had missed part of what he said. That was why she always stared so intently at his face when he spoke to her, why she sometimes seemed confused. Not realizing she was deaf, he had probably turned his head in the middle of a sentence. Or spoken indistinctly. Dear God. The girl was anything but stupid. That she had learned, all on her own, to lip-read and mimic speech was indicative of an intelligence well above average.

Talking more slowly and forming each word precisely so it would be easier for her to follow him, Alex repeated himself. Eyes large and luminous, she continued to stare at him for what seemed like endless minutes, each of which broke his heart just a little bit more. Moving cautiously so as not to frighten her, he extended his hand.

"Please, Annie?"

Trying to see things from her point of view, Alex

doubted she would find the courage to refuse him. He, the possessor of the razor strop? He was standing nearly on top of her now and blocked her path to escape. She either had to dance with him or suffer the consequences. He felt bad about using her fear to his advantage. It was a poor way to start a relationship. On the other hand, it was better than making no headway at all. There would be time later to revise her opinion of him.

Looking none too sure of her decision, she finally relented and set her other dance partner aside. The poor fellow took a tumble and landed in a lifeless heap, which was exactly where Alex hoped he would stay. This was his dance. His wife. He felt like a man who had accidentally stumbled upon the end of a rainbow.

No, not a rainbow, he thought nonsensically. More like a beautiful butterfly emerging, almost magically, from its chrysalis. In that moment, that was how he saw Annie. He didn't analyze the feeling. He had unveiled something incredibly precious, immeasurably lovely, and completely unexpected. When God saw fit to bestow such a gift, a man with any sense didn't ask questions.

Nervous of frightening her any more than he already had, he touched a palm lightly to her waist, took her hand in his, and gently moved into a waltz. Accustomed to leading, she stumbled slightly and tromped on his toes, but her weight was so slight that Alex scarcely noticed. As if he could *feel* his toes. Not with this girl in his arms. In the carriage that first morning, he had sensed the rightness, but he'd shied away from it, appalled by his feelings. Now he realized he should have trusted his instincts.

In retrospect, he looked back on the events that had drawn them together and believed with all his heart that an invisible hand had moved him and her about like pieces on a chessboard, aligning their positions, manipulating incidents, bringing them inexorably to a collision point. Fate? The Almighty? Alex didn't know, nor did he care to guess. All that mattered was this moment and the feeling that it was wonderfully and perfectly right.

After a few turns on their imaginary dance floor, Annie relaxed and began to take her cues from him, floating with the music as gracefully as a butterfly drifted with a breeze. The music . . . It was insane. He knew it was. But gazing down at her small face, he could almost hear the orchestra playing.

Annie, dancing to make-believe music, in a make-believe world, but no longer in the arms of a make-believe man. This fantasy world he'd invaded was all she had. Branded a moron. Shunned for most of her life. No education. No companions. An ugly secret that her parents had kept hidden. Rage roiled within him, but he tamped it down. Later he would let himself think about the how and why. Later he would place the blame.

For now, there was only the waltz and the girl he held in his arms.

It had been years since Alex had played make-believe. Too many years, perhaps, for there was a surreal feeling in the air around him. A feeling that anything might happen—if only he believed. He didn't want to shatter that.

Even holding her at a polite distance filled him with a sense of wonder. Though small and delicately made, she fitted to his body as though she'd been fashioned for him. Against the side of his hand, he could feel her hip moving. Beneath his thumb, he detected the swelling due to her pregnancy. He yearned to draw her closer, to press his cheek to the curls atop her head, to drown in the clean smell of rose-and-glycerin soap that Maddy used to bathe her.

Unable to resist, he did exactly that.

Momentarily startled by the sudden closeness, Annie stiffened. But when he continued to dance, she finally gave in to the strength of his arm and let her body mold to his. He pressed his face against her hair and let his eyes fall closed. *Precious.* It was the only word he could think of to describe her. God help him, he never wanted to let her go.

Not wishing to tire her, Alex eventually had to end the waltz. When he stopped and drew away from her, she looked slightly disoriented, eyes unfocused, cheeks flushed, lips parted with breathlessness.

"Thank you, Annie," he said slowly. "That was lovely."

A dimple flashed in her cheek as she returned his smile. *"Yes, lovely."*

The words she mouthed but didn't speak were nearly as audible to Alex as if she'd said them aloud, probably because they were the expected response. He had to learn to lip-read, he thought with a sense of panic. Straightaway, he needed to learn. Without circumstances to cue him, he would be at a loss when she tried to communicate with him.

Reluctant to leave the attic and this version of her, he cast his gaze about her parlor, searching almost frantically for an excuse, any excuse, to prolong the make-believe mood. Inspiration struck when he spotted the chipped china on the table. Pretending she had issued him an invitation, he took the male dummy's chair, picked up his empty cup, and extended it toward her for a refill. Even in the dimness, he could see the wariness returning to her eyes.

The magic of the waltz had ended. And now, like it or not, they were back to reality. Only Alex was no longer absolutely certain what reality was. Where it began, where it ended. He only knew this beautiful girl had been horribly wronged, and somehow he had to make it up to her.

To help her, the first thing he had to do was gain her trust.

He continued to hold out the cup, waiting, compelling her with his gaze. Something touched his pant leg. He ignored it. In that instant, nothing mattered to him but Annie. Then came a ticklish sensation through his sock. Little pinpricks. Unable to block out the sensation, Alex moved his foot slightly and bent to brush at his ankle. As he did, his fingertips connected with a small, furry body.

"Son of a—*Jeee*-sus Christ!"

He and the teacup parted company, the cup shooting upward, Alex diving to swat at his trousers. Dimly he heard china shatter.

"Son of a bitch!" He leaped to his feet. "It's going up my—Jesus Christ!"

A mouse. Up his trouser leg. Horror filled Alex. He started to dance again, alone this time and to a tune called hysteria. A goddamned *mouse*. And the little fiend was scrabbling for purchase, making a beeline for his *crotch*. Not in this lifetime.

Alex slapped at his leg. Big, mouse-squashing slaps, his intent murder. So fixed was his attention on the rodent that it took him a moment to realize Annie was hanging on his arm.

"Naah-ohh!" she cried.

No? Alex was so shocked to hear her make a sound that he forgot the damned mouse.

"Naah-ohh!" she cried again.

The word was distorted. An awful and not quite human sound. But to Alex, it was the most wonderful thing he'd ever heard. *No*. A simple expression, one that children learned at an early age and never forgot because adults said it to them so frequently. A word that Annie knew because she'd once heard it said herself.

Because she seemed so frantic to save the mouse, Alex

forced himself not to slap his leg again. The last thing he wanted was to kill the revolting little thing and break her heart. That would only drive another wedge between them. Panicked from the blows, the mouse continued its ascent. Alex clenched his teeth.

A scrabbling sensation well above his knee.

Then high on his thigh.

He stood it for one more second—undoubtedly the longest of his life—then swore and grabbed for the fly of his trousers. If that mouse gained a few more inches—well, it didn't bear thinking about. Alex could almost feel its small teeth sinking into his ballocks.

Forgetting about everything—Annie, propriety, decency—he dropped his pants. Its tiny claws hooked to his drawers, the mouse was hanging on for dear life. Seizing it by the tail, Alex jerked it loose and held it at arm's length. A squirming little body. Shrill squeaking. God, it was his worst nightmare. Not sure what to do with the creature, he glanced at Annie only to discover she had clamped a hand over her mouth and looked as if she were about to burst with laughter.

It struck Alex then how ridiculous he must look. A grown man, dancing around on his tiptoes like a hysterical woman. Trousers around his knees. Drawers flapping. A mouse dangling from one hand. He chuckled in spite of himself. Bending to release his small captive, he shook his head.

"You, young woman, will be the death of me yet."

Behind her hand, Annie made a sound that could only be stifled giggles. Alex refastened his trousers and belt. "You think it's funny, do you?" Measuring off a scant inch between thumb and forefinger, he grinned and said, "Your little friend came just that close to meeting his maker." Nudging a piece of china with the toe of his boot, he said, "Thanks to him, I think our tea party is over."

She crouched to pat the floor-length hem of her skirt, located the mouse, which had found sanctuary at her feet, and lifted it in her cupped hands. Alex's stomach did a turn when she kissed the rodent's small head and then held it to her cheek. As if it knew how close it had come to death, the creature curled into a quivering little ball. Annie kissed it again, stroked it with her fingertip, and then set it on the floor, shooing it away to safety with a light pat on its rump.

The moment she straightened and met his gaze, her smile vanished. Nervously, she toyed with the buttons at her bodice. Then she intertwined her fingers and cracked her knuckles. He wondered if the sensation was as soothing when one couldn't hear the hollow little pops. Judging by her tenseness, he didn't think so.

With a sigh, he concluded that one turn around a dance floor was not enough to instill trust in a wary girl. Not that he had expected miracles, but he had hoped to see a little less fear in her eyes.

He finished tucking in his shirt and hunkered to clean up the mess he had made. Keeping a safe distance, Annie knelt to assist him. When they both happened to reach for the same shard of china, she jerked her hand back as if she feared he might grab her. Alex tried his best not to take it personally. Earning her trust was going to take some time.

Acutely aware that the magic mood had been shattered as irreparably as the cup, he was filled with a profound sadness, but he pushed it away. There was no reason to feel sad. None at all. The waltz might be over, but Annie's life had just begun. If it was the last thing he ever did, he would see to that.

Conscious of Alex's gaze on her and growing more nervous by the second, Annie pretended to be oblivious of everything but the tiny shards of china that she was picking up and adding to the pile on her palm. *Foolish, so foolish.* She should never have sneaked up here to his attic in the first place. From the beginning, she had known her disappearances upset him and Maddy. If she'd had half a brain, she would have expected him to eventually discover where she was going.

Now he knew the truth about her, and he'd probably send her away to that awful place her mama was always warning her about—the place where girls like her were locked up in little rooms and fed wormy gruel. Not only would she never be allowed to go outdoors again, but her mama said they were mean to the people there, frightfully mean.

A lump rose in Annie's throat, and tears scalded her eyes. She dumped the shards onto the table and brushed her hands clean, avoiding Alex's gaze. If only he would leave. She could put her own clothes back on, take down her hair. Maybe, if she was very, very good and never came back up here again, he would forget all that he'd seen and not tell her papa.

She gave a little start when he suddenly grasped her chin and forced her to look at him. Annie blinked, but it was futile. The tears in her eyes had nowhere to go but out, and they spilled over her lashes onto her cheeks.

"Hey . . ."

She imagined his voice, low and laced with gentle scolding. For some reason, that made her want to cry all the harder. With leathery fingertips, he wiped the wetness from her cheeks. One corner of his mouth turned up in a crooked smile.

"Don't be afraid, Annie love. Everything is going to be all right. I promise you that."

It was easy for him to say. He wasn't the one who might have to eat worms. Disconcerted by his penetrating gaze, she lowered her lashes. In response, he strengthened his grip on her chin and gave her a slight shake. Startled, she looked at him again.

"Trust me," he said very slowly. "Do you know that word, *trust*? It means that I want you to believe I'm your friend. Can you try to do that?"

Annie gave him the blank look that she had perfected with fourteen years of practice. His smile deepened. "You can't fool me. I know damned well you understand what I'm saying."

With that, he released her and pushed to his feet. Uncertain what to do, Annie remained crouched at his feet. When she finally found the courage to lift her gaze to his, she found that he was smiling and had one hand extended to her. "Come on, let's go downstairs. Maddy isn't going to believe her eyes."

Annie's heart started to race. She cast a frantic glance at her own clothing, which she'd left folded over the rocker. He followed her gaze, then smiled and shook his head. "Just as you are. Come on." When she made no move to obey him, he leaned down to grasp her arm and draw her up. "I'll send a maid up to get your things," he assured her. "Except for the mouse, of course. I'm afraid he'll have to stay up here."

She shot an anxious glance into the shadows. When she looked back at him, Alex said, "I'll give strict orders that none of your little friends are to be hurt, I promise. So stop worrying. I can't say the same for the spiders, however." Following her example, he peered into the darkness that encroached upon them. "Tomorrow or the next day, I'm going to send a whole crew up. If you're going to spend time here, I want every inch of this place cleaned. As it is, it can't be safe."

Her sudden tenseness drew his gaze back to her.

''Don't worry, Annie. They'll leave everything the same. Just no more dust and cobwebs.''

Nothing would ever be the same again. Annie tried to tug her arm from his grasp. He not only wanted her to go downstairs dressed as she was, but he intended to send a whole bunch of people up here? All of them would see her secret place. All of them!

''Come on, Annie.''

Refusing to take no for an answer, he drew her resolutely along behind him. As the light from the dormers began to fade and the gloom around them grew more dense, so did Annie's dread. She *couldn't* go downstairs like this. And somehow, she had to stop him from sending people up here as well. The games she played in the attic were a secret. Her mama said they had to stay a secret. If people found out, she'd be sent away.

By the time they reached the attic door, Annie's fear had escalated to full-blown panic. She was shaking so badly, she felt sure Alex could feel it. Nonetheless, he drew open the door and pulled her out into the narrow stairway.

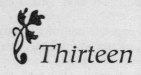

Thirteen

*A*lex *slammed* his fist against the Trimbles' front
door with such force that the wood shook in its frame.
He heard footsteps scurrying to answer his summons, and
the instant the portal swung wide, he shouldered his way
into the house, nearly knocking the startled butler off his
feet.

"Where is James?" he barked.

Clutching his lapels, the servant gave his shoulders a
shrug to straighten his jacket. "I beg your pardon, sir,
but—"

"Never mind. I'll find him myself."

Following a hunch, Alex strode directly to the parlor,
thinking that, given the hour, Annie's parents might be
there. He found the room empty. From there, he strode
purposely along the corridor and began throwing open
doors. He found James's study, the day room, sitting
room, and library unoccupied as well. At the end of the
hallway, he came upon a set of mahogany panels. Butting
them open with his shoulder, he burst through into the
dining room and surprised his in-laws at their supper
table.

One cheek bulging with food, James looked up, fork

and knife suspended above his plate. Recognizing Alex, he struggled to swallow and said, "My God, what's the matter? Is Annie all right?"

Edie, who was sitting at the opposite end of the long table with her back to the doors, sprang up from her chair, bumping her plate in the process and spilling her wine. Crimson splashed across the pristine white tablecloth and pooled around the base of a pretentiously ornate candlestick. "What on earth has happened?" she demanded. "Has she done something awful? What?"

Ignoring Edie, Alex stepped past her to advance on James. When he reached the end of the table, he grabbed the smaller man by the shoulder seams of his dinner jacket and hauled him unceremoniously to his feet. "You selfish, heartless little bastard!" Alex bit out. "How could you do something so monstrous to your own daughter?"

James's blue eyes went wide with fear, and his face drained of all color. "What in God's name are you talking about?" He clutched at Alex's wrists. "You're about to rip my suit, young man."

"Your *suit*?" Alex released the man so suddenly that he staggered, tripped backward over his chair, and sprawled on the floor. "If I rip anything, you miserable little worm, it'll be your head from your shoulders."

Struggling up on one knee, James grasped the chair arm to steady himself. "Explain yourself! You can't come barging in here like this, making threats and raising a ruckus! There are laws to—"

"Laws?" Alex brought his fist down on the table. The serving bowls and candlesticks leaped at the force of the blow, all landing simultaneously with a loud crash. "There are common laws of *decency*, my friend, that were never written in any of your precious law books. Did you ever once observe any of them? Not with your daughter, that's for damned sure." Alex leveled a finger at the other man's nose. "Understand this, you pitiful son of a bitch. Annie will never return to this house. Not as long as I draw breath. Consider my word on *that* part of our agreement broken, and you'd better give thanks to Almighty God that's *all* I've decided to break."

"I don't know what you're talking about," James said tremulously. "I've never mistreated our daughter."

"Never mistreated her?" Alex gave a harsh laugh. "Aside from beating on her every time she stepped out of line, you've neglected to educate her. There are schools for the deaf! And all manner of things that can be done to help them! In all these years, you've never even so much as bought her an ear trumpet! But worse than that, you've let everyone in this town believe she's a moron! How do you sleep at night? Can you tell me that? I sure as hell couldn't."

In the wake of that accusation, a stunned silence settled over the room. Through the haze of his anger, Alex brought James's face into clearer focus. What he saw in the other man's expression helped to douse his fury. Not guilt, as he expected, but incredulity mixed with profound relief. It struck Alex then that Annie's parents didn't know. As impossible as it seemed, they honestly didn't know.

Shaking with the last vestiges of rage, he jerked out a chair and dropped onto it as though someone had dealt a blow to the backs of his knees. "She's deaf," he said hoarsely. "Not mad, not stupid. Deaf."

Edie sank back onto her seat, one shaking hand clamped over her mouth, the other pressed to her waist. She stared at Alex over the tops of her white-knuckled fingers. After a moment, she dropped her hand. "Annie is *not* deaf! The girl can hear as well as you or I!"

Alex felt the anger building within him again. "That's an out-and-out lie, and you know it. The girl is deaf. I saw proof of it myself just this afternoon. And don't tell me you haven't. She didn't invent that fantasy world I found in my attic overnight. She's been playing those games for years. You had to have known about them! At one time or another, you must have come upon her when she was playing make-believe.''

The guilt that flashed in Edie's eyes spoke for itself. Never had Alex slapped a woman, but his palm itched to do so now. Just once, he wished she could see how it felt. She had certainly treated Annie to the experience often enough. ''How could you ignore the needs of your own daughter?'' he asked in a raw voice. ''If helped, deaf people can live nearly normal lives.''

''She *isn't* deaf!'' Edie shot to her feet. ''Do you think I wouldn't know if such a thing were true? That I haven't *wished* as much? Even prayed for it? She isn't deaf, I tell you. If she's turned once when I call her name, she's done so a thousand times. How dare you come bursting into our home, yelling obscenities and accusing us of mistreating her!'' She ground a fist against her mouth to stifle a sob. ''How dare you?''

His anger completely spent, disgust welling in its place, Alex stood up and pushed his chair back under the table. ''And I thought I was blind? My wife is deaf. Stone-deaf.'' He shot a glance at James, who stood behind his chair, gripping its back as though he couldn't stand without the support. ''Notice I said *wife*. I don't use the term lightly. From this moment on, Annie is a Montgomery and as such is no longer affiliated with this household or anyone in it.''

Edie spun to watch as Alex left the room. When he reached the doors, she cried out, the sound more moan than word. He paused to look back at her, seeing her pain, yet separated from it. There was no room within him for sympathy, not for anyone but Annie.

"You can't take our little girl completely away from us," she whispered raggedly. "You can't do such a thing! No one could be that heartless."

Alex regarded her with stony distaste. "Call it heartless if you wish, but that is exactly what I intend to do. I don't want either of you anywhere near my wife. Your love, if anyone in his right mind can call it that, has caused her nothing but injury." Looking directly at Edie, he said, "You, madam, are a pitiful excuse for a mother." Turning his gaze toward James, he added, "And you, sir, have made a mockery of the word *father*."

With that, Alex slammed out of the house, silently vowing that he would never again darken the Trimbles' doorstep.

During the ride home, however, something kept digging at his memory. An elusive something. Something Maddy had once said. He had nearly reached Montgomery Hall when he finally recalled what it was. He and Maddy had been in his study, discussing Annie, and during the course of their conversation, Maddy had ruled out the possibility that Annie might be deaf. *She turns when I call her name*, she'd said.

As Alex rubbed down his horse and put him away in his stall, those words kept coming back to him. Edie Trimble had said basically the same thing. *If she has turned once when I call her name, she has done so a thousand times.*

Alex couldn't find it in his heart to regret a single word he had said to the Trimbles. In his estimation, they had deserved all of that, and more. But he was filled with hope by what Edie had told him.

Could it be that Annie wasn't completely deaf? Was it possible that she could hear certain sounds? Alex hurried up to the house, so excited he could scarcely wait to discuss the possibility with Maddy.

*   *   *

At precisely ten o'clock the next morning, Alex hovered outside the nursery, watching Maddy and Annie through the partially open door. The girl, once again dressed in a childish frock, sat at the table, her unfinished breakfast shoved aside, her chin propped on the heel of her hand. Gazing out the barred window, she ignored Maddy, who was making a great show of straightening the bureau drawers.

As Alex had instructed her earlier, the housekeeper suddenly looked up from her task and loudly called, "Annie!"

Alex nearly whooped with excitement when Annie turned and fastened questioning eyes on the other woman. Pretending nothing was amiss, Maddy opened another drawer and began refolding the clothes that lay on top. She waited several minutes, allowing Annie plenty of time to direct her attention back outdoors. Then she called the girl's name again. As before, Annie glanced over her shoulder.

She could hear! Alex was so pleased he could scarcely contain himself. Maddy glanced toward the door, met his gaze through the crack, and winked conspiratorially. Alex grinned at her and nodded. After waiting a few minutes, he called Annie's name himself. At the sound of his voice, which was lower in pitch, she never so much as blinked. He called a little louder. Still nothing. After the third try, Maddy yelled her name again, and as before, Annie immediately turned.

"She hears you!" Alex proclaimed as he shoved the door open and strode into the room. "It's because you speak louder and your voice goes shrill when you call her, I think. Do you know what this means, Maddy?" Completely forgetting himself in his excitement, Alex snatched Maddy into his arms and swept her around the room in a two-step. "With the aid of ear trumpets, she may be able to hear us speaking to her. We'll be able to teach her her letters! And to read! Maybe even to talk! Maddy, this is wonderful."

Huffing from the unaccustomed exercise, Maddy cried, "Do stop, Master Alex. Me old heart cannot take all this dancing about!"

Releasing the older woman, Alex turned to Annie. She was watching him with her usual wariness, her blue eyes guarded. Flashing her a grin, Alex swept one arm across his waist and executed a courtly bow. After he straightened, he said, "May I have the honor of this dance?"

She stared up at him, clearly startled and more than a little suspicious. Then she slid a glance at Maddy. Dancing, Alex determined, was obviously a secret activity, one that could not be indulged in outside the attic.

To hell with that . . .

Determined, he closed the distance between them, grasped her hand, and drew her to her feet. Against her wishes, which she made quite apparent by going rigid and stumbling awkwardly within his arm, he swept her into a waltz step. Deciding his toes could take that punishment and more, Alex stubbornly drew her around the room, his gaze fixed on her averted face.

"I don't think she wants to dance," Maddy needlessly pointed out.

Alex only smiled more broadly. "She loves to dance. She simply doesn't want to dance with *me*." As he spoke, Annie glanced up. Alex looked into her frightened eyes, wishing with all his heart that she could tell him what was going through her head. Memories of Douglas? Fear of him? Acutely aware of the stiffness of her body and her diminutive stature, he felt his conscience begin to smote him. Slowly he drew to a stop, his gaze still holding hers.

"All right, Annie love, you win this battle. I won't force you to dance with me."

The relief that swept across her face was so unmistakable that Alex chuckled. She could give him that stupid look until hell was besieged by snowstorms, and he'd never again fall for it. As long as he looked right at her and spoke distinctly, she understood him perfectly.

"Before I turn you loose, however, you have to pay a price," he added softly.

At that, her blue eyes darkened, and he felt her body grow even more rigid. Oh, yes, she understood.

"If you don't want to dance with me," he pressed, "then tell me so."

Maddy drew in a sharp breath. "Master Alex! Fer shame. Ye know the poor wee lass can't speak."

"Oh, but she can," he said, never taking his gaze from Annie's. "And she *will*, or I'm going to hold her in my arms like this all day."

Annie's eyes widened. Alex grinned. "Well, Annie love? Turn me down, or dance with me. It's a very simple thing."

Her mouth thinned into a mutinous line. Taking care not to exert too much pressure, Alex tightened his arm around her waist and drew her a little more snugly against him. She raised her chin, the picture of defiance. In response, he began to move around the room again, forcing her to move with him. "Whisper it to me, Annie love. I know very well you can."

"Oh, Master Alex, have a pity!"

He smiled slowly into Annie's worried eyes. "Tell me no, Annie, or dance with me until dark. Your choice."

He saw her mouth tighten. Then she swallowed. Looking down at her, seeing the struggle she was going through, Alex felt his whole body tense. Fixing her gaze on one of his shirt buttons, she finally parted her lips. And then, so quickly he almost missed it, she formed the word, *"No."*

A burning sensation crawled up the back of Alex's throat. From her stony expression, he knew she hated him a little for forcing the issue, but he didn't care. By winning this small battle, he had claimed a large victory for both of them.

When he released her, she staggered at the sudden lack of support. Alex caught her elbow to steady her. When her beautiful eyes met his again, he touched a fingertip lightly to her cheek.

"Thank you," he whispered.

After leaving Annie, Alex closeted himself in his study to update his books. That order of business occupied him until lunch, which he ate at his desk. When the maid had cleared away the mess, he rocked back in his chair and propped his feet on his desktop, his folded arms tucked behind his head. Gazing thoughtfully into space, he contemplated yet another problem that involved Annie, one that, until this moment, he hadn't allowed himself to consider overmuch.

How could a man woo a timid deaf girl?

He allowed himself a few minutes to recall how he had felt while dancing with her in the attic yesterday, and he knew, beyond a shadow of a doubt, that he wanted her in his arms again. It was as simple and as complicated as that. The challenge would be to lure Annie back into his embrace. Judging by her reaction to their waltz that morning, she wasn't going to be an enthusiastic party to any sort of physical closeness.

Ordinarily, Alex might have gone about things in the usual way, but the direct approach wouldn't work on Annie, and he knew it. For one, she was frightened of him after what Douglas had done to her, and understandably so. For another, her life until now had not prepared her for openness. Her parents had done such a thorough job of keeping Annie and her affliction in the background of their lives that they had made her guarded and secretive as well.

Seduction was his ultimate aim. The question was, how should he go about it? Several minutes passed, during which Alex conceived and discarded several ideas. Then a slow smile touched his mouth. How did a man seduce any woman? He enticed her, of course, with something he knew she couldn't resist.

That afternoon when Maddy came downstairs to oversee the maids in their various household tasks, Annie trailed along behind her as she had been doing for well over a week, the only difference being that today there was a watcher in the house. When he saw that his wife was downstairs, he retired to his study, leaving the door carefully ajar.

Taking up his position in his favorite chair, Alex upended the cooking pot that he had taken from the kitchen. Clamping the pot firmly between his knees, he began to pound on its bottom with a large metal spoon. The resultant sound raised a din to wake the dead. Not satisfied with the tone, he repositioned the pot until the percussion produced a high-pitched *ping*. Having warned Maddy, the maids, and Frederick in advance, Alex knew that none of them would seek out the source of the sound. Only one person would come . . . if she could hear the noise.

Ping! Ping! Plunk! It was, without question, a godawful ruckus that he was raising, and he felt absolutely ridiculous. A grown man banging on a pot? He only prayed it would work. Forcing himself not to look toward the door, he pounded incessantly on the kettle, uncertain if Annie could even hear it.

He had about given up hope when he glimpsed movement from the corner of his eye. With renewed enthusiasm, he beat the pot, struggling not to reveal his elation by smiling. In a moment, Annie's worn shoes came into view, and he knew she was standing only a few feet away. He continued to wield the spoon, pretending he hadn't seen her.

Drawn to the noise like metal shavings to a magnet, she came closer. Then closer still. Finally Alex allowed himself to look up. The expression on her face made making a fool of himself worth the embarrassment. Eyes huge and bewildered, she stood there in thrall, her gaze riveted to the spoon.

Alex allowed himself to grin, albeit only slightly, and stopped pounding. At the silence, she jerked and fixed her gaze on him. He held the spoon out to her.

''Want to have a go at it?''

The yearning reflected in her eyes was unmistakable. Remembering what James had told him about Annie's embarrassing behavior years ago over an organ at church, Alex felt his heart catch. *Sound*. To Annie, it was elusive and infrequent, a miracle that occasionally broke through the wall of silence that enveloped her. As a child, to her parents' humiliation and her own damnation, she hadn't been able to resist its lure in church and had pressed herself against the organ, making what her father had called ''animalistic noises.'' As an adult, she was still helplessly drawn to it. *Sound*. A priceless gift to someone like Annie, and one that he could give her.

Watching the myriad emotions that crossed her face, Alex almost felt ashamed of himself for using sound as a seductive lure. *Almost*. She was his wife, and by fair means or foul, he meant for this to be more than a sham marriage, not just for his own sake, but hers. Given her affliction, she might never be able to lead a completely normal life, but he could give her something damned close. Love, laughter, companionship. Soon they would even have a child to raise. Annie was going to play an active role as its mother. He would see to that.

Alex held out the spoon, tempting her without mercy and with only a twinge of conscience. Her lovely eyes went stormy gray with wariness. But he also saw yearning. A yearning so sharp it made him ache for her. In his hand, he held magic. All she had to do was reach out and take it.

Her whole body trembled as she came closer and reached out to grasp the spoon handle. Their fingertips brushed in the exchange, an electrical feeling to Alex and clearly an unsettling one for her.

"Go ahead. Pound on it," he encouraged her.

She drew her gaze from his mouth back to the pot. A glint of excitement came into her eyes. Apparently reluctant to come too close, she leaned forward at the waist to clobber the pot. At the ensuing *clank*, she blinked. Actually blinked. Alex nearly shouted with jubilation.

"Go ahead! It won't bite you." And neither will I, he silently vowed. He couldn't ruin this for her, not today. Maybe not ever. So much for seduction.

His throat tightened as he watched her smack the kettle bottom again. At the resultant sound, an amazed look swept over her face. Then she smiled. The radiance of that smile so transformed her face that all Alex could do was stare. She lifted her gaze to his, and a feeling arced between them that had nothing to do with seduction and everything to do with budding friendship.

For Alex, it had to be enough. For Annie, it was a new beginning.

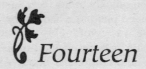

Fourteen

That evening, Annie expected to be served her supper in the nursery as usual, but instead Maddy escorted her downstairs and into the dining room. Though Annie had never been in the room directly before a meal, she had visited there several times with Maddy during the day. The room's hominess and sunshine-yellow accents had always appealed to her, probably because the color reminded her of being outdoors, which she sorely missed. A stone fireplace ran the length of one wall, its simplicity in keeping with the decor. Instead of Irish lace, the sideboard sported a simple, embroidered scarf with a tatted border. Upon it was arranged an assortment of rose-patterned china, utilitarian serving utensils, and a teapot with chipped gilt trim.

Despite its large dimensions, the room gave off an air of warmth, filling Annie's mind with visions of cheerful fires on cold winter evenings and a close-knit family gathering for hearty meals. Alex reclined on a chair at one end of the long table, his hair agleam in the light from a crystal chandelier, the room's only claim to elegance. With one arm hooked over the chair back and one booted foot propped on his opposite knee, he looked slightly bored and a whole lot impatient. When he spotted her coming into the room, he pushed quickly to his feet. Stepping around the table, he extended one large hand to her.

In keeping with the room, he was comfortably dressed in a V-necked silk shirt the color of fresh cream, his biscuit-brown riding pants tucked into tall, umber boots. As he approached, Annie took the moment to study him, noticing yet again that he was nothing at all like her papa or the men she'd seen visiting at her parents' house. Instead of the ruffles, jeweled stickpins, and ornate watch chains that those gentlemen usually favored, he wore a plain gold belt buckle and a simple watch chain, the latter tucked through a belt loop. No fancy silk vest. No sparkly rings. No funny-smelling perfume.

When Annie looked at Alex, she thought of sunshine and fresh air, not drawing rooms with the heavy draperies she so despised hanging over the windows. His tawny hair lay in wispy, sun-streaked waves over his forehead, slightly tousled, as though recently stirred by the wind. The collar of his shirt hung open, revealing the burnished planes of his chest. He even walked as if he were outdoors, with a careless air, his stride long and loose, his arms slightly bent and swinging at his sides.

When he came to a stop in front of her, he took her hand, then drew her back to the table, pulling out a chair to the immediate left of his. Realizing that the table had been set for two, she lifted a startled gaze to his. At home, she'd never been allowed to take her meals in the dining room.

"I think a wife should take the evening meal with her husband. Don't you?"

Annie felt as if the floor had vanished from beneath her feet. She stood there staring up at him in shocked amazement, convinced she must have misread his words. The disgruntled look on his face told her otherwise. He had obviously spoken without forethought and hadn't meant to divulge that bit of information to her.

Gently grasping her shoulder, he guided her around the chair, pushed her onto the seat, and then leaned down to lightly kiss her hair as he scooted her forward. Sitting sideways as she was, Annie's left arm was toward the table, and in her discomfiture, she accidentally bumped her elbow against her teacup. Alex shot out a hand to rescue the china, his eyebrows arched in mocking query. He had clearly decided that the best way to handle this situation was to make a joke of it.

"I take it that is *not* the best news you've received all day." At her horrified look, he asked, "Surely not all week?" When her expression remained one of appalled incredulity, he said, "I know I have my faults as a husband, but surely I'm not as bad as all *that*?"

Unable to tear her gaze from his, Annie carefully resettled her elbow near the edge of her plate. His *wife*? He had to be lying. He simply *had* to be. True, she knew very little about weddings. But she wasn't *that* ignorant about them. Not so ignorant that she could have participated in one without knowing it.

Not that long ago, her older sister Elise had been married. The ceremony, which Annie hadn't been allowed to attend, had been conducted at the church, and all manner of elaborate preparations had taken place beforehand, not the least of which had been the creation of a beautiful white wedding dress for the bride. As Annie recalled, her parents' house had been filled to the brim with flowers as well, and after the wedding, a horde of people had come there for a party, drinking punch, eating cake, and watching Elise open gifts. Lots of gifts. More gifts than Annie had ever seen at one time, even under the Christmas tree.

Alex resumed his place at the head of the table, his posture relaxed, his manner one of resignation laced with self-derision. Resting an elbow on the arm of the chair, he tugged on his ear and regarded her in thoughtful silence. After a long moment, he said, "I really didn't intend to break it to you in quite that way, Annie. It was thoughtless of me, and I'm sorry if I've upset you."

Upset? It was all Annie could do not to burst into angry tears. If she was married, then why hadn't her mama made her a dress? And why hadn't she gotten bunches of presents? She liked presents, and she liked pretty dresses even more. No party, no cake, no ceremony at the church. Nothing. How could she possibly be married?

Alex was beginning to look a little upset himself. Annie thought maybe it was because he knew she was about to cry. Trying to suppress the urge, she lowered her gaze to her hands where they rested on her lap. Then she noticed the grass-stain spots on her stockings, and the pressure behind her eyes grew even worse. Unlike her sisters, she never got anything. Instead of a white gown, silk slippers, and lace to wear over her face, all she got was icky old frocks, scuffed shoes, and stained stockings.

And no presents! Nary a one. That burned her most of all.

Alex caught her chin and forced her face up. Annie glared at him through a shimmer of tears. A muscle along his jaw started to twitch. "Sweetheart, don't cry. Just because I—well, we've been married all along, right? Just because you realize it now, that doesn't mean anything's going to change." He leaned down so he could look directly into her eyes, his manner cajoling. "I realize that you had an extremely unpleasant experience with Douglas."

Douglas? Annie didn't know a Douglas. She stared at him in bewilderment, wishing he'd stick to the subject, which in her mind was the pretty dress and gifts that she'd been cheated out of. And just when had their wedding taken place? she wanted to know. Had she somehow missed out on that as well?

He brushed the backs of his knuckles along her cheek. Little tingles spread over her skin wherever he touched her. At any other time, she thought it would probably be a wonderfully nice feeling, but as angry as she was, all it did was make her want to shudder.

"Annie, about what happened to you up at the falls that day . . . " He rubbed his thumb under her eye to catch a stray tear. "I don't suppose it's ever possible for a woman to completely forget something like that. But I want to make it clear to you, here and now, that I am nothing like my brother. What Douglas did to you was— well, it was despicable—and as long as I draw breath, no one will ever hurt you like that again. Do you understand me, Annie? Never."

At his words, Annie's heart started to jump around inside her chest like a frightened bird. The falls, that awful man. Douglas . . . Alex's brother.

"If and when the time comes that you and I—" He drew a fingertip across her lower lip, his amber eyes turning cloudy with what looked like tenderness. "Well, I guess it goes without saying that once you and I grow comfortable with each other, I'm hoping our relationship will change, that we'll be able to enjoy the special kind of closeness that other couples do."

Annie stiffened and tried to draw away. He tightened his grip on her chin, smiling gently. "Not right away, of course. Don't fly into a panic. And only if it's what you want as well. Unlike my brother, I'll never be rough with you or cause you any pain. I promise you that. You have absolutely nothing to fear from—"

Annie jerked from his grasp and shot up from her chair. The room suddenly seemed airless, and her lungs grabbed frantically for breath. Pressing a hand to her throat, she retreated a step from him, her horrified gaze fixed on his dark face. As she moved away, he rose slowly to his feet.

"Annie . . ."

She shook her head in violent denial, then spun and ran from the room.

When Annie ran, Alex went after her, a little amazed at how quick she was on her feet, especially when they reached the stairs. Like a gazelle, she took the ascent in graceful bounds. Right on her heels, Alex was about to catch her by the arm when she seemed to sense how close he was and turned to confront him. Pale with fright, she swung around, her small elbow glancing off his cheekbone. Alex knew it was an accident, but she was so appalled at having struck him, she nearly lost her footing. He reached to steady her. Seeing him make a move toward her, she flung herself beyond his grasp and literally scrabbled to ascend the rest of the stairs.

Afraid that she might fall, Alex wisely chose to let her get slightly ahead of him until she gained safe footing on the landing. As he resumed pursuit, he discovered that he had underestimated her speed. She reached the nursery well ahead of him, ran inside, and slammed the door. Just as he reached the room, he heard something thud against the wood. To his amazement, the door would only open about an inch when he tried it, and he realized the little minx had wedged a straight-backed chair under the knob.

"Annie?" Alex hauled in a calming breath and raked a hand through his hair. Of all the stupid, *asinine* stunts he had ever pulled, this took the prize. To drop it on her that way. He still couldn't quite believe he'd done it. Sooner or later, preferably sooner so she didn't learn it from someone else, he would have had to tell her about the marriage. But not like *this*. "Annie, honey, please open the door. Let me explain. What I said downstairs?

Well, you obviously mistook what I meant. If you'll just give me a chance, I'll clarify things.''

After delivering that nice little speech, it occurred to Alex he was talking to a deaf girl. *Christ.* He pinched the bridge of his nose and dragged in another bracing breath. What was she doing in there? His only comforting thought was that, no matter how frightened she was, she couldn't leap out the window. And wasn't that a fine kettle of fish? He shoved against the door. The damned chair held fast.

He would scare her half to death if he shouldered his way into the room. The chair would undoubtedly go flying, the door would probably sustain damage again, and in addition to all that, such an entrance wouldn't exactly pave the way for reassurance. Turning, Alex leaned his back against the wall, trying frantically to think of some way he might convince her to unblock the door. Since she couldn't hear, eloquent speeches weren't going to do the trick.

Ah . . . but she *could* hear, he reminded himself. What he needed was some kind of noisemaker. Something that would seem so wondrous to her that she wouldn't be able to resist it. Unfortunately he didn't have a church organ handy. Music, he guessed, would probably entice Annie to walk through fire.

Music . . . Alex pushed away from the wall. Music! Of course. He raced down the corridor to his bedchamber.

Huddling on the nursery floor with her shoulders squeezed between the bed and the wall, Annie peered out over her mattress at the dense shadows in her room. Without a lamp burning, everything looked bathed in blue, eerie and slightly ghostlike. With her nerves still leaping from the confrontation with Alex, it was all too easy for her to think she could see monstrous creatures hovering in the dark recesses, watching her and waiting to pounce.

She shook away the thought, refusing to let her vivid imagination run away with her. Right now, the only thing that was likely to pounce on her was Alex Montgomery, and she'd do well to watch the door instead of the shadows. If he decided to come in, that puny little chair she'd wedged under the knob wasn't likely to stop him.

His *wife*. Every time Annie thought the word, she cringed. And when she let herself ponder its implications, she started to sweat. A cold, shivery sweat that filmed her skin and ran in icy rivulets down her ribs. Douglas, her attacker, his brother. Oh, God! She'd guessed as much. From the very beginning, she'd guessed as much. But over time, she had stopped feeling constantly afraid.

Until now . . . He wanted to be close with her? He had admitted as much. Close with her as Douglas had been that day at the falls, only, of course, he promised not to hurt her. Did he really think she was stupid enough to believe that?

Tears filled her eyes. Of course, he believed it. She was Annie the dummy, after all, and dummies believed whatever they were told. Right? *Wrong*. Even if she were that stupid, it would make no difference. As if the pain she had suffered that day had been the only awful part? She didn't want to be touched like that ever again. Not ever. Not by anyone.

Memories slammed into Annie's mind, harsh with clarity. Since that day, she had tried very hard never to think about what happened. But sometimes, like now, she couldn't make the pictures go away. Alex wanted to do those things with her. And she was his *wife*.

Looking back on that morning now, it seemed so obvious. The minister, head bent and reading from the prayer book. Her mama making her nod her head. Her papa helping her to draw lines on the paper. She had been *married* that morning. To Alex Montgomery. That was why he'd brought her here, because he had made her his wife, not because she was fat and her parents didn't want her anymore.

Furious—with herself, with her parents, with Alex—Annie scrubbed her eyes with her fists and held her breath to keep from sobbing. If she started making noise, her *husband* might come. Oh, God, her husband . . . Annie had watched her mama enough to know that husbands were always the boss and that wives scurried around, trying frantically to keep them happy.

Well, if she was going to have to scurry for the rest of her life, the very *least* she deserved for her trouble was a pretty white dress and a gift from somebody. She didn't even care what it was, just as long as it was all wrapped up in fancy paper so she wouldn't know what was inside until she opened it. Ever since she was a little girl, she had always liked surprises.

Just not the kind she'd gotten tonight.

A high keening sound suddenly pierced the silence to rake against her raw nerve endings. Annie had no idea what it was. Tipping her head, she stared wide-eyed into the deepening shadows, trying to guess from which direction it came. The sound trailed through the quiet to her again, strange and lilting, never ceasing.

Curiosity drew Annie from her hiding place between the bed and the wall. A narrow band of light from the hallway spilled into her room through the cracked door. Her gaze fixed on the opening, she moved slowly forward. A few feet shy of the chair, she drew to a stop, went up on her tiptoes, and craned her neck. Through the narrow opening, she could see Alex. He sat on the floor outside her room, his back pressed against the opposite wall of the corridor. In his hands was something long and silver, which he held at an angle to his lips.

Music.

Annie stood there, transfixed. The sound made the little hairs on her arms stand on end. It was so very *beautiful*. Scarcely realizing she moved, she stepped closer to the door so she might hear it better, and still the lilting sound beckoned to her. She couldn't resist inching just a little bit nearer. Then nearer still. Before she knew it, her face was pressed to the crack, her gaze riveted to Alex. Nightmare or enchantment? To Annie, he seemed to be both, terrifying but tantalizing.

She could see his chest expanding, then expelling as he blew into the mouthpiece, his blunt fingertips gracefully depressing little round keys to produce certain notes. Sometimes, she couldn't hear them. But most of the time, she could, and they were wondrous.

Suddenly he stopped playing and looked directly at her. Annie sprang away from the crack, her heart slamming, but even standing a bit away, she could still see his face. He was holding out the silver thing, his eyes compelling. ''Would you like to play it, Annie?''

Play it? She pressed a hand to her throat, filled with a longing so sharp it nearly hurt. Music. To actually *hold* it in her hands . . .

Alex sprang to his feet, which sent her staggering backward again in retreat. With a lazy, unhurried air, he approached the door and held the silver thing up near the opening. ''It's easy to play, once you get the hang of it.'' He bent his head to peer through the crack at her, his smile reassuring. ''It's a flute. I used to take lessons as a young boy. I had nearly forgotten I still had it.''

Annie couldn't tear her gaze from his. The flute would never fit through the crack of the door, and he knew it. For him to hand it to her, she would have to move the chair a bit, and while she was doing that, he could shoulder his way inside.

''Come on, Annie. I know you're dying to try it.'' He

leaned closer and tapped on the edge of the door with a fingertip. Then he grinned, slowly and mischievously, his teeth gleaming white against the dark planes of his face. "Open sesame," he said with a slight jerk of his shoulders, an indication to her that he had chuckled. "The famous words of Ali Baba, the poor woodcutter. Have you been told that story?" He held up the flute again to tempt her. "How long has it been since anyone told you a story, Annie love? For that matter, have you *ever* made music? I'll be happy to share both the story and my flute with you. But, first, you have to open the door."

Annie backed up another step and gave her head another shake. Clearly frustrated by her obstinacy, he ran his fingers through his hair, shifted his weight from one foot to the other, and then puffed air into his cheeks. Reaching up with a fingertip to tap the door's edge again, he said, "I'll tell you what. If you'll open the door just a little wider, I'll pass the flute through to you. You have my word I won't grab you or force the door open. How's that for a deal?"

She glanced at the flute. To her, it looked magical, catching the light from the hallway and shimmering as brilliantly as a mirror.

"Trust me," he urged her. "My word is good. Wouldn't you like to try the flute? It's really sort of fun to play."

Fitting it to his mouth, he drew in a breath and blew into the mouthpiece again. A shrill sound came floating through the shadows to her. And it kept coming. Flowing around, over and through her. Annie closed her eyes, scarcely able to believe she was hearing it. And, oh, she never wanted it to stop. She felt like an empty cup that was being filled.

Lifting her lashes, she moved toward him, drawn by the music and his eyes, not entirely certain which had the strongest pull. When her knees bumped the chair, she halted, her gaze held prisoner by his, her senses spinning. He finally stopped playing and once again offered her the flute. This time, he actually tried to fit it through the opening, but the keys caught on the door frame.

"If you'd like to try it, you'll have to open the door just a bit wider." He tipped his head to peer down at the chair. "Move it about an inch toward you. I promise I won't shove my way in."

When she hesitated, he smiled slightly. "Annie, think. Do you honestly believe that chair could stop me if I wanted to get in? It would slow me down, but that's about all. I haven't broken the door down for one reason, and that was because I didn't want to scare you. I don't think it makes much sense that I'd decide to now."

Annie knew the chair wouldn't keep him out, not if he was determined. With shaking hands, she grasped the chair seat and lifted it slightly, drawing it toward her. Then she repositioned the head rail under the doorknob. Alex pushed the flute through the wider opening. After Annie took the instrument, he leaned a shoulder against the door frame, watching as she sputtered futilely into the mouthpiece.

"You're not holding it to your mouth right," he informed her.

She tried another way and blew with all her might into the hole, but no sound happened. He shook his head and started to reach to help her. The door was a barrier against him. "Can you open it just a little wider so I can show you how?"

Annie had the awful feeling he was trying to trick her. Her thoughts must have shown on her face, for he rolled his eyes and said, "I won't do a thing but teach you how to play it."

She searched his gaze for an endless moment. Then she mouthed the words, "*Do you promise?*"

He pressed his face to the crack. "Come again?"

"*Do you promise?*"

He shook his head. "Slower. I can't—"

"*Do you promise!*" As she repeated the words, Annie crossed her heart.

"Do I promise?" He pushed erect and raised his hands. "Honey, I promise. Cross my heart, hope to die." He made a snapping motion with his fingers. "I'll go one better and *swear* it. On a Bible, if you have one handy."

He looked so sincere that Annie nearly smiled. Then, against her better judgment, but following her heart, she removed the chair and drew the door open. Alex seemed startled that she had opened it all the way, and for a moment, he just stood there, looking at a loss. Then he scratched beside his nose and stepped over the threshold.

Annie shoved the flute into his hands. He took it and grinned one of those wonderfully crooked grins of his. "Come over here."

With that, he lit a lamp and went to sit on the bed. Patting the mattress beside him, he waited for her to join him. Annie glanced uneasily at the open door, not entirely sure she wanted to venture so far into the room while she was alone with him. When she turned to look at him again, his grin had gone mischievous. "You, young lady, do not trust easily."

Annie lifted one shoulder in an almost imperceptible shrug. He narrowed an eye at her and extended the flute. "You can't learn to play it standing clear across the room from me."

That was true, and she knew it. And, oh, how she wanted to learn. Slowly, she approached the bed. It made her tense to sit beside him. In the shifting light, he looked unnervingly large.

"First of all, you have to hold it to your mouth correctly," he said, and with that he encircled her shoulders with one arm so he could help her hold the instrument.

At his closeness, Annie jerked. When she shot him a questioning look, she found his face hovering a scant inch above hers. Her heart did a flip-flop, lurched to a sickening stop, and then sluggishly began to work again, each beat bumping against her ribs.

"My word, remember?" He hunched forward so she could see him speak as he showed her how to use the flute. "You have to hold your mouth right." To demonstrate, he drew his lips in over his teeth. "Then you press your mouth to the hole. There you go. Now blow."

Annie expelled air with all the force she could muster. No sound came out, but evidently something else did. Alex jerked his head back, laughed, and wiped under one eye. "Not that hard, goose. You'll bust a vessel."

Annie bent her head to try again. This time, Alex reared back out of the way, his eyes alight with silent laughter. A giggle wormed its way up her throat. Forgetting to stifle the sound, she gulped it back at the last possible second, nearly strangling herself in the process.

His smile suddenly vanished. "You can laugh, Annie. It's not against the rules here. Laugh all you like."

She grew still, staring at him over the flute keys, all urge to giggle gone. He glanced upward. "We have very sturdy rafters. I promise, the roof won't cave in. No one will get angry. I won't punish you. This is your home now. Anyone who complains about any noises you make can go whistle Dixie in a high wind, and at my invitation."

When she continued to stare at him incredulously, he shook his head. "Okay, fine. Don't laugh. Rome wasn't built in a day. We'll work our way up to it." With a wink, he added, "For tonight, we'll settle for your driving Maddy to distraction with off-key notes."

In the space of an hour, Annie was doing exactly that. Maddy appeared in the doorway, her hands clamped to the sides of her head. "Oh, Master Alex, have a pity!"

Alex laughed and waved her away. "Stuff some cotton in your ears. We're having fun."

Annie blew with all her might on the flute. The most beautiful noise in the world reverberated through her head. She hauled in another breath and did it again. She felt the bed shaking and knew Alex was laughing. She drew her mouth from the instrument and smiled at him.

Brushing away a tendril of hair at her temple, he smiled back. And then he took her totally by surprise by saying, "The flute is yours, Annie. You can play it all day tomorrow if you like. For tonight, though, maybe you'd better stop." He glanced toward Maddy, then turned back so Annie could read his lips as he spoke to her. "Before a certain housekeeper I know decides to scalp us both."

Annie lowered the flute to her lap and reverently stroked its keys. Alex had given her a wedding gift, after all, she thought. Something no one else had ever even *thought* to give her. Music . . . Beautiful music, wrapped in magic.

Fifteen

On his way downstairs the following morning, Alex encountered the maid, Yvonne, standing outside the nursery with a stack of freshly laundered sheets in her arms. Upon seeing her, he inclined his head and smiled.

"I take it your mistress is being a layabout again this morning?"

Yvonne shook her head. "No, Master Alex, she's up and about. She just isn't ready for her bed to be changed yet."

Since the door was ajar, Alex doubted that Annie was dressing. Curious, he poked his head around the door-frame to see Maddy standing in the center of the room, feet slightly parted, arms akimbo. Upon spying Alex at the door, she nodded in greeting.

"She's searchin' through the bedclothes again," she explained with a bewildered little shrug. "Every mornin' without fail. It's becomin' a regular ritual."

Moving into the room, Alex said, "Have you asked her what she's looking for?"

"Asked her?" Maddy shook her head. "No, I can't say as I have. It never occurred to me she could answer."

Pleased to have an excuse, any excuse, to linger, Alex

settled his gaze on Annie, who was going through her rumpled bedding with great care. As he'd noticed once before, her nightgown, though modestly cut, was thin and nearly transparent with wear. He made a mental note to add nightclothes to the list of things he wanted made for her. Not that he had any objection to sheer nightgowns. Far from it.

He was smiling with masculine appreciation by the time he drew up beside her. She gave a start when she spotted him and ceased patting the bedcovers.

He gestured at her bed. "What are you searching for, Annie? Maybe Maddy and I can help you look."

She drew her finely arched brows together, clearly unsettled, not only by his question, but by the fact that he expected an answer. Alex sighed. Patience had never been one of his virtues, but, since marrying Annie, he was beginning to see that it was one he needed to acquire. For fourteen years, she had been forced to follow strict rules, never making any sound or any attempt to communicate. He couldn't, in all fairness, expect her to change overnight.

"Answer my question, Annie, as best you can. No one here is going to punish you, I promise."

She looked none too certain of that. Alex hated to press her, but he knew it was either that or allow her to continue as she was.

"What are you looking for?" he asked again, assuming a stern expression that he hoped would encourage her to reply without frightening her half to death.

She plucked nervously at the bodice of her nightgown, which drew his attention from her face to her chest. At the sight he beheld, he clenched his teeth and jerked his gaze back to hers. Amazingly, she seemed totally unaware that his interest had momentarily strayed.

After what Douglas had done to her, he found her na-

ïvete more than a little incredible. But, then, he was looking at things from his perspective, not hers. Obviously,
Douglas's violent attack on her had been just that, violent.
No preliminary flirtation or attraction, only terror and
pain, which had taught her to be wary of men, but had
left her with little, if any, understanding of carnal pleasure
or what led up to it.

Gazing down at her, Alex felt like the proverbial wolf
stalking a helpless lamb.

His thoughts were snapped back into line by a movement of Annie's lips, which, because of his musings, he
nearly missed. Fixing his attention on her mouth, he said,
"Say it again, Annie. Slowly, so I can follow you. I'm
not nearly as good at lipreading as you are, I'm afraid."

She glanced nervously at Maddy. Then she mouthed
her reply again. When he couldn't read her lips, his heart
sank a little. This wasn't going to be as easy as he had
hoped. Lipreading, which seemed to come naturally to
her, was, for him, nearly an impossible feat. She said the
words again, this time with exaggerated lip and tongue
movements. He was still at a loss.

"Have you ever seen people play charades?" he asked.

She thought for a moment, then nodded with unmistakable reluctance. Alex guessed that she had come by her
knowledge of parlor games by spying on her parents when
they had guests. Evidently, that had been yet another forbidden activity in the Trimble home, one for which she
would have been punished if caught.

"Good. Then act out the words you're trying to say.
Give me some clues."

Forehead pleated in a frown, she gazed thoughtfully
into space for a moment. Then she brightened and held
up a small hand, forming a circle with her thumb and
forefinger.

"A bracelet!" Alex tried. "You're looking for a brace-let?"

She shook her head. Forming the circle again, she traced its shape with a fingertip, calling his attention to the fact that it was more oval than round. Alex stroked his chin. "A pendant?"

She made a moue with her lips and rolled her eyes, clearly frustrated at his dimwittedness. Pleased that she had dared reveal displeasure with him, even in so slight a way, he chuckled. "I know I'm slow. Be patient with me, hmm? After all, we've only just started, and if nothing else, we're having fun. We can do this. It'll just take some practice."

"A locket!" Maddy suggested.

Annie gave her head another shake. Then, looking absolutely adorable with her dark hair in disarray and a disgruntled expression on her face, she put her hands on her hips. After nibbling on the inside of her lip for a second, she seemed struck by sudden inspiration. Stepping back from Alex so she had a little room, she made a great show of pretending she held something in one hand. When he nodded his understanding, she pretended to tap the object against an imaginary surface, then break it in half.

Something about the gestures seemed very familiar, and Alex knew he should recognize them. At his blank look, Annie sighed. Then she tucked her hands under her arms and began to flap her elbows.

Alex hadn't a clue what the hell she was doing, but wanting to encourage her, he cried, "Very *good*, Annie. That's the spirit."

Her smile deepened, flashing dimples in her cheeks that he hadn't, until that moment, realized were there. Then, stretching her neck and bending her knees slightly, she began to walk in circles, still flapping her elbows.

So excited that he was almost yelling, Alex said, "A chicken!"

She nodded emphatically.

"A chicken, Maddy! She's looking for a chicken!"

Plainly baffled, the plump housekeeper nodded. "Of course! A chicken. I don't know why I didn't think of it."

Annie gave her head a vehement shake.

"Not a chicken," Alex amended.

She held up her hand and made another circle with her thumb and forefinger.

"An egg!" Maddy fairly shrieked. "Crackin' an egg! Yes!" She clapped her hands. "That's what she was doin', Master Alex, crackin' a bloomin' egg!"

Annie nodded excitedly, then folded her arms over her waist, one small hand curled protectively over her swollen stomach.

"An egg?" Alex threw a nonplussed glance at Maddy. "An egg, Annie? In your bed?"

She nodded again.

"I see," Alex said, only, of course, he didn't see at all. His confusion must have shown on his face because Annie pointed to her abdomen, made another egg-shaped circle with her fingers, and then made a sweeping motion from her waist to the floor.

"Holy Mother, pray fer us."

Alex turned a bewildered look on Maddy. "I'm not following."

Maddy looked mildly horrified. "An egg, don't ye see? The baby! The lass thinks—oh, dear God. She thinks she's goin' to lay an *egg*!"

"*What*?"

At Alex's appalled expression, Annie's eyes went even rounder than normal, and she retreated a step. Striving to regain his composure, which was no easy task, Alex shifted his gaze to the bed. Remembering how carefully he had seen her searching through the covers, he squeezed his eyes closed.

"Oh, dear," Maddy repeated softly. "The poor wee lass."

Alex opened his eyes and hauled in a bracing breath. "Now, Maddy. There's little point in making mountains out of molehills. Annie isn't the first young woman to have reached adulthood without a clear understanding of certain biological functions. It's a simple matter of addressing her ignorance. She's very good at lipreading."

"A simple matter, yes."

Alex smiled and started to leave the room, patting Maddy's arm as he walked by her. "After you girls have finished with your talk, why don't you join me downstairs for breakfast."

Maddy caught the sleeve of his shirt and brought him reeling to a stop. "Oh, no, ye don't! This is yer molehill to tend, not mine."

Alex patted her arm again. "Come now, Maddy. Don't be a faintheart. If I could explain it to her, you know I would. But a subject of this nature is too delicate for a man to address."

Maddy shot him a look that could have pulverized rock. "Ye're the lass's husband, and therefore 'tis yer duty, not mine. If ye'll recall, I was never married. What I know about such things could fit in a thimble."

"You surely have a grasp of the rudiments."

"Rudiments? Leave this room, and I'll settle the matter by lookin' in yon bedcovers for an egg, mark me words."

"You wouldn't!"

"I would."

Alex narrowed an eye at her. "Maddy, *someone* has to explain the facts of life to the girl, and it certainly can't be me. We can't let her continue to believe she's about to lay an *egg*, for Christ's sake. It's—well, it's—'' He broke off for lack of a word. Finally, he finished with, ''Irresponsible, that's what it is.''

''Then tend yer responsibilities.''

''This sort of thing is *not* my responsibility, not given the sort of relationship she and I have, which is no relationship at all.''

''Coward.''

''Don't be absurd. It wouldn't bother *me* to discuss the subject with her. The concern here is how *she* will feel if I do.''

Maddy folded her arms beneath her breasts. ''Then have her mama come talk to her. The way I see it, 'twas Mrs. Trimble's duty to educate the lass in the first place, and seein' as how she failed in that, it's her mess to tidy.''

''Over my dead body.''

''Well, then?''

Alex threw up his hands. ''All right, fine! But if she gets upset, the blame for it will be on *your* doorstep, not mine. A subject of this nature would best be handled by a kindly older woman, someone she trusts.''

Feigning a confidence he was far from feeling, he took Annie by the hand, led her over to the table, pushed her gently down onto a chair, and sat across from her. Resting his folded arms on the table, he leaned forward, holding her bewildered gaze with his. ''Annie, honey, there are a couple of things you need to understand.'' Listening from the sidelines, Maddy harrumphed and clicked her tongue. Alex chose to ignore her sarcasm. He would do this, and with a minimum of fuss. ''Babies and chicks—well, there are a few basic differences in the way they're born.''

Those eyes of hers. Alex looked into them and felt as if he were shriveling inside. How could he possibly enlighten her about something so . . . He couldn't even think of a word. Base? Personal? It was definitely not a subject men usually broached to young ladies. The trick, he decided, would be to give her an adequate explanation without becoming too explicit. Simple terms, that was his aim.

"You understand that there's a baby inside you. Correct?"

She nodded.

So far, so good. Acutely aware that Maddy was watching with a smug look on her face, Alex tapped his fingertips on the tabletop. "Mothers," he said softly, "have a special place inside them made just for babies. That's where their babies stay and grow until they're ready to be born, in that special place. Do you understand?"

Again, Annie nodded. Alex wanted to look anywhere but into her eyes. He saw so many questions there, and so much innocence. If he said the wrong thing—just one wrong word—he could send her into a panic and make this pregnancy one of dread for her.

"Good. I'm glad you understand." He tapped his fingers a little more sharply against the wood. "Anyway, when your baby is finally ready to be born," he went on, "the special place inside of you will open up and the baby will come out." At her look of bewilderment, he quickly added, "It's a very wonderful thing, the birth of a baby! Everyone will be really happy, and we—" He broke off and threw a helpless look at Maddy. "We'll probably have a big party to celebrate. Won't we, Maddy?"

"A party." Maddy pumped her chin up and down. "We'll have a shindig such as ye never saw, to be sure. A grand day, it'll be. A grand day!"

Annie's cheeks flushed with pleasure, and her face went radiant with a sweet smile. Convinced that he had said just enough to clear up her misconceptions without adding to them, Alex was about to heave a sigh of profound relief when she frowned slightly, poked a finger into her bellybutton, and arched inquisitive brows at him.

Rat-a-tat-tat. Rat-a-tat-tat, his fingers went on the tabletop, his gaze riveted to her navel. He greatly feared that if she didn't stop drilling her finger so deeply into the depression, she might do herself an injury. *Damn*. Thinking back to his childhood, Alex could distinctly recall his own youthful misconceptions about the birth process, namely his belief that the baby inside his stepmother's protruding belly would make its exit through her navel. At the time, it had seemed a perfectly reasonable explanation to him, and to this day, he could remember how shocked he had been when an older boy had told him differently.

"Not *there*, Annie," he hastened to explain in a gravelly voice. "The baby doesn't come out there."

She ceased poking her navel and fastened a perplexed gaze on his, clearly awaiting further explanation. *Rat-a-tat-tat*. Trying to think of a suitable way he might explain—or, for that matter, any way that he might explain without terrifying her—Alex swallowed a lump in his throat that felt as big as a rubber ball. Then, keeping his expression carefully blank, he pushed up from the table, brushed past Maddy, and descended on Annie's bed.

"Now what are ye about?" Maddy demanded.

Alex's only response was to gently lift one of Annie's blankets and give it a careful shake.

Alex spent the remainder of the morning closeted in his study. After making arrangements for the attic to be cleaned, he dispatched two messages, one to Dr. Daniel Muir requesting that he pay a house call to Montgomery Hall posthaste, another to Hooperville's one and only dressmaker, Pamela Grimes, saying that he wished to have his wife fitted for a new wardrobe.

Only after those three details were taken care of could Alex settle down to what he truly wanted to do, which was to pore over the Montgomery Ward & Company catalog for things he might buy Annie. Ear horns were at the top of his list. The company carried three styles, a trumpet-type contraption that came in three graduating sizes, a carryable horn in a convenient pocket size, and a conversation tube, one end of which sported a mouthpiece for the speaker, the other a listening device to fit into the deaf person's ear. Uncertain which type might work the best, Alex ordered a dozen of each style and size, determined that Annie would have at least one effective hearing aid in every room of his house. Other people had their ears with them wherever they went, he reasoned, and so should she.

The cost of so many ear trumpets was substantial, and Alex had always prided himself on being a frugal man. When it came to Annie, however, money was the least of his concerns. She had been given so little in her young life, and he had it in his power to change that. The way he saw it, he had been working his ass off all his life. And for what? So he might spoil his brother? Now, for the first time, Alex had someone in his life who truly had needs. He wanted to fulfill every single one of them.

Every time he remembered her parlor in the attic, his guts knotted. From this day on, he was making it his priority to turn the girl's fantasies into realities. Beautiful clothes. Delicate china. Music . . .

Remembering her enchantment with his old flute, Alex flipped to the musical section of the catalog. Before he was finished, he had ordered her a six-octave Windsor organ, a rosewood concertina with leather-bound bellows, a harmonica, a kazoo, a set of three-octave orchestra bells, a French horn, and a rack of musical sleigh bells.

From the music section he went to the toy section and ordered a toy zither, a game of Hopity, a parlor tennis set, a Ding Dong Bell game, tiddledywinks, a combination set of board games, including fish pond, checkers, and dominoes.

After tallying the amount of his order, Alex went from his desk to the liquor cabinet. Even as he poured himself a snifter of brandy, however, he knew he was more than happy to spend the money on her. In fact, he couldn't recall having had so much fun in a very long while. One smile from Annie—just one—would more than make up for the expenditure.

Shortly after lunch, Dr. Muir arrived. Once Alex had explained that he wanted Annie carefully examined and why, the two men went upstairs to the nursery. At first, Alex feared that, despite his earlier explanations to Annie, she might be frightened by the good doctor's unwanted attentions, but he soon realized that he had sorely under-estimated Daniel's abilities. As he might have with a timid child, the doctor made the process seem more like a game than a medical examination. To get a peek into Annie's ears, he first did a magic trick, pretending to pluck a piece of candy from her ear and feigning astonishment. Annie, of course, was astonished as well, and before Alex knew it, she was allowing Muir to insert an instrument into her ear canal, presumably to see if more pieces of candy were rattling about inside her head. Annie seemed to think it was all great fun. Alex, who stood off to one side, couldn't help but laugh at the amazed expressions that crossed her small face.

His urge to laugh faded abruptly when Daniel's examination of Annie moved from her ears to her torso. Here, he felt sure, the physician would find himself with a panicked young woman on his hands, and Alex was dreading the moment that he would be called upon to help subdue her. But, again, Daniel surprised him. Continuing to use sleight of hand, Muir plucked candy from the neckline of Annie's frock, from its sleeves, from under the hem. Before Alex knew it, the doctor had palpitated his wife's breasts and abdomen, evidently to his satisfaction, and had listened to her heart. In the end, Annie had a sizable collection of hard candy lying on the table, which Dr. Muir allowed her to keep.

On their way back downstairs, the physician related his findings to Alex. "As far as the immediate concerns go, her pregnancy seems to be progressing normally," he said. "Without doing a pelvic examination, I'm unable to be absolutely certain of that, but at this point, I believe a closer look would do the girl more harm than good."

Alex expressed his complete agreement with that and told the doctor of Annie's revelation to him and Maddy that morning.

"An *egg*?" Muir chuckled and shook his head as they entered Alex's study. "Ah, well, I can't see as how letting her continue to believe that will hurt. At least she has the general idea and understands that there *is* a baby growing inside her."

Alex felt a flush creeping up his neck. "She may be a little disappointed when it's born, minus the booties and bonnet." He described the picture he'd drawn for Annie to explain her pregnancy to her. "At the time, not realizing she could read lips, it was the only way I could think of to get my point across."

"It worked. That's all that matters." Muir deposited his satchel on the floor at his feet and sat down in one of the comfortable leather chairs positioned before the hearth. "You're correct in your diagnosis, by the way. The girl is deaf. It's only my guess, mind you, but judging by the scar tissue, I would wager that the fever that robbed her of her hearing was probably caused by a very severe ear infection."

"Which went untreated," Alex said bitterly, unable to hide the resentment he felt toward the Trimbles.

"True," Muir conceded, "but there's nothing to say I could have prevented the hearing loss, even if I'd treated her."

"They might have at least given you the opportunity to try."

Daniel sighed. "In all fairness to Edie, Alex, chronic ear problems aren't always easily detected by parents. I've seen cases where a child's ears were so bad that they were bleeding, and the frantic mother and father still hadn't a clue what was wrong. The child may be cranky, feverish, nauseated, yet manifest no sign of earache. One little boy I once treated was congested and had had a serious cough for days. In the mornings, when his mother found pus and blood on his pillow, she mistakenly believed that it was coming up from his lungs. She was terrified he had consumption."

"In other words, I shouldn't hold Annie's parents accountable?"

Muir pursed his lips and gazed sightlessly into the firebox for a moment. "For many things, yes, but not for the deafness. If Annie's middle ears were abscessed, which I believe they may have been, she could have run a raging fever until they broke and drained, which could have occurred in a matter of hours after the onset of the fever. Afterward, she may have seemed to be on the mend, and her mother may have believed she was fine. Kids get sick. Quite often, they run high fevers over the least little thing. A mother does her best, but she isn't infallible. Neither am I, for that matter."

Remembering Annie as he'd found her in the attic, Alex found it difficult to let go of his anger toward the Trimbles quite that easily.

"Would you mind my giving you just a bit of advice?" the doctor asked.

Alex smiled slightly. "Not at all. That's why I sent for you."

"Look forward," Daniel said softly. "For years, I've had to watch that girl live half a life. Now you have a chance to give her so much more. Concentrate on that, not on the Trimbles and the dozens of ways in which they have failed. You can't go back and undo all the injustices Annie has suffered. But you can try to make up for them. The girl can receive help now. Think of it that way."

"It's my hope to give her as normal a life as possible," Alex mused aloud. The admission turned his thoughts to other matters. Sitting straighter in his chair and clearing his throat, he said, "In regard to that . . ." He met the doctor's questioning gaze. "If things work out well between Annie and me, and I've every reason to hope, will it be harmful to her or the baby if—" Alex gestured vaguely. "I've heard it both ways, that it's okay for pregnant women to have marital relations and that it's not."

Pressing his hands to his knees and pushing to his feet, Daniel chuckled. "Trust me, Alex, you'll do no harm." He gave him a rakish wink. "Just take care not to dislodge the infant's booties. Annie may be a trifle upset if it's born missing a sock."

Alex grinned. "I'll bear that in mind."

"I'd appreciate it. After all that candy I just plucked from her various orifices, she may expect me to go bootie hunting."

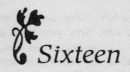

Sixteen

Over the next two weeks, Alex found it incredibly easy to follow doctor's orders and concentrate on Annie. As if he had a choice. From the time he opened his eyes each morning until he closed them at night, she was all he thought about. Other things he might buy her. Activities she might enjoy. About how her eyes lighted up when she smiled. He even began to contemplate building her a cage for her damnable pet mice.

Annie . . . For the first time in his adult life, Alex had someone deserving to care about, someone who mattered to him more than his work. He quickly came to realize just how lonely and utterly meaningless his life had been before now. He found himself spending less and less time at the rock quarry and the stables. After lunch each day, he closeted himself in his study with books that Dr. Muir had acquired for him. For three hours, without fail, he pored over the pages, trying to memorize the manual alphabet and learn how to speak sign language. Then he spent a half hour speaking to his reflection in a hand mirror to practice lipreading. At precisely three-thirty each afternoon, he abandoned those pursuits to spend the rest of the afternoon and evening with his wife.

In the beginning, Annie seemed none too pleased to be blessed with his company, but after several days, she seemed to accept, if not to enjoy, his presence. If she was in the attic, he followed her there. If she was downstairs with Maddy, he spirited her away outdoors for long walks. In the evenings, he insisted that she join him at the supper table, where he made her pour tea, pass serving dishes, and practice good table manners. After the meal was finished, they adjourned to his study, where he taught her how to play simple games, such as jacks and checkers, both of which required a minimum of verbal communication.

During that time, the dressmaker came to take Annie's measurements, and Alex ordered an entire new wardrobe for his wife, from the skin out. For a substantial bonus, Mrs. Grimes agreed to hire extra help so she could deliver at least three of the dresses within a week. Alex could scarcely wait to see Annie's eyes when she first saw the clothing. Though he'd had to choose styles with her steadily increasing waistline in mind, he felt sure she would be thrilled. No more moldy dresses spirited from dusty trunks in the attic. From now on, she would have beautiful gowns of her very own.

Madness . . . Alex seriously began to wonder if he wasn't losing his mind. He was falling in love, wildly in love, with a child-woman who believed the baby growing inside her wore a ruffled bonnet. The carnal bent of his thoughts was indecent, he felt sure, but when he looked into Annie's eyes, he wondered how anything that felt so right could possibly be wrong.

As luck would have it, Edie Trimble finally gathered the courage to come calling on the same afternoon that Mrs. Grimes arrived with the first finished garments of Annie's new wardrobe. Alex, who had been left to cool his heels outside the nursery door while Annie tried on the dresses, heard Frederick speaking to someone in the hall and went to the landing to see who was there. When he saw Edie, he nearly ordered her out of his house. Only the anguish he saw on the woman's face prevented him from doing exactly that.

"Mrs. Trimble," he said coldly. "I'm surprised to see you here."

Leaning her head back to meet his gaze, Edie wrung her hands, clearly afraid he would invite her to leave before she had a chance to say her piece. "I know you despise me, and perhaps with good reason, Mr. Montgomery. But, please, I'm begging you, let me see my daughter. I won't stay long. I swear it. And I won't do anything to upset her. But, please, let me see her?"

Alex curled his hands into fists over the banister rail, wanting nothing more than to tell the woman to go. But in the end, the pain in her eyes swayed him. Maybe Dr. Muir was right. Bitterness toward the Trimbles, no matter how well deserved, would only cast a pall over Annie's future. She loved her parents, he felt certain, despite their many faults, and she would probably be delighted to see them. He had no right to deny her that. Edie Trimble was and always would be the girl's mother, even though she had failed, more times than not, to behave like one.

"Right now, she's trying on new dresses," Alex finally said. "Come on up. Maybe you can be of assistance in choosing appropriate accessories. The dressmaker brought quite a nice selection with her."

Edie pressed a hand to her throat and closed her eyes, clearly overcome with relief. For a moment, Alex thought she might disintegrate into tears where she stood. But she finally managed to regain control. After handing her cloak to Frederick, she lifted her skirt and ascended the stairs. When she reached Alex on the landing, she met his gaze squarely.

"Thank you," she said shakily. "I know you'd much rather that I never see my little girl again and if you're correct about the deafness, I don't suppose that I can blame you."

"I'm absolutely correct," Alex couldn't resist saying. "I've had her examined. Dr. Muir concurs with my diagnosis completely."

Tears welled in Edie's eyes, and her mouth began to quiver. "Deaf," she whispered. "All these years, and she was only deaf? God forgive me."

It was those last three words, spoken with such heart-rending regret, that softened Alex. For totally different reasons, he had felt much the same way himself a few times over the years because of Douglas. "We all make mistakes, Edie," he said huskily. "Some worse than others, but the bottom line is that we can only do our best. Given the fact that Annie can register certain pitches of sound, I'm willing to concede that it may have appeared to you that she could hear. You acted out of ignorance, and in doing so, you made some grave errors. Let's leave it at that and move forward from here. Shall we?"

She gave a tearful nod and wiped her cheeks with tremulous fingers, making a visible effort to gather her composure. Alex waited until she had calmed down before he showed her to the nursery. Mrs. Grimes called out to him when she glimpsed him outside the door.

"Do come in, Mr. Montgomery, and tell us what you think."

Alex pushed the door farther open and preceded Edie into the room. The sight that greeted him brought him to a dead stop. Annie . . . only not the Annie he had come to know. Maddy and the dressmaker had combined their respective talents, finishing off her outfit with complementary accessories and styling her hair. The tousled child had disappeared. A lovely young woman had taken her place.

She stood in the center of the room, a vision in sapphire-blue. Her gown had a fitted bodice, just as Alex had specified, with a softly gathered skirt that fell gracefully from just beneath her breasts to the floor. Lace of a darker shade of blue edged the low scoop neckline, enough to draw the eye to her face, but not so much as to overwhelm her delicate features. Her large, luminous eyes clung to his, silently seeking his approval.

"Oh, Annie," Alex said softly. "You look absolutely beautiful."

A blush flooded to her face, flagging her cheeks with two bright spots of color. Alex gave her a slow grin, then motioned with his hand for her to turn in a complete circle. Catching the skirt to hold it wide, she turned on one toe, craning her neck so she might watch his reaction. It surprised and pleased Alex that she cared so much about what he thought. That told him more than she could know, and undoubtedly far more than she might wish—namely that his deepening feelings toward her weren't completely unreciprocated. He took more pleasure from that discovery than he did from the transformation the clothing had wrought.

Edie, who until that moment had lingered in the hall, finally entered the room. Upon seeing her daughter, she halted abruptly and stood there in frozen silence.

A joyous expression swept across Annie's face. Clearly eager to embrace her mother, she started forward, but before she could take more than a few steps, Edie clamped a hand over her mouth to stifle a sob, then whirled and fled from the room. The stricken expression that crossed Annie's face nearly broke Alex's heart.

"Annie love, she's crying because she's happy," Alex assured her. Closing the distance between them, he cupped her chin in his hand, determined that this moment was not going to be ruined for her. Forcing her gaze from the door to him, he looked deeply into her eyes. "She didn't know, sweetheart. She never knew that you were deaf. Seeing you like this makes her feel sad because she knows you should have had pretty dresses all along. Do you understand? She feels guilty. In a few minutes, she'll come back, and the two of you can have a lovely visit."

Tears filled her beautiful eyes. Alex gave her a confident smile. "I'll go get her, all right? Meanwhile, you put on another dress so we can see how beautiful you look in it when we come back."

Chin atremble, she gave a halfhearted nod. Alex shot a meaningful glance at Maddy, then quit the room. He found Edie downstairs in the hall, clinging to her cloak, which hung from the coat tree, her face buried in its black folds.

"God damn you," Alex ground out at her shaking back. "For once, just *once*, can't you put that girl before yourself? This is the very first time in her entire *life* that she's been given some beautiful clothes—something other girls take for granted, I might add—and you have to ruin the moment for her?"

Edie hunched her shoulders, sobbing wildly. Between ragged breaths, she managed to cry, "I'm sorry. I'm sorry! Seeing h-her like that. Oh, dear God, what have I done? My little girl . . . What have I done?"

Alex hauled in a deep breath, fighting to control his anger, acutely conscious and deeply grateful, for once, that Annie couldn't hear. "Mrs. Trimble, I realize that this must be difficult for you, but this is *not* the time to purge yourself. That girl is standing up there in the first pretty new gown she's ever owned and *tears* are streaming down her cheeks. Get a hold of yourself."

"You d-don't underst-stand," she cried. "I thought—

oh, God, I thought she had inherited Uncle Maxwell's madness. All these years! All the w-wasted years!''

Alex sighed, partly in exasperation, partly in sympathy. Taking the woman's arm, he guided her to his study, where she might at least weep in private. She sank weakly onto a chair, her face pressed to her knees. After a few minutes, when she had sobbed herself dry, she began to speak in a hushed, tremulous voice.

''I truly believed she was mad,'' she told him.

''I know you did,'' Alex admitted, sitting on the arm of her chair so he might place a hand on her shoulder. ''I realized it from the first. Why you thought that, I'm not sure, but I believe you honestly did.''

''I thought it for a hundred different reasons,'' she said shrilly. ''The awful sounds she made. My uncle made sounds almost exactly like them, animallike utterances and grunts. My aunt had to have him bound to a tree until attendants from a madhouse could come and get him!'' She pressed her hands over her face. ''And the kittens. Oh, God, the kittens.''

''What kittens?''

''She strangled and crushed two kittens,'' Edie said raggedly.

After having witnessed Annie's incredible gentleness with the mice in the attic, Alex found this story difficult to believe, but he didn't interrupt the woman.

''It was horrible. Horrible! I only left her alone with the litter for a little while, never dreaming she might hurt them. She seemed to love them so! And when I came back, she'd killed two of them. Killed them!''

She looked up, pinning Alex with an agonized gaze. ''I was terrified that James would find out what she'd done. Absolutely terrified! I lied and told him a tomcat had sneaked into the house. After that, I encouraged Annie to play in the woods, as was her wont, for I reasoned that the less she was about the house where he might accidentally witness her mean streak, the better. He would have sent her away. Don't you see? To one of those nightmarish places! I realized if I didn't restrict her activities, if I wasn't very, very stern, that she'd very likely end up living out the rest of her life in a cell. I couldn't bear for that to happen. Not to my little girl.

"That's why I wouldn't allow her to be examined by a physician. That's why I was so secretive about her activities in the attic, stressing that no one else could ever know. Don't you see? She's incredibly talented at sketching. And then there were the make-believe games and her pretending to talk. That wasn't the behavior of an imbecile! And because she seemed to hear when I called to her, I didn't believe she was deaf. What other explanation was there for her strangeness, if not that she was mad like my uncle?''

For the first time, Alex could begin to see things as Edie must have. A beautiful girl who behaved abnormally, who seemed unable to grasp the simplest concepts, whose ability to speak had steadily deteriorated. Yet in the attic, in her make-believe world, that same girl exhibited signs of keen intelligence.

"Now I realize that my fear made me blind, that if I'd only listened to Dr. Muir, we might have learned the truth years ago. But I couldn't take that chance. I was convinced she had inherited the illness from my uncle and that it would eventually progress to a point that I could no longer keep it from James. The way I saw it, the *only* thing I could do was delay that from happening for as long as possible.''

A burning sensation came up the back of Alex's throat. "Which is why you stressed to me that I should enforce your rules while Annie was here," he said softly. "You thought if I didn't, that I'd soon realize the truth and tell James she was crazy.''

"If you'll recall, I originally didn't want her to come here at all.''

Alex remembered that all too clearly.

"It was nothing personal,'' she rushed to explain. "From the beginning, I could see you had a kindly nature, and that you felt sorry for Annie. I was afraid that, in a misguided attempt to make retribution for what Douglas had done, you might indulge her.''

Alex smiled slightly. "Spoil her rotten, in other words?'' .

"Yes,'' she admitted. "I hoped that strangers who knew nothing of the circumstances would be more likely to follow my wishes and be regimental with her.'' She closed her eyes. "All I could think about was James learning the truth and sending her away. Someplace awful, where she'd be confused and alone, possibly mistreated.''

Alex tightened his hand over her shoulder, understanding all too well now what had driven the woman. After several minutes of silence, during which she grew calmer, he said, "You did what you thought was best for your daughter, Edie. It's terrible that it happened the way it did, yes. But for all of that, I believe she was reasonably happy in her own simple way. Now that part of her life's over. We have to put the past behind us and concentrate on her future. She can have a wonderful, reasonably normal life from here on out, if we all work together to make it happen. A moment ago, you expressed a fear that I might indulge her. I'm doing my level best to live up to your worst expectations. Care to lend me a hand?''

She fastened a hopeful gaze on his. "Oh, Alex, will you allow me that? To be a part of things? I have so *much* to make up for. So very much.''

Relinquishing the last traces of his anger, Alex sighed.

"Edie, your daughter loves you. I'm sure she wants to see you. I think it's time that all of us start paying attention to Annie's wishes for a change. Don't you?"

"Oh, yes," she said. "Oh, yes."

Drawing a handkerchief from his trouser pocket, Alex set himself to the task of cleaning up her face, a service he seemed to be providing to females frequently of late. Until now, he'd never realized the woman wore paint. A subtle amount, to be sure, but there were definite traces of kohl on her cheeks. "May I take the liberty of giving you a bit of well-intended advice, madam?"

"Not to cry in front of my daughter again?"

"That, too," he said with a half smile. "But I was thinking more along the lines of some marital advice. After you leave here, you need to go home and have an honest discussion with your husband. He is as much to blame for this tragedy as you are, if not more so."

"Oh, but I can't!" she said shrilly. "James—he doesn't *know*! About my uncle, I mean. When he asked me to marry him, I neglected to tell him. And, later, I couldn't find the courage." She gave her head a decisive shake. "You don't know James. If he even *suspected* that madness runs in my family, he'd divorce me. If he did that, I don't know what I'd do! Where would I live? How would I earn my keep?"

Alex pushed to his feet. "Edie, if the man tosses you out, you can always come to me. You are my wife's mother. I would see to it you had the necessary funds to get by."

She stared at him incredulously. "You would?"

He gave a startled laugh. "Yes, madam, I would. But I assure you, it won't come to that. For all his faults, and I could list a host of them, James cares for you. You say that I don't know him. I think it may be more accurate to say that you don't. And it's high time you do. Talk to

him. Tell him everything you've told me. I think you may
be surprised by what he says.''

"You know something I don't.''

"Let's just say that as much as I dislike the man, I
understand how he thinks.'' With that, Alex helped her
up from the chair. "Now, let's go upstairs and share in a
special moment, shall we?''

She nodded.

"No more histrionics?''

"None, I assure you.''

Alex could only hope.

After Edie and the dressmaker had departed, curiosity
prompted Alex to bring one of the barn cats into the
house. Seeking his wife, he found her in the kitchen with
Maddy, who was overseeing the preparations for supper.
Looking lovely in a pink, high-waisted gown, her hair
caught up in a cascade of sable curls at her crown, Annie
was perched on a stool at the counter. In the crook of one
arm, she held a green crockery bowl from which she was
scraping bits of cookie dough with a long-handled spoon.
When she spotted Alex, she froze, the spoon partway to
her mouth, her eyes fixed on the cat.

At her obvious fascination, Alex couldn't help but grin.
The girl didn't just like animals, she adored them. After
seeing her with the mice, he couldn't believe, even for an
instant, that she would ever inflict harm on any small creature, at least not deliberately.

"This is Mama Kitty, queen of the barnyard cats,''
Alex told her. "If not for her, we'd be overrun by''—
catching himself just in time, he finished with—"grass-
hoppers.''

Maddy slanted him a look, then shook her head. Annie,
thank goodness, didn't seem to notice his sudden change
of words. She was gazing in fascination at the tabby, the

cookie dough forgotten. Alex gestured with a nod. "Sit at the table, Annie love, and I'll let you hold her."

She didn't need to be told twice. Setting the crockery bowl on the counter with a resounding *thunk* that made everyone else in the kitchen wince, she slid off the stool and hurried to the table where she enthroned herself on a straight-backed chair. Scratching Mama Kitty behind an ear to keep her calm, Alex strode across the room. Annie reached for the cat with welcoming arms. With a smile, he relinquished his burden to her and took a seat nearby so he might observe her behavior with the animal.

Her small face aglow with pleasure, Annie immediately began stroking the cat's silken fur. Mama Kitty, unaccustomed to such loving attention, arched her back and rubbed a whiskered cheek against Annie's bodice. Then, so loudly that Alex could hear her, the tabby began to purr. Feeling the vibration, Annie ran her hands more firmly over the cat's body. A wondrous expression entered her eyes, and she glanced up at Alex, clearly amazed.

"She's purring," he explained. "Cats usually do when they're petted."

A maid bustled by with a tray of unbaked bread, her destination the oven. "All of them usually shed as well," she commented. "If there's hair in your soup tonight, don't be blaming me."

Alex chuckled. Then he returned his attention to Annie. What he saw made his heart catch. She hugged the tabby close to her breast, one cheek pressed against its ribs, her expression one of bedazzlement. Alex realized immediately that she was utterly captivated by the cat's purring, a sound she could feel even though she was unable to hear it.

The mystery of Annie and the suffocated kittens was solved. Alex could almost see her as a very young child, deaf and utterly captivated by the vibrations she felt when she held the kittens, her small hands and arms squeezing too tightly, her curiosity and elation making her forget to be careful. The kittens hadn't been killed with malicious intent, but by a deaf child's unbridled affection. Older now and more in control, she was being incredibly gentle with this cat, taking care not to hug it too tightly or to touch it too roughly.

Watching her with the cat brought home to Alex just how easily this girl was seduced by any sound that she could faintly hear or from which she could detect vibrations. And it explained so much. Her love of the woods, where she felt the wind on her skin. Her fascination with the waterfall, where she no doubt could feel the vibrations made by the water plunging against the rocks. Annie and the kittens. Annie and the church organ. All along, there had been so many signs of her deafness.

His throat suddenly tight with emotion, Alex swallowed and looked away for a moment. Funny that. Before meeting Annie, he hadn't felt close to tears since early childhood. Now it seemed to him that he was blinking away suspicious moisture or gulping back a lump in his throat more often than not. Watching her . . . coming to understand what her life had been like . . . Alex supposed that it would take someone with a heart of stone not to be affected, and when it came to this girl, his heart was definitely not made of stone.

In that moment, Alex accepted intellectually what his heart had been telling him for over two weeks. He was in love with her. Impossibly, hopelessly in love. He found her too incredibly sweet and precious to resist. If that was lecherous . . . if it was an unforgivable sin . . . well, then, he guessed he was doomed.

Contrary to the old saying, he wasn't entirely sure he'd go to hell with a smile on his face. Given Annie's effect on him, there was every possibility he'd have tears in his eyes when the moment of reckoning came. His only consolation was that they would definitely be tears of joy, not sorrow.

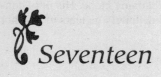

Seventeen

Time . . . For Annie, time, at least as it was interpreted by others, was a concept she didn't understand. For her, there were no clocks, no schedules, no calendars by which she could mark off the days, the weeks, the months. She only knew that the long, lazy days of butterfly season had grown shorter, that the leaves on the trees were beginning to turn color, and that the air had become cooler.

Rainy season was coming; she felt it in her bones. But for the first time in her memory, the thought didn't depress her. Alex's house, unlike that of her parents, was a place of excitement and discovery. She spent hours sitting on her bed each day, blowing on her flute. When she grew bored with that, she could sketch to her heart's content, for Alex had discovered her penchant for drawing and supplied her with charcoal pencils and sketchpads. In addition to that, her mother visited every few days, usually of an afternoon. She was trying to learn how to lip-read, and for the first time in years, Annie could actually communicate with her a little. With so much to occupy her time, she didn't dread being confined indoors as she once had.

Not that she would be confined. In addition to drawing

supplies, Alex had also given her an odd-looking contraption he called an umbrella, which Annie likened to a roof with a handle. According to him, when it rained, one opened the umbrella and held it over one's head, the result being that it rained all around a person but not on him. With the umbrella, she would be free to go walking in the rain whenever she wished without becoming wet.

If she was still *able* to walk by the time the rainy season arrived. Her stomach was growing so enormous she already felt as if she waddled like a duck. Going down the stairs worried her the most. Being front heavy as she was, she had to lean slightly backward to keep from losing her balance on the steps. It was ever so troublesome.

It was also becoming worrisome. Because of what Alex had told her—about babies being born in a different way than chicks—she no longer believed she might lay an egg. But, even so, there was no question in her mind that there *was* a baby growing inside her. Sometimes she could even feel it wiggling around, as though it were becoming anxious to get out. Given its size, Annie was beginning to wonder how it would ever manage. Not through her bellybutton, that was a certainty.

She wished she could ask someone how human babies were born, but for the life of her, she couldn't think how. Her mother was only just beginning to lip-read. Alex was much more accomplished at it, but not so much that he could grasp everything she said yet. Those few times when she had tried to act out her questions about babies for him, he didn't seem to understand. In fact, sometimes Annie got the feeling he didn't *want* to understand. That troubled her and gave her cause to wonder if having a baby wasn't a rather awful experience for the mother. Not that it mattered. She wanted a baby, and if she had to go through a bit of unpleasantness to get one, she was prepared to do whatever was necessary.

Late one afternoon, a time that Annie usually spent with Alex, he received a message requesting his immediate presence down at the stable. Shortly after he left the house, Annie grew bored and, since she'd been allowed more freedom of late to venture outside alone, she decided to take a stroll around the property. In her wandering, she ended up at the stable.

Immediately upon entering, she came to an abrupt stop and tipped her head, held in thrall by a faint sound that broke through the silence that always surrounded her. Since she was so seldom able to detect noise, this was not only a novelty but also a curiosity. It was a shrill sound, unlike anything she could recall ever having heard. Drawn to it, she moved hesitantly through the stable, her footsteps picking up pace slightly as it became louder and easier to follow.

Halfway down the shadowy alleyway that ran through the stable, Annie came to an intersecting corridor. To her left, she saw a bright dome of lantern light, men milling about in its nimbus. Fascinated, she moved toward them. As she drew close enough to see, she realized they were gathered outside a horse stall. Craning her neck to look past them, she saw Alex kneeling beside a prostrate mare inside the enclosure.

The shrill, piercing noise was coming from the horse. The poor animal was screaming, throwing its head, and trying frantically to gain her feet. Alex, face contorted and neck veins bulging, was straining to help the mare stand. During those intervals when the horse fell limp with exhaustion, he stroked her swollen belly and said, over and over, "It'll be okay, girl. It'll be okay."

Following the movements of his hands, Annie noticed that his arms were smeared with blood to his shirt sleeves, which had been shoved back to his elbows. Concern etched the chiseled lines of his dark face, and when she caught a glimpse of his eyes, she saw they were filled with sorrow. Her gaze moved to the horse. Something was terribly wrong with the poor thing, Annie realized. Judging by the blood, she guessed that the mare had been injured somehow.

"Easy, girl. Easy."

Behind Alex, Deiter, the stable master, was wrestling frantically with some sort of pulley contraption that had been attached to the rafters. Annie guessed, by the mechanism's design, that the canvas straps would be fitted around the mare's body so she could be hoisted to her feet.

Her heart aching for the poor mare, Annie drew closer so she could see better. The mare chose that moment to give a powerful lunge, throwing Alex aside as she pushed to her knees. At a shout from Alex—Annie knew he shouted by the way the muscles along his throat grew distended—Deiter abandoned what he was doing and ran to help. With the assistance of both men, the horse staggered to her feet.

Frantic—probably with pain—the mare seemed not to appreciate the help of the men and wheeled about, throwing her head and lashing out at Alex with a forehoof. The stable master, trying to dodge her feet, grabbed for her harness but missed. The animal, in her frenzy to escape, came about yet again, this time turning her hindquarters toward the open stall door.

Annie nearly fainted. The mare's backside was dilated and streaming blood, and from it protruded miniature horse legs, the hooves of which were covered with white stuff that resembled clumps of clabbered milk. A baby . . . The mare was giving birth.

Annie stood paralyzed, her gaze riveted. The mare's sides were heaving and lathered in sweat. Alex grabbed one of the straps hanging from the ceiling and quickly looped it around her girth. When he got the band fastened, he ran to the wall, unhooked a pulley rope, and, leaping high into the air, pulled on it with his entire weight.

As he tied off the hoist, he glanced over his shoulder at Deiter. "Get the foal turned! Hurry, Deiter, or we're going to lose her, goddamn it!"

Provided with a perfect view of the mare's backside, Annie watched in horror as Deiter shoved his arm, clear to the elbow, up inside the mare. *Inside* of her! Black spots swam before Annie's eyes. An awful, rubbery feeling attacked her legs. A baby, the mare was having a baby. A baby that had been growing inside her in a special place. Only it wasn't wonderful, as Alex had told her. It was *horrible*. More horrible than anything Annie might have imagined. The mare was suffering, suffering terribly. And if Alex and Deiter couldn't do something to help her, she was obviously going to die.

A strong hand clamped over Annie's elbow. Blinking to see through the spots that swam in her vision, she looked up into the concerned face of a man she'd never seen. He said something to her, but she was in such a state, she couldn't focus on his mouth.

All she wanted was to get away. From the man. From the stable. From Alex, who had lied to her. Away to someplace safe—someplace where she could hide— someplace where the screams welling within her could be released without anyone hearing.

She whirled and ran, blindly and in a panic, the thought going through her head that maybe, if she ran fast enough, she could escape the fate that nature held in store for her. As she exited the stables, however, all thought of running fled her mind. Her legs felt like melted rubber, wobbly and incapable of bearing her weight. The world around her seemed to be doing a slow, undulating turn, vertically one minute, then shifting on its axis, making her feel as if she were being flipped upside down and then sideways.

And she felt sick, so awfully sick. In the blur of her vision, she saw the house, and she broke into a staggering run toward it. There was a hiding place there. A safe place.

Alex had just finished washing up and was drying his arms when Maddy came tearing into the stable, her green eyes bugged, her face blanched. As she skidded to a stop before him, she began working her mouth, but several seconds passed before any sound came out.

"Annie," she finally managed to cry. "Up in the attic! She's screamin' and carryin' on somethin' awful. Come, Master Alex. Come quick!"

One of the hands, who had washed up just before Alex and stood nearby rebuttoning his shirt, said, "Oh, damn."

Both Maddy and Alex whirled toward him. At their questioning stares, he shrugged. "The missus was in here a little bit ago," he explained, looking shamefaced. "She seemed purty upset when she ran out."

"In here?" Alex barked. "What d'you mean, in here, Parkins? You mean she saw the mare?" At the man's nod, Alex nearly snarled. "Why in God's name didn't you tell me?"

"Well, you was busy. With the mare and all. If I'd've bothered you, we would've lost her for sure."

Alex had an unholy urge to knock the man's teeth down his throat. "My wife is far more important to me than a damned horse, Parkins. She shouldn't have been in here. The minute you saw her, you should have—"

Alex broke off, realizing how futile it was to jump all over the fellow. The damage had already been done. Tossing down the towel he'd been using, he pushed by Maddy and broke into a run for the house.

The instant he entered the hall, Alex heard the screaming. It was like nothing he had ever heard in his life, a horrible, demented wailing that reverberated eerily along the landing and down the stairway. Grasping the banister rail, he swung onto the first step and took the others in flying leaps, his heart slamming like a sledge against his ribs. When he reached the second flight of stairs, the screams seemed louder, more frightening, shrieks one moment, guttural moans the next, the intermittent sobs so deep and tearing that he began to fear Annie might do some serious harm to herself.

Tearing along the third-floor corridor to the west wing. Hitting the narrow, dangerously steep staircase. Falling to one knee. Scrabbling to regain his feet. Alex moved in a blur, scarcely conscious of anything but the screams and his sense of urgency to reach his wife.

He hit the closed attic door as though the barrier of wood wasn't there. Darkness. Objects in his path. What he couldn't leap over, he plowed through, scarcely noticing the pain as sharp projections barked his shins and slammed into his thighs. Annie . . . Dear God. The panic and pain he heard in her cries nearly dropped him to his knees. The mare, he thought wildly. She had seen the mare giving birth. That she had come into the stable, that she had witnessed something so awful, made him feel sick. Physically sick. No pregnant woman should see something like that, least of all someone like Annie.

Alex finally reached the dividing wall that separated her small parlor from the rest of the attic. As he staggered around the partition, Annie's screams came to a sudden stop. The silence was so absolute it seemed deafening, crashing against his ears, resounding. Dimly, he was aware of the rasp of his own breathing.

The fading light of the late autumn afternoon spilled anemically through the dormer windows, doing little to illuminate the room. Alex searched the gloom, trying frantically to locate her. As his eyes grew accustomed to the dimness, he finally spotted her pale oval face. Stepping closer, straining to see, he began to make out her features.

Thinking only to comfort her, he ate up the distance with three strides to where she sat huddled in a corner. "Annie, sweetheart." He grasped her violently shaking shoulders. "Honey . . ."

It hit Alex then. The silence. The sudden and awful silence. Dear God, she was holding her breath. To stop herself from screaming. She was afraid. Of him. She had broken the rule of silence, and now she thought he might punish her.

"Annie, no. Sweetheart, go ahead and cry. I don't care."

In her panicked state, Alex didn't think she was registering anything he said. Her slender body jerked fiercely with suppressed sobs. He stared down at her, helpless to breach the chasm that stretched between them. Deafness. A lifetime of observing rules and being harshly reprimanded when she broke them. Even in the dimness, he could see her pinched little face turning a frightening, dull red. The veins at her temples and along her throat bulged, bluish purple beneath her skin, throbbing and swelling with pressure.

Impotent rage exploded within Alex. He shoved to his feet with such suddenness that his head spun. James Trimble. The goddamned razor strop.

He turned and ran from the attic, taking the narrow, steep staircase as though it weren't there. Almost immediately after his departure from the attic, Annie began to cry again. Bless her heart, she had no way of knowing how loud her screams were.

Nearly blind with tears, he passed through the house, feeling as if he were slogging through waist high molasses, each step an effort, every movement agonizingly slow. Alex hit his study like a man gone mad. The strop.

That damned strop. He couldn't remember where he had put it.

When he reached his desk, he began jerking drawers open with such force that they departed from their runners, spilling the contents onto the floor. Dimly, Alex realized that Maddy had run into the study. As if from a distance, he heard her talking, but he couldn't make out the words. What she was saying didn't matter. Nothing mattered to him at that moment but the girl upstairs.

He finally found the razor strop in the bottom right drawer of the desk. He closed his fist around it and raced past Maddy, never sparing her a glance. Retracing his steps, he returned to the attic. He knew now that Annie would quiet the minute she saw him. That was the *rule*.

Well, he had had it with the Trimbles' idiotic rules, and he was going to show Annie that, once and for all.

When he stepped into her parlor again, she reacted just as she had before, gasping and then holding her breath to stifle any sounds that tried to erupt. Alex strode directly to her wobbly three-legged table. With a violent sweep of his arm, he sent her mismatched collection of china flying. Cups and saucers hit the wall, shattering upon impact, particles and shards ricocheting. He didn't care. He could buy her more china, a whole houseful of it if that would make her happy. But he couldn't buy her another chance at life!

Shaking with rage, Alex slapped the strop across the table's surface. Then he fished his pocketknife from his trousers. With jerky movements, he unfolded the blade, and then he set upon the length of leather in a frenzy, hacking it into pieces, then hacking the pieces into pieces.

"Scream!" he roared at her. "Scream, yell, cry! I don't care, Annie! Do you understand me? I won't punish you for making noise. I will *never* punish you. *Never!*"

Hack, hack, hack! In his frenzy, Alex mutilated the

length of leather until it lay before him in minuscule bits. Then, and only then, did he stop. Tossing down the knife, he planted his hands on the tabletop and hung his head, breathing as though he had run a mile. When he finally looked up, he saw that Annie was still huddled in the corner, her slender arms locked around her knees. Against her breathlessly red face, her gigantic, tear-filled eyes were inky splashes of blue.

Alex held her gaze. "I love you, Annie," he whispered hoarsely, and then he opened his arms to her.

For a moment that seemed to last an eternity, Alex waited, silently praying for a miracle as he hadn't since childhood. Just one little miracle.

"Please . . ." he whispered raggedly. "Come here, Annie love."

With a low, broken cry, she pushed up so suddenly from the floor that she seemed to move in a blur. Then she launched herself at him, plowing into him with the foremost part of her small body, which at this stage of pregnancy happened to be her belly. Afraid she might hurt herself, Alex gave with her weight to lessen the impact and nearly lost his balance in the attempt. Catching her against him, he staggered back a step, then managed to regain his footing.

Annie . . . Her slender arms were hooked around his neck, clinging to him as though she hung off a cliff and he were her only purchase. Her deep, shuddering sobs, which she still stifled against his shoulder, weren't that loud, but they jolted through him. He was just glad she no longer held her breath.

"Oh, God, Annie . . ." Gently, Alex gathered her closer, if indeed that was possible, for she had melted against him like a pat of butter on a hot griddle cake. "Forgive me, sweetheart. Forgive me."

With her face buried in his shoulder, Alex knew she

couldn't know what he was saying, and perhaps that was just as well. Before he could hope to soothe her, he had to calm down himself, and right now, he was far from calm. This was all his fault. He'd had an opportunity to sit down with her once and explain the birth process, and out of some misguided sense of chivalry, he'd shirked the responsibility, telling himself ignorance was bliss.

How wrong he had been. By avoiding the issue, he'd left her vulnerable in a way that no woman should be. Because of him and his stupidity, she was terrified now and in a panic. Senseless and totally unnecessary. If he had only talked to her. All it would have taken to avoid this mess was a little honesty.

Nearly frantic in her attempt to get close to him, she stepped up on the toes of his boots and clung more tightly to his neck. Her weight was so slight that Alex scarcely felt the pressure on his feet. Angling an arm under her rump, he lifted her against him, smiling through tears at how sweet she felt. Annie, big belly and all, was the most precious armful he'd ever held. As he pressed his face against her hair, she let loose with a wail. A terrible, tearing cry that came jaggedly from her chest.

To Alex, the sound was heartbreaking, not a practiced cry designed to gain sympathy, not a delicate sob, carefully measured to seem feminine. This cry came from her soul, raw with pain, ugly in its honesty. Nothing was held back or modulated. Even so, to Alex, it was the most beautiful sound on earth. The very fact that she had dared to utter it was a gift of trust.

That realization brought fresh tears to his eyes. Forgetting her delicate condition, forgetting everything, he tightened his arms around her, acutely conscious of the fragile ladder of her ribs beneath one of his palms, of the narrow span of her shoulders, of her lightness. There wasn't much of her, but somehow, she had filled up his world. To hold her in his arms. To know that she trusted him as she had never trusted anyone else . . .

The gift of Annie . . . Holding her as he was now, Alex could scarcely believe that there had been a time when he had railed against fate, when he had viewed his marriage to her as an obligatory sacrifice to set a wrong right. He had wrongs to rectify, certainly, but they had nothing to do with duty and nothing to do with sacrifice. Loving this girl, being a part of her world, was a blessing.

Bending low, Alex swept her into his arms and carried her to the rocker in one corner of the room. Sinking down on it, he cradled her across his lap, letting her head rest against his arm, not so much so that he could see her face, but so that she might see his. Her eyes, dark with panic, clung almost desperately to his. Until that moment, Alex had intended to talk to her, to explain away what she'd seen in the stables. But that look in her eyes silenced him. Now was not the time for talking. At least not in the conventional way.

Instead, he gathered her close, much as he might have a child, and began to rock her. As he rocked, he whispered words he knew she couldn't hear. But it wasn't what he said that mattered. What Annie needed right now were messages that couldn't be expressed with words, anyway. With a shaking hand, he stroked her hair. Then he pressed his cheek atop her head and closed his eyes, not at all surprised when he felt more tears running down his cheeks. Each one of her sobs cut through him like a knife.

He had felt guilty a few times in his life, but never more so than now. Because he knew she needed to, he allowed her to cry. God knew she deserved that much. When she finally began to quiet, he resettled her in his arms so their faces were only inches apart. ''Annie,'' he said, and hauled in a deep breath, ''I think we need to have a talk. About the baby, and what it will be like when—''

Her eyes going wide with unmistakable dread, she gave her head a violent shake. ''*Naah-ooh!*''

Alex caught her chin in his hand and forced her to look at him. When she finally grew still and he felt he had her full attention, he said, ''Have I ever told you a lie? Ever?''

Almost imperceptibly, she shook her head.

''Then trust me not to lie to you now. Having a baby is *not*''—he stressed the word *not,* saying it slowly and with exaggerated clarity—''like what you saw happening in the stable.''

Her gaze clung to his, filled with questions and disbelief.

Alex swallowed, not looking forward to this conversation, but knowing he had to get through it. Uncertain where to start, he simply began talking. Word for word, he wasn't certain exactly what he said, only that he told her about the foal's breech birth, following up with a description of normal childbirth. He held nothing back and was completely honest, even about the pain of labor. As he explained how the child would exit her body, her eyes grew dark with fear, which caught at his heart but also made him smile.

''Annie love, your mama gave birth to you. Mine gave birth to me. All the living things we see around us were born, and in much the same way that your baby will be born. It may not be pleasant, but you're going to survive it, and I'll be there to help you, I promise.'' He traced a fingertip along the hollow of her cheek. ''It's going to be beautiful, sweetheart, not awful. Trust me on that. And when it's all over, you're going to have a baby all your very own to love.''

At that bit of news, she looked dubious. Alex couldn't help but grin. ''Do you think I'd fib to you?''

When she continued to look doubtful, he said, "Well, it looks to me as if a walk to the stable is in order. Breech birth and all, the mare is fine. And she's the proud mama of the cutest little colt you ever saw." Determined, Alex set her off his lap and pushed to his feet. "I'll prove to you I'm not lying."

She gave her head a vehement shake, clearly frightened at the thought of returning to the stable.

Alex took her hand. "Trust me, Annie. You saw the worst thing an expectant mother can possibly see. Now I want you to see the sweetest."

The last place Annie wanted to go was back to that stable. But Alex insisted, and since he was a good deal larger than she, she had no choice but to comply. To her surprise, darkness had fallen during the time she was indoors. Moonlight and shadows fell across them as they stepped out into the dooryard. As if he sensed her jumpiness, Alex curled an arm around her shoulders and drew her against him as they walked.

His unaccustomed closeness served to distract her from her worries more than anything else he could have done. Where her shoulder pressed against his side, he felt like lightly padded silk over steel. His arm around her felt wonderfully strong and warm. As they moved in unison through the dark garden, it occurred to her that he must be matching his stride to hers, for his legs were longer, by far, than her own. The rotation of his hip bumped against her side at a point well above her waist.

She sneaked a glance at his dark profile, unnerved by him in a way that she'd never felt before, sort of fluttery in the stomach, yet oddly excited. As if he sensed her regard, he looked down, caught her gaze, and smiled one of those slow, slightly crooked grins. "We've never walked together in the moonlight, have we?"

Annie shook her head.

His long fingers shifted where they were curled over her shoulder, and the friction of his touch through the sleeve of her dress made her skin tingle. "We'll have to do it more often. You're beautiful in the moonlight. Absolutely beautiful."

Somehow, Annie doubted that. Though she had not indulged in bouts of weeping very often, the few times that she had, she'd looked awful afterward, all puffy-eyed and red in the face.

As though he guessed her thoughts, he chuckled, the low laugh vibrating into her shoulder and radiating down the length of her arm. "You *are* beautiful, Annie love. Trust me on that. Without question, one of the loveliest young women I've ever had the pleasure of clapping eyes on."

A hot feeling crept slowly up Annie's neck and pooled like fire in her cheeks. She glanced quickly away. She immediately felt his body shift, and the next thing she knew, he'd stooped down and forward to put his face in front of hers. She reared back in startlement, which made him laugh again.

"I'm talking to you, goose. How can you know what I'm saying if you don't look at me?"

As he straightened, Annie followed him with her gaze, about to smile in spite of herself. Since the *last* thing she'd felt like doing a few minutes ago was smile, that gave her pause.

"That's better," he said. "I feel like a damned fool, walking along in the dark, talking to myself."

Her mouth quivered at one corner. He touched a fingertip to the dimple in her cheek. "You also have the most glorious smile I've ever seen, by the way. The kind of smile that drives grown men to make utter fools of themselves."

Annie shook her head. He nodded just as emphatically. Gulping back a giggle, she shook her head harder.

He arched an eyebrow and assumed a disgruntled expression. "My God, our first argument."

At that, Annie lost control. The giggle she'd been swallowing back erupted from her throat. At the sound, Alex spun to a stop. Annie's first thought was instinctive, that he was going to reprimand her. But even in the moonlight, she could see the mischievous twinkle in his eyes.

"Was that a *laugh* I just heard?" Tightening his arm around her shoulders, he drew her gently against him. "Nah! Not my Annie." He studied her for a moment. "You poor girl, you've got the hiccups, don't you? The bane of every expectant mother's existence, chronic indigestion."

Annie giggled again. She couldn't seem to stop herself. And when she did, the most incredible thing happened. Alex's grin vanished, and after gazing down at her for what seemed to her several endless seconds, he got tears in his eyes.

"Thank you," he said. Only that, just a simple "thank you." But to Annie, those were the two most wonderful words she'd ever seen spoken, and they meant more to her than a thousand others might have. With them, he told her a wealth of things, namely that he had meant everything he'd said to her in the attic, that he not only wouldn't punish her for making noise, but that he *wanted* her to.

A wondrously free feeling filled her, a light sensation, almost as if she'd become buoyant. She could trust this man, she realized. With everything. And with his gaze to embolden her, she dared to mouth the words, "*You're welcome.*"

Incredibly, he seemed to read her lips, for his smile deepened. Catching her chin on the edge of his hand, he tipped her face so the moonlight fell across it. "Say it again."

Annie obliged him. As she finished, he slanted his thumb across her lips, his eyes warm with laughter as they delved into hers. "Isn't that just like a woman? Encourage her to talk, and the first thing you know, she's a chatterbox."

With that proclamation, he shook his head and drew her back into a walk. Fixing her gaze on the stables, Annie realized that she no longer felt afraid to go there and see the mare. Even if Alex was wrong, and the horse was in pitiful condition, she could face it.

As long as Alex went with her, she thought she could face almost anything.

When they entered the stable, Annie's courage dwindled. It was so *dark* inside the building. And utterly silent. It was how she imagined death would be, black nothingness. For a few moments, Alex left her standing there in the void alone. She had no idea why, only that he'd left her and she felt as though her skin was going to turn inside out.

Then he was beside her again. Big and muscular and warm. He took her hands and placed them on something made of metal and glass. Annie searched out its contours with her fingers and identified it as a lantern. She smiled slightly at his thoughtfulness. By letting her touch the lamp, he was explaining why he'd left her for a minute.

Clutching his arm, she leaned against him as they walked, wishing he would decide they didn't have to do this, after all. No such luck. He pressed forward, drawing her along beside him in the blackness. When they turned left, she knew they had entered the intersecting corridor and that the mare's stall lay just ahead. Peering futilely

through the blackness, she tried to see Alex's face. She
wanted, no, needed to see him.

As he drew to a stop, he pulled away from her again.
Never in her life had Annie resented her deafness so in-
tensely. It seemed to her that the silence had become a
living thing with cold, clawing fingers that were curling
around her. *Alex?* Oh, God, he had left her. All alone. She
groped a little wildly. Her palm encountered rough wood.

The next instant, light exploded beside her. Startled,
Annie leaped back. Then she saw that Alex had only
struck a match. Amber flickered across his dark face,
making his eyes glow eerily. Lifting the lantern globe, he
touched the flame to the mantle, and a blinding whiteness
flared. Waving the match out, he stuck the hot end in his
mouth to make sure it was dead out before he tossed it
away. After turning the fuel valve to adjust the light, he
hung the lamp from a long nail protruding from a wall
stud above him.

He said something to her. Then, when she didn't react,
he placed his hands on his hips, his weight on one booted
foot, his other leg slightly bent. Clenching the match between his teeth, he spoke again. Because he was talking
through his teeth, Annie had no idea what he was saying,
only that he was getting aggravated because she wasn't
complying. When he started to speak again, she stepped
quickly forward and jerked the match from between his
teeth.

He looked nonplussed for a second and then slowly
grinned. "Oh. Sorry about that."

She lifted an eyebrow.

"I was telling you to take a look and see for yourself."
He inclined his head at the stall. "Mama and baby, safe
and sound."

As Annie turned to look over the gate, he stepped up
behind her and encircled her waist with his strong arms,

one large hand splayed over her swollen stomach, his fingertips lightly caressing. For just an instant, she stiffened, unnerved by the familiarity. But then she felt her tension slipping away under the gentle strokes of his hands. *Alex.* She leaned back against him and closed her eyes, imagining that she felt his strength seeping into her. Against her shoulder, she felt the steady thumping of his heart, a sturdy, soothing rhythm that seemed oddly harmonious with the flutter of her own pulse.

A smile touched her mouth, and, opening her eyes, she looked into the stall. The mare stood in the center of the enclosure, her liquid brown eyes resting curiously on the two humans who had intruded upon her peace. Beside her, his long, gangly legs spread wide for balance, was her colt. Head tucked under his mama's belly, he was eagerly suckling, his small broom of a tail uplifted and making quick little rotations.

Alex leaned forward so she could see him. "See that tail? It's his pump handle. Every time he sucks, his tail goes up and down."

Annie giggled.

"I'm glad you like him. Before winter's over, he'll probably seem like part of the family. He's out of season. Most foals come in the spring, which gives them plenty of time to mature before harsh weather hits. We'll have to pamper this little fellow."

That said, Alex hunched his shoulders to rest his chin beside her ear. Just below her temple, she could feel the slight rasp of whiskers. The scent of bergamot from his shaving cologne filled her senses.

Suddenly, as though disturbed by the unaccustomed weight of his hands, the baby inside her wiggled. Not a little wiggle as she usually felt, but a big one. She jumped with a start, and she felt Alex's chest jerk with a laugh, the deep vibrations of it moving through her like sunshine.

Repositioning his hands, he gently palpitated her hard roundness. The baby accommodated him, shifting to escape the intrusive pressure. Annie felt a warm flush creeping up her neck.

Alex must have felt the heat rising against his cheek, for he leaned around to regard her face with twinkling amber eyes. "Don't be shy, Annie love. This is *my* baby, just as you are mine. Feeling the life inside you is like touching a miracle."

Placing her hands over his, Annie let her eyes fall closed again. For reasons beyond her, being held like this by him felt absolutely right. Wonderfully right. She didn't want to move, never wanted him to take his arms away. Their baby. The sweetness of that nearly brought tears to her eyes again, only this time, tears of happiness.

For a long while, they simply stood there, Annie leaning against him, he supporting her weight. The feeling that filled her was very like the feeling she got when she watched the sunrise, as if God had sent her a song.

As they left the stable, Alex's thoughts were focused entirely on the girl who walked within the circle of his arm. She had made no objection when he told her the baby was his, that she was his. He prayed to God she had no objections. He was in too deep to turn back now. Head over heels in love. Irrevocably so. She had brought joy into his life beyond his wildest dreams, a sweet, wondrous joy that made every breath he took seem worthwhile. Seeing the world through her eyes had given him a new appreciation of it. Newborn foals. Mice in the attic. Waltzing to silent melodies. Drinking tea that didn't exist. She was both child and woman, wrapped up in one, a delightful blend, and he loved both.

To lose her now . . . Just the thought made Alex ache, so he pushed it from his mind. She belonged to him in the eyes of God and man. The child she carried was his. Nothing was ever going to change that. He wouldn't allow it to, because to lose her, now that he had found her, would be to die inside.

Eighteen

The following morning, a wagonload of merchandise was delivered to Montgomery Hall, all of it for Annie. Alex felt like a kid at Christmas as he directed the men through the house to his study, which from now on was going to be a combination study and music room.

When Maddy saw the organ, she raised dubious eyebrows. "Master Alex, are ye sure ye want a noisemaker like that in yer study? How will ye ever be able to concentrate?"

Alex intended to have complete concentration, just not necessarily on his accounts. Weeks ago, he had decided that the way to court his wife was with sound. He'd be damned if he'd put all his lures in another room.

"Where is Annie now?" he asked Maddy.

"Up in the nursery. Drawing again, I think."

Alex smiled, so anxious to show Annie all that he'd bought her that he ran out to the wagon and grabbed a crate of merchandise himself. "We can git it, Mr. Montgomery," one of the men assured him. "This is our job."

"I don't mind helping."

Alex carried the box into his study and set it on his desk. Fishing his knife from his pocket, he cut the binding and tape, then folded the lid back. Ear trumpets. Almost reverently, Alex lifted one from the box. He flashed a grin at Maddy. "Annie's hearing aids! Now I can start her lessons."

"You playin' teacher! Rememberin' yer marks in school, that'll be a sight to see."

"I'm going to teach her the manual alphabet and sign language," Alex pronounced. "Just you watch. I'll be a great tutor. I just didn't want to start until these came." He held up an ear trumpet. "With any luck at all, Maddy, she'll be able to hear with these. Maybe not clearly, but anything will help."

Maddy moved to the desk and took a medium-sized ear trumpet from the box. Peeling away the paper, she inserted the earpiece into her ear. Alex leaned forward and said "hello" into the bell flare. She jumped, jerked the trumpet from her head, and cried, "Blessed Mother!"

Alex laughed and grabbed the horn from her. Putting it to his ear, he said, "Say something to me."

"Ye busted me eardrum!" Maddy nearly shouted.

"*Jeee*-sus Christ!" He rubbed the side of his head, gazing at the trumpet with new respect. "That's amazing. Absolutely amazing."

After the deliverymen left, Alex spent nearly an hour arranging all Annie's instruments about the room. He refrained from trying any of them out, fearful that she might hear the sounds and be drawn to the study before he was ready for her.

Finally, the moment of presentation arrived. So excited to see her face that he could scarcely bear the suspense, Alex took his seat at the organ. With a deep breath and a prayer, he experimentally worked the foot pedals. Then he began to play. Well, not exactly *play*. He hadn't a clue how to make music on the damned thing. But the noise was glorious. Within just a few minutes, the door to his study crashed open and Annie came in, hands folded over her swollen waist, eyes round with wonder.

Alex continued to fill the room with sound, grinning at her over his shoulder. As though mesmerized, she moved toward him, her gaze glued to the organ. When she was finally within arm's reach, she put out a hand, touching the polished wood almost prayerfully. Then she moved closer, running both hands over the organ's surface. The look that came over her face made the organ worth every penny he'd spent on it. Blissful, that was how she looked. Absolutely blissful. Keeping her hands pressed to the wood, she closed her eyes, her rapturous smile so sweet that he ached.

Alex stopped playing, grabbed her hand, and drew her down to the bench. "You play it," he encouraged her.

She folded her hands again and pressed them to her bodice as if she were afraid to touch the keys. Alex clasped her wrists, forced her arms down, and guided her rigid fingers onto the slats of ivory. After catching her eye, he said, "It's yours, Annie. I bought it for you."

She gave him an incredulous look. Then she swung her gaze back to the organ. Chuckling, Alex showed her how to work the thing. Within seconds, she was about to blast him out of the room. He stood back to watch her. Of all the things he might have given her, he realized, the musical instruments had been inspirational.

In the organ, Annie had found a dream come true. That seemed fitting. Since knowing her, she had made some dreams come true for him as well. Impossible dreams. Finding and marrying an angel. Loving someone more than he loved himself. Having a real reason for living.

Until suppertime, Annie stayed in his study, not because he insisted this time, but because nothing could have dragged her away. From the organ, she went to the sleigh bells. From that instrument, she moved on to others.

The house was filled with noise. A rather earsplitting, awful noise, to be sure, but it was made beautiful for Alex by one fact, that Annie could hear some of the chords. He didn't care that she quickly learned how to strike those notes she heard best and repeated them, over and over, over and over. She was having the time of her life.

At mealtime, Alex made her stop playing with the instruments long enough to eat. As they began to partake of the first course, Maddy came in with a pot of tea, which she sat in the middle of the table with a rather loud *plunk*. Alex shot her a questioning glance.

"Is something amiss, Maddy?"

"Eh?"

Alex repeated himself.

Maddy cocked her head. "What's that ye say?"

Convinced she was being sarcastic about all the noise Annie had been making, Alex settled back in his chair, eyeing her with a level gaze. "I don't find this amusing, Maddy."

With a disgruntled frown, the housekeeper poked a finger in one ear, fished about for a moment, and plucked out a ball of cotton. "I'm sorry, Master Alex. I didn't catch that."

Alex stared at the woman for a moment, then threw back his head and barked with laughter. Annie, busily shoveling food into her mouth so she could finish eating and return to the study, never looked up.

The following morning, Alex decided it was high time that he begin Annie's lessons. The instant he tried to act on that decision, however, he found himself with a very unhappy young lady on his hands. Annie, fascinated with all the noisemakers he had provided for her, wanted to do nothing but play with them. When Alex drew her to his desk and made her sit down, she got a mutinous expression on her face and then proceeded to pout. Actually *pout*. His angel, Alex realized, was getting just a little spoiled around her edges.

Drawing up his chair, he sat down beside her and reached for the publications Dr. Muir had procured for him, James S. Brown's *A Vocabulary of Mute Signs* and W. P. Clark's *The Indian Sign Language* which, to Alex's delight, contained about a thousand verbally described entries and related each to the equivalent in American Sign Language, thus making the book a dictionary of both Indian and American sign. In addition to the publications were two carbon copied pamphlets that had been compiled especially for Alex by a woman in Albany who worked extensively with the deaf in a classroom environment.

"Work before play," he told his wife firmly. "It's time you began filling that pretty little head of yours with some knowledge, Annie love."

He opened a publication and began leafing through the pages to locate the manual alphabet. When he glanced back up, Annie had lifted an ear trumpet off his desk and was blowing with all her might into the earpiece. Alex watched her for a moment with an indulgent smile, then he plucked the hearing aid from her hands and poked one end of it in her ear. Holding up his right hand, fingers folded against his palm, thumb extended upward and pressed against them, he leaned forward and boomed into the flare bell, "*A!*"

Annie jumped as though he'd stuck her with a pin and jerked the trumpet from her ear to stare at it. After a moment, she thrust it into her ear again, her expression expectant. Alex realized she thought the trumpet had made the noise all by itself.

"No, no, Annie love. That was me." Elated that she actually seemed to have heard him, Alex made certain she kept it in her ear while he made a great show of putting his mouth to the flare bell. "That was *me*, Annie," he yelled.

She jumped again. But this time she didn't pluck the horn from her ear. Instead she grabbed Alex by the hair of his head and stuffed the lower half of his face into the bell. By this point, he was laughing so hard he couldn't have spoken if he tried. As his mirth subsided, he met her gaze over the bell wire. All urge to laugh left him. Her eyes held more raw emotion than he'd ever seen before. Guarded hope. Disbelief. Wary joy. His chest tightened. Drawing back so she might see his mouth as he spoke, he loudly proclaimed, "I love you."

She stared at him for a moment, tears gathering and sparkling like diamonds in her blue eyes. Then, to his dismay, the tears spilled over her lashes to run in glistening rivulets down her cheeks. As he watched, it seemed to him her entire face began to quiver, first her mouth, then her chin, then the little muscles beneath her eyes. Alex drew back from the trumpet bell. "Honey, don't cry. I thought this would make you happy."

The trumpet went flying as she launched herself into his arms. Shaken by her reaction, he pressed a hand over her back and ran his other through her hair. He felt her body jerk with a sob. Then, as though her heart were breaking, she scrambled out of his arms and ran from the study.

Concerned, Alex followed her upstairs, only to find that she had once again levered the door closed with a chair. And this time, no matter how he tried to tempt her, she wouldn't open it.

Annie sat in the middle of her bed, rocking back and forth, hands covering her face. Holding her breath to stifle her sobs, she wept disconsolately. He *loved* her. He had told her as much the night before last. But until a few moments ago when she'd looked into his eyes as he said the words, she hadn't thought about the consequences of such an attachment—not for herself, but for him.

He loved her. Seeing his expression as he said the words—oh, God! Annie choked on a strangled breath, recalling the sense of helplessness that had filled her when she couldn't say the words back to him.

Half a person, that was she. *Deaf.* Nothing he did, nothing he gave her, could ever change that. *Nothing.* All her life, she'd been shunned by normal people, an outcast wherever she went, unable to make friends, unable to attend church, forbidden even to go to town. Not that she'd really wanted to do any of those things, for doing them only brought her pain. It wasn't any fun to be gaped at and tormented, or to have people whisper about her, thinking she didn't know what they said. She *did* know because, whispers or no, she could read their lips. *There's that Annie Trimble, the dummy. Poor thing. Annie the dummy. Annie the dummy.*

Was that to be her gift to Alex? Nothing but pain? Was that what she wanted to bring into his life? To avoid hurt, she'd been *content* to stay apart from people, *content* to live half a life. For years, she'd understood that half of a life was all that she could expect. But Alex could have so much more. Fresh tears filled Annie's eyes, setting fire to the back of her throat. Alex was *wonderful.* Not just handsome, but gentle and kind as well. He could have any woman he wanted. Annie felt certain that every pretty lady in town would adore being in her shoes, the sole recipient of all his attention. Why should he have to settle for a deaf girl? Not only a deaf girl, but a girl who couldn't even tell him she loved him.

Annie knew what would happen if she let this situation continue. Soon people would start to shun Alex, not over anything he'd done, but because he was associated with her. Before he knew it, he'd have no friends. He wouldn't even be invited to go to people's houses to visit. And no one would want to visit him here because of her. Annie the dummy. All she was good for, all she'd ever be good for, was to give people something to stare at.

Annie had never known anyone quite like Alex. Since she'd come to Montgomery Hall, he had changed her life. She loved him better than she'd ever loved anyone. She couldn't bear to see bad things start happening to him because of her. He needed someone else to love. Someone who could make *him* happy, not the other way around.

Having reached that decision, Annie cried until she was exhausted and had no tears left to shed. Then she contemplated ways in which she might inform Alex of her feelings. He wasn't good enough at lipreading yet for her to communicate with him that way, and trying to act it out would be impossible. Pondering the problem, she suddenly remembered the night he had drawn her a picture to tell her about the baby.

Alex paced. Across the hall. Up the stairs. To the nursery. Then he retraced his steps. Again and again. Then again. Pretty soon, he lost count of how many times he ascended the stairway. Something was horribly wrong. He'd seen it in her eyes. But he couldn't imagine what. He'd thought the ear trumpets would make her wildly happy. Instead she had burst into tears. Why? No matter how Alex circled it, he could find no answer.

When he finally heard the telltale creak of door hinges, he was midway up the staircase, executing what seemed to him the thousandth climb. The slight sound of her opening the door sent him flying up the remainder of the steps. Racing along the hall, he braked to a stop outside her door. Annie stood just inside the room, her small hand on the doorknob, her face as white as milk. By the redness around her eyes, he knew she'd been crying.

Backing up a step, she motioned for him to come in. Alex had a bad feeling about this. She avoided his gaze as he stepped into the room. Then, with a decisive little click, she closed the door behind him. Still not looking at him, she crossed quickly to the table where she picked up a sheet of paper and held it out to him.

"What's this?" Alex closed the distance between them and took the paper in a tense hand. After studying the drawing she'd done, he said, "Annie, this is astounding. You're very talented."

She had sketched their head-and-shoulder likenesses, and her attention to detail was incredible. Aside from the work of professional artists, Alex had never seen such mastery. With nothing but charcoal and paper, she'd brought him to life. He smiled slightly at the expression she'd captured on his face. Did he truly look at her that way, with a rakish grin and a lascivious gleam in his eyes? He supposed he must and couldn't help but marvel that she hadn't slapped him silly a couple of times for the affront. Not that Annie would recognize lecherousness if it ran up and bit her on the behind.

His gaze drifted to her image, which seemed a little off-plumb to him somehow. After studying the likeness for a moment, he realized that she had captured herself on paper much as she probably appeared to herself in a mirror, unsmiling, with no trace of the innocent sweetness or candid expressions that had stolen his heart. The eyes held no emotion or sparkle. No dimple flashed in her cheek. Annie, with no lustrous glow, still beautiful, but a face without any soul.

There was something else that didn't seem quite right. Something missing. But for a moment, he couldn't pinpoint what it was. After studying the drawing awhile longer, Alex finally noted the flaw and looked up at her, his heart in his throat.

Annie had drawn herself without ears.

With a trembling hand, Alex put the drawing back on the table. He was about to speak when she snatched up another and shoved it into his hands. He glanced down and saw another perfectly executed sketch of Annie's face, only it was minus the ears as well as a mouth.

Alex's first instinct was to rip the drawing into tiny pieces and tell her to stop being ridiculous. But the bruised look in her eyes forestalled him. This was very serious business to her, and judging by the pinched tightness of her mouth, calling attention to what she obviously believed were her inadequacies was painful for her. Extremely painful.

Tossing down the drawing, Alex sat on one of the chairs. Patting a knee, he said, "Come here, sweetheart."

She folded her arms under her breasts and shook her head, the stubborn set to her chin making her look more adorable than anything else. Alex also couldn't help noticing that the position of her slender arms was causing an upward thrust of certain parts of her anatomy. The dressmaker, following his explicit instructions, had cut the necklines of her gowns a bit low. Nothing immodest, but low enough to provide a lovely display of her feminine attributes, which had become more generous with her advancing pregnancy. The way Alex saw it, if he couldn't partake of the meal, the least he deserved was an occasional glimpse of the menu.

He patted his knee again. "Come on, honey. I just want to talk with you." That was, without a doubt, the biggest falsehood he'd ever told.

She shook her head and mouthed the words, "*I want to go home.*"

With daily practice, Alex's lipreading skills had improved to a point that he could, with great effort, make out simple sentences. "Home? To your parents, you mean?"

"*Yes.*"

He had only one answer for that. "Absolutely not." Leaning forward, he grasped her wrist and drew her to him. Ignoring her protests, which was rather easy to do since she didn't voice them aloud, he pulled her down onto his knee and curled an arm around her. "This is your home now. You belong here with me."

She jerked her gaze from his lips and stared resolutely at the window. Realizing immediately what her game was, he tugged gently on a curl at her temple. When she still persisted in not looking at him, his mouth quirked at the corners. Catching her by the chin, he forced her face back around to his.

"Annie, I don't care about your being deaf. You're beautiful and warm and funny. Being with you makes me happy as I haven't been in a very long—" Alex saw that she was staring fixedly at his nose. He chuckled in spite of himself. "You little minx. So, it's your plan to ignore me, is it?"

Tweaking the tip of her nose, he succeeded in reclaiming her attention. "I love you," he whispered hoarsely. "If you go away, Annie, you'll break my heart. Is that what you want, to make me sad?"

Shadows of pain shifted in her lovely eyes. Touching a small hand to his jaw, she said, "*I want you to be happy. You can't be with someone like me. You should find someone who can hear, someone who can talk.*"

Following her lips movements, Alex struggled to make sense of the few words he'd been able to make out. The effort gave him cause to appreciate Annie's intelligence. So many of the mouth positions that formed certain sounds looked exactly like those that formed others. Yet

Annie managed to lip-read with amazing adeptness. He knew that to do so she not only had to keep up with the speaker, but had to second guess him half the time to figure out any unclear words.

"Someone else can't make me happy," he assured her when he had finally made sense of what she'd said. "Only you, Annie. So, you see? You can't leave me. If you do, I'll be sad forever."

"*I can't hear. I can't talk. People think I'm an idiot, and they hate me. If I stay with you, they'll hate you, too!*" She made a frustrated little gesture with her hands. "*I want you to be happy. Let me go home.*"

Those last four words were easy enough for Alex to interpret. "No," he shot back. "Never. If you leave, Annie love, I'm leaving with you."

A glisten of tears touched her luminous eyes. She gazed at him for several endless seconds before a smile started to quirk at the corners of her lips. Finally she said,"*You are the stupid one, not me.*"

After stumbling his way through that sentence, Alex grinned. "Stupid, yes. A big, bungling oaf without any sense whatsoever. I guess you'll just have to stay here and look after me."

She rolled her eyes, clearly exasperated with his logic. Or perhaps with his lack of it. "*I can't stay here.*"

He had other ideas, and sliding his hand around to the nape of her neck, he quickly acted upon them, settling his mouth over hers. There were more ways for a man and woman to communicate than simply with words, and he was determined she should learn that lesson before he finished with her. *No mouth?* The girl had a mouth most men would kill for.

Fully expecting her to resist his kisses, Alex tensed his arm at her back, prepared to subdue her until she began to relax. But, to his pleasant surprise, she acquiesced, allowing him to part her lips and touch his tongue to the moist recesses of her mouth.

Dear God. Just that quickly, and Alex was lost. Never had a kiss been so wonderfully sweet. She surrendered to him like a blossom to sunshine, opening, pressing upward, so soft and delicately fragrant that he felt intoxicated. His heart started to pound. His breath became ragged. Tightening his arm around her, he slid his lips from her mouth to her throat. He wanted her. Like embers fanned to a sudden flame, the passion he had so ruthlessly tamped for weeks ignited within him.

At the touch of his lips on her throat, Annie leaned her head back and moaned low in her chest. Alex lifted his free hand to her bodice. The tempting softness of her breast filled his palm. Obviously aroused, she began to breathe in quick, whining little pants. The sound alone was enough to drive Alex half-mad. With a practiced touch, he grazed his thumb across the peak of her breast, delighting in the instant hardening of her nipple. But there were too many layers of cloth. He wanted so badly to feel the silken warmth of her skin that he burned.

The buttons at the front of her bodice were frustratingly small. He fumbled, managing to unfasten one, then two, his sense of urgency mounting. In the back of his mind, he kept expecting Annie to start struggling, and he was prepared to stop himself if she did. But instead she ran her small hands into his hair, her breathing still as fast and irregular as his. Finally Alex slipped the last button free. Gently, his senses electrified with anticipation, he drew the panels back and encountered . . . a chemise.

''Shit.''

He drew back to survey the undergarment, acutely conscious of Annie's blue eyes, large and feverish, on his face. Pleased to find that her chemise had a drawstring neckline instead of damnable buttons, he seized the ribbon and tugged sharply. Instead of pulling free, the strands of satin knotted. Alex clenched his teeth, biting back another curse, knowing, even as he began to untangle the snag, that Annie might regain her senses during the delay and start to panic before he ever got her breasts bared.

Taking a deep breath and giving her what he hoped was a reassuring smile, Alex leaned farther back so he might see better. Then he set upon the knot, so frustrated that it took all his restraint not to rip the chemise off her. *Keep smiling*. After all, it was just a little knot, he told himself. He felt sweat start to bead on his forehead. One *stubborn* knot. He could scarcely believe his miserable luck. The most beautiful girl he'd ever seen was sitting on his knee, not only willing but patiently *waiting* for him to get her clothes off her, and he was fumbling around like a goddamned *idiot*!

Alex glanced up to find that Annie was watching his hands, her beautiful eyes filled with bewildered curiosity, her mouth slightly pursed. She didn't seem in the least afraid, and for that, he was grateful. On the other hand, he wasn't at all sure she knew what he meant to do, either. Whatever Douglas's offenses against her had been, he had clearly not trespassed on her upper torso, at least not in such a fashion that he had left Annie with an aversion to being touched there.

Alex felt a pang of guilt as the knot finally came loose. But he chased it away. The girl was deaf, not dead from the eyebrows down. And at twenty, she was no longer a child. In addition to that, she was his wife. Another man, given the opportunities Alex had had, would have long since consummated the marriage. Besides, it wasn't as if she were struggling. Or frightened. She only seemed curious about what he found so fascinating beneath her chemise.

Alex was more than willing to satisfy her curiosity.

His heart was slamming inside his chest like a threshing machine as he loosened the gathered neckline of the chemise. The white cloth fell loose to underscore her breasts. Milky white globes with swollen pink crests. Reverently, Alex brushed a fingertip across her skin. It was warm and silky, just as he had imagined. He trailed his touch lightly to her nipple, watching the swollen aureole grow pebbled, the peak erect. Annie jumped when he captured the sensitive protrusion between his thumb and forefinger. Her startled eyes flew to his. As he rolled her flesh gently, she made tight fists in his hair and her eyes darkened to a stormy blue, her lashes drifting low over her pupils.

Bending his head, Alex flicked her other nipple with his tongue. She emitted a strangled little cry and arched her back to better accommodate him, her sudden yearning expressed to him in a language as old as womankind. Alex was happy—no, elated—to attend her needs. In fact, he couldn't quite believe that she had surrendered to him so easily and was responding as she was, pressing herself forward, eager for his touch and the ministrations of his mouth.

Taking care not to hurt her, for he guessed her breasts were probably tender, he nibbled the swollen bud of her nipple. When it grew distended and hard, he captured it between his teeth, then started to tease it mercilessly with his tongue. He knew exactly how sharply to nip that sensitive flange of hardened flesh, exactly how hard to suckle it, to drive her beyond reason. With quick, relentless flicks of his tongue, he rasped the responsive tip, making it swell until it throbbed with her every pulsebeat. Then, and only then, did he deliver the killing blow to her senses, tugging hard on her with his teeth.

With the first tug, Annie shrieked. Not a little, whimpering cry. An earsplitting, rafter-shaking shriek. Caught off-guard, Alex was so startled, he jerked back and nearly dumped her on the floor. He might have if she hadn't grabbed him by his ears.

"Annie, hush!" Her head was thrown back and her eyes were closed, so she couldn't see him speaking. "Annie, don't scream." Alex threw a horrified glance at the door, which was unlocked. Clearly frustrated, she wrenched on his ears and arched upward, offering him her breast in a very determined way. "Maddy'll come barging in on us, sure as—"

Her nipple grazed his lips. At the contact, she mewled with urgency and jerked him forward by his ears. "Ah—hhh!" she caterwauled.

"Jesus Christ."

In one fluid motion, Alex pushed up from the chair, lay her atop the table on her back, sending paper and charcoal flying, and clamped a hand over her lips. Then, and only then, did he give her what she wanted. It was the first time in his life that he had ever been *laughing* when he drew a woman's nipple into his mouth.

With the first rasp of his tongue over her crest, Annie shrieked into his palm and twisted on his ears again. Alex decided his ears could take the punishment. In a heartbeat, he could no longer even feel his ears, anyway.

Annie was like a miracle unfolding in his arms. So incredibly sweet, so absolutely guileless. No stranger to women and ways to please them, Alex knew exactly where and how to touch her, and she responded to each new sensation with hungry eagerness and complete trust.

When she was panting and trembling with need, he ran his free hand under her skirt and up her leg. Imagining his goal, the apex of her thighs, he groped for the slit in her bloomers, so eager to run his fingertips over her warm wetness that he was nearly mindless. So mindless that it took him several seconds to realize that Annie had gone rigid and was pushing in earnest against his shoulders. He reared back and fixed passion-glazed eyes on her fearful ones.

Looking into her eyes, slowly registering her reaction, he froze and hauled in a deep breath, trying to get control of himself. Then, with great reluctance, he drew his hand from under her skirt. It seemed that Douglas's ghost was going to haunt them, after all.

"It's all right, sweetheart." Braced on an elbow, Alex leaned a hip against the table and bent his head to kiss her swollen mouth. "Don't be afraid. I won't hurt you."

The tension slowly eased from her body. The fear slipped from her eyes. Lying there on the table, her lovely breasts bared and only inches from his lips, she tempted Alex in a way no woman ever had, and he congratulated himself on his almost saintly forbearance. Remembering how the little minx had nearly yanked his ears off, he gave her a heavy-lidded, satisfied smile, confident that the moment would come, and soon, when she wouldn't call a halt to their lovemaking. All he needed was patience and other opportunities to arouse her.

He started to push up. At his movement, Annie grabbed the front of his shirt and held fast. He arched a questioning brow. "What, sweet?"

She silently whispered something, but in his feverish state of unsatisfied passion, he had difficulty concentrating on her lip movements. "What?"

Her eyes darkened to a cloudy gray blue. Then she brushed her fingertips over her nipple and dimpled a cheek at him. Alex's gaze shot to her breast. As he watched her tease her own nipple erect, he felt a certain part of himself getting painfully more erect as well.

"Annie, no," he said hoarsely.

She tugged urgently on his shirt.

"I can't," he said with a ragged laugh. "You don't know what you're asking."

She pouted her lips and looped her arms around his neck. "*Please?*"

Grabbing her above the elbows, Alex hauled her up to a sitting position, pretending he didn't understand. It was a lie, of course. But the way he saw it, all sin was relative, and it was better that he lie to her by omission than risk becoming so aroused that he lost control. To force himself on her would be unforgivable and cause irreparable damage. She was only just now starting to trust him.

With trembling hands, Alex groped for her chemise ribbons, which was no easy task with Annie's slender fingers running interference. He glanced down to see what she was doing and nearly groaned when he realized she was lightly tweaking the swollen peaks of her breasts. Jerking his gaze back to her face, he took measure of her expression, which was drawn taut with desire, her eyes heavy-lidded and dark with need.

"Christ!"

He caught her wrists and drew her hands away. He had clearly opened a Pandora's box, he decided, and set himself to the task of putting his treasures back where he had found them. As he tightened the drawstring of her chemise and drew a bow, she sighed resignedly.

"You liked that, did you?" he couldn't resist asking.

She smiled an angelic little smile and nodded. Alex drew her bodice together and began fastening buttons as though his life hung in the balance. "Well, we'll have to do it again sometime," he said in an oddly twangy voice.

She nodded again. He grinned and met her gaze as he worked the last button into its hole. "Next time, don't ask me to stop, and I'll show you how nice the other things can feel."

A troubled frown drew her delicate brows together. Alex bent to kiss the wrinkles away. When he straightened, he rasped the back of his knuckle across her lower lip. "Trust me, Annie. What I would have done if you hadn't stopped me would have felt a hundred times nicer." When she looked unconvinced, he said, "Maybe even a *thousand* times nicer." She still looked dubious. He studied her for a long moment, and then he said in a monotone, "You can't count."

She whispered, "*I can so!*" Then she promptly held up a fist and began unfurling her fingers, one at a time. "*One—two—three—*"

Alex closed a hand over hers, laughing in spite of himself. "Never mind, you've convinced me. How high can you go?"

"*Forty*," she informed him proudly. "*No mistakes.*"

"Forty? As high as that?" He considered that for a moment. Then, determined to explain things in terms she could grasp, he said, "What we just did? It was"—he held up a finger—"one nice feeling. But what we could have done?" He held up all ten fingers, then folded and unfolded them three times in quick succession. "What we *could* have done if you hadn't made me stop would have been *forty* nice feelings."

She narrowed her eyes suspiciously.

"Seriously. Lots and lots of *very* nice feelings," he assured her. Bracing the heels of his hands against the table on either side of her, he brought his face within inches of hers. "And let me tell you, sweetheart, if the time comes when you want more of *that*, I'll oblige you, anyplace, any time."

She wrinkled her nose, which set him to laughing again. Then he caught her chin on the edge of his finger and tipped her face up. "As for your going home, forget it. I love you, Annie. It doesn't matter to me that you can't hear. Not a whit. Understand? And as for your not being able to talk, you'll learn because I'm going to teach you."

She looked troubled by that pronouncement.

"Until you can talk," he whispered, "you have a beautiful mouth, and I can think of dozens of nice uses for it besides talking."

With that, he settled his lips over hers to prove his point.

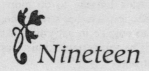

Nineteen

For Alex, the word *courtship* took on new meaning
over the next few weeks. Instead of wooing Annie with
softly spoken words of love, he made cacophonous music.
Instead of writing her romantic poems, he drew letters for
her and painstakingly tried to teach her the manual alphabet. Instead of entertaining her with brilliant conversation,
he stuck a horn in her ear and yelled, or he fixed one eye
on a book and, as he read, awkwardly tried to execute
signs according to the instructions.

In the beginning, Annie was an unreceptive pupil.
While he was in a sweat, trying to make a sign perfectly,
he would glance up and discover that her attention had
drifted to the window behind him or that she was eyeing
one of her noisemakers with abject yearning. On occasion,
he even caught her looking at *him* with the same longing,
which played havoc with his nerves. Since that day in the
nursery, he had initiated no more embraces, not because
he didn't want to hold her in his arms, but because he
feared he might lose control if he became too highly
aroused.

Annie had no such concern, apparently. To her, the
foreplay they had engaged in had been a highly pleasur-

able experience, and she obviously made no connection between their doing that and Alex longing to do more. Unfortunately, there *was* a connection, a rather strong one, and Alex was determined not to engage in activities that might get out of hand. Not until he felt certain Annie was ready to consummate their marriage.

One morning in the middle of a lesson on the manual alphabet, Alex glanced up from the instructional guide to find Annie leaning across his desk, her weight resting in equal part upon her elbows and her swollen stomach. Her mischievous grin and the sultry gray cast to her eyes set his heart to thudding.

"Annie, we're supposed to be working," he said sternly.

The dimple in her cheek deepened, and as she gazed at his mouth, he got the distinct impression she was thinking about other things besides lipreading. Lifting one hand to her bodice, she toyed with her buttons, then lifted her darkened gaze to his, her smile filled with unmistakable invitation. Jerking his eyes from hers, Alex started leafing almost frantically through the pages of the book. The little minx scooted closer.

"Annie . . ." He glanced up. "Please get off my desk. You're going to scatter my papers everywh—" His gaze dropped like a rock to her slender fingers, which had moved from the line of small buttons on her bodice to the crest of her breast. Through the layers of her clothing, she was lightly stroking herself. Alex could see her nipple thrusting against the material, a sharp little peak that beckoned to him irresistibly. "Annie, don't. That isn't—"

She smiled and caught her bottom lip in her teeth.

Alex shoved up from his chair and took a turn before the window. "You mustn't—" He couldn't keep his eyes off her hand and what she was doing. His guts knotted painfully. It was on the tip of his tongue to tell her that such behavior was unladylike, but in truth, as long as she only did such things when they were alone, he didn't find it objectionable. Far from it. "Don't ever do that in front of other people," he amended hoarsely. "Not in front of Maddy or anyone. You understand?"

She nodded. Alex dragged in a shaky breath. "As for doing it in front of me," he went on, "you have to understand that *if* I should take you up on your offer, I'll want to do the other things we talked about. Last time, when I tried, you grew frightened. Unless you've had a change of heart, then I'd suggest you stop"—he swallowed, hard—"issuing me the invitation."

She stood up so suddenly that he felt sure it made her head spin. Watching her sultry expression change to one of wariness, he gave a halfhearted smile. "Somehow, I was afraid that would be your reaction." He glanced at her bodice. "Which is a shame. Making love to you is one of the few activities I'd deem worthy of interrupting our lessons. As I explained before, it's extremely pleasurable."

She promptly sat down and looked pointedly at the lesson book. Alex chuckled and resumed his seat as well. Ignoring her resigned expression, he relocated his place in the manual. Five minutes later, Annie was yawning and gazing out the window again.

Alex began to despair that he would ever be able to impart to her the importance of what he was trying to teach her, that if she would only pay attention, a whole new world could be opened up to her. Then one morning, quite by accident, he hit upon the strategy of teaching her signs that were meaningful to her. Midway through their lesson, which had thus far inspired Annie to do nothing but fidget, Alex glanced over and saw her gazing with longing at her organ.

Capturing her attention with a wave of his hand, he

said, ''Would you like to play the organ, Annie?''

''*Yes!*'' she said, and pushed eagerly up from her chair.

''Not so fast,'' Alex said, feeling more than a little out of sorts with her. ''First you must ask permission.''

''*Please?*''

He shook his head and tapped the book. ''In sign.''

She shrugged helplessly. ''*I don't know the sign.*''

Nearly as accomplished at lipreading now as she, Alex hooked an arm over the back of his chair and fixed a challenging gaze on her. ''Then you'll just have to learn it, won't you? It's either that or give up playing the instruments. From now on, unless you ask permission in sign, you can't play them.''

Her eyes widened with incredulity. Alex grinned at her and began flipping pages. He located the sign he was looking for. ''*Make.*'' He placed his right fist upon his left and made a twisting motion as though he were unscrewing something. ''*Music.*'' He waved the flat of his right hand from left to right in front of his flattened left hand, palm facing right. ''*Please.*'' Smiling, he made a counterclockwise circle with the flat of his right hand over his heart. ''That's all there is to it.'' Making the signs again, this time more rapidly, with no hesitation between, he repeated the words, ''*Make music, please?*'' Settling back in his chair, he eyed her with lazy arrogance. ''Now, you do it. Or forget playing the organ today. Your choice.''

Mouthing the word, *make*, Annie stacked her fists and gave a pretend twist. As she said, *music*, Alex guided her through the hand movements. The only mistake she made signing the word *please* was going clockwise as she circled the flat of her hand over her heart. He corrected her error.

''Now do it with no help,'' he challenged.

Frowning in concentration, she executed the sign again,

this time perfectly and without his assistance.

"Very good, Annie! Perfect!" Alex slapped the book closed and glanced at his watch. "For that, you deserve a ten-minute break."

To his surprise, she didn't immediately move from her chair. Swinging his gaze back to her, he arched an eyebrow. "Don't you want to play the organ?"

She nodded, but her expression said otherwise. In her eyes he saw a certain guardedness, but he also saw yearning. "What, sweet?"

She inclined her head at the book. "*Is there a sign for love?*"

Alex's chest tightened. "I'm sure there is." Feigning a nonchalance he was far from feeling, he reopened the book. "Let me see. Ah, here it is." He crossed his hands over his heart, palms toward his chest. "Love. That's a simple one."

She leaned slightly forward, looking frustrated. "*Is there a sign for 'I love you'?*"

"That's simple as well. To speak in sign, you string the signs together much as you do with words. To say 'I love you,' you first make the sign for *I*." To demonstrate, he placed his folded right hand against his sternum, palm facing left, thumb touching his chest, little finger thrust upward. "Then you make the sign for *love*, which you just learned." He showed her the sign a second time. "Then you make the sign for *you*." With a slow grin, he pointed the index finger of his right hand at her. "And I do love you, by the way."

Her cheeks turned a pretty pink, and she averted her face. Alex waited, expectant, filled with yearning, wanting her to tell him she loved him in sign more than he could recall ever having wanted anything. He waited in vain. After a moment, Annie pushed up from her chair and wandered to the organ. A few seconds later, the room was filled with deafening noise.

The cacophony lasted for only a few minutes, however, before Annie pushed up from the bench and wandered back to Alex's desk, her gaze fixed curiously on the book that lay beside him. Toying with the lace at her neckline, she finally looked into his eyes. "*How do you say 'Alex'?*" she asked.

He shoved his account book aside. "There aren't any signs for most names. They have to be spelled out." Grabbing another book, he flipped it open to the section that contained the manual alphabet. Slowly, so she could absorb the hand positions, he spelled out his name, saying each letter as he made the sign for it. "A—L—E—X."

Annie sat down across from him, her attention shifting rapidly from his hand to his mouth, her expression intent. Then she duplicated the hand motions and smiled at her accomplishment. "*Alex!*" she cried, looking inordinately pleased. "*I spelled Alex!*"

"You certainly did! But, Annie, that's only a beginning. With the manual alphabet, which is simply a collection of signs for the regular alphabet, you can learn to spell every word in our language. Did you know that? Once you've memorized the alphabet, you'll be able to master reading." At her uncomprehending look, he gestured toward his bookshelves. "Books, Annie. You'll be able to read books. There are wonderful stories in some of them, about exciting people and faraway places."

She glanced at the book-filled shelves. "*Me? I can learn to read?*"

"You certainly can. You're a very intelligent young woman."

She made a face, clearly unconvinced she was even halfway smart. "*Stupid,*" she said. "*Mama says I'm stupid.*"

Alex sighed. "You are *not* stupid. Trust me on that. And your mama doesn't say that you are. Not anymore. I'm not saying it'll be easy, but if you pay attention during lessons and work very, very hard, you can learn to read, Annie. And you can learn to write as well."

Looking suddenly purposeful, she folded her arms and sat perfectly erect. "*Teach me, then.*"

He chuckled. "Well, we won't accomplish it this morning. We can only make a start."

"*Teach me!*" she repeated. "*Please?*" And to Alex's delight, she made the sign for *please* as she mouthed the last word.

Trying not to reveal his sense of victory, Alex set himself to the task of doing just that.

Learning to speak in sign . . . It was the most difficult thing Annie had ever tried to accomplish, but it was also the most fascinating. Under orders from Alex, her mother and everyone at Montgomery Hall began studying the manual alphabet so Annie would one day be able to communicate with them. To that end, they all studied the alphabet at least one hour every day. Henry and Deiter, neither of whom could read or write, were the only individuals in his employ who were excused.

Within two weeks, Edie Trimble, Annie, and everyone who lived at Montgomery Hall had memorized the manual alphabet. Once that was accomplished, Alex compiled a list of words he insisted Annie learn to spell before she advanced any further in her lessons: sick, help, hot, cold, drink, eat, and Alex, the last because he alone could read lips and, if summoned, would be able to understand what she needed if no one else could.

It was a heady feeling for Annie the first time she entered the kitchen and was able to ask for a drink. The maid to whom she spelled out the word immediately understood and drew her a glass of water. It was the first time in over fourteen years that Annie had been able to ask anyone for anything. After drinking the water, she left the kitchen, sought privacy in the nursery, and wept. To speak, even if it was with her hands, was to her a priceless gift.

Thinking back to her early days at Montgomery Hall, Annie remembered how angry she had felt when she first learned that she was married. She had believed then that she had received no gifts on her wedding day and had felt cheated. Now she realized she had been given a priceless gift, a tall, tawny-haired man with amber eyes and a lazy grin. He was, without question, a maker of miracles. Knowing him had altered her world in so many ways that she could no longer even count them.

Loving him as she did put her in a difficult position. On three different occasions, he had expressed, ever so clearly, his desire to be *close* with her, not just by kissing and touching her bubbies, which she'd found delightful, but down below as well, as his brother Douglas had once done. Annie couldn't bear the thought of letting anyone, not even Alex, do that to her again.

But he wanted to. Lately, she sensed that whenever she was with him. The message was there in his eyes when he looked at her, in his hands when he touched her, and it was always in the air between them, a heavy, expectant feeling.

The most difficult part was that Annie wasn't entirely certain that being close with Alex would be so terrible. That day when he had touched her and kissed her in the nursery, it had been glorious, and because it had, she couldn't help wondering if the other things he wanted to do would be delightful as well. According to Alex, they would be, and as far as Annie knew, he had never lied to her.

What a quandary . . . She wanted to make Alex as happy as he had made her, and she sensed that he would be very happy indeed if she would let him put his hand under her skirt. The question was, could she bear it once she let him? Annie didn't know, and because she didn't, she procrastinated about reaching a decision, one way or another.

September gave way to October, October to November—Annie knew the names of the months now because Alex had made her memorize them—and the days grew increasingly chilly. When the last cutting of hay had been baled, Alex spent less time working, and more time with Annie. On some afternoons, he bundled her up in a cloak he'd had made for her and took her for long walks. On others, they stayed in his study by a warm fire and engaged in pleasant pastimes, sometimes playing games, other times simply talking. He had become very accomplished at lipreading, and both of them were becoming fluent in sign language.

One afternoon, he asked her, "If you could name one thing that you want more than anything else, Annie, what would it be?"

Annie gnawed her lip. Alex had given her so much. So very much. It seemed ungrateful to admit there was anything else she still yearned for.

"Come on. This is a time for honesty." Sitting close to the fire as he was, the golden light from the flames played over his dark face and flickered in shadows across his cream silk shirt, which complemented his broad shoulders. His gaze searched hers. "Jewelry?"

She laughed and shook her head. "*No, not jewelry. Where would I wear it?*"

"You'd like to go to town," he guessed. When she shook her head, he said, "To a dance, then?"

"*There's nothing I really want,*" she fibbed.

"Annie . . ." he said in a scolding way. "Tell me."

Already loving the child within her, Annie pressed her hands over her stomach and drew up her shoulders in a shrug. "*When the baby comes, I probably won't even want one anymore.*"

"What difference does that make? Tell me."

"*A dog.*"

He narrowed an eye. "A dog? They're big, hairy, drooling, and ill-mannered. Why on *earth* would you want a dog?"

She shrugged again. "*I don't know. I just always wished for one.*"

He shook his head and gazed into the fire for a moment. When he glanced back at her, she asked, "*And you? If you could name one thing you really, really want, what would it be?*"

His gaze delved deeply into hers. "You won't like my answer."

She rolled her eyes. "*That isn't fair. I told you.*"

He didn't release her gaze. "I want you."

Annie felt a flush sliding up her neck.

"In my arms, in my bed," he said. "I want to make love to you, Annie. I want that more than anything in the world." His gaze touched on her swollen waist, then returned to her eyes. "I love you. And I love our baby. I want us to be a real family." His eyes ached with yearning. "All my life, I've been alone. Until you came, I didn't realize how empty I felt. Now you and the baby are bringing about changes. Good changes. Maybe it's greedy, but I'm like a kid in a candy shop. I want it all. Does that make sense? A real marriage, you in my arms when I go to sleep at night and wake up in the morning."

She finally managed to jerk her gaze from his and stared into the flames. She jumped when he touched her cheek to draw her face back around.

"I know you're frightened," he whispered. "And I don't blame you for that. But I think I've earned your trust, if nothing else, so will you at least think about it?"

Her face felt as though it had been smeared with egg white.

"I'll make you a promise," he told her. "If you'll trust me enough to let me try, I won't do anything you don't want me to do. And if you ask me to stop, I swear I will."

Annie could scarcely bear looking into his eyes. In them, all she saw was love for her. How could she possibly deny him the one thing he had ever asked of her?

"As I said, just think about it. There's no need to give me an answer right now. Will you do that? Think about it?"

She nodded.

He rewarded her with a slow smile. "While you're thinking about it, think about how nice it was that day in the nursery. I guarantee you that what comes after is even better."

Annie wished she could be certain of that. Oh, how she wished she could be certain.

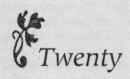

Twenty

A sound jerked Alex from a deep sleep. Momentarily disoriented, he rolled onto his side and gazed through the darkness. Blessed with good night vision, he had little difficulty seeing even on a moonless night, which tonight definitely was not. Silver light bathed his bedchamber, pooling on the floor before the armoire and casting dappled shadows over his dresser.

Annie . . . Remembering their talk that afternoon, he allowed himself to hope she might be sneaking into his room. His heart sank when he glanced at the door and saw that it was firmly closed. Not Annie. He frowned slightly and pushed up on an elbow, trying to estimate the time. Midnight, perhaps a bit later, he decided. He didn't feel as though he'd been sleeping very long.

The sound that had disturbed his rest came again, a muted thumping and rattling from somewhere downstairs. Slipping from bed, he bypassed his robe in favor of trousers and boots. In the event that he had to confront an intruder, he wanted to be halfway prepared. Not that he believed someone had broken into the house. He'd lived at Montgomery Hall since birth, and never in all those years had there been any trouble. The people in and around Hooperville were a wholesome, God-fearing lot, and crime was almost nonexistent. Douglas had been the most frequent perpetrator of foul deeds hereabouts, and now he was gone.

Douglas . . . Alex's pulse quickened. Then he discarded the thought. For all his faults, his brother was no fool. No, it was probably one of the servants, he decided. Sometimes Frederick had trouble sleeping and rattled around in the kitchen during the wee hours to heat himself some milk.

En route down the hall, Alex made a quick stop at the nursery to be certain Annie was all right. Walking lightly, he approached her bed, assured himself she was sound asleep, then retraced his steps, quietly closing the door as he went back out into the hall.

The steps on the stairway creaked under his weight as he crept downstairs. During the day, Alex never noticed the noise, and he made a mental note to have a carpenter check the stairwell supports. A place the size of Montgomery Hall required constant maintenance.

As he gained the hall, Alex froze. Something about the sounds he heard raised gooseflesh along his arms. It wasn't the haphazard rattling about that one would expect from a servant. It was more a stealthy sound, as if someone were searching for something and desperately afraid of being heard. Alex followed the noise to the dining room.

Pushing open the door, he stepped inside. Enough moonlight came in through the partially draped French windows to illuminate the room, which made lighting a lamp unnecessary. A man hunkered before the sideboard. Beside him on the floor rested a white bag, into which he was stuffing objects he withdrew from the cabinets. Recognizing him instantly by the tawny cast of his hair, Alex wasn't certain which emotion was stronger within him,

anger or sadness. After loving his brother so long and so
well, it was no easy task to completely despise him, no
matter what he had done.

"Douglas," he finally said, "what the hell are you doing?"

His brother withdrew from the cupboard so abruptly he
cracked his head. Swearing under his breath, he clamped
a hand over the smarting spot. "Alex?"

"Who do you suppose?" Alex folded his arms over his
bare chest. "You should probably wrap the crystal in
something. The good linen, perhaps? Clattering around in
that bag, some of the pieces may get chipped."

"What crystal? A few pieces, and that's it. And hardly
any silver. I swear Alex, for a man of means, you spare
pitifully few coins for finery."

"I apologize. How shortsighted and inconsiderate of
me."

Douglas pushed to his feet. After standing there for a
second, looking defiant, he rubbed his nose with his
sleeve. "As you have probably guessed, I've met with
financial difficulties."

An ache filled Alex's chest. If only his brother would
beg for forgiveness and promise to straighten up. If he'd
just reveal some sign of guilt or—Alex cut the thought
short. It was a path he had walked a thousand times, and
he knew where it would end. The heartbreak of it was
that, regardless, he wanted and needed to forgive him.
This was his brother, not some stranger. He had told him
bedtime stories when he was small, taught him to ride his
first horse, watched him grow to manhood. To forget all
that, to pretend it had never happened, was impossible.

"If you need some money, Douglas, I have some loose
cash in the safe," he offered gruffly.

"You'd give it to me? When I saw that you'd changed
the safe—well, I figured it was because—"

''I might be afraid you'd sneak in and steal me blind?'' Alex finished for him.

Douglas had the good grace to look a little shamefaced. ''I would've taken only enough to get by.''

Alex was tempted to say that he also believed pigs could fly. But his brother's lack of compunction was beside the point. Not that he was entirely sure what the point *was*. Aside from the fact that he was a fool, of course. Where Douglas was concerned, it seemed he always would be. Since the day of their father's death, Alex had been trying to atone for the loss, never able to forget, even for a moment, that he was responsible. Guilt had a way of grabbing hold of a man and never letting go.

He sighed and thought fleetingly of Annie. Loving her as he did, it was wrong to give Douglas anything. *Wrong*. If she saw his brother in this house, Alex doubted she would ever forgive him, and he wouldn't blame her. Douglas had raped her, cruelly, consciencelessly. To help him in any way was a betrayal of the worst kind, and Alex knew it. On the other hand, he couldn't hate his own brother so much that he would see him beggared and starving.

''Come to the study. I'll give you some cash and a bank draft. Then I want you out of here, Douglas.'' Hearing a slight clatter, Alex turned back from the doors in amazement. ''Leave the silver, for Christ's sake. I said I'd give you some money.''

Praying that Annie, with her uncanny ability to detect vibrations in the floor, wouldn't awaken and wander out to the landing to see who was there, Alex hustled his brother through the hall and into his study. Closing the doors, he wasted no time in approaching the safe. As he turned the dial, taking care to conceal its face, he heard Douglas's weight settle onto one of the leather chairs.

''Don't get comfortable.''

Douglas laughed. "Oh, yes. I don't suppose your little wife would like it too well if she found me here. I understand, Alex. All men have their priorities. It's obvious what yours are."

The door to the safe swung open at just that moment. His body suddenly rigid, Alex turned and asked in a deceptively calm voice, "Just what the hell does that mean?"

"Nothing! Don't be so touchy." In the moonlight, Douglas's face seemed featureless from across the room. He finger combed his hair and stood up. Strolling casually to the mantel, he lit a lamp, then turned to survey his surroundings. "Lord, how I've missed this study. I'll bet I've imagined being here a dozen times. When did you get the organ?"

"Only recently."

Taking in the other instruments, he said, "Developing an interest in music, are you?"

"You might say that."

Douglas trailed his fingertips over the small table that sat between the two chairs before the hearth. "Do you remember all the times I beat you at chess, sitting right here before this fireplace?"

"I remember how often you cheated."

Douglas chuckled. "That, too. Moving the pieces when your head was turned was the only way I could win." A moment of silence ensued. Then he added, "Those were good days."

"Those days are over, and it's entirely your own fault that they are." Alex took the small packet of money from the safe. Crossing to his desk, he said, "I'm going to write you a sizable bank draft. Handle it wisely. Once this is gone, you'll get nothing more. I never want to see you here again. Is that clear?"

There was an echo in those words. With relentless clarity, Alex could recall saying them to Douglas once before and believing with all his heart that he meant them. Now here he stood, handing over more funds. It made no sense, not even to him, and yet he felt powerless to do otherwise. He pictured himself, a dozen years from now, reenacting this same scene for the dozenth time, mocking himself for repeating the same meaningless words.

Douglas leaned a shoulder against the rock face of the fireplace. "Jesus, Alex, I *am* your brother. I realize I committed a grave sin by raping the girl. If I had it to do over again, I wouldn't. But I can't undo the past. Haven't you got it in your heart to forgive me?"

Alex looked up from the draft he was signing. "Unfortunately, yes. But I've always been a fool where you're concerned, haven't I? Do you know that I sometimes lie awake until nearly dawn, asking myself what I did wrong in raising you? Blaming myself. If I had been sterner, stricter, if I had kicked your ass from here to hell and back a few times, would you have turned out differently?"

"You did a fine job of raising me," Douglas assured him. "I just did something stupid, that's all. It wasn't your fault. Maybe it wasn't even mine. I was drunk. Not thinking straight. It just happened, Alex. Before I knew what I was doing. You know how I get when I drink. Mean as a snake. I admit it."

Knowing where his brother was headed, Alex said, "Douglas, don't. A pretty speech can't make everything better between us, not this time. You'll only succeed in making it worse."

"Worse?" His brother moved a step away from the hearth, his hands uplifted imploringly. "At least *listen* to me. I've lain awake at night, too. Feeling bad. Not just over what I did to the girl, but for disappointing you. Please, give me one more chance. Just one more. I've sworn off drinking. I haven't touched a drop since I left.''

"Oh? And what was that I smelled on your breath in the dining room? Tea?''

"It's freezing out tonight. I took one little nip to stay warm, that's all. One little nip.''

Alex shook his head. "Was I really such a fool that you can stand there now and actually expect me to *believe* this horseshit?'' He raked a hand through his hair. "You're right, you know. I think liquor is three-fourths of your problem, that when you drink, you do things you'd never do otherwise. Unfortunately, the other fourth of your problem is that you will always be able to justify taking just one little nip. And then another. And then another. Lie to yourself if you must, but not to me.''

"Alex, please. Give me another chance. Just one, and I'll never ask again. I swear, this time I won't mess it up. I won't so much as *touch* the whiskey. I *won't*. Not for any reason, not ever!''

With grim determination, Alex resumed writing the draft. "I can't do that, Douglas, and you know it. It isn't just myself I have to think about now. I have a wife. I owe her my loyalty, first and foremost. Quit drinking, if you can. Straighten out your life, if you can. But do it away from Montgomery Hall.''

Douglas straightened his jacket, a heavy wool garment that had seen better days. "Ah, yes. Your wife. Abbie, isn't that her name?''

"Annie.''

"Right. Annie. How could I forget? Although I must admit, the most memorable thing about her was her legs.''

"Don't,'' Alex warned him softly. "I have very few fond memories left of you. Don't destroy them by lashing out.''

"Lashing out?'' Douglas said bitterly. "You're turning your back on me. I'm your brother, for Christ's sake.''

Alex's stomach did a slow revolution. He quickly finished filling out the draft, ripped it from the book, and slid it across the desk. "There you are. Take it and get out."

Douglas walked slowly to the desk. He picked up the draft, folded it precisely into thirds, and slipped it into the breast pocket of his jacket. Their gazes met, amber striking amber. Alex had seen that look in his brother's eyes before and knew it portended some form of retaliation. No big surprise. When Douglas didn't get his own way, when Alex denied him anything, he always retaliated.

Smiling slowly, Douglas said, "Annie . . . Nice little ass, if I remember right. Are you enjoying your little idiot, Alex? When I plowed her, you called it rape. When you do, I suppose it's a noble sacrifice. Good old Alex, cleaning up his brother's messes. What a cross for you to bear."

Alex braced his weight on his hands, which had suddenly formed fists. It always came to this, he realized. Staring at Douglas, trying to understand him, and running facefirst into a brick wall. Some things were beyond understanding. "Don't," he said again, knowing even as he spoke that Douglas would have his pound of flesh before he left. That was his way. It always had been.

"Don't what? Confront you with the bald truth?" His eyes aglitter, Douglas said, "You're pathetic, you know that?" He indicated the well-appointed study with a sweep of his hand. "What if the brat she whelps is a girl, Alex? Ever thought of that? Being half a man like you are, how will you sire a son? Or don't you want a male heir?"

Alex couldn't speak. And even if he had been able to, there were no words.

"At least with me around, you might get another brat or two out of her. Or maybe you're just too selfish to share that sweet little honeypot of hers. I'll bet you've been wetting your nose in it every night since you married her.''

Alex had started to shake. A horrible shaking.

Douglas smiled. ''Or are you one of those men who prefers that particular service to be rendered? I can almost see you, a snifter of brandy in one hand, the other holding her by the hair of her head to show her how you like your—''

Alex planted his fist squarely in his brother's mouth. Just that quickly. Without forethought, without intent. He simply hit him, throwing all his weight into the blow. With a startled look on his face, Douglas staggered backward. Scarcely realizing he moved, Alex vaulted over the desk after him. In a flurry of motion, the two of them collided and hit the floor rolling. Gaining the advantage, Alex sprang to his feet, drew back a leg, and buried a boot in his brother's midsection. Then he grabbed him by the hair of his head and jerked him to his feet.

While pummeling his face, he roared, ''You *miserable* little sack of shit! You aren't fit to kiss that girl's feet, let alone speak her name!''

To Alex, time seemed to move as slowly as a fly crawling over tacky paper. Each time he drew back his fist, it seemed to him he moved a fraction of an inch at a time. He was out of control, and he knew it. His brother's face was turning to a bloody pulp under the punishment of his knuckles. If he didn't stop, he'd kill him. But his conscience seemed to have taken leave. The next thing he knew, he had Douglas pinned on his back to the floor and was strangling him. As if from a distance, he watched his hands squeezing, watched his brother's face go from dull red to swollen scarlet.

Alex wasn't sure what finally brought him to his senses. A fleeting thought of Annie? Of what might happen to her if he ended up swinging from the gallows? He didn't know. He only knew that something, perhaps the Almighty Himself, made him jerk his hands from his brother's throat.

Douglas rolled to his side, clawing at his larynx and making horrible gargling noises as he struggled for breath. Alex pushed to his feet and turned away, not caring if his brother lay there and suffocated. Not caring, and almost hoping he did. Bracing his hands on the desk, he hung his head and closed his eyes. When the rasping noises began to subside, he said, "Get out. Get out before I kill you."

He heard Douglas scramble to his feet. But he didn't hear him running for the door.

"I mean it, Douglas. I'll murder you with my bare hands."

Staggering footsteps. The creak of hinges. The resounding slam of the doors. Alex expelled a breath he hadn't realized he'd been holding. Then, feeling as though his lungs were being ripped from his chest, he sobbed. A dry, horrible sob. His knees buckled and he sank down to cradle his head on the desktop.

Death. Not of a man, but of love. The end did not come easily.

Annie clawed at the door to Alex's bedchamber. For a nightmarish moment, she thought it was locked. Half blinded by the darkness in the hall, she threw terrified glances toward the landing. *Here. He was here.* The door suddenly gave, and she spilled into the suite. Moonlight, feeble and patchy, fell across the room. She ran for the bed, her breath tearing from her chest, her movements jerky with hysteria.

Alex. Wildly, she patted the rumpled covers. Gone. She whirled and stared at the door, her hands over her mouth to stifle any sound she might be making. *Douglas, here*. If he heard her sobbing, he might come and find her. Had she made any noise? Oh, God . . . She had to hide. She took several frantic turns, looking for a place. Then, too terrified to remain exposed, she dived into Alex's bed, scrambling to get way down under the covers, to shrink into the mattress and make herself small.

The smell of Alex surrounded her. *Alex*. Shaking violently, Annie hugged her belly and drew up her knees. That man was in the house, and Alex was gone. She caught her breath. *No sound. She couldn't make any sound*. She would stay here, safe in Alex's bed, hidden. He would come back. He had to. And when he did, he wouldn't let anyone hurt her.

Alex stepped into his bedchamber, closed the door, and leaned his back against the panel of wood for a moment with his eyes closed. Annie . . . Now more than ever before, he ached to hold her. Suppressing the urge to go to the nursery, he imagined her smile—the way her mouth curved up so sweetly at the corners, the dimple that flashed in her cheek, her lovely eyes, so softly blue and utterly guileless. Picturing her made him feel less empty inside.

Pressing the barked knuckles of one hand to his mouth, Alex remembered once again how satisfying it had felt to pummel his brother's face. That first punch had marked the end of a lifetime's commitment, and now that it had happened, he felt oddly liberated. Sad, of course. And hollow. But undeniably free. For the first time since the death of his father, his responsibility to his brother was finished.

Straightening from the door, Alex sauntered toward his bed, his gaze on the window and the swaying branches of the willow tree beyond the moon-silvered glass.

Leaves, flattened against the pane by the night wind, made eerie squeaking noises that reminded him of fingernails trailing over a chalkboard. *Sound.* Since knowing Annie, Alex had become acutely conscious of everything audible and frequently found himself trying to perceive the world as she must. Leaves trailing over the glass, birds in the trees, the wind blowing, all with no sound. For all his trying, he found total silence difficult to imagine. She was missing out on so much. So very much.

Sighing, Alex sank down on the edge of his bed and leaned over to yank his boots off. From behind him came a shaky squeak, which for a moment he believed was made by the tree branch outside. Then he froze. Skin prickling, he glanced over his shoulder.

Under the covers at the center of his bed, there was a lump. A trembling lump. Forgetting about his boots, he twisted around, bracing a bent leg on the mattress. As he lifted the coverlet, he heard a shallow panting sound.

"Annie," he whispered incredulously.

With a little grunt, she came up off the mattress at him like a projectile from a slingshot, teeth and claws bared. Alex was so startled that she raked his jaw with her fingernails before he could react.

"Annie!"

Grabbing for her wrists, he ducked to avoid her blows. As he captured her hands, she let loose with a wail of terror. Using his greater strength and weight to best advantage, he quickly pinned her to the bed, holding her arms anchored above her head and immobilizing her thrashing legs with an angled thigh. She arched her back, her lungs whining for breath, as she strained helplessly to break his hold.

"Annie love, it's me." Alex reared up so his face was above hers. "It's me, sweetheart."

In the moonlight, her eyes were large, luminescent

spheres in her pale face, her spiked lashes casting shadows on her cheeks. Unable to move, she stared up at him. Slowly her expression went from one of panic to relief. With a ragged sob, she went totally limp.

Releasing her arms, Alex gathered her against his chest. Like a terrified child, she looped her arms around his neck and clung to him, her entire body convulsing with sobs and a horrible shaking. Heartsick, he pressed his face against her sweet-smelling hair, knowing without having to ask that she must have seen Douglas in the hall. Seeking protection, she had come here, only to find him gone.

Taking care not to hurt her, Alex rolled onto his back, carrying her with him, never loosening his hold on her. He could only imagine how frightened she must have been. Douglas, her rapist, inside the house. His guts knotted on a wave of shame. He was at fault for this. Cupping a hand over the back of her neck, Alex pressed a kiss to her temple.

Momentarily forgetting she couldn't hear him, he whispered hoarsely, "Oh, Annie, forgive me. I'm sorry. So very sorry."

Her violent shivering didn't relent. Running a hand over her back, he felt coolness seeping through her flannel nightgown. Hiding as she had been under the blankets, he knew she couldn't actually be cold. But there was still no denying that she felt chilled. Judging by the way she trembled, she was chilled clear to the bone.

Tucking in his chin, he repositioned her head on his shoulder so she might see his face. "It's all right, Annie. He's gone."

She gave a jerky nod and squeezed her eyes closed. Alex ran his hands briskly over her back and hip, trying in the only way he knew to restore her circulation. Despite his ministrations, her teeth continued to clack. When several more minutes passed and she still hadn't stopped shaking, he began to grow alarmed.

"What you need, young lady, is a long, hot soak in the tub and some of Maddy's Irish coffee."

She clung more tightly to Alex's shoulders when he started to move.

"Annie . . ." Turning onto his side, Alex brushed his fingertips along her cheek and forced a smile. "I'm just going downstairs to get some hot water from the range reservoir. I'll be back before you can count to—" He nearly said "a hundred" but caught himself. "Before you can count to forty. You'll be safe here, I promise. Have I ever lied to you?"

She gave her head a little shake and loosened her arms from around his neck. The look on her face caught at his heart, and he kissed the end of her nose. "There's a good girl. I'll be right back. You stay here. Keep the blankets over yourself, all right?"

Again, her only response was to nod. Alex slipped from the bed, hating to leave her. When he turned to look back at her, though, the shuddering he saw going on under the coverlet convinced him he had no choice.

A few minutes later when he returned to the bedroom, he was carrying two five-gallon buckets filled with hot water. After taking them to the water closet, he lighted the lamps in there and set himself to the task of preparing her a bath. When he had drawn enough cold water from the tap to partly fill the tub, he added the hot water from the buckets and tested the temperature with the inside of his wrist.

When he returned to the bed, he drew the coverlet down from Annie's face. "Up you go. Let's get you in the tub."

Teeth chattering, her small body shaking, she managed to sit up and swing her slender legs over the side of the mattress. Alex helped her to stand and walk to the water closet. Afraid she might think he intended to disrobe her, he leaned slightly forward so she could read his lips as he explained, "While you're undressing and taking a soak, I'm going to go back down to the kitchen and make you some Irish coffee. Maddy's special recipe, guaranteed to warm you clear to the marrow of your bones."

At the edge of the tub, she reached to unfasten the small buttons on the bodice of her gown, but her hands and body were shaking so badly that her fingers couldn't home in on their target. Alex smoothed her hair back from her shoulders and took over the task, his concern mounting with each button he popped free. In his memory, he had seen only two individuals suffering from shock, and as he recalled, both of them had been stricken with violent shakes. Had Annie's terror of Douglas been so great that she was in shock?

Alex didn't know. He only knew that she seemed frighteningly fragile to him in that moment, swollen tummy and all. Slender little hands, lined with delicate bones. Narrow shoulders. Upper arms he could encompass with the span of his fingers. He wanted to gather her close and infuse his body heat into hers. To hold her until all thought of Douglas fled her mind.

As he finished unbuttoning her gown, she plucked shakily at the wristband of one sleeve, her intent obviously to work her arm out. Looking on, Alex could see that she'd never manage to get the garment off by herself. *Shit.*

Ducking down to get her attention, he arched his eyebrows. "You want me to help, sweet?"

Shivering violently, she shook her head, planted the heel of one hand against his shoulder, and gave him a little push. He recognized an invitation to leave when he received one. He just hoped she could manage without him. "I'll be right back, okay?" Grabbing a linen towel from the rack, he laid it over the edge of the oblong tub. "Cover yourself with that once you get in. It doesn't matter if you get it wet. That way, when I come back, you won't feel uncomfortable. All right?"

She nodded jerkily. Against his better judgment, Alex turned on his heel, closing the door of the water closet as he exited. En route from the bedroom, he paused at his armoire to grab a shirt, which he donned but didn't button as he strode down the hall.

Once downstairs, he hastened to build a small fire in the cookstove to reheat the pot of coffee that sat on a burner. That done, he partially filled a mug, added a dollop of cream, and then topped off the cup with whiskey. After adding some sugar to taste, he headed back upstairs, expecting to find Annie up to her armpits in steaming hot water. Instead he found her sitting on the chamber pot commode, still wearing her gown, her arms hugging her middle.

"Annie . . ."

Alex set the mug of Irish coffee on the washstand and hunkered down in front of her. Never had he seen anyone shake like this. If the hot bath and whiskey-laced coffee didn't help, he would have to send for Dr. Muir. Given her pregnancy, he wasn't about to take any chances.

Fleetingly, Alex considered wakening Maddy to come help Annie into her bath, but he quickly discarded the thought. The housekeeper was sound asleep in another wing of the house. In the time it would take for her to get up, find a robe and slippers, and come to Alex's suite, the damned water would be getting tepid.

Grimly determined, he grasped one of Annie's hands, pried it from her ribs, and unfastened the button on her cuff. "I'm going to help you just a bit," he informed her as he unfastened her other sleeve. At her dismayed expression, he flashed a grin. "Honey, I'll have you out of that gown and into the tub so fast, all I'll see is a blur.''

She didn't look convinced, but, concerned for her health, Alex gave her no opportunity to balk. Grasping her by the shoulders, he drew her up from the commode and got handfuls of the nightgown, all in one fell swoop. ''Up with your arms.''

He wasn't sure if she obliged him or if he dragged her arms up as he tugged the gown over her head. No matter. The instant she felt the hem lifting, she assisted him in the endeavor by jerking her arms free so she could attempt to cover herself. Alex couldn't help smiling slightly at what she chose to hide. Not her chest as most females might. Instead she angled one arm over her protruding stomach and clamped her other hand over the dark triangle of hair at the apex of her slender thighs. He was afforded a delightful display of her breasts, the tips of which had darkened with her advancing pregnancy to a deep rose.

He jerked his gaze away and made a valiant effort not to let it wander back. That proved a little difficult as he tried to assist her into the tub. Given her shaking, he didn't trust her footing or the strength of her arms to lower herself in. Where to grab a naked and very pregnant lady? Alex steered away from her waist, afraid he might hurt her or the babe. Her hips were out of the question. Too tantalizing. Too everything. He settled for grasping her under the arms.

Big mistake. He clenched his teeth and made a heroic attempt to think about baseball scores as he helped her step into the water. His palms felt on fire, and, facing her as he was, there was no place to put his thumbs but under her breasts. The silken brush of her skin against his knuckles brought beads of sweat to his brow. Ungainly and awkward, she bent at the knees, legs quivering. Alex continued to support her weight as she sank into the water.

Baseball scores? Jesus. He couldn't even recollect the names of the teams.

"There you go. Now that wasn't so bad, was it?"

The ache in Alex's groin made him think of the time a colt had kicked him in the crotch, but that seemed beside the point. There was something seriously wrong with him, he decided. A normal man should *not* find a pregnant woman attractive. But to him, Annie was beautiful.

He sat on the commode lid and braced his elbows on his knees, hoping to God she hadn't noticed his arousal. His gaze shifted to the towel he'd left out for her, and he willed her to reach for it. Instead, shivering and shuddering, she pressed her back to the sloped end of the tub and sank down in the hot water, which came to her nipples and buoyed her breasts. Counting his blessings, however small, Alex was thankful that, from his present position, he could see her breasts, the upper swell of her tummy, and nothing more. More, he couldn't handle.

Leaning her head back, she closed her eyes and clenched her teeth to stop their clacking. Alex fixed his gaze on the floor and spent several tense moments counting squares of tile. When that quickly grew tiresome, he regarded the toes of his boots. From there, he turned his attention to his fingernails, then to his cuticles. When he glanced at Annie again, it seemed to him she was shivering less.

He pushed to his feet. At his movement, which she must have felt through the floor, she opened her eyes. "How's about some of Maddy's coffee now?"

She grabbed for the towel. Quickly unfolding it, she shook it out over the water and covered herself from the belly down, leaving her breasts exposed. Alex handed her the mug, which, due to her shakiness, she took into both hands. The instant she released the towel, it went floating away. She grabbed for it, sloshing coffee onto her upper chest.

"Here," he said in a gravelly voice. "Let me handle the cup. You tend to the towel."

As he took the mug, she jerked the square of linen over her abdomen again and anchored it there with tight little fists. Hunkering beside the tub, Alex struggled not to chuckle. It was patently obvious to him that for all her modesty and wariness, she was mainly concerned with hiding her swollen waistline and what was nestled between those lovely thighs of hers, the devil take her breasts.

That puzzled Alex. He'd met a few females who weren't shy about displaying their charms, but never anyone like Annie. She wasn't trying to be provocative, that was plain. She honestly didn't seem to realize that it was as important to keep her chest concealed from a man's admiring gaze as it was the rest of her. It was as if no one had ever bothered to explain to her that—

A sudden memory struck Alex. As clearly as if it were yesterday, he recalled going wading up near the falls as a young child. There had been a community celebration of some kind up there, a picnic of sorts, with outdoor games and food galore. In the heat of the afternoon, most of the small children, under adult supervision, had been allowed to go wading. Stripped to their underdrawers, boys and girls alike had romped in the water. Alex had been about five at the time, but there had been kids as old as six or seven in the stream as well. None of the little girls had seemed embarrassed about being seen bare chested. In that stage of their development, there had been nothing for them to feel embarrassed about.

Pressing the mug to Annie's lips, Alex watched with growing tenderness as she took a dainty sip of Maddy's remedy. At the taste of the liquor, she wrinkled her nose.

Alex coaxed her to take another sip, then reached to smooth a damp tendril of dark hair from her cheek.

"It'll rid you of the shivers," he assured her when she cast him another look of distaste.

She fiddled with the towel, the loose end of which kept catching air and floating off to one side, baring her nether regions. As he studied her, he recalled the morning of their wedding and how she had sat on the landing above him, apparently unconcerned about the view he might have up her frock. And the day in the nursery, when he had kissed her breasts? He had expected her to be frightened, but instead she had watched him fumble with her buttons and chemise, curious but unafraid. Until he had tried to put a hand up her skirt, she hadn't seemed aware that there was a connection between his kissing her breasts and what Douglas had done to her.

Annie . . . robbed of her hearing at six and shuffled away into the shadows, where she had been kept ignorant of people and their social mores. Even to Alex, the rules of society didn't make much sense half the time. Naturally this girl didn't clutch the towel to her breasts. What had she to hide? Little girls of six kept their lower anatomy covered because they were taught to do so from an early age. Shyness about their upper bodies came later, an attitude that was taught to them by their mothers a year or so prior to their developing breasts. By the time Annie reached puberty, she had already been a pariah, her social circle limited to immediate family and trusted servants, her only contact with the outside world, aside from accidental encounters with people, with wild animals and attic mice.

Putting the mug to her lips again, Alex said, "Two big gulps this time, Annie love." When she obeyed him, he smiled. "There's my girl. A little more. Come on."

She gulped twice more. "*I don't like it.*"

"I didn't figure you would," he admitted. "I made it pretty strong." Pleased to note that her shaking had all but stopped, he looked deeply into her eyes. "I'm sorry about all this, Annie." Averting his gaze, he swallowed. "I, um . . ." He looked back at her. "If you never forgive me, I won't blame you."

She studied him, looking slightly bewildered. "*For what? It wasn't your fault.*"

For a fleeting instant, Alex considered taking the easy way out. But he loved her too much to lie to her, even if the truth made her think less of him. "For being so—where Douglas is concerned, I'm weak. I always have been. I should have kicked him out of the house, straight off. I knew when I didn't that it was wrong, that I was betraying your trust. But I—"

He set the mug back on the washstand, avoiding her gaze. "Before it was over, I regretted not showing him the door, believe me."

She reached out suddenly, touching tremulous fingertips to his broken knuckles. He glanced up, straight into the bluest, most honest eyes he'd ever seen. For several endless seconds, neither of them moved. He had the awful feeling she was looking clear to his soul and seeing far more than he wanted her to. "*Oh, Alex.*"

"I'm sorry," he managed to say once more. "You'll never know how sorry. Douglas is rotten, and he's mean. He deserves anything he gets. But I gave him money anyway. I know that must seem crazy to you. Probably to everyone."

She deserved more of an explanation than that, and Alex knew it. But now didn't seem the time to discuss it. He wasn't sure there would ever be a good time.

As if she sensed his turmoil, her eyes darkened with concern. He looked quickly away, knowing that if he didn't, he might end up telling her everything. Suddenly the air in the water closet seemed too thin. He needed to get out of there. So he could lick his wounds. So he could come to grips with his feelings.

Forcing himself to return his gaze to hers, he said, "He won't be back, Annie. What happened tonight—it's ended between him and me, once and for all. We'll never see him again."

She gave an almost imperceptible nod, her eyes filled with questions. Questions Alex couldn't answer. Not right now. He pushed to his feet and shoved a hand through his hair.

Watching his movements, her gaze snagged on the barked knuckles of his right hand again. A stricken look came over her face, an indication that it had finally dawned on her how he might have come by the abrasions.

"That water must be getting cool by now," he said, grabbing for any excuse he could think of to leave. "You should probably be getting out before you get the shivers again. If you can manage by yourself, I'll go in the other room and build a fire so you can dry your hair."

"*I can manage.*"

"Good. I—a fire will take the chill off the room."

He reached behind him for the doorknob, gave it a vicious twist, and nearly tripped over his own feet getting out of there.

Twenty-one

As *Alex* closed the door of the water closet, a rush of air swept across Annie's damp skin, raising goose bumps on her upper arms and shoulders. His soap and shaving paraphernalia sat on the washstand beside her, and the scent surrounded her, a common enough blend of bay rum, bergamot, and masculine cologne, but one that she had come to associate only with him.

Alex. He was troubled about seeing his brother tonight. Deeply troubled. And because he was, she knew he needed her now in a way he never had. If she truly cared about him, she would get out of the tub, towel herself dry, throw on her nightgown, and go to him.

And then what? When he turned to her, when he drew her into his arms, what if he wanted more from her by way of comfort than she was prepared to give? He had already made it clear to her on a number of occasions that he wanted to be physically close with her. In his present frame of mind, he might press her to accommodate him.

An awful, slithery feeling attacked Annie's stomach at the thought, and she shivered with dread. After seeing Douglas such a short while ago, the memories of what he had done to her were impossible to hold at bay. Like images from her nightmares, they rushed at her from the darkest corners of her mind. The pain, that awful sense of helplessness, and the shame. Hot tears stung her eyes.

To walk into the other room, knowing in advance that Alex might try to do those things to her? She wasn't sure she could go through with it. Or if she even wanted to. She loved him, yes. And she wanted to be his friend. But there were limits, to save her sanity, if nothing else.

Limits . . . It seemed such a selfish word. Annie sank her teeth into her bottom lip and squeezed her eyes closed. From the beginning, Alex had given her everything he could, holding nothing of himself in reserve and demanding nothing in return. How could she, in good conscience, hold back a part of herself from him?

Alex . . . dancing the waltz with her in the attic, tempting her with music from his flute, giving her the organ, teaching her how to speak in sign. When Annie thought back over the last few months, she realized, not for the first time, that their relationship had always been one-sided, with him doing all the giving, she all the taking. At some point, that had to change, and it would be up to her to see that it did. Alex might express his desire to be close with her physically, he might even press her to that end, but he would never force her.

Pushing to her feet, she watched the water stream from her body into the tub. The soppy towel slipped from her fingers and fell with a splash. *Silence*. No trickling sound of water. No wet plop. Just an awful nothingness that had been the ruling force in her life for so long that, until meeting Alex, she had grown to expect nothing beyond it. Hour after hour, day after day, year after year of silence and loneliness. Knowing Alex had changed all that.

With a sad smile, Annie recalled how bitter she had once felt at having been cheated out of getting any wedding gifts. How mistaken she had been. Alex had come into her life bearing so many gifts she'd long since lost count, each wrapped in a wealth of love. No pretty paper. No fancy ribbons. The things he had given to her couldn't be placed in a box. But they were no less wonderful for all of that. How could she deny such a man anything?

She stared hard at the closed door. Then, not allowing herself to think past the moment, she reached for a dry towel to wrap her damp hair. All too soon—at least it seemed so to her—she had redonned her nightgown and fastened every button. With a trembling hand, she grasped the doorknob, gave it a decisive turn, and drew the door open.

At first glance, the room beyond seemed dark, but then her eyes grew accustomed to the dimness. As she exited the water closet, her silhouette, cast by the lamp behind her, danced eerily over the floor and walls, the disrupted light shifting and reflecting off the highly polished mahogany of the armoire and dresser. Earlier Annie hadn't taken time to look closely at the bedchamber. Now she saw that, like the man who inhabited it, the room was almost stark in its simplicity, the furniture straight and sturdy, the draperies and bed hangings unpretentious. In the poor light, she couldn't be sure, but the walls looked cream-colored, as did the draperies, reminding her of the silk shirts Alex wore. Indeed, bathed in firelight as it was, the entire room seemed a mirror image of him, solid and comfortable, painted in shades of burnished darkness and tawny gold.

He stood before the fireplace, one arm braced on the mantel, head bent, a booted foot resting on a small pile of extra logs at one end of the stone hearth. Her gaze settled on his shoulders and the breadth of his back, where his shirt, stretched taut by the lift of his arm, molded like a second skin to the muscle that roped his torso. Studying him, she recalled his strength and the ease with which he could overpower her. But even as those memories slithered into her mind, she also recalled his gentleness, the many times he had touched her with a caress so light it made her breath catch.

Like a moth attracted to flame, she moved toward him, her heart bumping hard against her ribs. With each step she took, a little voice whispered inside her head, "Once there, you can't turn back. Once there, you can't turn back." But her decision was made. And now that she'd made it, she wondered why it had taken her so long. Some things were destined to be, and she instinctively knew that having this man in her life was one of them.

He glanced up when she reached him. As she had so many times before, Annie looked into his eyes and thought of Christmas toffee still warm from the pan. His eyes were a rich, golden brown, so deep and clear she could get lost in them. Like the candy she loved so well, they beckoned irresistibly to her, tempting her, filling her with a yearning that she had, until now, been afraid to acknowledge. She came to a halt several steps shy of him, knowing even as she did that a mere arm's length between them would not be enough to save her, not necessarily from him, but from herself.

His eyes . . . Tonight there was something more than warmth reflected in those amber depths, an awful, bone-deep sadness. It drew her a step closer to him, held her fast. She touched his shirt sleeve with quivering fingertips, her heart aching for him. Shifting his arm on the mantel, he turned more fully toward her. His shirt hung open to reveal his furry chest and hard belly, the well-padded planes defined by firelight and shadow. His skin gleamed as if he'd been dipped in bronze. Annie wanted to touch him to see what he felt like, but to do so would be tantamount to leaping off a cliff, and she was a little too wary of the consequences to initiate familiarity so quickly.

Alex had no such problem. As he studied her, his firm mouth lifted slightly at one corner, and he reached out to run the backs of his knuckles along her cheek. In that moment, it seemed to Annie that the air between them became so electrified that the friction of his skin against hers produced static. As he trailed his knuckles lightly to her neck, she gulped for breath as though she had just surfaced from under water.

His smile deepened and his eyes took on a knowing twinkle. "You look like a condemned Christian about to face the lions."

Annie frowned slightly, not entirely certain what he meant.

"Christians were once sentenced to death for their religious convictions," he explained. "Right now, you have the look of a little martyr who's afraid she's about to be devoured." He rubbed his thumb over her bottom lip. "Determined to sacrifice yourself for a cause, Annie, love? Why do I have the feeling I'm it?"

Embarrassed to be so easily read, she lowered her gaze. When she glanced back up, his smile had vanished and the muscles in his face had drawn taut. He regarded her for several seconds—endless seconds for Annie. "You're trembling again, and I know damned well it isn't with cold."

Annie couldn't deny the obvious. She was trembling, and it wasn't because she was cold. She was nervous, horribly nervous. And more than a little afraid. Though she knew Alex would never hurt her on purpose, that wasn't much comfort when she recalled how bad the pain had been with Douglas.

Her mouth suddenly felt as dry as sun-parched grass. "*You asked me to think about*—" Whatever else she meant to say fled her mind. How did one refer to such an act? Alex had called it a "special closeness" and "making love,'' but those terms seemed too embarrassingly explicit to repeat. *''I've thought about it,''* she finished lamely, praying he would understand what ''it'' meant. *''Remember? This afternoon, you asked me to think about it?''*

His hand still at her throat, he began to make light, circular motions with the leathery pads of his fingers directly beneath her ear. Her skin there was so sensitive that every drag of his fingertips set her nerve endings afire. She gulped, realizing too late that his thumb was pressed gently over her larynx.

''And because you know I'm feeling sad, you've decided to grant me my request,'' he finished for her.

Annie started to shake her head, but he forestalled her by grasping her chin. His gaze held hers in a grip that was just as relentless as that of his hand. ''If nothing else, Annie, let's keep this honest. If you start coloring the truth to save my feelings and I start doing the same to save yours, the first thing we know, we'll have a mountain of white lies looming between us.''

''But I want—''

He cut her off yet again, this time by touching a finger to her lips. ''No, Annie, you don't want. That's the unvarnished truth.'' In the firelight, his eyes, usually so clear, turned cloudy, the color reminding her of matte gold. ''Given what happened to you, I don't expect you to *want* any part of a physical joining. This afternoon, I asked you to consider the possibility and to trust me enough to allow me a chance to show you how wonderful it can be between us. That's all. Just a chance. It was never my expectation that you would come to me burning with need or *wanting* any part of it.''

As though he found that thought mildly amusing, he continued to regard her, his mouth quirking slightly at one corner.

"*Well, I've thought about it!*" she told him, feeling a little put out because he seemed to be laughing at her expense. "*And I have decided to give you a chance to show me.*"

"Why?"

"*Well, because . . .*" She licked her lips and fixed her gaze on the hollow at the base of his throat. "*Because I—*" She broke off and returned her eyes to his.

"Because you know I'm very upset?" he finished for her. "And because you feel obligated?" He shook his head. "You've made the right decision, Annie, love, but for all the wrong reasons." With another smile that didn't quite touch his eyes, he reached to draw the towel from her head. "I think I'll wait until you come to me for all the right ones. For now, let's get that hair of yours dried before you take a chill." He motioned for her to sit on the rug before the hearth, then left her to get his hairbrush off the dresser. As he walked back toward her, he said, "Don't frown. It'll give you wrinkles."

Annie couldn't help but frown. As perverse as she knew it was, she felt irritated and a little bit hurt. For all the wrong reasons, he said. And just what reasons would he deem the right ones? She loved him and cared about him. Tonight he felt sad, and she wanted to make him feel better. What better reasons could she have?

Resting a hand on her shoulder, he pressed her down onto the rug and then sat beside her, one long leg tucked beneath him, his other knee raised. The position was so blatantly masculine and he had assumed it with such ease that she felt awkward in comparison. The hem of her nightgown got caught under one foot, which caused an uncomfortable tightness across the shoulders. She spent a moment trying to untangle herself. When she finally got comfortable and looked back up, Alex set himself to the task of brushing her hair. Expecting him to hit snags and bring tears to her eyes as her mother had always done, Annie was tense at first. But his gentleness soon soothed the rigidity from her neck and shoulders.

Long, slow strokes. Big, slightly callused hands. Warmth from both him and the fire. Her eyelashes drifted low, and her body, loose with relaxation, moved with the pull of the bristles. As the damp ends of her hair began to dry, he lifted the brush with each stroke, separating the strands and letting them fall slowly back around her shoulders. Annie gazed at the firelight through an ever shifting veil of sable, feeling oddly drowsy and separate from reality.

When at last he set the brush aside, she felt so lazy she didn't want to move. A log in the fire rolled forward, sending up a spray of sparks. She could almost hear the snap of the pitch and the crackling of the flames. Bracing his weight on one hand, he smoothed her hair from her face, his eyes searching hers. Annie sensed that there was something he wanted—no, needed—to say. It was there in the tautness of his features, in the firm set of his mouth, in the slightly pleated frown on his forehead.

"*What is it?*" she finally asked.

His gaze skittered from hers. For several seconds, he stared into the fire, the sharp definition of his face catching the amber light, the crevices etched with shadows. Several different times, his mouth tightened and he swallowed, as if he were on the verge of speaking. But in the end, he remained silent.

Annie leaned forward to rest her hand over his. At the touch, he squeezed his eyes closed. "I need—" His throat worked as though the words were snagging on his larynx. "About tonight—Douglas and everything—I need to explain. I don't want you to think that I'd ever choose him over you, and I know that's how it must have seemed to you tonight."

A hundred times, at least, he had caught her chin to make her look at him. Now Annie did the same to him. At her touch, he opened his eyes, apparently startled. His gaze, darkened with emotions she couldn't quite define, met hers and delved deeply.

"*You love him*," she said. "*Just because he does bad things, that doesn't mean you can stop caring about him. I understand that.*"

"He doesn't deserve my affection, not in any measure."

"*Neither does my papa, but I still love him.*"

That got his attention. As she finished speaking, he dragged his gaze to hers, his expression slightly bewildered, as if he'd registered the words but couldn't quite make sense of them. "I don't know why, but I always assumed you loved your father because you didn't know any better."

Annie hugged her knees and smiled, more amused by his admission than disgruntled. "*I'm deaf, not stupid.*"

His response was a smile. There was no mistaking the admiration that gleamed in his eyes. "I'm glad you're finally beginning to realize that."

"*You're changing the subject.*"

"Trust you to notice."

"*You were going to explain. About Douglas and what happened tonight.*"

"I just wanted to assure you that, no matter how it may have looked, I will never put him before you. Not for any reason. For tonight, I think that's enough on the subject. As upset as you were at seeing him, I can't think a discussion about him would be good for you or the baby right now."

"*The baby and I are perfectly fine. You're upset. I want to help. Is that so wrong?*"

"No, of course not."

"*Well, then? I offered to be*"—she broke off and gestured vaguely—"*close with you, and you didn't feel my reasons were sound. Now you're refusing to talk about what's troubling you. How can I help if you won't let me?*"

He smiled lazily. "Uncooperative, am I?"

"*Very.*"

"I apologize." He seemed to consider the accusation. Then his smile deepened. "I guess I am being difficult, aren't I?"

She nodded.

"What it boils down to is a choice between being close and talking. Correct?" He arched a tawny eyebrow at her. "Faced with that ultimatum, I choose the first."

A frown pleated Annie's forehead. "*Pardon?*"

"The first," he repeated. "I don't feel like talking about my brother. That leaves being close, which is something I always feel like doing. No problem there."

Annie narrowed an eye at him again. At her expression, his shoulders jerked with a laugh and his eyes took on a mischievous twinkle. "Correct me if I'm wrong, but I believe your enthusiasm is waning. I thought you wanted to make me feel better. Trust me, Annie, being close will do it."

"*Coward.*"

He draped an arm over his upraised knee. "In this instance, I believe the term applies to both of us. Maybe we should hold hands and face our dragons together, hmm?"

Annie grasped his dangling hand. "You first."

He threw back his head and laughed. Somehow, she knew the sound was rich and deep, the kind of laugh that would have warmed her clear through had she been able to hear it. As his mirth subsided, he turned his hand to curl his fingers around hers. "Me first, huh? You're priceless, Annie, girl. Two hours ago, I felt as if someone had sliced my insides to pieces with a knife, and now you have me laughing.''

"*I didn't mean it to be funny.*''

He grew suddenly sober. "No, I don't believe you did.'' After studying her for a moment, he said, "You're actually serious, aren't you? If I take you up on it, you're prepared to let me make love to you.''

"*Not prepared, exactly, but ready.*''

He tightened his hand around hers. "That means a lot to me. That you trust me enough to take a chance like that. It means more than I can say.''

Annie's throat felt achy and tight. "*I wish you trusted me half as much.*''

He sighed deeply and closed his eyes. "Oh, Annie. It's not that I don't trust you. It's just that—well, you have no idea what you're asking.'' He raised his lashes to regard her. "Talking. It sounds so simple. But it isn't. My feelings about Douglas are anything but simple, and they stem, in part, from something that happened years ago.''

"*What?*''

A muscle along his jaw bunched, and his grip on her hand tightened until it was almost painful. "I killed our parents. My father and Douglas's mother, Alicia. I killed them. It was my fault Douglas was left an orphan at only six. All my fault.''

Of all the things Annie had expected him to say, that wasn't it. She stared at him in stunned disbelief, convinced she must have misread his words. The stricken expression on his face told her otherwise. "*Oh, Alex . . .*''

His grip on her hand grew more bruising. "I didn't mean to do it. It was an accident. But in the end, they were both just as dead as if I'd put a gun to their heads and pulled the trigger. The guilt I felt—'' He took a deep breath and exhaled through pursed lips. "Jesus. It never turned loose of me. I've spent the last fourteen years trying to make it up to Douglas, and now, looking back on it, I think I did him more harm than good.''

Annie didn't try to draw her hand from his. Despite the pain of his grip, she was afraid to move for fear she'd distract him, stop him from talking. As though the dam had finally burst, the ugliness was pouring from him. He scarcely paused between sentences to draw breath as he told her about the accident that had killed his father and stepmother.

''I was, um . . . about sixteen when it happened. I had just started college that year up in Portland, and I'd come home for the summer to work for my father at the rock quarry.'' He fell silent for a bit, his gaze growing distant with memories. ''Boys that age—well, I was feeling pretty full of myself that summer. It was heady stuff, coming home from college, working alongside grown men, having my father ask me my opinion about business matters.'' He smiled slightly and shook his head. ''It was the first time he'd ever really treated me like an adult. I was part of everything. On a work crew. Helping fill orders. I wanted to prove myself. You understand? I saw everything as some sort of test, pass or fail, the cumulative score a measure of my manhood.''

Annie had no idea what ''cumulative'' meant, but she got his gist and nodded, wishing with all her heart that his smile would reach his eyes. But all she saw in those amber depths was pain. An awful pain that had been with him far too long.

''Toward the last part of June,'' he went on, ''everybody was getting excited about the approach of Independence Day and the celebration they were going to have in town. Up at the quarry, we had access to explosives of all types, and some of the men started experimenting, their original intent to create their own firecrackers.'' At her puzzled look, he quickly explained what a firecracker was, describing the loud blast one made. "Anyway, one thing led to another, and men being men, they started playing pranks. One day when I was in the privy, my father lit a homemade firecracker and tossed it in the door. It went off right at my feet and scared the—"

His face turned a dull red, and he chuckled. Envisioning what must have happened, Annie couldn't help but smile as well. It had been a long while since a loud noise had startled her, but she could still recall the feeling.

"Let's just say it scared the orneriness right out of me," he said. "After that, all I could think about was playing a prank on my father to pay him back, doing him one better if possible." His smile faded abruptly and the sadness returned to his eyes. "A few days after the outhouse incident, one of the men who worked for my father got creative with black powder and made this tiny explosive, enclosed in a minuscule wad of paper. After setting off a few of them, he made another and stuck it in the end of a fellow worker's cigar. Later, when the man lit his smoke, he only took a few puffs before it blew up in his face. I thought it was hilariously funny, and since my father smoked cigars, I decided to load one of his with explosive. It was harmless. No injury would come of it. All I intended was to give him a good scare."

Annie's throat went tight at the haunted expression that crossed his face.

"Since I wanted to catch him totally by surprise, I waited until I got home and loaded one of the cigars in his study. I figured he'd be doing his books some evening, and *bang* would go his cigar, right?" He looked into her eyes, not moving or speaking. "That wasn't how it happened. He received a new order of cigars and put them in his cigar box. Not realizing that he rotated his stock, putting his fresh cigars under the older ones, I figured the one I had tampered with was probably clear at the bottom of the box. Days went by, and like a kid, I forgot all about the prank. One evening, my father and Alicia were invited to the home of a friend. My father had the buggy brought around. They got in. Douglas and I were standing on the porch to wave them off.''

The muscles along each side of his throat grew distended. Annie guessed what he was about to tell her, and she wanted nothing more than to hold him in her arms to ease his pain. Only if she did that, she wouldn't be able to read his lips, so she had to be content with holding his hand.

''Just before he reached for the reins, my father lit a cigar. He took a long drag. There was a loud bang and the horses bolted. When it was all over, he and my stepmother were both dead.'' Turning loose of her, he turned his hands and stared at his palms as if he might find answers there. ''I killed them.''

She put her hands over his, gripping tightly. ''*It was an accident.*''

He shook his head. ''Accidents can't be helped. That could have been. If I hadn't been so stupid, so thoughtless, it never would have happened.''

''*You didn't mean to hurt anyone.*''

''They were still just as dead.'' He stared into the fire for a long while. When he finally looked back at her, there were shutters over his eyes, as though he'd closed his feelings away inside himself. ''I didn't tell you to make you feel sorry for me, Annie. I just hoped—well, that it might be easier for you to understand. About Douglas. About my giving him money tonight. I wanted to send him packing. Honestly I did. But I couldn't.'' He shook his head. ''That's the story of my life, never being able to tell him no. Out of guilt. Maybe if I hadn't spoiled him so, he'd have turned out better.''

Annie pressed her lips to his knuckles and closed her eyes, wishing with all her heart she could turn back time for him and make everything better. When she looked at him again, she saw that his eyes held a distant expression, and she knew he was far away from her, remembering.

"From the day of our parents' deaths, all I could think to do was try to make it up to Douglas. He was a frightened little boy—an orphan—and it was my fault. I could never forget that or forgive myself. Later, when he got older and his pranks became more serious, I blamed myself because our father wasn't around to discipline him and set an example for him. So I tried to make up for that as well. Anything he wanted, he got. Anything he wanted to do, I allowed. If he got into trouble, I bailed him out. In short, I killed his parents, and then I ruined him. Douglas is what he is today because his every whim has been gratified for most of his life."

Unable to bear seeing him this way, Annie caught his face between her hands. "*No!*" she cried. "*Blame yourself for what happened to your parents, if you must, but not for the way Douglas is. Being spoiled doesn't make people mean. Not the way he is.*"

"I blame myself because he hurt you," he admitted. "By then, I was beginning to suspect how vicious he could get, especially when he drank, but I refused to face it. If I had, I might have prevented what happened up at the falls that day."

Since words weren't seeming to reach him, Annie looped her arms around his neck. He caught her close, his embrace almost painful, he held her so tight. She felt his chest vibrate against hers. She knew without seeing his lips that he was saying, "I'm sorry." Over and over again. She didn't want him to do this to himself. What Douglas had done—what had happened to her—none of that could be laid at his door.

Because she could feel that he was still talking, she drew back and took his face between her hands so she might see. Tears, shot through with gold by the firelight, trailed over his cheeks.

"Every time I think about him hurting you, I feel sick," he told her. "Just the thought of him putting his filthy hands on you makes me want—"

Annie couldn't bear to let him finish. Without weighing the possible consequences, she covered his mouth with hers and kissed him with a ferocity that startled her nearly as much as it seemed to startle him. Whatever else he meant to say spilled with his breath into her mouth. He tasted warm and sweet. His lips beneath hers felt like wet silk. Remembering how he had kissed her that day in the nursery, she touched the tip of her tongue to his. She didn't need ears to know that he groaned. It erupted from him, raw and ragged, with such force that it vibrated clear through her. Running a hand up her back, he made a tight fist in her unbound hair. With the force of his grip, he tipped her head slightly and resettled his mouth over hers.

Annie knew control had changed from her hands to his the instant he deepened the kiss. The sudden hardness of his body unnerved her. Beneath her hands, she felt the flesh over his shoulders bunch into steely knots. The muscles in his arms had tensed as well, their circle forming an unbreakable band around her. Steel and fire, need and urgency, possessiveness and determination, all were evidenced by the changes that came over him.

His mouth ground against hers, and suddenly his hands seemed to be everywhere. His touch was feverish, bold. There was nothing gentle about it. Annie had the terrifying feeling that he was no longer even aware of her as a person, that in a twinkling, she had become naught but a body to him. A body he meant to possess.

This was not the Alex she knew. A stranger had taken his place.

Twenty-two

Alex had unbuttoned his wife's nightgown and was groping for the hem when he came to his senses enough to realize exactly what he was doing and with whom he was doing it. *Annie.* He dragged his mouth from hers. His brain feverish with passion, his thoughts in a jumble, he blinked and glanced around. Measure by measure, reality returned to him. On the floor? *Jesus Christ.* When he saw what he had nearly done, a chill as jolting as a dash of ice water washed over him.

Hauling in a ragged breath, he groped almost frantically for his self-control, which at the moment seemed as elusive as the sparkles in dust motes. *Need.* It burned in his guts like a hot coal. In his temples, his pulse went *swi-swish, swi-swish*, each thrum sending a knifelike pain behind his eyes. *Annie.* He blinked and tried to bring her small face into sharper focus, to concentrate on her and only her, a sweet, frightened, and very pregnant girl who not only deserved but needed gentle handling.

Somehow he had pulled her across his lap. His upraised knee formed a support for her back. His arm around her swollen middle was the anchor that held her fast. Glancing down, he saw that he'd jerked her gown up to her knees, that he'd been perilously close to fondling forbidden treasures. He swallowed and lifted a trembling hand to her rumpled hair. Beneath his fingertips, the strands felt like sun-warmed silk. Her eyes, wide and wary, jerked from his hand to his face. She clearly feared what he might do next. Alex couldn't blame her. In another two seconds, he would have had her on her back and been driving it home.

"Annie," he said in a throbbing whisper, "I'm sorry. I didn't mean to frighten you, sweetheart. It's just that—" He broke off, uncertain what to say, whether he should be brutally honest or lie to keep from frightening her even more. In the end, he decided on honesty. This girl had been held apart from reality for too many years already. "I want you very badly. I've been wanting you for weeks. When a man is around a woman for such a long period of time, as I have been you, and can never . . ." His voice trailed away. "I'm sorry. The wanting got away with me there for a minute, that's all, and I nearly lost control."

Alex almost made her a promise that he wouldn't let it happen again but checked himself. The truth was that he might. She was one sweet armful. Everything about her tempted him, from the translucent pinkness of her small toenails to the glistening moisture on her full bottom lip. He'd never wanted a woman so badly.

Slowly—a little too slowly to suit him—the fear left her beautiful eyes. Alex smiled at her, feeling more than a little relieved when she smiled back. She still looked uncertain and a little shaken, but she seemed willing to give him the benefit of the doubt.

Thank God.

Feeling like a lowdown skunk, he cupped his hand over her cheek, his gaze holding hers. "That was, without question, the sweetest kiss I've ever gotten. I'm sorry I went after you like I did. I didn't hurt you, did I?"

A little hesitantly, she finally shook her head. He could

see that she was trembling, and this time he couldn't blame it on Douglas. Rubbing his thumb over her mouth, he whispered, ''I know I don't deserve it, but will you give me one more chance? To do it right this time?''

Her eyes went dark, with fear or uncertainty, he wasn't sure which. He held his breath, waiting for her answer. When she gave an almost imperceptible nod, he nearly whooped with relief, which wouldn't have been at all the thing, considering her lack of enthusiasm for this undertaking. ''Thank you.''

He made another pass with his thumb over her precious mouth. His guts knotted when he saw that her bottom lip looked slightly swollen. Though he had no clear recollection of having done so, he knew he must have ground his mouth against hers. What a prince he was. With one bit of encouragement, he'd gone after her like a bear for honey.

He had some fences to mend, no question about it. He instinctively knew it wouldn't be wise to leave the task for later. Given too much time to contemplate his behavior, she'd very likely grow even more frightened at the prospect of making love. If there was anything he didn't need right now, it was another hurdle to jump.

Very gently, he moved his hand from her cheek to her neck, running his fingertips around to her nape. Pressing the pad of his thumb against the underside of her fragile jaw, he lifted her face. Angling his head, he touched his mouth lightly to hers. For an instant, she stiffened, but when he didn't increase the pressure or drag her back into his arms, she finally began to relax.

Doing it right. It wasn't as simple as it sounded. He wanted her. God, how he wanted her. With a feverish urgency. There was nothing gentle about his need or anything gentlemanly about the thoughts that kept sweeping through his head. Kissing her breasts until she was mindless. Tasting the honeyed wetness nestled between her silken thighs. Driving his shaft into her slick, hot channel. Nibbling lightly at her mouth when he really wanted to devour every inch of her was not the easiest thing he'd ever done.

The end result was ample reward for the effort, however. The tenseness slowly eased from her body, and like a child seeking warmth, she pressed against him. Alex steeled himself against the urge to take advantage of her acquiescence. Not yet, he cautioned himself. He had to gain ground inch by inch, not by leaps and bounds. Otherwise, he'd frighten her again. If he did that, he wouldn't achieve his ultimate goal, which was to make love to her. Not tomorrow. Not next week. But tonight.

And so he kissed her. Slowly. Gently. As if that were all in the world he wanted to do. One minute . . . two . . . Kisses so whisper-soft he scarcely felt them. Like the silken brush of butterfly wings. When she finally looped her arms around his neck, he pressed his face against her hair for a moment, inhaling the scent of her, smiling tenderly at the trusting way she molded herself against him. Very carefully, he looped an arm around her waist, and splayed a hand over her side, slowly tightening his hold. Her spine gave way to his arm, and her head fell back slightly. Alex kissed the hollow of her throat, taking measure of her pulse with the tip of his tongue. Fast, irregular. He smiled again, savoring this one small taste of her, his mind leaping ahead to other places he hoped to kiss.

Moving back so she could see him, he said, "I don't want you to get chilled, honey. Let me put some wood on the fire."

Her expression still a little guarded, she blinked as he set her off his lap. He pushed quickly to his feet and added logs onto the grate, nudging them with his boot to position them. Sparks shot up the flue. Then the flames caught on the wood. Alex rubbed his hands clean on his trousers as he turned back to his wife, who knelt on the rug, looking a little too innocent for his peace of mind. Gilded by firelight, in the flowing white gown, with her hair like a cloud around her shoulders, she might have been a religious painting. Or an angel. *Sweet, so impossibly sweet.* He felt as though he were about to defile something sacred, not a good feeling to have when his conscience was at war with pent-up passion. Whether she was angelic or not, he meant to have her, the devil take his scruples.

He held out a hand to her. "Come here, Annie, love."

As though she sensed his intent, she searched his gaze. Alex bent slightly and grasped her by the upper arms, taking the choice away from her by pulling her to her feet.

"I don't want you to get cold," he said as he drew her closer to the fire.

Blue eyes, shot through with gold from the firelight . . . Looking into them, Alex accepted that she had every reason to be wary. Given his behavior a few minutes past, he was fortunate she wasn't panicky. She had given him her trust, which he knew hadn't come easily, and he'd nearly broken it. Now, though he was far from deserving, she was willing to trust him yet again.

When he contemplated that, Alex found it a little overwhelming. Trust was a gift, and coming from her, priceless beyond measure. He swept his gaze slowly over her. In his frenzy a few minutes ago, he had unbuttoned her gown, which saved him the trouble of having to do so now. With a nonchalance he was far from feeling, he unfastened one of her cuffs, tugged it off over her hand, and began working her arm out of the sleeve.

"Let's get you out of this, shall we?"

Her pointed little elbow caught in the armhole of her

gown. He made fast work of wiggling it free. Then he turned his attention to her other sleeve. From the corner of his eye, he saw her lips moving and knew that, as much as he might wish to, he couldn't ignore her protests. He stopped what he was doing to search her gaze.

His voice oddly thin, he said, "Sweetheart, if you're afraid and want me to stop, all you have to do is say so."

Alex felt fairly certain that she'd been telling him exactly that, right up until he looked into her eyes. But now she said nothing. He waited, in an agony of suspense, determined to work her arm back into her sleeve, refasten her cuff, and take it with good grace. Instead, she raised her chin a notch, took a deep breath, and squared her small shoulders. "*No, don't stop.*"

Alex knew what it had cost her to say those three words. To him, making love with her was a natural culmination, but to her? "You won't be sorry. I swear it." Not wanting to draw out the torture for her, he quickly maneuvered her other arm out of its sleeve. "There we go."

Reaching down, he grabbed handfuls of cotton, studiously avoiding eye contact with her as he drew the hem of her nightgown upward. At the last second, her courage deserted her. Knowing how frightened she must be, Alex was half expecting some reflexive resistance, and when she tried to foil him by grabbing handfuls of cloth, he gave a jerk, successfully breaking her hold. In one smooth motion, he drew the gown off over her head and gave it a toss.

When he turned back, his heart skipped a beat. Though she made a valiant attempt to hide herself from him with crossed arms and splayed hands, she was still a vision, naked and gilded by firelight. Swollen pink nipples peeked out at him through the parted curtains of her sable hair. Helpless to resist, he reached out and brushed the backs of his knuckles over a sensitive crest. At his touch, she jerked as if he'd stuck her with a pin.

He lowered his gaze, filled with tenderness as he observed her frantic attempts to conceal more territory than two small hands could possibly cover. By the way she tried to hug herself, he guessed she couldn't decide what part of her was most important to hide, her protruding belly, her navel, or the tantalizing triangle of dark hair at the apex of her thighs.

In the end, she hugged one arm over her belly and clamped her other hand over her navel, a choice that stymied him. But he couldn't quarrel with the result. No man in his right mind yearned for a glimpse of bellybutton when he had an unobstructed view of—

No suitable word came to his mind for that tantalizing thatch of sable curls. In the past, Alex, like most men, had referred to that particular part of a woman's body with little reverence, the list of names as base as they were numerous. To even think one of those words in connection with Annie seemed a sacrilege.

He raised his gaze to her swollen waist, a perverse curiosity niggling at him as he studied the hand she held clamped over her navel. That she was bent on hiding something was blatantly obvious, but for the life of him, he couldn't think what. One navel looked pretty much like another. Dying to know what she felt so embarrassed for him to see, he barely resisted the urge to pry her fingers away.

Given the feast of sights she was providing him with, however, he decided he could allow the poor girl one secret. For the moment, at any rate. Later, there would be no room for secrets between them.

Even hugging herself as she was, a wealth of her skin was left bare. The color of cream, it looked luminescent in the light cast by the fire. Like shimmering silk. Or a trembling leaf . . .

With a start, Alex realized she was shaking. Jerking his gaze to hers, he saw in the depths of her eyes that she was perilously close to bolting. Not that he blamed her. He was gaping at her like a damned idiot. *Jesus*. From the get-go, he hadn't handled this well, and judging by her expression, things were quickly going from bad to worse.

For all his experience with women over the years, he suddenly felt like a bungling oaf. So horribly nervous. His voice a throbbing whisper, he said, "I'm sorry for—for staring at you, sweetheart. It's just that—my God, Annie, you're so beautiful. I can hardly take my—"

Her small face flooded with scarlet. His gaze darted to her protruding belly and her ineffectual attempt to keep it hidden with her thin arms. *Stupid! So stupid*! He nearly thumped himself on the forehead with the heel of his hand. The girl was in the advanced stages of pregnancy. Naturally she didn't feel very beautiful.

Only she was. The most beautiful thing he'd ever clapped eyes on, barring none. *So, tell her that, you damned fool*. Alex tried to moisten his lips with a tongue that had gone as dry as beef jerky. He wasn't much good at spouting flattery. Never had been. For some reason, he'd always felt a little silly when he tried to get poetic.

"Annie, don't feel self-conscious about your stomach," he started. "I think it's—cute."

Her big blue eyes went bright with a rush of tears. Alex couldn't feel the rug under his feet. *Christ*. At least he could *see* his feet.

"Sweetheart, your tummy is beautiful. Honestly."

Actually, now that he was taking its measure, he might have added that it was remarkable as well. She looked about ready to pop her seams. Beneath the hand that she held over her navel, dark hair ran in a tapering line down to her pelvis.

"Annie . . ." He stepped closer. With hands that were suddenly shaky, he brushed the tears from her cheeks, wishing with all his heart that he knew what to say to her. There was no denying the fact that she was misshapen and ungainly. But that didn't dampen his desire for her. If anything, it heightened it. His wife, heavy with child. To him, that was a miracle beyond measure. If given half a chance, he'd worshipfully kiss every inch of her. But he wasn't sure how to convince her of that.

It occurred to Alex that he might be going about this all wrong. Annie wasn't stupid. She knew her feminine shape was temporarily distorted, and no pretty words were likely to convince her otherwise. It might be more fruitful if he were to make light of the situation and try to tease a smile from her. If he seemed to take her pregnancy in stride, perhaps she would relax about it as well.

Bending to plant a kiss on the end of her nose, he flashed her a slow grin. "It has just occurred to me that there seems to be something coming between us."

Her eyes went huge. Then she blinked, spilling another rush of tears over her lashes. The next thing Alex knew, she planted a hand in the center of his chest and shoved him with surprising strength. Caught unprepared, he staggered a step. Annie, still hugging her belly, made a dash for her discarded nightgown. Alex caught her wrist just before she reclaimed the garment.

"No, sweetheart, don't," he said, forcing her to straighten. "Please?"

She tried to jerk her arm from his grasp. Taking care not to bruise her with his grip, Alex held fast. "Annie . . . You're being silly about this. It isn't as if I've never seen a nude pregnant woman before." That was one of the biggest whoppers he'd ever told. "And, whether you believe me or not, I think you're beautiful. Honestly, I do!''

Her mouth quivered. The next thing he knew, the spasm spread to her small chin. Alex nearly groaned. Releasing her wrist, he framed her face between his hands and set himself to the task of kissing her tears away. In between kisses, he drew back so she could see his mouth and whispered, ''Honey, I'm sorry. Forgive me? I didn't mean to hurt your feelings. I think you're beautiful. I swear it.''

She attempted to twist her face from his grasp. *''I'm not beautiful. Ugly, I'm ugly.''*

''Ugly? Honey, no. Pregnant women are . . . special.'' Alex nearly winced at that. Special? A sheer genius with words, that was he. ''To me, seeing you like this is—''

''You haven't seen my bellybutton!''

Alex traced the arch of her brows with his lips, then leaned back. ''I'll bet you have a gorgeous bellybutton.''

''It pooches!''

''It what?''

''Pooches!''

Tiny muscles had begun to jerk beneath her eyes, a sure sign to Alex that she was perilously close to weeping. She was clearly very upset about her navel, which seemed a small point to him, considering her impressive girth. ''It pooches? What do you mean, it pooches?''

''It's turned inside out!''

Convinced he'd misread her lips, he said, ''I beg your pardon?''

''Inside out!'' she repeated.

Alex glanced down between their bodies. Feeling certain that, in her self-consciousness, she was exaggerating the condition, he drew her fingers away from the spot. Mouth and chin atremble, Annie stared down at the protrusion. His heart caught at the distress on her face. ''Honey, it's not *that* bad.''

''Ugly, ugly, ugly!''

"No! How can a bellybutton be ugly? I think it's sort of—" He broke off, groping for a word. "Adorable. That is, without question, the cutest bellybutton I've ever clapped eyes on."

Not stopping to think about how she might perceive the move, he gathered her close and pressed his face against her hair. He ran a hand up her silken back, learning her spine with searching fingertips, his eyes falling closed on a wave of contentment. To hold her like this, to feel her softness pressed so firmly against him, was as close to heaven as he ever hoped to get.

"Don't cry, Annie, love." It suddenly struck Alex that he was whispering into the ear of a deaf girl. Sheer frustration crashed over him, and he drew back again so she could see his face. Feeling a movement between them, he glanced down to see that she was pushing at her protruding navel with a fingertip, trying without success to tuck it back where it belonged. Afraid she might hurt herself, he brushed her hand aside and covered the spot with his own. Tenderness swamped him as he looked into her eyes. "Once the baby comes, your body will return to its former shape," he assured her. "Until then, honey, trust me when I say that I think you're beautiful. Big tummy, inside-out bellybutton, and all." He brushed a hand over her hair. "There's not a single thing about you I'd change. Except maybe to see you smile."

She fixed him with an incredulous gaze, clearly unconvinced.

"You are absolutely perfect," he assured her.

She wrinkled her nose and shook her head again. Alex released her and stepped back. "Show me one thing about you that's not perfect," he challenged.

She started to hug herself again, but he forestalled her by catching her wrists and drawing her arms back down to her sides. Then, his throat aching with love for her, he made a great show of stepping around her to examine her from all angles. As he came full circle and faced her again, he rested his hands on his hips, settled his gaze on her flushed face, and said, with complete honesty, "You are, without question, the sweetest, most beautiful girl I've ever seen."

She placed a hand over her swollen stomach, her gaze skittering from his. Alex leaned around so they were nose to nose again. "Line up forty skinny women, give me a choice, and I'd pick you every time."

She sniffed and swiped at her chin to catch a tear before it fell. Alex was more interested in catching another tear that had already fallen and was now making a glistening trail over her breast to her nipple.

"I mean that, Annie, love." The dark shadows in her eyes made him wish with all his heart that he were more silver-tongued. "I want you, and only you, just the way you are right now."

She made a small sound, low in her throat.

He held out a hand to her. "Come here, sweetheart."

She stared down at his palm for several long seconds. Then she finally crossed it with her delicate fingers. Alex couldn't speak, and even if he'd been able to, he doubted he could express the emotions that rolled through him. Tugging her toward him, he enfolded her in his arms. For a long while, he simply held her, instinctively knowing that she needed time to grow accustomed to the closeness, that she needed to know he wanted more from her than just the physical.

And he did . . . So very much more.

When he felt her begin to relax a little, he drew back and slid up a hand to cup her breast. As his fingertips grazed her silken skin, she gave a little squeak and caught her breath. Lightly, ever so gently, he dragged his thumb over her nipple, which was still slightly damp from her tears. Her aureoles were swollen and an even deeper color of pink than he'd judged them to be earlier. He suspected they were tender and extremely sensitive as well.

Drawing her back into his arms, he hugged her close and pressed his face against the silken slope of her shoulder. In a voice that shook with emotions he couldn't separate or define, he whispered, "Dear Lord, you are so incredibly precious." He knew she couldn't hear him, but for the moment, his usual feeling of frustration gave way to vague relief. He could scarcely think, holding her like this, let alone guard his every word. In making love to a deaf girl, there were advantages as well as drawbacks, he realized. "God, how I want you. It's probably a blessing you have no idea how much."

She nuzzled close, bringing a reluctant smile to his mouth, for he knew damned well she'd be making for the door if she could hear him. Turning his head, he traced the shape of her ear with his lips, then caught her lobe in his teeth and flicked it with his tongue. At the titillation, she gave a low moan. "Ah, you like that, do you?" He ran his mouth down the curve of her neck, nibbling lightly at her skin. "It's a damned good thing because I'm going to love every inch of you just that way." He closed his eyes as his mouth covered the pulsebeat at the hollow of her throat. "Ah, Annie, love . . ."

When her head fell back, he pressed his mouth to hers. She made a soft, mewling sound, her sweet breath spilling against his lips. He thrust his tongue deeply into her moistness, then withdrew, emulating the rhythm of lovemaking, imagining how it would feel to bury himself inside her. The muscles in his thighs knotted as he slid his hands over her, glorying in her softness, in the velvety texture of her skin. Molding his cupped palms to her pliable buttocks, he drew her hips closer. At the contact, she stiffened and jerked her mouth from his.

Alex lifted his head, sliding a hand from her rump to her back to steady her and hold her, just in case she got frantic. By her expression and the flutter of pulse he saw in the hollow of her throat, he knew she was remembering that day at the falls. He didn't suppose he could blame her for that.

The enormity of what he was about to do struck him. One wrong move, one wrong word . . . ''I won't hurt you, Annie, girl. I promise.''

Her frightened gaze clung to his. Alex looked into those eyes and felt as if he were drowning. He swallowed, the sound echoing through his head, testimony to his nervousness. He wanted to make this beautiful for her. He wanted to erase every bad memory from her mind and replace them with glorious ones.

Bending slightly, he caught her up in his arms and carried her to the bed. After gently lowering her to the mattress, he stripped off his shirt and kicked off his boots. She tugged at the corner of the rumpled coverlet, drawing it over her lower body. Alex smiled and braced a knee next to her hip. Settling a hand on either side of her, he leaned down to kiss her eyes closed. Then he traced her features with his lips, lightly, ever so slowly. He wanted her to feel cherished, for he did cherish her, feeling as if God had sent him an angel. She made soft, pleased little sounds and smiled.

Alex smiled as well, for he noticed that she was still clutching the coverlet for dear life over her lower body. Against her closed eyelids, he whispered, ''Make tight little fists and don't turn loose. It'll suit me just fine to have your hands occupied elsewhere.'' He trailed his mouth along her sculpted cheekbone, down to her lips, then to her throat. ''By the time I'm finished with you, you aren't going to care where that coverlet is, I promise you that.''

Moving lower, he licked lightly at her skin, drawing closer and closer to the peak of one breast. Her aureole, swollen and throbbing with her every heartbeat, felt like velvet when he drew it into his mouth. At the first drag of his tongue, her muscles jerked, and she made fists in his hair as though to push him away. Alex realized she was even more sensitive than he'd guessed and gentled his ministrations, using light flicks of his tongue to coax her tender flesh to a pebbled hardness. When he judged her ready, he drew sharply on her. She gasped and arched against him, her throat convulsing on shrill whimpers of need. Her breath became quick and shallow as he flicked her with his tongue.

This time, Alex didn't mind if she gave a passionate outcry. The door was locked, and all the servants, including Maddy, slept in another wing. She could shriek all she liked. He not only didn't mind, but felt sure he'd find the sounds arousing. Capturing the throbbing nubbin of flesh at the crest of her nipple between his teeth, he gave it a roll. She immediately started to pant. Shrill, desperate little panting sounds that worked on his senses like a powerful aphrodisiac. Quickly, so as not to allow her time to resurface, he switched his attention to her other breast and gave it the same treatment.

When she finally grabbed hold of his ears, he knew he had succeeded in his initial goal. She was so aroused, he doubted she could think clearly, let alone feel afraid. Then and only then did he slip a hand under the coverlet.

To Alex's surprise, she parted her thighs, welcoming the touch of his hand. Cautiously, he sought the sweet center of her, smiling when she moaned with pleasure. Like shavings drawn to a magnet, his fingertips homed in on the patch of curls at the apex of her thighs. Gently, carefully, he parted the silken folds. White-hot. Slick with wetness. At the invasion of his touch, she bucked her hips and released her hold on his ears to raise up on her elbows. With his chest, he rode her back down to the bed. His face hovering scant inches from hers, he held her frightened gaze.

"Annie, trust me," he whispered huskily. "Will you do that? Just for a few minutes. Then, if you want me to stop, I will. I promise."

Her delicate brows drew together. But in the end, she nodded her assent.

Taut with tension, Alex found her sensitive feminine flesh. With light strokes, he teased her to arousal, watching the subtle changes in her expression. Pleasing her was his one concern. Annie came first. With him, she would always come first.

She never so much as blinked when he drew the coverlet off her. Never a man to pass up an opportunity, Alex took full advantage of her preoccupation. Bringing his mouth into play, he launched a gentle but relentless sensual attack to take possession of her sweetness.

With the first flick of his tongue against her sensitive nerve endings, she shrieked. With the second, she groaned low in her throat. With the third, she made tight little fists in the bottom sheet, dug her heels into the mattress, and arched her hips to better accommodate him. Her shrill pants and throaty little moans were the sweetest sounds he'd ever heard.

"Oh, yes, Annie, girl," he whispered raggedly. "Give yourself to me."

"Aaa-aah!" She arched higher, offering him what he sought, her breathing quick and shallow. "Aaa-aah—aah!"

Alex caught her tortured flesh between his teeth and began a slow, firm rotation with his tongue. She caught handfuls of his hair and pressed upward, clearly aroused beyond thought. Quickening his rhythm, he brought her to her first climax, marveling at how responsive and uninhibited she was.

When she finally lay spent and trembling, Alex drew away only long enough to shed his trousers. Then he positioned himself between her thighs and grasped her hips, nudging her open with the head of his shaft. She raised her lashes and gazed up at him with a dazed little smile, her eyes still dark with desire. Quickly, not giving her time to realize what he meant to do, he thrust smoothly into her.

Alex saw her eyes go wide with startlement. Then, for several seconds, he was aware of nothing but the sensation of being inside her. She was ready for him, hot and slick with desire, the walls of her womb snug around his shaft and still pulsating from orgasm. It took all his self-control not to spend himself, right then and there.

But before he could, her small face swam back into focus, and he was reminded that it was Annie's pleasure he needed to be concerned with, not his own. Taking care not to crush her with his weight, he suspended himself on his arms and managed to flash her a slow grin, withdrawing slightly, then driving deep. She gasped and made fists in the sheet again. Rejoicing in her response, Alex slowly picked up the pace, thrusting deeper and harder, intending to deny himself completion until he made certain she reached hers.

The tension slowly building, Alex leveled out to a rhythmic thrust, withdrawing, then driving himself deeply into her, ever aware of her expressions so he wouldn't hurt her. He needn't have worried. With the artless abandon that had captivated him from the beginning, Annie arched her neck, whimpered with pleasure, and wrapped her slender legs around his hips so she might undulate and intensify the impact. The need within Alex became an unbearable ache.

The best laid plans . . . Despite his determination to maintain control, when she cried out and quickened around him, the need inside him exploded into a mind-numbing pleasure that was like nothing he'd ever experienced or even imagined could exist.

Annie . . . Her breathless, panting little cries told Alex she was going to climax with him. Then the walls of her womb suddenly spasmed. Red flashed inside his head. Unable to see, no longer capable of thought, he surrendered to the need and plummeted into a swirl of sensation with her.

Annie . . . Fire and blackness. In some distant part of his mind, Alex was aware of her shrill cries of release. Then, completely drained of both energy and strength, he plummeted with her into the blackness of oblivion.

Annie drifted back to reality as though from a dream, becoming aware of her surroundings measure by measure, registering first the flicker of amber light, then the weave of the sheet beneath her, the heat of Alex's body pressed against hers, the heat of his breath against her hair, the weight of his arm over her waist. She blinked and drifted, feeling completely at peace and happier than she could recall ever being.

Alex. She lay with her back to his chest, her bottom fitted snugly into the crook of his body, his thighs, coarse with hair, pressed firmly against the backs of hers. Taking a deep breath, she absorbed the scents of him—faint traces of soap and cologne, tangy leather, the male musk-iness of his skin. Against her shoulder blades, she felt his heart thudding, the beat strong and even. It felt absolutely right to lie there, cradled against him, her body limp, her thoughts muddled.

Alex. Just once, she wished she'd heard his name so

she might imagine it now. She loved him. She loved him so much.

Heat rushed to her cheeks when she recalled the things he had done to her body. At the memories, a funny, achy, tingly feeling spread through her lower stomach. A smile curved her mouth, and she couldn't help but wish he'd wake up and do it all again.

To that end, she rolled over to face him. In the fire glow, she thought she'd never seen anyone so beautiful. His golden hair lay in tousled waves over his forehead, the wispy ends catching the light. In sleep, his carved features looked almost boyish, his lashes casting shadows over his bronzed cheeks, his lower lip relaxed and vibrating slightly with each breath he expelled. He pillowed his head on one bent arm, its underside a shade paler from lack of sunlight, the skin there stretched tight over thick muscle and tendon. Curious, she touched his chest, teasing the coarse tufts of hair to curl around her fingertip. When she grew bored with that, she gingerly explored one of his nipples, which were small and copper brown. When she flicked one with her fingernail, it hardened slightly, but somehow she didn't think it felt the same for him as for her.

She gave a start when she looked up and found that his golden eyes had come open. When their gazes met, he flashed a slow, lazy grin at her. "Why do I have this feeling my wife is refreshed and ready to go again?"

Annie dimpled a cheek at him and gave his nipple another flick. His grin deepened. "Is that a request that I return the favor?" he asked.

She shifted so the tips of her nipples grazed his chest. At the contact, they went instantly hard. She raised her eyebrows.

"You little minx."

He drew his arm from over her waist to cup her breast

in his hand. With a rub of his thumb, he coaxed her nipple more erect. Then he dipped his head forward to suckle her. Annie's eyes fell closed. The pleasure she felt was so intense, she could have lain there forever, letting him kiss her.

Alex had other ideas. After only a few kisses, he fell back against the pillow and regarded her from beneath lowered lashes, his smile mischievous. "If you want more, bring it on up here. I'm tired."

Annie knew he wasn't that tired. The gleam in his eyes told her differently. Feeling suddenly shy, she gazed with yearning at his mouth. Noticing her regard, his shoulders shook on a chuckle, and he grasped her by the arm to draw her to her knees.

"Come here," he said. "I don't bite."

As if to belie those words, he suddenly rose up to catch her gently in his teeth. One flick of his tongue was all it took to coax Annie closer. With an arm braced on either side of his head, she lowered her breasts to give him easy access. With lazy slowness, he accommodated her until she was trembling. She ended the torment by pulling away and covering his mouth with hers.

Catching her in his arms, he rolled with her, taking care not to crush her with his weight. Once on her back, Annie hooked her legs around his, thinking that he would make love to her again.

"Oh, no . . . Not so fast, Annie, love. We have the rest of our lives, so why get in a rush?"

The rest of their lives . . . Annie liked the thought of that. Night after night in Alex's arms. It was a promise fulfilled, definitely forty times better than what they'd done that long ago day in the nursery.

Twenty-three

The rest of their lives . . .

Over the next few days, Alex thought of little else, dreaming grand dreams of the future that he and Annie could share. He saw no reason that those dreams couldn't become a reality. In January, shortly after Christmas, their child would be born. From that moment on, they would be a family. Whether Alex could father more children was a question that remained to be answered and one that no longer even seemed important. Boy or girl, this first child would be his heir, and that was all that had ever mattered to him.

In Alex's mind, the child Annie carried was his as surely as if he'd planted the seed. He no longer thought about Douglas and what he'd done. Now that Annie had put it behind her, Alex found that he was able to as well. The past was forgotten. The future awaited them like a brilliant promise.

Loving Annie. To Alex, the girl was a precious gift. Given her experience at the falls, she had turned out to be a far more responsive lover than he could have ever dreamed possible, and he found it difficult to keep his hands off her. Fortunately, the feeling seemed to be mu-

tual. Once she got over her shyness, she initiated lovemaking almost as often as he did and was sometimes far
more creative. When it came to sex, she seemed to have
no idea that there were some things a lady simply never
did. One night while working in his study, he glanced up
from his paperwork to find Annie's naked bosom hovering just inches from his nose. The next thing he knew,
his papers were scattered on the floor and his wife was
sprawled across his desk.

Alex soon came to realize that Annie, who had never
been required to follow schedules or been dictated to by
clocks, was a creature of impulse. One night during supper, directly after Maddy had served dessert, she rose from
the table and advanced on him with a seductive little smile
that heated Alex's blood so quickly his ice cream was in
danger of melting.

"What are you up to, you little minx?"

With a flick of her hand, Annie shoved his dish of ice
cream aside and planted her lush derriere in its place. Her
lashes sweeping low over her eyes, which had turned a
dark, sultry blue, she said, "*I want to be your ice cream.*"

"My ice cream?" Alex repeated in bewilderment.

Curling her hands over his shoulders, she leaned forward and touched the tip of her tongue to his cheek, licking his skin and pretending to savor the taste, just as he
had done with his frozen dessert just moments ago.

"Jesus Christ," he said in a ragged whisper. "Annie,
sweetheart, a—"

He was about to explain to her that a proper lady would
never dream of making this sort of suggestion. But then
her hot little tongue found his ear, and he forgot what he
meant to say. Not that he had really wanted to say it,
anyway. What man in his right mind wanted his wife to
be a proper lady behind closed doors? Alex knew that
most husbands got stuck with prudish wives who were

total bores in bed. It was his good fortune that Annie had come into their marriage with no preconceived notions of what was proper. He would be a million times a fool if he filled her head with a bunch of ridiculous social mores.

With deft fingers, Alex unfastened her bodice and made short work of unlacing her chemise. Her breasts spilled forth like plump melons tipped from a basket. Strike that, he thought, as his heated gaze settled on her nipples. They were more the delicate pink of strawberry juice mixed with cream.

While he was busy admiring her bounty, Annie was reaching behind her for his dessert dish. Alex watched in stunned amazement as she dipped a dainty fingertip into the fast-melting ice cream and then rubbed the cold sweetness on her nipple. Her pink flesh turned instantly hard and seemed to thrust toward his mouth, eager for attention. As if to demonstrate what she had in mind, she leaned forward again to lick lightly at his lips.

Alex, who had always prided himself on being a quick study, shoved up from his chair. In his recollection, he had never covered ground quite so quickly as he did that which stretched between the table and the dining room doors. After throwing the lock so no one could disturb them, he returned to accommodate his wife, who was now covering her other breast with sweetness.

Thoroughly aroused, but trying not to show it, Alex reclaimed his seat and waited to see what else she had in mind. When she looked up, her expression was impish. Locking gazes with him, she slowly and suggestively suckled each of her fingers clean. Alex's guts knotted with yearning, but he was enjoying the display too much to bring it to an early end. Not just yet.

As he hoped, Annie pressed her bare breasts upon him, teasing his lips with her warm, sticky nipples until he could resist the temptation no longer and began to lick the sweetness away. Her flesh went instantly hard and pebbled. She ran her hands into his hair and arched her back to make her breasts more accessible. Alex licked and suckled the sensitive peaks, smiling at her whimpering sounds of pleasure.

Her whimpering soon grew louder. Groping behind her, he located his discarded napkin and pressed it against her mouth. As if she realized his intent, she took it between her teeth to muffle her cries.

No longer concerned about the noise she might make, Alex was able to concentrate solely on Annie and pleasing her. While groping for his napkin, he'd bumped his dessert dish. He reached for it now and dipped his fingertips into the froth of melting ice cream. He repainted Annie's nipples with the sweetness. Strawberries and cream . . . Never had Alex tasted anything like it. It was deliciously wicked, the sort of eroticism a man dreamed of but never experienced. But with Annie, who was blissfully ignorant of the rules, there were none to follow. She was governed only by sensation.

That had always been fine by Alex, but never more so than now. Vaguely, he heard dishes clattering as he swept them out of the way to lay his wife upon the table. Feverishly, he fumbled with her clothing. Skirts, petticoats, pantalets, garters, hose. Christ. Recalling the morn of their wedding, when she'd perched on the landing above him and displayed herself for his perusal, he wished she were wearing that simple attire again. Now that he'd gotten a taste of how delightful ice cream and his sweet little wife tasted together, he wanted to try the blend elsewhere.

When he had peeled away enough clothing to find what he sought, Alex leaned back a moment to regard her from under passion-heavy eyelids. The folds of her femininity glistened up at him, the delicate pink reminding him once again of strawberries . . . which always begged for cream.

Above the crumpled napkin, Annie's huge blue eyes sought his. Alex smiled slowly. She had started this game. Now he meant to take it to new lengths. As he dipped his fingertips into the ice cream, she seemed to guess his intent. Evidently even Annie realized that this was carrying things a bit too far.

"Aah . . ."

Halfheartedly, she tried to twist away. There was nothing halfhearted about Alex's move to stop her. After laving his fingertips, he found her hot, throbbing center with deft aim. Her shocked little cry was muffled by the napkin as he smeared the coldness over her silken folds. Her entire body jerked when he caught the sensitive nubbin of flesh hidden there between his thumb and forefinger. Giving it a hard roll, Alex watched her eyes drift closed. She moaned low in her chest and ground her hips upward, clearly overcome.

Annie, for dessert. It was the sweetest ending to a meal that Alex had ever experienced. If, in future, she found him more appealing than the food served for supper, he would be more than happy to make himself available. It was the least a husband could do for his sweet, biddable, insatiable little wife.

Annie . . . For such a small woman, she had a very large presence in Alex's life, filling his days with laughter, his nights with lovemaking, and his sleep with dreams of her.

Around the middle of December, Dr. Muir paid a visit, supposedly to see Annie, but in truth to speak privately with Alex. Afraid that Annie might become upset during the medical examination, which was, by necessity, more invasive than the one Muir had done during the early months of her pregnancy, Alex remained with his wife while the doctor was with her. Afterward, both men retired to the study to have a brandy and discuss the doctor's findings.

Coming right to the point, Muir said, "Everything looks normal, Alex, so stop looking so worried."

Alex smiled as he handed the good doctor a drink. Taking the chair catty-corner to him, he said, "Am I so obvious?"

"You've become very fond of her. That's apparent."

Alex rested a booted foot on his knee. "I am that."

"And the lessons? How are those coming?"

"Very well. She's mastered a goodly number of signs and knows her alphabet now. As of last week, we graduated to a first-year primer."

Muir raised his glass. "Congratulations. That's quite a feat."

Alex lowered his foot to the floor and leaned forward to rest his arms on his knees. "I think so. To be honest, I was hoping the ear horns might be more of a help than they're proving to be. Even though, with the horns, she seems able to hear me if I speak loudly, she can't seem to reproduce the sounds correctly. The few words she has actually tried to say are grossly distorted."

Daniel nodded. "That's probably to be expected. She lost her hearing at six. It's been fourteen years since she's been allowed to speak. She's forgotten how. With a hearing disability, it's bound to take time for her to relearn all she's forgotten."

Alex sighed. "So I keep reminding myself." He shrugged and smiled. "Now that I can lip-read, we manage to communicate well enough."

"What about when the child comes? It would be nice if Annie were to master at least a small vocabulary before it begins learning to talk."

Alex considered that for a moment. "We'll just have to see how she progresses."

Daniel tapped his finger against his glass, eyeing Alex

over its rim. "I know you want what's best for Annie and the child."

"Of course I do."

"I was just wondering if you'd considered sending her away to school."

"School?"

Daniel raised an eyebrow. "She needs special instruction, Alex. I know you're doing wonders. I take nothing away from you. But to truly recover her speech, Annie should have specialized tutors, people who know how to help her. The school in Albany is reputable. Irene Small, the headmistress, is a fantastic instructor, and in addition to addressing her pupils' educational needs, she sees to it they're enriched culturally and socially. It would be very good for Annie to go there, at least for two or three years. That isn't so long a time. She'd still be a young woman when she finished her instruction. And just think how much the experience would benefit her."

Alex's heart felt as if it had fallen to the floor. "Two or three years?"

Daniel smiled. "Albany isn't that far away. You look as though I just suggested we send her to a foreign country." He, too, sat forward in his chair, his gaze direct and filled with concern. "Alex, please, at least think about it. I think I could convince Irene to make room for Annie. Since Annie will have a child, she could be a nonresident student. Maybe Maddy could move to Albany with her. The two of them could rent a small house near the school. Somewhere close enough that Annie could walk to classes."

Alex shot up from his chair, spilling brandy in his agitation. "No. It's out of the question. We're discussing my wife here. I'm not going to send her away for two to three years." He raked a hand through his hair and started to pace. "Jesus Christ, Daniel, I don't know how you can even suggest such a thing. If you think Annie needs a special tutor, I'll hire one. But she's staying here at Montgomery Hall where she belongs, end of discussion.''

Daniel set his drink aside and pushed to his feet, retrieving his bag as he stood. ''Alex, with all your money and good intentions, you can't buy Annie the things she needs most. Up there in Albany, the students produce their own plays. They have dances and socials and musicals, all geared expressly for the deaf. Annie would be around other people like herself for the first time in her life. There's no way you can provide all of those experiences for her here.''

Alex turned a fiery gaze on him. ''Maybe not. But you're asking me to send my wife and child away. I can't do that. I won't. It wouldn't be right.''

''Right for who, you or Annie? Think about it, Alex.'' Daniel strode slowly to the study door. He paused before opening it to look back at Alex over his shoulder. ''If you truly love the girl, and I believe you do, then in the end, you'll do what's best for her. I'm convinced of that. As I said, I believe I can convince Irene to take her. If you'd like, I'll check into it for you. I think Annie could start instruction in March. She will be sufficiently recovered from childbirth by that time to travel and make the move.''

Struggling to regain his composure, Alex finally replied, ''I guess it couldn't hurt for you to look into it for me. As long as you understand that it's highly unlikely I'd seriously consider it.''

Daniel smiled slightly. ''You'll do the right thing. You always do.''

With that, Daniel quit the room.

Over the next few days, Alex considered what Daniel had said. So great was his indecision that he even consulted Edie Trimble, who agreed wholeheartedly with Dr. Muir that sending Annie away to school was a wonderful idea. No matter how he circled it, deep down he knew his mother-in-law and the physician were probably right. At a school for the deaf, a whole new world would be opened up for Annie. She'd learn not only to speak, but to read and write, things Alex wasn't absolutely sure he could teach her. And in addition to that, she would have a chance to be around other people like herself. In Albany, she could make friends, something that had always been denied her.

Dances . . . parties . . . plays . . . In short, a social life. That was something Alex could not buy for her. If he kept her here with him at Montgomery Hall, he would be cheating her out of those experiences.

For a short time, Alex considered hiring a competent foreman to oversee Montgomery Hall so he might move to Albany and be with Annie while she attended school. But, after he really thought about it, he knew that would be almost as selfish as keeping her in Hooperville. If he were there in Albany, always backstage, always waiting, she wouldn't feel free to participate in all the social activities she would enjoy otherwise. As much as he wanted to be with her, he didn't want to be a proverbial chain around her neck, either. Other people were allowed to experience life to its fullest before being tied down in marriage. Annie deserved the same privilege.

Two or three years . . . As Daniel said, it wasn't that long a time. If all went well, Annie would only be twenty-three when she completed her schooling and came back to live permanently at Montgomery Hall. In the meanwhile, Alex could visit her in Albany occasionally, and she could come home during holidays. He could live with that. He had to.

For Annie's sake, he had no choice.

Once his decision was made, Alex wasted no time in speaking to Maddy. The housekeeper, though initially against the idea, eventually agreed to accompany Annie to Albany so she could help care for the baby while Annie was attending school. Once that was settled, Alex began corresponding regularly with Irene Small to ensure Annie's enrollment, to secure off-campus housing for her, and to pay her tuition in advance. After doing all that, only one thing remained to be done, and that was to tell Annie. Alex decided it would be best not to risk upsetting her with the news until after the baby was born.

Over the next few weeks, Alex cherished every moment with her, for he knew their time together was destined to end all too soon. Long walks in the rain. Making love by firelight. Planning for the baby. Through it all, Alex pretended they had all the time in the world stretching before them. He never let on to Annie that he sometimes looked at her and imagined how empty his life was going to be without her.

Life without her . . . It was a possibility Alex couldn't completely discount. Annie had become his wife not by choice, but against her will. Over the months, she had learned to love him; he didn't doubt the sincerity of her feelings, not for a minute. But the bottom line was, it hadn't been an instant attraction. Most young women— and Annie was no different than any other—harbored romantic notions of meeting someone special, of being swept into his arms and carried off to live happily ever after. The fact that the fantasy usually lasted only as long as the honeymoon was beside the point and didn't stop girls from dreaming their dreams.

What if? Those two words haunted Alex, awake or asleep. What if, when Annie went away to school, she met a deaf man and fell wildly in love? He imagined her looking across a crowded room, straight into the eyes of

Mr. Right. He pictured her waltzing in his arms, attending a play with him, laughing with him. A faceless man, a nameless man, someone with whom Annie would have things in common, most importantly a shared affliction and an inherent understanding of the difficulties that arose from it. At best, Alex could only guess how frustrated she must feel sometimes, not being able to communicate with other people, not being able to read their lips if they turned away while speaking to her. He tried. He truly did. But no matter how much he wanted to understand what it was like for her, he knew he never really would, not without experiencing deafness himself.

In dark moments, Alex remembered the sketch Annie had once drawn of herself without ears. In Albany, she would be like everyone else. If she met a man there, if she fell in love, who could blame her for not wanting to return to Hooperville, where she'd suffered so much pain and humiliation at the hands of others? Alex knew he couldn't. And therein lay the heartbreak. It was damned easy to love a woman enough to spend a lifetime with her. Loving her enough to set her free was another matter entirely.

It seemed to Alex that time flew by, carrying them relentlessly toward the day when Annie would leave him. Christmas came and went. December gave way to January, and they began to mark off the days until Annie's due date. On the evening of the eighth, which was several days early, according to Daniel's calculations, Alex was in the water closet, washing up before going to bed, when he heard Annie cry out. Heart in throat, he tore into the bedroom to find her standing before the armoire, her white nightgown soaked with pinkish fluid, her face pale with fright.

"Honey, it's all right. Your water just broke, that's all."

Christ! The baby was coming. Alex tore open dresser drawers, searching for a dry nightgown. Striving to appear calm when he actually was terrified, he helped her to change and then got her into bed before racing downstairs to find Maddy.

"Send Henry for Dr. Muir," he yelled. "Annie's having the baby! Her water broke. It's coming, Maddy. We have to get Daniel over here. Fast!"

Maddy stared at him long and hard. "Alex, methinks ye'd better calm down. It'll likely be hours before the lass gives birth."

Alex gulped and rubbed a hand over his face. "Are you absolutely sure?"

Maddy calmly took off her soiled apron and put on a fresh one. "Of course I'm not sure. But, as I understand it, that's the usual way of things with the first baby."

Alex relaxed slightly and took a deep breath. "I guess you're right. I am overreacting a little, aren't I?" He gestured weakly and chuckled. "It *is* just a baby coming, after all. I mean—well, women have babies every day. Right?"

Maddy marched past him. Throwing open the kitchen door, she poked her head into the room beyond and screamed, "Henry! Get yer arse down here! The baby's comin'!"

So much for everyone remaining calm. On the way upstairs, Alex discovered that when she was scared, Maddy could damned near outrun him, even going uphill. He also discovered that, jogging abreast of each other, they tended to become stuck when they tried to pass through doorways.

During all this excitement, Annie had drifted off into a restless sleep. When Alex and Maddy reached his bedchamber and found her napping, they each pulled up a chair, one at either side of the bed, and sat down to stare at her stomach. Every once in a while Annie would moan softly, at which times Alex felt sure her belly tightened. When he said as much to Maddy, she leaned forward to watch more closely.

'Ach! I believe ye're right. She's havin' a slight contraction.''

Alex opened his watch. "It's fifteen after. Help me remember so we can accurately time them, all right?"

That was how Daniel found the three of them, Annie sound asleep, Alex and Maddy counting her pains. Upon seeing the doctor, Maddy said, "Now that the moment's upon us, me thinks egg layin' would've been easier."

Daniel couldn't help chuckling. "From the look of things, I'd say Annie's faring better than either of you. It may be a few hours before we get down to serious business, you know. I can sit with Annie while you two get some sleep, if you'd like."

"Sleep?" they echoed.

Daniel chuckled. "I suppose not." He rubbed his chin. "Hmm . . . Well, when there's a change, call me. I'll be stretched out in the study. If neither of you intends to get some rest, I can't see why I shouldn't."

Right before dawn, Alex ran down to the study to shake the doctor awake. "It's coming," he said shakily. "Hurry, Daniel. She's in a bad way."

The physician sat up and rubbed the sleep from his eyes, apparently in no hurry. "I could use a cup of coffee."

"Coffee?" Alex grabbed the man by his arm and jerked him up from the sofa. "My wife is giving birth! You don't have time for a goddamned cup of coffee."

Several cups of coffee and nearly ten hours later, Annie went into hard labor. Alex refused to leave her side, much to Daniel's dismay. As a general rule, he didn't allow fathers to attend births. In his experience, most men didn't handle it well, and thus far, Alex hadn't shown any sign that he might prove to be an exception. As Annie's pains grew worse, however, Alex dug in and weathered the storm quite well, outwardly calm and doing all he could to soothe Annie when she became frightened.

"It's all right, sweetheart," he said, over and over. "I'm here."

Watching the two of them together, Daniel realized he had underestimated the love they felt for each other. No matter how excruciating her pain, Annie never took her gaze off Alex or let go of his hand. And, exhausted though Alex was, he never left the girl's side, not to have a meal, not to rest, not even to stretch his legs.

What touched Daniel most of all, though, was watching the two of them communicate in sign. More than once, he saw Alex moving his fingers against Annie's palm, talking to her—Daniel suspected he was saying he loved her—in an intimate way that no one else could interpret.

When the climactic moment finally arrived, Daniel delivered the baby, but it was Alex who coached Annie through the ordeal, Alex who mopped her face and smoothed her hair, Alex who placed her son in her arms. "A boy, Annie," he said huskily. "Isn't he something? We have a son."

When Daniel saw the tears in Alex Montgomery's eyes, he took it as his cue to leave the room and give the couple some privacy. Once in the hall, he leaned wearily against the wall, his gaze fixed blankly on the floor, his thoughts on Annie, Alex, and their marriage, which, until today, he had believed was little more than a convenient arrangement. Not so, he realized now. If ever he'd seen two people deeply in love, it was those two.

Albany . . . In March, Annie would go away to school, leaving her husband behind. Daniel had sincerely believed it was the best thing for the girl. Now he was no longer so sure.

Watching Alex's face as he looked down at his son in her arms, Annie was filled with an indescribable joy. He looked both tender and fiercely protective, every line of his face taut with emotion. She understood the feelings, for she was experiencing them herself. Her baby. Her own tiny baby. In the space of only a few minutes, she loved this tiny person so completely it was almost frightening.

Alex knelt beside the bed and curled an arm around the two of them. Blinking to keep her eyes open, for she was absolutely exhausted, Annie looked into his beloved face and smiled. She'd never felt so complete. In that moment, it struck her that, for the first time in her life, she could love without reservation. There were two people who needed her. Really needed her. She'd never felt needed before.

From girl to woman . . . Annie felt as though she'd made the journey almost overnight. But, oh, it was wonderful. Sleepily, she traced the handsome lines of Alex's dark face with her gaze. Then she looked down at her son. The warmth of his tiny body pressed against her breast was the most wondrous feeling she'd ever experienced. He resembled his papa, she decided. A good thing. It would be a shame if he were to grow up and look like her.

On that thought, she closed her eyes, losing the battle against exhaustion. As she drifted off to sleep, she was filled with a sense of purpose. For years, she had slipped away to the attic to pretend she was somebody. From now on, there would be no need to pretend. Through this man and child, she had found definition.

Annie Montgomery . . . wife and mother.

* * *

"Thank God I'm sterile," Alex said to Daniel a short while later when they met downstairs in the study. "Never again. I *never* want her to go through that again."

Daniel smiled to himself and leaned a shoulder against the rock face of the fireplace. "I don't mean to be the voice of doom, my man, but what if you aren't?"

"Castrate me."

Daniel threw back his head and laughed.

Alex shot him a glare. "I don't know what you think is so damned funny. That poor girl. My God, I've never seen anything like it." His eyes darkened with worry. "Will she heal? Back like she was, I mean?"

Daniel considered the question. "Well, a certain amount of stretching has occurred. A woman can never provide as tight a fit for her husband after the babies start coming along."

A fiery glint entered Alex's eyes. "Jesus Christ, Daniel! I don't care if I have to tie a two-by-four to my ass to keep from falling in. That wasn't what I was asking. I want to know if she's going to be all right inside. Has this caused any permanent injury?"

"Of course not. She'll be right as rain in four weeks. If you're truly dead set against putting any more bread in her oven, come see me before the time has elapsed and I'll advise you on precautionary measures. You needn't worry about it now."

Alex sank into a chair and sighed. "I don't need to worry about it, period."

"If you don't want more children, I suggest you take precautions, nonetheless. True, you had the mumps and there were complications. But I've seen men recover from worse cases and go on to sire children."

"Not me. I'm sterile, I tell you."

"You've been associating only with prostitutes, Alex.

That kind of woman protects herself. How the hell can you possibly know if you're sterile?''

''How do you know what kind of women I've associated with?''

''Gossip.''

''Gossip?''

Muir smiled slightly. ''You're a very eligible bachelor and not given to promiscuous behavior. On those rare occasions when you went into town, tongues wagged about it for a month. I presumed you were patronizing Kate's place. Was I wrong?''

Alex ran a hand over his face. ''No, you weren't wrong.'' Now that he thought about it, Alex supposed Kate's girls did take precautions to prevent pregnancy. ''And your point is well-taken, Daniel. I suppose there is a minute possibility that I'm not sterile.'' He flashed the doctor a stricken look. ''God help me, if I get that girl pregnant again, I'll shoot myself.''

Daniel couldn't help chuckling at his horrified expression. ''The next time will be easier on her, son. Trust me, she's perfectly made to deliver a dozen healthy babies.''

''A dozen? Jesus Christ!'' Alex shot up from his chair and started to pace. ''That's it then. I'm not touching her. Maybe it's a damned good thing I'm sending her away to school, after all.''

Daniel pushed away from the fireplace and thrust his hands in his pockets. He'd heard many a man make the same vow directly after his wife delivered their first child. ''You'll begin to feel differently as time wears on.''

Alex shook his head. ''No. She is not going to suffer like that again. Not if I can help it, and there's no question there. It's a simple matter of abstinence.''

Highly amused, Daniel asked, ''What will you do? Go into town every Saturday night? Annie may have something to say about that.''

"My nights in town are over. I'm married, for God's sake."

Daniel grinned. "We'll see how things go. As I said, there are some precautions you can take. When Annie comes home for visits or you go to Albany to see her, abstinence may be rather—constraining."

Alex glanced back over his shoulder. "Are the precautions absolutely safe?"

"Nothing is absolutely safe."

"Then I'll suffer."

It was a promise Alex meant to keep.

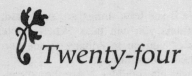

Twenty-four

During the first month of his life, Bartholomew Alexander Montgomery, named after Alex's father, grew at an impressive rate, thriving on his mother's milk and the limitless love that was showered upon him by all the adults in his world. But even with his added inches, at the end of four weeks, he still wasn't as long as his name. What he lacked in length, however, he compensated for with lung power. When he cried, everyone in the house but his mother heard him and came running.

Little Bart, Alex called him. It was a name that underwent subtle changes when he woke up Alex at three o'clock in the morning. As he scooped his son from the cradle to pace the floor with him, Alex would whisper, "You little fart. It's the middle of the night." Bart, like his mother, seemed to have no concept of time and was a creature of impulse. Predawn socializing had never been one of Alex's favorite activities. But, after four weeks, he had to admit that the habit was beginning to grow on him. A little too much for his peace of mind. It was already the tenth of February and the first of March was only three weeks away.

For several different reasons, Alex had waited to tell

Annie that he meant to send her away to school. For one, he wanted what little time they had left together untarnished by sadness, and the minute he told Annie, they were both going to feel sad. For another, he fully expected her to take the news badly, and he couldn't see much point in upsetting her weeks before it was necessary. For fourteen years, she'd been forced to live in veritable seclusion. To suddenly be thrust into the world, to be expected to attend classes and socialize, would not be easy for her.

There was also the inescapable fact that Alex had discovered a very broad yellow streak running up his spine. The long and short of it was, he didn't look forward to telling Annie of his decision because he knew she was going to hate him for it. Attending school in Albany was the best thing for her. Alex was convinced of that, and eventually Annie would realize it as well. But, like bitter medicine, what was best for a person wasn't always very palatable.

Well in advance, Alex thought of a dozen different ways he might break the news to her, but when the moment finally arrived, all his well-rehearsed speeches went the way of dandelion fluff on the wind. They were in the study, a checkerboard unfolded on the game table between them, the baby well-bundled and asleep on the horsehair sofa nearby. Gathering his courage, Alex looked into his wife's beautiful blue eyes and said, "I have a wonderful surprise for you, Annie. It's something I've been waiting to tell you about for weeks now."

In the flickering light from the fire, her smile seemed even more radiant than usual. Looking at her, Alex knew he'd never seen anyone more beautiful. Two days ago, the dressmaker had completed her postnatal wardrobe, and she was absolutely stunning in a deep rose skirt and pale pink cotton blouse with ruffled cap sleeves. The outfit

conformed to her figure, revealing her now slender waist
and gently flaring hips.

"*A surprise? What is it? A puppy?*"

Alex's throat went tight. He hadn't forgotten her yearning for a dog. Before deciding to send her away, he'd
planned to buy her one for Christmas. Now that would
have to wait until she finished school. "No, not a dog,
sweetheart." He forced a smile. "It's something better
than that." Leaning forward over the checkerboard, he
looked deeply into her eyes. "I've decided to send you
to school, Annie. A school for the deaf."

Her eyes darkened, and a bewildered expression came
across her small face. "*School?*" She smiled hesitantly.
"*When?*"

"In three weeks," Alex said huskily. "Oh, Annie,
you're going to love it. The students there put on their
own plays. You'll be very good at that. You've been
dressing up and putting on plays in the attic for years!
And they have dances there. Real dances. You'll get to
wear pretty dresses and waltz until you drop. Won't that
be fun?"

The darkness left her eyes to be replaced by a sparkle
of excitement. "*Dances?*"

"Absolutely. With music and everything." As he
watched her, Alex sent up a quick, heartfelt prayer that
his facial expressions weren't as revealing as hers, that
she would never guess that with every word he spoke, his
heart was breaking. "You'll make friends there, Annie.
With deaf people just like you. People who know how to
speak in sign. Before you know it, you'll be able to read
and write. Won't that be grand?"

She clasped her hands and held them to her chest. "*Oh,
yes! In three weeks? How long is three weeks?*"

"Not very long. About twenty days." It wasn't nearly
long enough, not in his books. "You'll leave on the

twenty-eighth. That'll give you plenty of time to get settled in before your classes start.''

Her excited smile became frozen. After staring at him for several long seconds, she said, ''*Leave?*''

Alex swallowed. ''Um, yes. The school is up in Albany. You'll go by train. Maddy will be with you, though, so that won't be a problem. While you're at school during the day, she'll take care of Bart.''

Annie continued to stare at him. ''*How long?*''

Alex knew what she was asking, but he chose to pretend he didn't. ''How long? The train ride, you mean? Several hours. I'll have to check the schedule. Albany is about two hundred miles from here.'' He smiled again. ''That's five sets of forty, in case you're wondering. It sounds like a long way, but it really isn't, not in this day and age with modern modes of transportation.''

Her gaze clung to his. ''*No . . . I meant how long will I be at school?*''

''Only as long as it takes for you to learn all you need to know. How to speak, how to read and write, how to do arithmetic.''

''*A very long time.*''

''No . . . At the very most, Annie, it'll be two or three years. Because you went deaf after acquiring language skills, you're going to pass the other students as if they're standing still. Before you know it, you'll graduate. Meanwhile, we'll visit back and forth. It won't seem like a very long time at all.''

For an awful moment, Alex thought she might burst into tears. Then she brought her chin up, squared her shoulders and flashed a smile that didn't quite reach her eyes. ''*How exciting. I can hardly wait!*''

With that, she pushed up from her chair, avoiding his gaze, but keeping her face turned toward him so he might read her lips. "*I think I'm too excited to play checkers anymore. Please, excuse me.*"

"Annie!" Alex called. "Honey, wait . . ."

Quickly gathering up the baby, she headed for the door, never turning, never looking back. As she exited the study, Alex fell back in his chair and closed his eyes. Then, with a violent sweep of his arm, he sent the checkerboard flying.

Annie held Bartholomew snugly against her breast and stared sightlessly into the fire, the toes of her slippers touching the floor periodically to keep the rocking chair in motion. She didn't look left or right, up or down, just stared straight ahead, the pain in her chest so intense that she found it difficult to breathe.

School . . . for two or three years. In Albany, where she would learn to speak, read and write, and do arithmetic. In Albany, where she would not be a part of Alex's life until she was sufficiently accomplished to no longer be an embarrassment to him.

Annie the dummy . . .

She closed her eyes, determined not to cry, no matter how much it hurt. She couldn't blame him. Not really. From the first, she'd known she wasn't good for him, that her deafness made her unsuitable as a wife. If she went away to school, she might learn to talk. That alone would help. When Alex took her into town, people wouldn't be as likely to stare and whisper if she could speak. It would be better for Bartholomew as well. The last thing Annie wanted was for him to be teased and taunted because his mother was a dummy. She knew how it hurt to be constantly ridiculed.

Albany . . . A school for the deaf. Where she could make friends. A special place, where everyone else was a dummy, too. A place where the dummies put on plays and went to dances and pretended they were normal. A place where Alex could send her so people wouldn't see her with him all the time and laugh at him.

Bartholomew began to squirm. Opening her eyes, Annie unfastened her bodice and put him to her breast. As he snuggled down to suckle, she ran her fingertips over his silken little head. Rocking, constantly rocking. Inside her head, the word *Albany* became a singsong. In three weeks, she would go there. In three years, if she learned quickly, she could come home. It was as simple and horrible as that.

Creak—creak—creak—creak. The sound was enough to drive Alex crazy. He sat on the edge of the bed, patiently waiting for Annie to finish feeding Bart so he could talk to her about going away to school. From the look he'd seen in her eyes downstairs, he knew she believed he didn't want her with him, that he was sending her away expressly to get her out of his way.

Nothing was farther from the truth. He loved her more than he'd ever loved anyone. Just the thought of spending a day without her was torture, let alone months at a time. He'd rather cut off his arm.

From his vantage point, he had a clear frontal view of her. Bart had long since grown bored with nursing and was pacifying himself, nothing more. Halfhearted suckles, gumming the crest of her nipple. Annie just sat there, letting him rout, her small feet rhythmically pushing to keep the rocker in constant motion. *Creak—creak—creak.* Alex was tempted to take the goddamned chair and throw it out the window. Instead, he sat there, the epitome of patience, willing his wife to at least look at him.

Bart finally began to doze. Catching her nipple between index and middle fingers, Annie teased his little mouth, apparently reluctant to end the feeding and thus find herself with no excuse to ignore her husband. Watching her, Alex bit down hard on his back teeth, not because she was ignoring him, but because seeing her naked breasts was driving him half-mad.

He pushed up from the bed and began to pace. Four weeks was a hell of a long time to abstain from touching one's wife. He felt like the head of a match held too close to a flame, ready to ignite at any second. Between listening to the chair creak incessantly, which she couldn't hear, and watching her fiddle with herself, he was perilously close to either strangling her or seducing her, the latter of which seemed a lot more tempting.

Now that her ordeal in childbirth had faded a bit from his mind, Alex wasn't quite so appalled by the thought of siring another child. Dr. Muir had assured him the second birth wouldn't be as difficult for Annie, and that she was perfectly made to bear children. As if such a thing were even possible. If he truly wasn't sterile, it seemed rather fortuitous that he'd never left his calling card anywhere. Surely the vinegar-soaked sponges prostitutes used weren't failure-free as a means of preventing pregnancy.

He strode to the window and pulled back the ivory drape to gaze out into the darkness. Staring at nothing had to be better than torturing himself. After several endless seconds, he glanced over his shoulder, hoping and praying that she had fastened her bodice. But, of course, she hadn't. Not Annie. She had, however, stopped enticing Bart to nurse. Alex was thankful for small blessings.

He turned and moved decisively toward her. At his approach, she raised blue eyes to his. One look from her, and his irritation vanished. His decision to send her away had hurt her deeply. Somehow, he had to make her understand that it hurt him just as badly to think about letting her go.

Bending over her, he scooped the baby from her arms and put him in his cradle. Then he hunkered beside her rocker, watching dry-mouthed as she tucked her breasts back into her chemise and tied the drawstring into a neat little bow.

"Annie . . ." He caught her chin and made her look at him. "I don't *want* to send you away. I know that's what you're thinking. Don't deny it. I promise you, sweetheart, you couldn't be more wrong."

Eyes luminous with unshed tears and aching with pain, she sat there glaring at him. He had a very bad feeling.

"I love you, damn it. I'm not sending you to school to get rid of you." Enfolding her hands in his, he listed all his reasons for having made the decision, ending with, "I don't want to deny you those experiences, sweetheart. If I did, I'd be the most selfish bastard who ever walked."

"*What about what I want?*" she finally asked.

Alex sighed. "Honey, you don't *know* what you want. Can't you understand that? How can you know if you'd rather stay here than see a play? You've never even seen one. And dances. It's easy to think you don't care about those things, but that's only because you've never done any of them. I have." He leaned down to look into her slightly downcast eyes. "I know what you've missed, Annie, love. And I want you to experience life at its fullest. Making friends, having fun with them. Being able to go to school, like other people. Once you're there, you're going to love it. I promise you that."

She shook her head and gestured around her. "*This is the life I want. To be here with you. To be your wife.*"

"You only think that because you've never experienced anything else." Alex took a deep breath. He needed strength. It was so tempting, so damnably tempting, to let her stay with him. "I'll tell you what. Let's make a bargain, hmm? You go to school and stick it out for one whole year. If, after that long a time, you still want to come home, I—''

She sprang from the chair. After taking several steps away, she swung around to fasten tear-bright eyes on him. Lifting her hands, she cried, *"You don't want me. That's the truth of it. And you don't love me. Not like I love you! If you did, you couldn't do this."*

Alex rose to his feet. "That is *not* true. I love you so much it hurts. Just the thought of your leaving makes me feel sick. I don't—''

She cupped her hands over her eyes. *"Just go away!"*

He closed the distance between them and drew her hands down. "Annie, sweetheart, please, don't make this any more difficult than it has to be.''

"Go away! You don't want me. I don't want you. So go away!"

"I do want you.''

Her mouth twisted and the tears welling in her eyes spilled over her dark lashes onto her cheeks. *"No, you don't. You don't even kiss me anymore."*

The accusation hit Alex like a fist in the gut. It was true; he didn't kiss her anymore. He feared that if he did, he'd lose control and make love to her. What if he wasn't sterile? When he was thinking rationally, which he damned well wouldn't be if he kissed her, he knew that getting her pregnant was a risk he couldn't take. Another baby . . . She wouldn't be able to go away to school if he got her with child again. If Dr. Muir was right, if there was even a slight chance . . .

His voice gravelly with a longing he couldn't slake, Alex whispered, "I'd like nothing better than to kiss you, Annie, girl. But if I do, I may do more than just kiss you. If I make love to you, you could get pregnant again.''

Her eyes widened and she pressed a hand over her waist. *"With a baby?"*

"Of course, with a baby."

"*Making love. That's what makes babies?*"

Alex swallowed. "Well, yes. How'd you think?"

Looking stricken, she whispered something he didn't catch.

"What?"

"*Fairies,*" she repeated. "*Mama told me fairies brought them.*"

A sudden headache was developing behind Alex's eyes. "Fairies?" He gave a low chuckle, but there was no humor in it. "Surely you didn't *believe* that, Annie. I mean, when you thought about it, surely you—" He broke off, staring down at her pale face. "I, um . . . I guess, maybe, if no one ever explained, then it's understandable that you didn't—"

He broke off, watching her with a sinking heart as she turned an agonized gaze toward the cradle. After a long moment, she stiffened as though someone had struck her, then closed her eyes. A low, keening sound issued from her throat. Alex reached for her, but she shook him off. When she finally opened her eyes again, the look she gave him was pulverizing.

"*You lied.*"

The nape of Alex's neck prickled. "Annie, no. I didn't lie."

She had begun to shake. An awful, horrible shaking. "*Douglas!*"

"Annie . . ."

She whirled and ran before Alex could stop her. The door slammed behind her with a resounding crash. The retort startled Bart awake, and he began to fuss. Alex ran out into the hall. He caught a glimpse of pink at the end of the corridor and guessed that Annie was going up to the attic, her favorite hiding place. Hurrying to the landing, he called down for Maddy to come and tend the baby.

* * *

The attic was as dark as pitch. His mind racing, Alex held the lamp high as he made his way toward Annie's little parlor. When he finally reached the area he sought, he expected to find her huddled in a corner crying. Instead she was sitting in the old rocker. Moving the lamp so the light played over her, he studied her face, trying to think of something, anything, he might say to soothe her. There was nothing. Not one damned thing.

He set the lamp on her wobbly table and took a seat on one of the straight-backed chairs. For a long while, they simply gazed into each other's eyes, his aching with regret, hers burning with unvoiced accusations. Looking at it from her side, Alex could see how it must seem, that he had deliberately kept the truth from her. The heartbreak of it was, no one had bothered to lie to her. Not him, not her parents. They hadn't deemed it necessary because all of them had believed they were dealing with a moron. Later, when Alex learned the truth, the identity of the child's biological father had seemed irrelevant. In Alex's heart, he was the father, and that was all that seemed to matter. In his heart, it was still all that mattered.

In a throbbing voice, he said as much. Annie continued to stare at him in accusing silence. Alex sighed and pinched the bridge of his nose. When he looked back at her, he said, ''In the beginning, it was my intention to stay married to you only until after the baby came. Then I planned to divorce you and raise the child as my own. From the very beginning, long before I started to love you, Annie, I thought of the baby as mine. When I said as much, I wasn't lying, I was just telling it the way I saw it.'' As briefly as possible, he told her about the case of mumps he had contracted in his early twenties. ''Ever since, I've assumed I was sterile, that I couldn't have babies. Recently, Dr. Muir told me I may be mistaken, but that's beside the point. On the night your father came to me to tell me you were pregnant with my brother's child, I believed with all my heart that I could never have a child of my own. I saw your baby as the answer to a prayer, a child that would be closely related to me that I could raise as my own.''

"*You were going to steal my baby?*" she asked with a horrified look on her face.

Alex groaned. "I didn't think of it as stealing. Not then. You were—I thought you were incapable of raising the child, that you were mentally disabled. When I began to realize that you were capable of feeling affection, that you might love the baby and pine for it, I decided to keep you here at Montgomery Hall.''

"*And that's why you kept me? So we could share the baby?*"

"No!" Alex rubbed a hand over his face. "No . . . In the beginning, Annie. Only in the beginning. Then I started to fall in love with you. Everything changed after that. Everything . . .'' He gave a shaky laugh and gestured with a hand. "To the point that now I'm sending Bart away with you. If he was all I cared about, do you truly believe I'd do that?''

She caught her bottom lip between her teeth and looked up at the rafters. When she lowered her gaze, she said, "*I feel like you're sending me away because I embarrass you, that you don't want me around until I learn not to act like a dummy.*"

"Oh, Annie, no." Alex shot up from his chair and crossed the room to her. Going down on one knee before her, he grasped her by the shoulders. Her eyes made him think of wet velvet. "I'm not sending you away to school because you embarrass me. I love you with all my heart, and I'd be proud to go anywhere with you on my arm. Just as you are! Embarrassed?" He shook his head.

"Never, not in a million years. It's just that there are so many things you've missed. Fun things. Wonderful things. Because I love you so much, I want you to have a chance to do all of them, and you can't do them here. That's all."

"*Are you sure?*" she asked, her lips tremulous.

"Oh, honey, yes, of course, I'm sure."

Before Alex quite realized what he was about, he was covering her mouth with his. The next instant, she melted against him. Inside his head, his pulse sounded like a drumbeat. *Don't do this. Don't do this*, it seemed to say. But Alex was beyond warnings. Beyond being cautious. With so many other emotions pelting him, the remote possibility of pregnancy didn't even enter his mind.

Annie . . . Pulling her up with him, he came to his feet. She felt like pure heaven in his arms. He ran his hands over her body, familiarizing himself with her shape, which had altered since childbirth. A slim waist. Gently flared hips. Lord, he wanted to hug the breath right out of her. He moved his hands to her breasts, cupping their softness, reveling in their heat. At his touch, she moaned into his mouth. The sound, thick with need, drove him beyond rational thought.

He fumbled with the buttons of her bodice. As the cloth fell away, he attacked the drawstring of her chemise. Soft, warm skin. Nipples that eagerly pushed up for the brush of his fingertips. He ran his mouth from her lips to her throat, then lower. She arched her back over his arm, offering herself to him. Alex didn't need an engraved invitation.

As he drew her nipple into his mouth, the sweetness of her milk spilled over his tongue. Encircling her waist with his hands, he lifted her slightly, feverishly suckling first one nipple, then the other, teasing each with his teeth and tongue. She cried out, a long, low wail that trailed off into a moan.

Alex peeled her clothing away as he might have the skin from a delectable piece of fruit, his lips following in the wake of his hands to taste every sweet inch of her the instant he got it uncovered. When he had her stripped, he took a moment to simply adore her with his gaze. Heavy with child, she had been precious to him beyond measure and beautiful in a way he couldn't put into words. But now? She was every man's dream, with full, rose-tipped breasts, a tiny waist, ample hips, and long, shapely legs, every inch of her flawless. So lovely, he was almost afraid to touch her. Yet so tempting, he couldn't resist. He wanted her, had to have her, the devil take all the reasons why he shouldn't.

He lowered her back into the rocker, jerked his fly open, and buried his shaft into her hot wetness. She looped her legs around his waist, meeting him thrust for thrust, the motion of the rocker heightening their rhythm. *Creak—creak—creak.* Vaguely, Alex was aware of the sound, but for some reason, it no longer wore on his nerves.

Some time later, he returned to his senses to find that he was lying on the attic floor, his lovely wife sprawled naked on top of him, her face pressed to the hollow of his neck. As his vision sharpened, he found himself staring into a pair of beady little eyes. A mouse was perched on Annie's slender shoulder. Alex blinked, then smiled as he stroked the tiny creature with a fingertip.

Madness. Making love in a mouse-infested attic? He closed his eyes, perfectly content to go crazy as long as this woman he held in his arms was with him.

Three weeks. He could hold her and love her for three more weeks, and he intended to make the most of every second. He'd confer with Dr. Muir about ways he might avoid getting her pregnant, and he'd take every precaution. But love her, he would. As much as he could, for as long as he could.

Three more weeks . . . After that, his wife and child would be gone, and his arms would be empty.

So would his life.

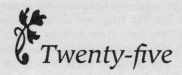

Twenty-five

Three weeks later, when Alex took Annie and Maddy to the station in Medford to see them off, the morning was cold, gloomy, and damp, a perfect reflection of his mood, which was dismal, to say the least. He had been dreading this moment for over two months, didn't want to face it, and could have thought of a dozen perfectly rational reasons to do an about-face and take his wife and baby home.

"Have you got your tickets?"

Wincing, Alex realized he was yelling so Annie might hear him over the train's engine. Reaching under the thick folds of her wool cloak, he caught her arm and drew her to a stop, leaning around so she could see his face as he repeated the question. She opened her reticule, a blue silk bag embroidered with jet beads, and started to fish through the jumbled contents. Alex glimpsed something small and brown wriggling among the papers. Before he could register what it was or react, it took a flying leap.

"Naah-ooh!" Annie shrieked.

"Christ!" Alex swore.

"Mouse!" a fat lady screamed.

From that moment on, all hell broke loose, women

screeching and jumping on benches, men stomping about in an attempt to squash the scurrying little creature under their heels. Alex leaped into the fray, not entirely sure what he hoped to accomplish, aside from making a complete ass of himself. With all the noise and confusion, he doubted the poor mouse was going to stand still so he might catch it. But with Annie's worshipful gaze fixed on him, her expression hailing him as her hero, he couldn't just stand there and do nothing.

The mouse took cover between a trash receptacle and a post, whereupon a woman, skirts bunched around her knees with one hand, launched an attack on the mouse's hiding place with wild swings of her purse. All Alex could think about was Annie's pet being bludgeoned to death before her very eyes. He dived between the woman and the garbage can, rendering her blows harmless by taking the brunt of them across his shoulders. When his fingertips connected with a furry little body, he made a none-too-gentle grab. Tiny teeth sank into his index finger.

"Jesus Christ! You ungrateful little shit!"

"Watch your language, sir!" *Kerwhack*. The woman's purse hit him squarely on the ear. As he straightened, Alex raised an arm to protect his face. "How *dare* you turn a mouse loose in a public place!" she cried. "I nearly had heart failure!"

She looked in fine form to Alex. He dodged another swing of her purse. "Madam, kindly stop swinging that reticule at me."

She thumped him on the shoulder. "Disturbing the peace! Terrifying innocent people! And a grown man, no less. Such pranks are to be expected from young boys. But you? I've a good mind to report you. Rodents are diseased. Rabies! The plague! How dare you subject other people to—" Alex cupped the rescued mouse against his coat lapel. "This is no ordinary mouse. It's a"—he grabbed at the first words that came to him—"genus attica. It's very rare. My wife wouldn't take a thousand dollars for it."

The woman blinked. "Rare, you say?"

"You have no idea."

She pursed her lips, the movement twitching the end of her nose and making her nostrils flare. "Did I understand you to say it's worth over a *thousand* dollars?"

"That and more."

"Oh, my . . ." She touched a hand to her throat. "Oh, I am *so* sorry. At a glance, it certainly looked like an ordinary mouse."

"Madam," Alex said with his most well-practiced smile, "only a damned fool would charge through a train station trying to catch an ordinary mouse. Thank your lucky stars that you did it no serious injury."

She raised her penciled eyebrows and leaned sideways to peer at his cupped hand. "You don't say? A genus attica? You know, now that you mention it, I've heard of them. In fact, I think I saw one exhibited at the fair last year. Oh, yes, I'm sure—a genus attica. Yes, that was it. How absolutely extraordinary!"

"You won't see many people packing one around, I can tell you that."

She gestured for a thin little man standing nearby. "Horace, come and look. This man has a genus attica. Isn't that amazing? We saw one at the fair last year, remember?"

Tweaking his mustache and rocking back onto his heels, Horace looked surprised to hear that. "Hmm . . . Ah, yes. A genus—what was that you said?"

"A genus attica! They're valuable beyond measure. You remember." She came closer to Alex. "May I see?"

Several other people were gathering around. Alex captured the mouse in his cupped hands and parted his thumbs so the woman could have a peek. She assumed a knowledgeable air and nodded. "Oh, yes. Upon closer inspection, I can see that this is no ordinary mouse. The ears of the genus attica are quite distinctive, are they not?"

A well-dressed man leaned forward to look over the woman's shoulder at the mouse. "The nose is quite distinctive as well. Dear God, a genus attica. It's a miracle some damned fool didn't smash it."

"Oh, isn't he cute?" another woman cried. "Paul, I'd love to have one of those. What a conversation piece. Where on earth did you buy him, sir?"

"Actually, I didn't," Alex replied. "You might say I came by him through a special liaison. Connections, you know. As I said, not just everybody has one."

Annie dashed up just then. Alex relinquished the mouse to her. She held it to her cheek, making soft cooing noises. None of the onlookers seemed to think that was strange, not now that they realized the mouse was a rare and expensive genus attica.

Alex knew when to retreat. He seized Annie by the arm and hotfooted it away from there. He spied Maddy standing near the steps of the train and veered in her direction. "Did ye catch the bloomin' mouse?" she asked as they joined her.

"Keep your voice down," Alex whispered. "That woman over there nearly sent for the authorities. Said mice were a health hazard, of all the crazy things."

"Well, I never!" Maddy huffed.

"From here on, it's a genus attica. Very rare, very expensive. Otherwise, they might discover it later and put you off the train."

Maddy shot a look at Annie, who was carefully stowing her pet back in her reticule. "We can't have that."

"No, we cannot."

"A genus attica." Maddy nodded. "It has a certain ring to it. Have ye got the tickets?"

Alex's heart leaped when he saw Annie reopen her reticule to get the tickets, but this time she caught the mouse in one hand while she searched. When she came up with the fare vouchers, he nearly sighed with relief. If she and Maddy missed this train, they wouldn't be able to leave for Albany until tomorrow. As much as he would have enjoyed keeping them home another day, he didn't think he could survive saying all the goodbyes again. Last night, holding Annie in his arms, not knowing how long it might be before he saw her again, had been agony.

After taking the tickets, Alex made sure she got her mouse tucked safely away. "Don't take it out on the train," he cautioned her. "Not everyone has a fondness for"—he lowered his voice—"mice, you know. In fact, some people are downright peculiar about them."

"All aboard!" the conductor yelled.

Alex caught Annie's arm, drawing her quickly along to catch up with Maddy, who was already harkening to the conductor's call.

"All aboard! All aboard!" the conductor yelled again.

When they reached Maddy, Alex stuffed the tickets in her hand and took little Bart from her to give him one last hug. Tears burned in his eyes as he nuzzled aside the blanket and pressed his cheek against the baby's downy hair. After returning the infant to the housekeeper's waiting arms, he turned to Annie. Her mouth was quivering and her eyes were swimming.

"I'll write," he assured her. "It won't be so bad, sweetheart. You'll see. Once you get started at school, you're going to love it."

She nodded, looking so dismal and forlorn that it was all he could do not to call the whole thing off.

"I love you, Annie, girl. I'm going to miss you every second of every day."

The end of her nose started turning red. Alex bent to kiss the tip, then gathered her into his arms. He closed his eyes, pressed his face against her hair, and dragged in a deep breath, trying to memorize her scent. He was shaking when he drew away from her.

"*I don't want to go,*" she said.

Pretending he hadn't noticed, Alex kissed her forehead. Then he turned to Maddy. "You'll write? Once a week, at least."

"Lands, yes. I told ye, Master Alex, I'll write ye every week without fail!" She handed the tickets to the conductor, then, cradling the baby in one arm, grabbed Annie's wrist. "Come along, lass. They're gonna leave without us."

"If anything goes wrong, wire me. I'll be there as quickly as I can."

"Not to worry," Maddy called. "I'll wire if we need ye."

Alex clenched his teeth and shifted his gaze to Annie. Big blue eyes, clinging to his. As Maddy started up the steps, Annie craned her neck to look back at him. He lifted a hand to wave. Then, just like that, she was gone.

He walked alongside the train, searching for her face at one of the windows. The train began to move. He picked up his pace, desperately searching, determined to get one more glimpse of her. Just one. When the train pulled away from him, he staggered to a stop, staring after it, feeling more desolate than he ever had in his life.

When Alex returned to Montgomery Hall, the house seemed utterly silent. Feeling indescribably lonely, he wandered from room to room, seeing Annie or the baby everywhere he looked. *Gone.* In his study, he sat before the fireplace, stared into the soot-blackened firebox, and thought to himself that the darkness was an omen. They were gone, and there was every chance they might never come back. As difficult as it was, he had to accept that.

Frederick tapped on the study door. "Might I get you something, Master Alex? A cup of coffee, perhaps? Or have one of the maids bring you in some lunch?"

Alex sighed. "I'm not really hungry, Frederick. Thank you, anyway."

The butler walked farther into the room. When he reached the hearth, he did the unprecedented and sat in the opposite chair. "I know it's no consolation, but you've done the right thing, sir. Difficult, I know. But, in the end, it will be what's best for her, and for the babe."

That realization was small comfort. Alex said nothing.

"Maddy will write regularly, I'm sure. And before you know it, Annie will be sending letters."

Alex nodded. "It'll be easier then, I suppose. But it'll be a spell before she learns to read and write, Frederick."

"Yessir, I know." The man fell silent for a moment, hands turned toward the fireplace as if to warm them even though no fire burned in the grate. "What you need are some projects to keep you busy. One thing the two of us might set our minds to is a mouse cage. I hate to complain, but since Annie sprang all the traps in the attic, we're being overrun. Droppings in the flour this morning, no less."

"Dear God. You tossed it out, I hope."

"Well, sir, not exactly. Given the fact that the creatures seem taken with it, I, um . . . took it upstairs. I thought maybe—well, if they have food up there, perhaps they'll stay out of the kitchen."

Alex groaned and rubbed his forehead. Then he gave a halfhearted laugh. "Frederick, that's mad. Feeding the attic mice? Have you any idea how quickly they multiply?

I can't recall the exact figures I learned in college, but the multiplication factor is phenomenal.''

"You're right, of course. Quite mad, feeding the mice." He slanted a look at Alex. "I'll let you be the one to reset the traps, if you'd be so kind."

Alex groaned again. "I can't do that. Sure as hell, I'd catch a favorite of hers. Maybe you have a point. I'll have to build a cage for them." Recalling the incident at the train station, he recounted the story to Frederick. "Maybe we could go into business and sell the buggers," he joked. "Five hundred a head. What a bargain!"

Frederick grinned. "I'd be pleased to just give them away, sir."

"No problem. I could have gotten rid of two dozen this morning, easily. Incredible, isn't it? Tell people something is rare and expensive, and they immediately want one."

As Alex fell silent again, Frederick said, "If you want help with a cage, I'm handy with a hammer and nails."

"Thank you, Frederick. I appreciate the offer."

"After we've rounded up Annie's little friends, perhaps we can reset the traps?"

"There's a thought."

"As for their multiplying, perhaps I can"—the butler cleared his throat and lowered his voice—"discreetly dispose of any unwanted offspring."

"We'll have to do something," Alex agreed listlessly, and returned his gaze to the firebox.

"Don't feel too down at the mouth, Master Alex. It's not as if you can't go visit her whenever you wish."

"Not any time soon. I need to give her a chance to settle in or she'll beg to come home, and quite frankly, I don't know if I could refuse her, not feeling the way I do right now. Everywhere I look, there's something to remind me of her or Bart. I keep thinking of all I'll miss. He'll grow so much between visits, I probably won't recognize him.'' What really bothered Alex was that the same would undoubtedly be true in reverse. Just the thought nearly broke his heart. He finally had a son, and now he couldn't be part of his babyhood.

Frederick sighed and stood up. ''I'm a fair hand at checkers, if you should like some company now and again.''

The offer made Alex smile. ''You sound as blue as I am.''

''Yes, well . . . It won't seem quite the same around here without Maddy to harp at me, will it?''

Alex glanced up. After searching the butler's gaze for a long moment, he chuckled. ''I'll be damned.''

Color flooded Frederick's face. ''You won't let on to her, I hope. I haven't declared myself. She's rather . . . prickly, our Maddy.''

''My lips are sealed.''

The butler straightened his black jacket, then picked at a bit of imaginary lint on the sleeve. ''I only mentioned it because—'' He cleared his throat. ''Well, as the old saying goes, sir, misery sometimes enjoys a spot of company, and without a dose of Irish temper once a day to keep my life interesting, I will be a tad miserable.''

''When I go to Albany for visits, maybe you'd like to go along?''

Frederick sniffed. ''It's certainly a thought, my schedule allowing.''

After the other man left, Alex pushed up from his chair and moved aimlessly around the room. When he reached the organ, he trailed a hand over the highly polished surface. Moving on from there, he paused to tap out a couple of notes on the sleigh bells. Then he went to his desk. One of Annie's ear trumpets lay on the blotter. He picked it up, stared at it for a long while, and then closed his eyes on a wave of pain so intense he felt physically sick.

*   *   *

From that day on, Alex's life narrowed down to one focal point, letters from Maddy. A week and a half later, the first arrived. He closeted himself in his study and opened it with shaking hands.

Well, we've arrived, Maddy wrote. *As small a place as Albany is, Annie was terrified when we first got here, but she is settling down some now and seems to like her classes.*

Alex gulped. He didn't want her to like it there, damn it. At the thought, guilt rolled through him. He forced himself to keep reading.

The teachers seem to be a kindly lot, and on the very first day, she made several new friends. She wants to come home, of course. Each afternoon, when I walk to the school to escort her home, the teacher conveys to me that Annie is constantly expressing a desire to leave. I'm sure she'll get past it, eventually, but for right now it's difficult for her, and for me as well. I can't help but feel sorry for the poor wee lass.

The letter went on to update him on how Bart was doing and to describe the small town of Albany and the house where Annie and Maddy lived. Alex read it, reread it, and then read it yet again. It was a short missive, and he soon had every word of it memorized.

News of Annie. Updates on Bart. Alex knew it was madness, but he honestly felt that was all he had left to live for. Edie Trimble dropped by one afternoon. Alex shared Maddy's letter with her. After reading it, she glanced up and smiled tremulously.

"I know how you must miss them," she said.

Alex doubted that. It wasn't just that he missed his wife and child. He felt as if his heart had been ripped from his breast. "It's . . . difficult. There are moments when I'm not so sure I've made the right choice."

Edie leaned close to touch his hand. "Don't think it, not for a minute. This is, without question, the most precious gift you could have given her, Alex. She doesn't understand that now, but she will. Down the road, she will."

Alex could only hope.

A week later, another missive from Maddy arrived. Annie was doing well, she said, and Bart was growing by leaps and bounds. The weather had turned unseasonably warm and flowers were blooming in their dooryard. In regard to school, only one difficulty had arisen thus far; when Annie spoke in sign, she was making many of the hand motions incorrectly. Nothing serious, just slight variances. Annie's teacher said that, given the situation, Alex had done a wonderful job of tutoring her. It was a simple case of his having misinterpreted the instructions in the manuals, a common enough occurrence, and one that was usually easily rectified. Annie, however, refused to cooperate, explaining to her teacher, over and over, that if she began making the signs differently, then Alex wouldn't be able to understand her anymore.

That brought tears to Alex's eyes. He wrote back to Maddy and asked her to tell Annie that she needn't worry about his not understanding her. While she was away, he would ask Irene Small for clearer instructional material and teach himself how to talk in sign correctly. Immediately after sealing the envelope addressed to Maddy, he penned a note to Mrs. Small to carry through on that promise.

Around the middle of April, Alex received a letter that, according to the postmarks, had gotten sidetracked and gone clear to San Francisco. When he perused the awkwardly printed letters on the outside of the envelope, he wasn't surprised. *Hopervile, Orgen*? There was no return address, and he didn't recognize the scrawled printing. He tore open the seal and withdrew a folded piece of widely ruled tablet paper. As he smoothed the sheet, his attention was caught by the letter's closing. *Luv, Anie.* His heart caught. Incredulous, he struggled to interpret the roughly composed sentences, marveling at how much she had learned in so short a time. *I mis yu. I wan to cum hom. Pleze.*

On the last line, she had written, *I mis yu big.* Alex read those last words through a blur of tears. He sank onto the corner of his desk and lifted the paper to his nose. The faint scent of roses clung to it. He closed his eyes, imagining how it would be to hold her in his arms, to bury his face against the sweet curve of her neck. The longing that filled him was so acute, he trembled with it.

When he had recovered his composure sufficiently, he penned a letter back to her, printing the words, keeping the sentences short and simple. A cheerful note, encouraging her to do well in school, to enjoy the social activities.

Those few short sentences were the most difficult he had ever written in his life.

As regularly as clockwork, letters from Maddy arrived once a week from that point on. She kept Alex abreast of all the news, but there wasn't much. Annie was doing well in school. The baby was growing. They were all three fine.

The first of May, Alex received another letter from Annie. This time, in addition to pleading with him to let her come home, she wrote three sentences that made his blood turn to ice. *I hav a nu frend. He is def. We laff a lot.*

Alex's first reaction, bone-deep fear, finally gave way to fatalistic acceptance. If Annie found someone else, if she fell in love, then their marriage had never been meant. All her life, she'd been denied everything other people took for granted. If he loved her, truly loved her, then he wouldn't let his own selfish yearnings deprive her of this one chance at a normal life.

Shortly thereafter, another letter from Maddy arrived. She described Annie's new friend, Bruce, as a pleasant, handsome young fellow. *He clearly adores her, and he's wonderful with the baby, which endears him to her.* After finishing the letter, Alex sat in his study, staring at nothing. Was Maddy issuing a warning? The thought made him ache. Bruce . . . Without ever clapping eyes on the man, Alex detested him. Wonderful with the baby, was he? The lowdown skunk, using the child to worm his way into Annie's affections. It was the oldest trick in the book. What frightened Alex was that it just might work.

Was he about to lose Annie? Without her and the baby, he wasn't sure the rest of his life would be worth living.

Agonizing over the news, he went to the stable and worked late into the night, pushing himself to the point of exhaustion so he could sleep. When he finally dropped into bed, it was only to be haunted by dreams. Dreams of Annie . . . dancing the waltz in the arms of another man.

On May 15, another letter from Annie arrived. After Maddy's subtle warning about good old Bruce, Alex was almost afraid to open the envelope. Inside he found only a sketch. As he smoothed it on his desk to examine it, he frowned. As she had done that long ago day in the nursery, Annie had drawn a lifelike sketch of his face and hers, the attention to detail amazing. Only in this sketch, Annie had ears and Alex didn't. No message. Nothing to explain. Only a picture of him without ears?

Alex studied the drawing endlessly, not knowing what to make of it. Then, like a mule kick between the eyes, it finally struck him what she was trying to say.

I wan to cum hom, she had written. *I mis yu big*. And he had ignored the plea, writing back to her as though he'd never read the message, encouraging her to do well in her studies and enjoy the social activities. In his determination to do what was best for her, he had turned a deaf ear to what she thought and what she wanted, as if her feelings and wishes counted for nothing.

He had tried to lay the world at her feet, and in the trying, he had cheated her out of the most important thing of all, the right to make her own choices.

"Oh, Annie, love . . ."

Alex closed his eyes on a wave of regret. He should never have listened to Dr. Muir and Edie Trimble. No one knew Annie better than Alex. No one understood her better. And no one loved her more.

In a twinkling, he saw himself with her that long ago afternoon in the attic, picking up shattered china, thinking to himself that the tea party was over, but that Annie's life had just begun. In that moment, he had made a vow to do everything in his power to turn all her fantasies into realities. Looking back, he reconstructed the scene in his mind. A cozy parlor. Annie, serving tea in mismatched pieces of china. Annie, dancing in the arms of her dream man to imaginary music. No thick tomes. No classroom. No hordes of strangers. Just a simple little world, arranged to her liking, peopled by individuals who allowed her to be somebody.

A normal life . . . That had been her dream. To be recognized as a person with needs and thoughts and emotions. To be loved. To be accepted for who she was. Instead of giving her all that, he had started trying to change her. Why he'd done so was a mystery, for he loved Annie just the way she was.

Pictures of her flashed through his mind, all bringing a smile to his lips. Annie, searching through her bedding for an egg. Annie, sitting on his knee, lips pursed, eyes filled with bewilderment, as he unfastened her chemise. Annie, repeatedly striking one note on the organ, her expression blissful. Annie, sprawled on the dining room table, skirts above her waist, a napkin stuffed in her mouth so no one would hear her scream as he brought her to climax. Annie, replete from lovemaking, with a mouse perched on her shoulder. Annie, with her luminous eyes and her gentle smile.

She was perfect just as she was. Absolutely perfect.

Twenty-six

Alex stood at the white picket gate and gazed at the large white house. Set well back from the street, it had sloping green lawns, well-tended flower beds, and large shade trees, one of which sported a swing hanging from one of its thick limbs. On the front veranda, several young people sat in wicker chairs, drinking what looked like iced tea and engaging in conversation. Watching their quick hand movements, Alex smiled slightly. He clearly had a lot of practicing to do if he hoped to become proficient in sign language.

The gate creaked loudly when he opened it. No one on the porch turned to look. As Alex made his way up the walk, he searched the windows of the house, half hoping he might see Annie. When he reached the steps, a good-looking young man on the porch noticed his approach and stood to greet him.

"Hello. May I help you?"

Startled, Alex hesitated with one foot on the bottom step. The man's speech was rather flat and oddly nasal, but each word was pronounced perfectly and distinctly. "Perhaps. I'm Alex Montgomery. My wife, Annie, is a student here."

The man's blue eyes warmed at the mention of Annie's name. He smiled, making no secret of the fact that he was looking Alex over. "You aren't as handsome as she says you are."

The comment took Alex aback, and he laughed. "I'm sorry to disappoint you."

"I'm not disappointed. I consider you to be my competition." An unmistakable twinkle lit up his eyes. He extended his right hand. "My name is Bruce Johnson."

Alex glanced at his outstretched palm. After a moment's hesitation, he shook it. "I recognize the name. My housekeeper, Maddy, has mentioned you in several letters. I understand you've been actively courting my wife."

Bruce chuckled. "Trying."

"Any luck?"

"Not yet."

Alex laughed in spite of himself. As much as he hated to admit it, he liked the man. "I'm relieved to hear that."

"Annie is very loyal. We're good friends, nothing more."

Alex moved on up the steps. "She is here, isn't she?"

"She's in class right now." He drew a watch from his vest pocket. "Ten minutes more, and she'll be done for the day."

Alex didn't want to wait ten minutes, but he supposed he had no choice. He leaned against the porch railing and folded his arms. "How long have you been a student here?"

"I'm a teacher."

"Oh."

Bruce grinned. "Many of the teachers here are deaf. Believe it or not, being deaf makes it easier for us to teach. We understand better. There are hearing teachers, too. We need them for the speech classes. I obviously can't be sure if a student is getting his phonetics right."

Alex nodded. "How is Annie progressing?"

Bruce's smile faded. "She's very smart, and she has the advantage of having once been lingual. But she isn't learning as fast as she could."

"Oh? She's been sending me letters. The words are misspelled, but I—" Alex shrugged. "I naturally assumed she must be learning by leaps and bounds."

Bruce turned an embarrassed pink. "Yes, well, I helped her a bit." His mouth quirked. "I didn't correct her spelling. If you saw how hard she works to print just one letter in a word, you'd understand why. I didn't have the heart to make her do it all over, and I thought you'd rather have a letter she'd done herself, mistakes and all, than one I corrected."

Alex couldn't think what to say. In his breast pocket, he had all of Annie's letters. He'd traced each word with his fingertips a hundred times.

"Annie's . . . homesick. Aside from the letter writing, her heart hasn't really been in her studies."

Alex met Bruce's gaze. "Why do I have this feeling that you're campaigning in her behalf?"

"Probably because I am. All of us could learn more, you included. How's your Latin?"

"Not worth a shit."

Bruce raised an eyebrow. "Then perhaps you should go away to school for a few years and learn the language. After your Latin is perfect, you can go home and be with your wife."

The man was butting in where he had no business, but for the life of him, Alex couldn't be angry. "Point taken." He smiled slightly. "The lecture isn't necessary, though. I've come to take her home. Since sending her here, I've realized it was a mistake."

Bruce's blue eyes darkened. Alex could see that the news of Annie's departure hit him hard. He recovered quickly. "I'm glad you've changed your mind. For her sake." He lifted one shoulder. "Why learn to speak if the one person you want to talk to is far away? Annie's heart isn't here. It never will be. Let her learn at a slower pace at home with you. It's where she belongs."

With that, he started to turn away. Alex reached out and touched his arm. "I'd like to surprise her. Please don't tell her I'm here."

Bruce smiled. "I was going to catch her so I could tell her goodbye. Once she sees you, she'll be so excited . . ." He lifted his hands. "Will you tell her for me then?"

"Happily," Alex said with a laugh. Then he sobered. "We'll be staying the night here in Albany and taking the morning train. Why don't you join us for supper? That way you can say your own goodbyes and spend some time with her before she leaves."

Bruce brightened at the invitation. He made a show of studying Alex for a minute before he turned and went in the house. "You grow on a person," he said over his shoulder.

Alex chuckled and drew out his watch to check the time. Annie's class would end in three more minutes, which converted into one hundred and eighty seconds, each the longest of his life.

When the front door finally swung open and students began spilling out onto the porch, Alex straightened, his heart leaping whenever he spied a dark head. Two young men came out, three young women. No Annie. Alex realized he was shaking, and from the way his stomach felt, he could have sworn he'd swallowed a handful of jumping beans.

Then, like a vision, she appeared. Alex stood there, frozen, his gaze riveted to her. Sable hair, ivory skin, eyes as clear and endlessly deep as a summer sky. She held a stack of books in one arm and was trying to fasten her cloak. Another student exited behind her and bumped her shoulder. She stepped out of the way, which put her directly in front of Alex. Still, she didn't look up.

"Annie . . ."

No response. Her gaze caught on his shoes. She slowly looked up. When her eyes found his face, she went perfectly still. No smile. No surprise. She just stared at him, her lips slightly parted, her hand hovering over the clasp of her cloak. For an awful moment, Alex started to wonder if her feelings for him had changed, if she was dismayed to see him.

Then she dropped the books. They hit the porch with a resounding crash, the report of which only Alex seemed to notice. Papers scattered, some catching air and drifting past him down the steps.

"Aluck!"

With that, she launched herself into his arms. Alex caught her to his chest, knowing as he tightened his embrace that this was where she belonged, where she had always belonged.

Sobbing, trembling horribly, she wrapped both arms around his neck. "Aluck!"

Her pronunciation of his name was flat and imperfect, but to Alex, it was the most beautiful sound he'd ever heard.

Annie . . . He swung with her in his arms, so happy he ached. He didn't care that everyone on the porch was staring. He didn't care when he felt tears streaming down his cheeks. He held his world in his arms. He had been a fool to send her away. He'd never make the mistake again.

Keeping one arm firmly around her, he drew her down the steps. When she spied her papers, which were scattering with the breeze, Alex caught her from going after them. "Leave them," he told her.

She looked deeply into his eyes, hers swimming with tears.

Alex hauled her closer and caught her chin on the edge of his hand. "You won't be needing them. We're going home."

"*Home?*"

"Home," he assured her. "You and I and the baby. Home. No more school. I'll hire you a tutor."

"*Home, for always?*"

"For always."

Alex caught the gate with his hip and swung it open, unwilling to release his hold on her for even a moment. He glanced up the tree-lined street, then returned his gaze to her sweet face.

"Home, for always."

As he said the words, he felt at peace as he hadn't in months. Home, where their future awaited them. Home, where fantasies could become realities. On impulse, he swung Annie into a waltz step. The breeze caught her cloak, lifting it around her. She let her head fall back, her expression blissful. Alex knew she was imagining they danced to music. The strange thing was, he thought he could hear it as well. Faint, lilting, elusive.

Annie's song, and now his, magical notes only they could hear.

Epilogue

Sunlight streamed through the dining room window, creating a golden nimbus around Annie, who sat at the table, head bent, gaze fixed intently on something in her lap. Even after nearly three years of marriage, Alex was ever thankful that God had blessed his life with someone so sweet, and he hesitated just inside the doorway to watch her for a moment. From the looks of her plate, she had picked at her breakfast again for the third day running.

Unable to help feeling a little concerned, Alex strode across the room. Gabby, the shaggy white dog Alex had given Annie two years earlier, must have felt his master's footsteps vibrating through the floor, for he leaped up from his nap and began to dance around Annie's chair, barking shrilly all the while. Detecting the sound, Annie looked up from what Alex could now see was a piece of embroidery work.

"Good morning," she said with a warm smile.

"Good morning."

With a pained expression, Alex glanced down at the noisy dog. Because the animal's shrill bark was one of the few sounds his wife could hear, he resisted the urge

406

to complain. As useless as the dog was otherwise, he always barked to alert Annie when Bart began to cry, and that made the shaggy creature worth his weight in gold. Gabby, whose name suited him perfectly, also barked to let Annie know if someone was calling to her or knocking at the door, enabling her to respond to sounds she otherwise might have missed.

With a soft laugh, Annie set her needlework aside and leaned down to curl her fingers over Gabby's muzzle. "Enough," she told the dog softly.

Gabby, who adored his mistress nearly as much as Alex did, quivered and twisted about, so pleased at her touch that he looked nearly beside himself. Alex understood the feeling. With a sigh, he drew out a chair from the table and sat down, his gaze returning to his wife's breakfast plate.

"Annie, love, you can't continue to do without your morning meal. It isn't good for you. Are you feeling poorly or something?"

Shifting her gaze to her plate, she wrinkled her nose and pressed a hand over her waist. "I just don't want to eat it. I'm getting fat."

"That is sheer nonsense, if ever I—"

Alex broke off. Annie had puffed air into her cheeks, trying to make herself look plump. The gesture was so reminiscent of that never-to-be-forgotten night when he'd first realized how intelligent she was that it gave him chill bumps. He looked deeply into her guileless blue eyes. No . . . It couldn't be. He flicked a glance at her waist. Was it a little thicker than normal? he wondered. Or was he imagining it? When he looked back up, he could have sworn he glimpsed a fleeting smile on her sweet mouth.

"Annie?" he said under his breath. "Sweetheart, are you—"

She lifted one delicately drawn eyebrow. There was definitely a smile playing about her mouth, Alex decided. A mischievous smile. His stomach felt as though it dropped to the floor. It couldn't be. He already had everything a man could want, an absolutely wonderful wife and a beautiful little boy. To wish for more . . . well, as much as Alex adored children, he had never allowed himself to hope for more babies, mainly because he was afraid he'd only be disappointed.

"Annie, don't tease me," he cautioned her solemnly. "Not about this. Are you pregnant?"

Her eyes grew suspiciously bright as she slowly nodded. Alex couldn't contain the sudden joy that burst inside him. Before he thought it through, he was out of the chair and grabbing Annie into his arms. Her embroidery went flying. Gabby scrambled to get out of the way as Alex swept his wife around the room in a waltz step.

"Pregnant!" he cried. "I can't believe it!"

Clinging to his arms, Annie allowed him to swing her feet clear off the floor. She gave a shrill laugh when he drew her against his chest to hug her. "Careful," she warned. "Don't squeeze too hard."

Alex instantly gentled his hold. "Oh, sweetheart." He bent to kiss her. The instant their lips touched, she melted against him, making him think about all the times they'd started out just this way and ended up locking the dining room doors so they could make love. Against her responsive mouth, he murmured, "I love you. God, how I love you."

He had no sooner finished making this profession than he heard whispering. Abruptly ending the kiss, he glanced over Annie's head to see Frederick the butler standing just inside the dining room doors, Bart riding piggyback on his shoulders. "Yes, Frederick?"

Before the butler could state his business, Maddy's red head poked around his arm. "Well, has she told ye yet?"

Alex felt Annie wiggle and glanced down to see her shaking her head emphatically at Maddy and touching a finger to her lips. In response, Maddy winced. It was as clear to Alex as a freckle on a pig's back that his housekeeper and butler already knew about Annie's pregnancy. So much for a husband's being told first. Disgruntled, he narrowed an eye at his wife, but in truth, he couldn't be angry. In the three years since their marriage, Annie had come to regard Maddy as a second mother. He couldn't fault her for sharing her feminine concerns with the older woman. Unfortunately, since her marriage to Frederick a year ago, Maddy had developed an irritating habit of telling him absolutely everything, secret or no.

"Baby!" Little Bart chortled. Then, clucking his tongue as though to a horse, he tugged on Frederick's hair and kicked his small feet. "Go fast, Fwedwick! Go fast."

Ever ready to spoil the young master of the house, Frederick began to run in place, putting plenty of bounce into his step to satisfy his adventurous young rider. "I am sorry, Master Alex, but I came by the knowledge before you did only because—"

"I told him," Maddy inserted with a huff. "Besides, it isn't as if it's something to be kept secret, now is it?"

She had Alex there. No secret this, but a precious gift. He gathered Annie close again, so happy that he couldn't express it with mere words. Fortunately, she seemed to understand and returned his embrace. From the corner of his eye, Alex caught a glimpse of Little Bart, still bouncing about on Frederick's shoulders. Maddy was beaming as proudly as if the unborn infant were her grandchild. Alex supposed that under the circumstances, that was fitting. Maddy was as much a mother to him and his wife as their own had ever been.

I want a girl, Alex thought. He already had a fine son. Oh, yes, a daughter. Not that he would really care either way as long as the child was healthy. But secretly, in his heart of hearts, he wanted a little girl. One with silken sable hair and huge, incredibly expressive blue eyes. The happy clamor of voices seemed to fade away as Alex gazed down at his wife's precious face.

Oh, yes, a little girl exactly like Annie. . . .